BUBBLE

Also by Anders de la Motte

Game

Buzz

ANDERS DE LA MOTTE

BUBBLE

Translated from the Swedish by Neil Smith

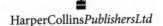

HarperCollins*PublishersLtd*

Published by HarperCollins Publishers Ltd, by agreement
with the Salomonsson Agency.

First Canadian edition

HarperCollins Publishers Ltd
2 Bloor Street East, 20th Floor
Toronto, Ontario, Canada
M4W 1A8

www.harpercollins.ca

Library and Archives Canada Cataloguing in Publication
information is available upon request

ISBN 978-1-44341-742-6

Printed and bound in Canada
WEB 9 8 7 6 5 4 3 2 1

For Anette

He who owns the past controls the future

My warmest thanks to all the Ants out there, without whose advice and achievements the Game could never have become a reality.

The Author

Bubble [ˈbLbəl]
A small quantity of air or gas within a liquid body
A small, hollow, floating bead or globe
Anything that is more spacious than real; a false show
A cheat or fraud; a delusive scheme; an empty project;
a dishonest speculation
A person deceived by an empty project; a gull
A small spherical cavity in a solid material
To cheat, to delude (verb)
A (usually temporary) state of existence, in which what
you see, touch, hear, feel, and smell are under close
control either by those around you or a system
When an electronic device or person is remotely under
surveillance (bubbled)
A fantasy/dream that is so far-fetched it couldn't ever
be true

www.brainyquote.com
www.urbandictionary.com
www.wiktionary.com

'In a personalized world, we will increasingly be typed and fed only news that is pleasant, familiar, and confirms our beliefs and because these filters are invisible, we won't know what is being hidden from us. Our past interests will determine what we are exposed to in the future, leaving less room for the unexpected encounters that spark creativity, innovation, and the democratic exchange of ideas.'

Eli Pariser

'Knowledge is power. Information is power. The secreting or hoarding of knowledge or information may be an act of tyranny camouflaged as humility.'

Robin Morgan

'It is not so important who starts the game, but who finishes it.'

John Wooden

Outbox: 1 pending message.

From: goodboy.821@gmail.com
To: magnus.sandstrom@farookalhassan.se
Subject: the Game

Fuck it, Manga, how did things end up like this?
It was all so easy back at the start. So innocent.

A mobile phone someone left behind on the train.
A phone that knew who I was, called me by my name.

Do you want to play a Game, Henrik Pettersson?
YES or NO?

To start with everything went like clockwork. The tasks they gave me were pretty simple. Nick an umbrella, loosen the wheel-nuts on a flash car, stop the clock on top of the NK department store.
The film clips looked good, the fans liked what they saw and I started climbing the high-score list. Soaking up their praise and approval, aiming for the top, and trying to depose Kent Hasselqvist a.k.a. player number fifty-eight from his throne.
At almost any price. . .
That grass in Birkagatan whose door I spray-painted, followed by his face. The attack on the royal procession. The stone I dropped on those police cars from the Traneberg Bridge. . .
I didn't even blink, Manga, I didn't hesitate for a single fucking second. . .
I just did all I could to get to the top, to get the audience to love me. To get a bit of recognition.

But then I blew it. I broke rule number one:
Never talk about the Game to anyone.

First they chucked me out, then they gave me a warning. Set fire to my flat, and tried to do the same to your computer shop. Not to mention Erman the nutter, the hermit who got too involved and was now trying to live a low-tech life out in the sticks.

Didn't do him much good, did it. . .?

You are always playing the game, whether you like it or not.

So I fought back, big time. Blew their server-farm sky-high. Emptied their bank account and took off. Lived the easy life on Asian beaches like everyone dreams of doing, really tried to enjoy my early retirement.

It was kind of okay. . .

You have to be careful about what you wish for. . .

I managed to lie low for fourteen months, until they caught up with me down in Dubai. They framed me for the murder of Anna Argos, and I ended up getting locked up and tortured. But I managed to wriggle out of their trap. And I decided to find out who wanted Anna dead. And me too, for that matter. . .

The answer seemed to lead back to her company, Argoseye.com, and their undeniably shady business practices. Bribed bloggers, thousands of fake internet identities, all making comments and giving scores that suited the company's clients. All the different techno-logical tools they used to suppress things and keep them hidden. Making certain things on the net seem invisible.

Like the Game, for instance. . .

But we beat them as well, even if it was at a cost. The trojan you designed that I planted in their computer system did exactly what it was supposed to.

It dragged the trolls out into daylight, and they burst. And shafted Philip Argos, the creepy bastard, and gave the rest of his little gang what they deserved.

Everything would have been fine.

If it hadn't been for him.

Tage Sammer, or Uncle Tage as Becca calls him.

He claims he's an old colleague of Dad's from the military.

The old man might have fooled my sister, but I know who he really is. The Game Master. The brains behind the whole thing.

He's given me a task, Manga.

One last task that will make me famous.

I'm trying to figure out a plan to get out of it.

To free both me and Becca from his grasp.

If you get this email, it'll mean I've failed.

That they forced me to carry out the task.

And that I'm very probably dead. . .

It's quiet at the moment. Too quiet.

But I know they're out there, watching every step I take.

Soon it's all going to kick off.

The question is: am I prepared to play one last game?

What do you think?

YES or NO?

Your old friend,
   HP

This message is set to send at a future date

Like a punch in the chest – that was pretty much what it felt like. In a weird way the blow seemed to slow everything down even more. All of a sudden he could appreciate the tiniest details around him. The gun aimed at his chest, the drawn out, panic-stricken screams from the surrounding crowd. All around him, bodies crushed together in slow motion. Trying to get as far away from him as possible.

But in spite of the evidence, in spite of the gunpowder stinging his nostrils and the shot still reverberating in his eardrums, his brain refused to accept what was happening. As if it were fending off the impossible, the unthinkable, the incomprehensible . . .

This simply couldn't be happening.

Not now!

She had shot him . . .

SHE

HAD

SHOT

HIM!!!

The pistol was still pointing straight at his chest. The look on her face behind the barrel was ice-cold, completely emotionless. As if it belonged to someone else. A stranger.

1

He tried to raise his hand towards her, opened his mouth to say something. But the only sound that passed his lips was a sort of whimper. Suddenly and without any warning time speeded up and returned to normal. The pain spread like a wave from his ribcage, out through his body, making the tarmac beneath him lurch. His knees gave way and he took a couple of stumbling steps backwards in an attempt to keep his balance.

His heel hit the edge of the kerb.

A second of weightlessness as he fought the law of gravity.

Then a dreamlike sensation of falling freely.

And with that his part in the Game was over.

1

A whole new Game?

The moment he woke up HP knew something was wrong. It took him a few seconds to put his finger on what it was.

It was quiet.

Far *too* quiet . . .

The bedroom faced out onto Guldgränd and he had long since got used to the constant sound of traffic on the Söderleden motorway a few hundred metres away. He hardly ever thought about it any more.

But instead of the usual low rumble of traffic interspersed with the occasional siren, the summer night outside was completely silent.

He glanced at the clock-radio: 03.58.

Roadworks, he thought. Söderleden, Söder Mälarstrand and the Slussen junction closed off for yet another round of make-do-and-mend . . . But besides the fact that Bob the Builder would have to be working in stealth mode, it was also slowly dawning on him that there were other noises missing. No-one rattling doors as they delivered the morning papers, no drunks shouting down on Hornsgatan. In fact hardly any sound at all to indicate that there was actually a vibrant capital city out there. As if his bedroom had been enclosed in a huge bubble, shutting the rest of the world out. Forcing him to live in his own little universe where the usual rules no longer applied.

Which, in some ways, was actually true . . .

He noticed that his heart was starting to beat faster. A quiet rustling sound from somewhere inside the flat made him jump.

A burglar?

No, impossible. He'd locked the high-security door, all three locks, just like he always did. The door had cost a fortune, but it was worth every single damn penny. Steel frame, double cylinder hook-bolt locks, you name it – so, logically, no-one could have broken into the flat. But the umbrella of paranoia wasn't about to let itself be taken down so easily . . .

He crept out of bed, padded across the bedroom floor and peered cautiously into the living room. It took a few seconds for his eyes to get used to the gloom, but the results were unambiguous. Nothing, no movement at all, either in the living room or the little kitchen beyond. Everything was fine, there was no sign of any danger. Just the unnatural, oppressive silence that still hadn't broken . . .

He crept carefully over to the window and looked out. Not a soul out on the street, not that that was particularly surprising given the time. Maria Trappgränd was hardly a busy street at any time of day.

Closed off for roadworks, that had to be it. Half of Södermalm already looked like some fucking archaeological dig, so why not go for a complete overnight shut-down? All the little Bobs were probably just having a coffee break.

Plausible – sure! But the uneasy feeling still wouldn't let go.

4

Only the hall left.

He tiptoed across the new floorboards over to the front door, taking care to avoid the third and fifth ones because he knew they creaked.

When he was about a metre away he thought he saw the letterbox move. He froze mid-step as his pulse switched up a gear.

Two years ago someone had poured lighter fluid through his door and set fire to it. A seriously unpleasant experience, and one which had ended with him lying in Södermalm Hospital with an oxygen mask over his face. It wasn't until much later that he had realized the whole thing was just a warning shot to remind him about the rules of the Game.

He sniffed carefully at the stagnant air, but couldn't smell paraffin or anything similar. But by now he was quite certain. The sounds had come from the front door.

Maybe someone delivering papers after all?

He crept a couple of steps closer to the door and carefully put his eye to the peephole.

The sudden noise was so violent that he staggered back into the hall.

Fuck!

For a few seconds he saw stars, and his heart almost seemed to have stopped.

Then another violent crash jolted him out of the shock.

Someone was smashing his door in!

The steel frame was already starting to bow, so whoever it was basically had to be stronger than the Hulk. A third crash, metal against metal, no bastard Bruce Banner but probably a serious sledgehammer – if not more than one.

The frame moved another few centimetres and he could suddenly see the bolts of the locks in the gap. A couple more blows was all it would take.

He spun round, stumbling over his own feet, and fell flat on the floor. Another crash from the door sent a rattling shower of plaster over his bare legs.

His feet slid on the floor as his hands tried to get a grip. He was up.

Quickly into the living room, then the bedroom.

Another crash on the door!

He could taste blood in his mouth, and his heart was pounding fit to burst.

His hands were shaking so much he had trouble turning the key in the lock.

Whatinthenameofholyfucksgoingon . . .?

A further blow from the hall, this time followed by a splintering sound that almost certainly meant that the door frame had given way.

He grabbed the chest of drawers, and almost fell over when it glided easily in front of the bedroom door.

Fucking chipboard crap!

If the steel door out there hadn't been able to stop his attackers, then a bit of self-assembly furniture from the other side of the Baltic wasn't going to win him more than a couple of seconds at most. He leapt at the bed and fumbled about on the bedside table, which was covered with magazines and paperbacks.

The phone, where the hell was the phone?

There! No, shit, that was the remote for the television . . .

He heard rapid steps in the living room, gruff voices shouting to each other, but he was concentrating too hard on his search to hear what they were saying.

Suddenly his fingers hit the phone, so hard that it fell to the floor.

Fucking hell!

The door handle rattled, then a rough voice shouting: 'In here!'

HP threw himself on the floor, fumbling wildly with his arms.

There it was, right next to his left hand.

He grabbed the phone, scrabbled at the buttons. His fingers were twitching as if he had Parkinson's.

One, one, two is easy to do . . . like fuck it was!

A crash from the door and the Ikea chest of drawers almost fell over.

'Hello, emergency services, how can I help you?' a dry, professional voice said.

'Police!' HP yelled. 'Help m . . .'

A sudden flash of light blinded him, burning onto his retina.

Then a blow that was so strong he was left gasping for air.

And then they had him.

'It's back.'

'The van,' she added when he didn't react immediately.

He glanced quickly in the rear-view mirror.

'The same one as yesterday?'

'Mmh,' she said, without taking her eyes off the extra mirror fixed to the windscreen above the passenger seat.

What else would it be? she wondered quietly to herself.

'Four cars behind us. It's been there a while now . . . Just like yesterday, and in almost the same place.'

'Are you sure it's the same one? There are plenty of white vans in the city . . .'

'I'm sure,' she said abruptly. 'Slow down a bit and let him get closer.'

'But then I'll lose the VIP . . .' He gestured towards the open-topped sports car in front of them.

'Just forget the Security Police handbook, Kjellgren, and

7

try to be a bit flexible,' she snapped with unnecessary sharpness.

He took his foot off the accelerator more abruptly than he needed to. The car behind blew its horn angrily, and then overtook them a little too closely. Another car followed it.

Rebecca opened the glove compartment and took out the camera. She held it low and close, so that the van-driver wouldn't see it through the rear window.

Another glance in the rear-view mirror.

The zoom lens was pretty good, but the van was still two cars away and partially obscured.

'A bit more,' she muttered to Kjellgren, getting the camera ready in her lap.

She was fighting the urge to look round.

Suddenly the VIP in front of them changed lane, crossing a solid white line, and headed up towards Kungsgatan.

Kjellgren had no choice but to follow it.

She swore quietly to herself – so much for that chance. But a couple of seconds later she realized that the van was still following them. Another of the cars between them was gone and it was much closer now. Considerably closer than she would have been if she was tailing someone.

The sudden change of lane must have taken the driver by surprise. Forced him into making a mistake.

She slowly turned her upper body, pressing her left elbow against the seat and holding herself in place with her legs. The van's licence plate was still hidden by the car between them, but she could see the top halves of the two people in the driver's cab through the tinted windscreen. Long-sleeved, pale-coloured clothing, some sort of overalls, just like yesterday. But last time she hadn't managed to get the camera out quickly enough. She was planning to make up for that mistake today.

The car directly behind them suddenly indicated to change lane and she saw her chance. She turned round in a flash, raised the camera and aimed at the point where the licence plate was about to become visible.

She pressed the button halfway down. The car between them pulled out. There was a short bleep as the automatic focus adjusted the image.

Button down. She fired off a couple of pictures. Perfect!

Then she quickly raised the camera towards the cab of the van. She focused on the driver and pressed the button. The telephoto lens whirred and the fuzzy shape behind the wheel suddenly became much sharper. But just as the automatic focus bleeped, Kjellgren suddenly accelerated hard and the rapid movement threw her off balance.

By the time she got the cab back into view, the van was already a long way behind them.

'What the hell are you playing at, Kjellgren?' she snapped as she took a series of shots, almost at random, of the diminishing silhouette in the van.

'The VIP, Wennergren junior.' He pointed ahead at the little sports car which was almost out of sight. 'He suddenly took off like a scalded troll. Didn't want to risk losing him.'

She lowered the camera and sank back into her seat.
Shit!

A quick glance in the mirror, but she already knew what it would tell her. The van was gone.

She clicked through the pictures on the little screen of the camera. The licence plate was clearly visible, but just as she suspected the images of the cab were pretty much useless.
Bloody hell!

Call it police intuition or whatever the hell you liked, but there was something about that van that worried her.

As soon as she got back to the office she'd check the licence plate, maybe even make a couple of calls and double check with Surveillance if the Highways Agency didn't come up with anything . . .

She suddenly regretted snapping at Kjellgren. His priorities had been totally correct. The VIP was the most important thing, after all, and she would have done exactly the same if she had been the one driving.

Kjellgren was an excellent driver, which was one of the reasons why she'd brought him across from the Security Police. He had already made up the distance to the VIP's car and they were in their customary position immediately behind him.

'You made exactly the right call, Kjellgren,' she said, doing her best to sound neutral.

He merely nodded and for a few minutes they sat in silence as they took it in turns to check their rear-view mirrors.

'So when did you say we'd be going up to the Fortress?' Kjellgren said eventually, in a rather too-friendly voice.

'That depends a bit on Black's schedule.' She made an effort to return his smile.

'Okay. By the way, did you see that article in *Dagens Nyheter*? A big piece about the new uses people have found for old military installations. Apart from using underground bunkers as server rooms, they've also fixed the old communication tunnel to the coast so it brings in water for the cooling system. Seriously advanced stuff.

'The security up there's supposed to be quite something as well.'

He pulled closer to Wennergren's car and did a quick

swerve to scare off a car that was trying to squeeze in between them.

'Apparently PayTag want to retain its status as a high security installation, which is pretty understandable. Because then their security staff up there can be armed . . .'

Kjellgren looked away from the car in front to give her a quick sideways glance.

She could hear the question coming before he had opened his mouth.

'By the way, how are things going for us on the weapons front, boss . . .?'

'The licensing authority is still looking at our application . . .'

. . . *again*, she almost added, but her mobile started to vibrate in her jacket pocket. Number withheld. Probably another marketing call, or some former police colleague fishing for a job . . .

She moved her thumb towards the red icon to reject the call, but changed her mind at the last moment. Kjellgren kept glancing at her, evidently keen to carry on the conversation about weapons licences. And he wasn't alone in that.

Pretty much all of the new recruits to her bodyguard team had taken the job on the assumption that they'd be able to bear arms in the course of their duties. So if the application got rejected . . .

She quickly pressed the green icon on her phone.

'Sentry Security, Rebecca Normén,' she said, in an exaggeratedly businesslike tone.

'Personal Protection Unit, Detective Superintendent Ludvig Runeberg,' her old boss said at the other end.

'Hi, Ludvig, it's been a while. Good to hear from you . . .'

'I'm not sure you're going to think that by the time we've finished, Normén . . .'

Something in his tone of voice made her straighten up unconsciously.

'You should probably come up here to Police Headquarters, right away if you can manage that . . .'

The connection crackled and his voice vanished for a few seconds. But part of her had already worked out what he was going to say. Her stomach contracted into a hard little lump.

No, no, no . . .

'. . . your younger brother.'

Opening

His body was slumped motionless across the table. His eyes were shut and it almost looked like he was asleep.

The last time she had seen him his hair had been cropped short, but now it had grown again and was hanging in greasy clumps over his chalk-white face. The fluorescent lighting in the claustrophobic little room made the rings under his eyes look darker than ever against his pale, yellowish skin. As if she were really looking at a wax doll rather than an inert human body through the large glass window.

She had been worried that this would happen. Ever since Henke threw a rock through her windscreen two years ago and almost killed her and Kruse, her colleague, she had been dreading this moment. Well, longer than that, really. Much, much longer . . .

'He was brought in last night,' Runeberg said somewhere behind her right shoulder, but she hardly heard him.

'I was only informed an hour or so ago. I called you at once. Not quite going by the rules, but I thought you'd want to know straight away. I know I would if it was my brother . . .'

She tore her eyes away from the glass and turned to look at him.

'Thanks, Ludvig, I appreciate it . . .' The words caught in her throat.

They stood in silence for a while.

'Terrible business,' he said eventually.

He put his hand clumsily on her arm.

Suddenly and without warning the door opened and a skinny man in his sixties with thinning hair walked in. He was carrying a file of papers under one arm and, even though it was summer, he was wearing a dark three-piece suit topped off with a perfectly centred tie. The man nodded curtly to Runeberg, then turned to Rebecca.

'You must be the sister.'

'Rebecca Normén,' she said, holding out her hand.

But instead of taking her hand, the man pulled out a pair of narrow reading glasses from the pocket of his waistcoat, planted them firmly on the end of his nose and then opened the file.

'You said she used to work for the Firm, Runeberg?'

'She still does, at least officially, Stigsson,' her former boss replied in an ingratiating tone that she didn't recognize at all.

'Normén is on leave of absence until the end of the year,' he explained. 'Then she has to make up her mind which she prefers, the Security Police or private enterprise . . .' Runeberg attempted a smile, but the other man's face didn't move a muscle.

'I see . . .' Stigsson turned his head and looked at Rebecca over his glasses.

'Since you're still employed by the Security Police, Normén, your security clearance holds, as does the oath of confidentiality you signed when you first joined. Whether or not you're his sister, everything you hear in

14

here is confidential, and any attempt to communicate it to anyone else is strictly forbidden, is that understood?'

'Yes,' she nodded.

'Of course,' she added when he didn't seem happy with her response. 'So, what's this all about, then?'

In the room on the other side of the glass a door suddenly opened and two people, a man and a woman in dark suits, entered. For a few seconds no-one in the room moved. Then Henke opened his eyes.

He raised his head, sat up in the chair. Slowly and elaborately he stretched, as if he had just woken up. He said something that she couldn't hear through the glass, and she was seized momentarily with an urge to burst in and give him a good slap.

Stigsson's bone-dry voice changed her mind.

'Your brother is suspected of conspiracy, and possibly planning a gross act of terrorism.'

'Well, Henrik, I repeat: you are suspected of planning and possibly making preparations for a crime intended to seriously destabilize or disrupt the fundamental political, constitutional, economic and social structures of the country,' said the lead interviewer, a forty-something woman with short, dark hair, as she fixed her eyes on him.

But HP hardly noticed her. His weary brain was still trying to make sense of everything. At least there was one thing he was reasonably sure of. Unlike two years ago, when he thought he had been arrested but was actually the victim of a huge hoax, this time every single detail was right, from the armed unit's break-in to his flat down to the scorched taste of the instant coffee in the brown plastic cup on the table next to him. It all seemed genuine. *Was* genuine, in all likelihood. Which meant . . .?

The subject is conspiracy theories, and here comes your thousand-kronor question . . .

'Mmm . . .' he muttered, seeing as he was evidently expected to say something. He closed his eyes and rubbed his temples to buy himself a bit of thinking time. What the fuck was the woman banging on about? Destabilizing the political what . . .?

'I've already told you at least a dozen times, I want a lawyer present during the interview,' he said quietly.

The woman, whose name was Roslund or Roskvist, something like that, exchanged a quick glance with her colleague.

'Yes, we heard you, Henrik,' the policeman said. HP had already forgotten his name. 'But we've been waiting several hours. At least we can get some of the formalities out of the way before your lawyer shows up.

'He is coming, isn't he – or she? How many law firms have you called?' He tilted his head and smiled in a way that left no room for misinterpretation.

'Of course there's a lawyer coming . . .' Henrik mumbled.

'Well then, how about making a start? To save us all a bit of time,' the policeman added with another smile.

'Unless there's anyone else you'd like to call? Someone close to you . . .?'

'No!' HP interrupted, slightly too loudly, as he sat himself up.

He saw the look in their eyes. *Bollocks*, he'd been trying to play it cool . . .

'I've got all the time in the world, and I'm not going to say anything until I've got a lawyer,' he said as calmly as he could, staring down at the tabletop.

'But by all means – feel free to talk away . . .' he muttered a couple of seconds later, mainly to break the oppressive silence.

16

'Good suggestion, Henrik.' The male police officer, whose name HP still couldn't remember, pulled out a chair and sat down. He took out a little digital recorder from the pocket of his jacket and put it on the table between them.

'Interview with Henrik Pettersson, known as HP, third of June, time 15.13. Officers present, Police Inspectors Roswall and . . .'

'. . . Hellström.'

Stigsson had pressed a button next to the window and suddenly the lead interviewer's voice could be heard from the speakers.

'So what exactly is Henke supposed to have done?' Rebecca said to no-one in particular, while Hellström went on talking to the recording device.

She was doing her best to sound calm, as if she wasn't that worried about the answer.

'We've received information which suggests that your brother is planning some sort of terrorist attack against the state, possibly connected to the princess's wedding . . .'

'You're kidding!' she exclaimed, unable to stop herself.

Stigsson gave her a quick look and she bit her tongue. Obviously, this was all just a big practical joke, the Security Police were renowned for their sense of humour, and Stigsson here was a brilliant stand-up comedian . . .

Pull yourself together, for God's sake, Normén!

A mistake – this was clearly some sort of huge mistake. They must have got Henke mixed up with someone else and broken into the wrong flat. It would hardly be the first time information was wrong, after all . . .

'We've also been made aware that this is by no means the first time your brother has been involved in this sort of criminal activity . . .'

17

'You mean that business with Dag,' she cut him off. 'Henke was only trying to protect me. Besides, that was almost fifteen years ago . . .'

Stigsson shook his head.

'No, no, not the incident in which your boyfriend was killed, even if that isn't entirely without interest as part of the bigger picture . . . This is about something else entirely. See for yourself.'

He gestured towards the interview room, where one of the officers had just switched on a video projector. A recording from a shaky hand-held camera appeared on one wall, blue sky and some dark buildings. Then slender trees and a row of pavement cafés. Kungsträdgården, more specifically: Kungsträdgårdsgatan. In the background there was a clattering sound that was getting louder and louder. It took her a few moments before she suddenly realized what it was. Horses' hooves . . . A lot of horses' hooves on tarmac. When the royal cortege appeared in shot she noticed she was trembling . . .

He recognized the film at once. Kungsträdgårdsgatan, exactly two years ago, the cortege with the royal couple and the Greek president.

The soldiers bobbing along on their horses, the spectators on the pavements fiddling with their mobiles. He'd seen it on film hundreds of times, recognized every face, every expression. The guy with the dog, the woman in the white hat, the German tourists with their huge rucksacks . . . He knew the rest of it by heart. Any moment now a flash would bleach the image, and a bang like the one he had experienced in his flat would make the hand holding the camera shake. Then complete chaos, galloping horses, soldiers on the ground, people screaming in panic.

But instead of focusing on the cortege as he had

18

expected, the camera suddenly began to pan round. It wavered for a few seconds, then slid along the crowd lining one side of the road.

And it came to rest on a familiar figure, then zoomed in slowly until the person filled almost the entire screen.

HP couldn't help squirming. Suddenly he felt a bit sick.

A man dressed in black sitting on an EU moped. The tinted helmet might be obscuring his face, but Rebecca had no trouble recognizing him. His posture, jerky movements, the way he held his head slightly tilted. There was no doubt at all . . .

She had suspected it at the time, but had deliberately not asked because she hadn't wanted to know the answer . . .

The man on the screen reached into a plastic bag that was hanging from the handlebar, pulled out a cylindrical object and started to fiddle with it. The noise of horses' hooves got steadily louder as the cortege approached. The camera zoomed in even closer. The man looked up, waiting for a moment with the object in both hands. Then he suddenly jerked one hand and raised his arm. She already knew what he was about to throw.

The blast from the grenade made this film shake as well, but the cameraman didn't shift his focus from the moped. According to the timer in one corner of the screen, he sat there impassively for ten seconds, watching the effects of what he had done, before putting the bike into gear, making a sharp u-turn and disappearing down Wahrendorffsgatan.

The film stopped abruptly and the room fell silent. HP shifted on his chair and swallowed uneasily a couple of times. A couple of clicks on the computer and suddenly

19

a still of him covered the whole screen. A freeze-frame image of the precise moment when he threw the grenade.

His arm in the air, his body coiled like a spring. When you added the tinted helmet, he looked pretty alarming, to put it mildly.

'So, Henrik,' Hellström began, in a considerably less friendly tone of voice than before. 'Is that . . .'

'. . . your brother on the screen?'

Stigsson and Runeberg were both looking at her now, and for a few seconds her head was completely blank. Her blouse was sticking under her jacket, and the air in the little room suddenly felt stale and difficult to breathe. Their eyes seemed to be boring right through her.

She glanced into the interview room, but there was total silence in there as well. She had to try to gain a bit of time, get a chance to think things through . . . But to judge from the looks on both men's faces they were expecting an immediate answer.

So what was she supposed to do? Lie, or tell the truth? *Make a decision, for God's sake!*

She gulped a couple of times to clear the lump in her throat.

'Well . . .' she began.

'You don't have to answer, Henrik!'

The door to the interview room opened and a tall man with slicked back grey hair walked in. With a flourish the man undid the gold buttons on his blazer and sat down on the empty chair beside Henke. At that moment Rebecca realized that she knew him.

'My client declines to answer that question,' the man said, this time looking at the police officers as he lifted his briefcase onto the table and snapped it open. He took out a folder.

'Well, now I'd like to know why this interview has already started even though my client clearly stated that he wished to have his legal representative present. As I'm sure you are aware, this is in breach of chapter twenty-one of the Penal Code . . .'

'Johan Sandels!'

Runeberg's surprised exclamation drowned out the rest of the lawyer's speech.

'How the hell did your brother manage to get hold of a heavyweight like that at such short notice?'

'I've got no idea,' she replied with a shrug.

That much was completely true.

What the hell was going on?

3

Timeout

The metal gate swung shut behind him and he took a couple of steps out into Bergsgatan. Freedom again – fuck, what a relief!

The prosecutor had backed down almost immediately. A blurry film-clip was evidently not sufficient grounds to hold him, at least not if Johan Sandels was involved.

The cops clearly hadn't done their homework, and still thought he was the sort of small fry they could scare the shit out of with a nocturnal break-in, a few hours waiting and then a stint in the hot seat.

A couple of years ago that might well have worked, and indeed probably *had* worked. But he was a totally different person now, and was playing in a considerably higher league than the cops could possibly realize.

Even if he *had* chosen to break rule number one and tell them what had actually happened, their tiny little cop brains would never have been able to accept the truth.

I found a mobile phone on a train, a shiny silvery thing with a glass touch-screen, and through that I got invited to play a game. An alternative reality game that altered my reality forever. But I broke out, or at least I tried to . . .

Someone had shopped him, that much was obvious. Sent in the film clip and gave the Security Police his name.

The clip was hardly a new Zapruder film, captured by some tourist who had got more than he had bargained for. The cameraman had focused specifically on him, had known exactly where he was going to be. Which must mean that the film came from the Game.

But the Game had nothing to gain from getting him locked up – on the contrary. They'd already got their hands on him again and they needed him out in the open if he was to stand any chance of fulfilling the task they were asking of him. Were trying to force on him.

He had actually considered trying to get himself locked up. Come up with some poxy little crime that would land him inside for a few months and quite literally get him out of the Game. But, like so many of his other brilliant ideas, he had chosen to park it for the time being. Prison really wasn't his thing.

Been there, done that . . .

Fucking lucky that Sandels bloke showed up.

He had called four of the biggest law firms, asking for their most famous lawyers, and each time he got stuck with some snippy little underling who gave him a half-hearted promise that they'd be in touch. He'd decided to make do with some junior lawyer from the B-team and a few nights on a hard bunk.

But suddenly Sandels had popped up like a jack-in-the-box . . .

Maybe the lawyer had got fed up of life in the country with his family, and was grateful for an excuse to come into the city and see his mistress?

A stroke of luck, anyway. Unless it wasn't . . .

Either way, he had been severely roughed up, banned from travelling, and the cops had seized his passport.

But at least he was out.

He took a few more deep breaths, then set off towards the tobacconist's a few blocks away.

They had let him go far too easily.

They could hold a suspect for seventy-two hours, and in terrorism cases the court usually followed the Security Police line and agreed to remand suspects. Yet Henke had been held for less than thirteen hours. That couldn't only be down to the fact that he'd got hold of a famous lawyer.

'Stigsson. How long has he been with the Firm?' she asked Runeberg when they were sitting in the police canteen.

'Why do you ask?'

'I thought I knew most people in the Security Police, but he's new to me . . .'

Runeberg shuffled slightly, enough for her to notice.

'Okay, he isn't new, he was actually my supervisor back in the day. But then he worked abroad for years. UN, OSCE, that sort of thing, but right now we're pulling in all available resources. Have you had a letter yet, by the way?'

'A letter?'

'Anyone on leave of absence is being asked to return to duty to cover the wedding. We're going to need every trained bodyguard we've got. We're already stretched as it is, with all these rightwing Sweden Democrats needing protection from the voters. How about it? It would only be a couple of weeks . . .'

She shook her head.

'Not at the moment, Ludvig, we're only just getting things sorted at Sentry. It's a bit of a muddle with all the new staff and the buy-out. I've got more balls in the air than I care to think about . . .'

It suddenly dawned on her that he had managed to change the subject.

'Okay, it's more or less like this,' he said. 'New general director and all that. Well, will you promise to think about it? Do you want more coffee, by the way, they're about to close?'

She shook her head and stood up.

'I have to get home, Micke will have dinner ready and I'm already late.'

'Okay,' he said, pushing his chair back. 'How have things been going on the home front . . .? I mean, after . . .'

'Tobbe Lundh? Oh, we got through it. Micke's the forgiving sort.'

'Good.' Runeberg looked away for a few seconds. 'Well, I have to show you out. New bosses, new routines, you know how it is.'

HP emerged from the tobacconist's, tore the cellophane from the packet of cigarettes and pulled out a Marlboro.

His hands were still trembling slightly, but that was probably due to his nicotine withdrawal. Well, that was his preferred explanation . . .

A couple of deep drags on the pavement to calm the worst of the pangs, then he set off towards the underground. Time to go home and inspect the damage. The cops had no doubt turned his flat upside down. Good job he had nothing there that he was worried about.

He opened the door to the underground station then, without deigning to look at the ticket booth, jumped over the barrier as he usually did, and carried on towards the escalator.

On the way down he was passed by a tall, platinum blonde woman roughly the same age as him. Mostly out of habit he watched the movement of her hips for a few

25

seconds before returning to the maelstrom of thoughts in his head.

He had to try to make some sort of sense of whatever the fuck was going on, and who had grassed on him. And, above all, why . . .

But first he had to get a few hours sleep.

He got to the bottom of the escalator and strolled slowly along the platform towards an empty bench.

The blonde was sitting a short distance away. The music in her massive headphones had to be seriously absorbing, because she was staring ahead of her with a glassy look in her eyes, and didn't even seem to have noticed him.

Never mind, women were the least of his problems right now, and besides, to judge by her black nail varnish, fringe and gloomy clothes, she looked like she was probably a bit emo. Not really his cup of tea . . .

A faint gust of wind against his legs made him turn his head towards the opening of the tunnel. He got slowly to his feet as the train thundered into the station.

'Well, it was still good to see you, Normén,' Runeberg said as they approached the reception area. 'Even if the circumstances could have been rather happier . . .'

He held his card up to a little black reader beside the door. It looked new – the pale outline of the old card-reader was still visible on the wall behind it.

Runeberg pulled at the handle, but the door remained locked. He muttered something and repeated the procedure, with the same result.

'Bloody security system,' he muttered. 'Two years of planning, millions of kronor, and the crap still doesn't work properly . . .'

Taking it more slowly, he repeated the procedure for a third time, and suddenly the lock clicked. Over by the reception desk two people appeared to be having a heated discussion with the guards. Runeberg quickly ushered Rebecca past them and off towards the main door.

She opened her mouth to say something, but Runeberg was quicker.

'I'll be in touch . . .' He gestured towards the ceiling and it took her a couple of seconds to realize that they were standing right beneath the dark globe of a little camera. Just like the card-reader, it looked very new.

She frowned and for a few seconds they stood opposite each other without speaking. Then she gave him a quick hug and opened the door.

'Bye, Ludvig,' she said as she left, but for some reason Runeberg didn't answer, just pulled an involuntary grimace. It only lasted a fraction of a second, then his face went back to normal. But for the second time in just a few hours she couldn't shake the feeling that something wasn't right.

The note was on his front door, and he came close to just crumpling it up and throwing it down the stairwell. A little greyish-white scrap of recycled paper, with a tiny bit of tape to hold it up, just like all the ones that had gone before it. *Please don't play loud music at night,* or *We would like to remind you of the housing association's rules about blah blah blah . . .*

A nocturnal Nescafé visit by the anti-terrorism squad had probably made the committee shit themselves. He could easily imagine the discussion downstairs in the communal area. *We need to let our feelings be known, Gösta. Use capital letters this time . . .*

In previous years he had always just moved the notes onto the Goat's door. Which probably wasn't a very nice thing to do, in the pale light of hindsight. The little hash pixie was already paranoid enough. It still seemed a bit odd that he hadn't said anything about moving out, or knocked on his door to ask for help.

But on the other hand he hadn't exactly been very sociable himself in recent months, and he'd long since cut the wires to the doorbell.

Oh well, his new and as yet unknown neighbour might as well have a little welcome message.

He pulled the note off and fixed it to the door of the neighbouring flat. His hands were still shaking slightly, which irritated him more than he was prepared to admit.

There, welcome to Housing Association block number 6, mofo!

He stepped back and was just about to turn away when he realized that the note didn't look the same as usual. Instead of the chairman's old man's handwriting, this note was written in rounded, almost feminine letters.

Problems?
Don't give up, we can help you!
070-931151

He peered suspiciously at the message for a few seconds. Admittedly, he could do with a bit of instant salvation, but a subscription to *Watchtower* was hardly going to help.

At least the cops had had the decency to fix the door, he noted. More or less, at any rate. Two of the locks were completely buggered, but the third seemed to have survived pretty much unscathed.

The crooked frame creaked in complaint as he pushed the door open.

Just as he stepped inside he thought he heard a noise from the neighbour's door, and for a few moments he imagined someone was about to come out.

He quickly closed the door behind him and then put his eye to the spyhole, but his new neighbour must have had a change of heart because nothing happened.

Oh well, sooner or later they were bound to bump into each other. Right now he had other things to think about. Considerably more important things . . .

The cops evidently hadn't found the USB memory stick he had hidden in a jar of coffee in the kitchen, but otherwise the flat looked pretty much as he had expected. Every drawer had been emptied, the shelves cleared and the stained mattress on the bed turned upside down.

Some of his things were missing, he knew that already. He had been given a copy of the list of items they had seized before he was turfed out of the police station. The only question was how much wiser the cops would be after examining a few dog-eared paperbacks and a collection of action films. Not to mention his extensive collection of adult movies . . .

As luck would have it, he hadn't had any dope in the flat for months, he could hardly even remember the last time he had smoked a joint. Must have been in Dubai after that fake Frenchman-slash-hitman had given him a bad trip and then tried to frame him for the murder of sex goddess Anna Argos.

These days he steered clear of dope – he was paranoid enough as it was.

He spent ten minutes clearing up the worst of the mess, then threw himself down on the bed.

'Oh, a letter came for you . . .' Micke said when they had almost finished eating. 'Something about a safe deposit box.'

She started, but he seemed to misinterpret her reaction.

29

'Sorry, I didn't mean to open your post. I just saw the SEB bank logo on the envelope and assumed it must be for me. I've just got a bit too much on my mind right now . . .'

'Don't worry,' she muttered. 'I've got no secrets from you . . .'

. . . any more, a little voice inside her head added, and to judge by Micke's reaction he must have heard it as well.

He stood up quickly and came back with the torn-open envelope.

Dear Rebecca Normén,
The contract regarding safe deposit box 0679406948, listing you as one of the key-holders, is about to expire.
Please contact our branch at 6 Sveavägen in Stockholm to discuss the extension of the contract.
If we fail to hear from you within thirty (30) days from the date of this letter, the box will be opened in the presence of a public notary and the contents stored by the bank for a further sixty (60) days. After that the contents will be disposed of at auction and any eventual profit, minus a handling charge, will be placed in a bank account in the names of the key-holders.
Yours faithfully,
L. Helander
SEB

'I thought safe deposit boxes disappeared years ago,' Micke said in an exaggeratedly amused voice. 'A tin box hidden in an underground vault feels like a pretty old-fashioned way to store valuables. More the sort of thing my parents or grandparents would do. I didn't know you had one . . .?'

'Nor did I,' she returned blandly.

He opened his mouth to say something, but seemed to change his mind.

'So what do you want to do?' he asked a few seconds later.

'W-what?' She looked up from the letter.

'It's Friday evening, and just for once we're both off at the same time. How about the cinema?'

'Don't you want to work? I thought you were up to your neck . . .?'

'I am, but it can wait till tomorrow. The new Clooney looks interesting.'

He was still acting with exaggerated cheerfulness, but neither his tone of voice nor his smile convinced her. Okay, so they had talked through everything. She had told him the least hurtful details about her affair with her colleague, Tobbe Lundh, and Micke had said that he forgave her. That he believed her assurance that the whole thing had been a stupid mistake and that he was the one she loved.

But even though six months had passed since her confession, and even though he had never raised the subject again – not even during one of their rare quarrels – she had no trouble at all picking up the emotion that was bubbling beneath his urbane exterior.

He didn't trust her . . .

And he was hardly alone in that . . .

He picked up the paper from one of the kitchen chairs and leafed through until he found the right page.

'It's on at Filmstaden on Södermalm, we could aim for the nine o'clock screening and grab a beer afterwards . . .'

Her first instinct was to say no. Her computer was full

of work she needed to do, things that couldn't really wait. But a film and a few beers might manage to reinforce the illusion that their relationship was still working. It might even get her brain to skip the usual nightmare and make it easier for her to sleep.

She could always hope.

'Sure, great! Let's go for it!' She tried to sound as though she meant it. 'Do you want to get the tickets now?'

'Yep!'

He got up to fetch his laptop and she took the chance to read the letter once more.

A tin box hidden in an underground vault . . .

For some reason she couldn't help shivering.

4

Knowledge is power

'Hello, my name's Rebecca Normén. Apparently I've got a safe deposit box here?'

She held out the letter and her driving licence to the man behind the counter.

She was in a small reception area behind an anonymous door right next to Sergels torg in the centre of the city. She must have walked past it a thousand times without ever noticing it. A buzzer and an entry-phone, a reception desk and one solitary man in a suit. Behind him a short flight of steps led down to a dark steel door. It would all have looked perfectly innocent if it hadn't been for the unobtrusive little round cameras in the ceiling. Five of them, exactly the same sort as in Police Headquarters, which had to be at least three more than necessary. Every point in the room was covered from at least two angles.

'You need to use your card . . .'

'Sorry?'

'Your passcard . . . To get into the vault you need to use your passcard,' the man explained, gesturing backwards with his thumb at the metal door behind him.

'It also opens the right section of the vault. Then you use the key to open the box itself. You have got a key?'

She shook her head.

'I've haven't got a passcard or a key. To be honest, I didn't even know I had a deposit box until I received this letter from you. I was hoping you might be able to give me a bit more information . . .' She nodded at the sheet of paper in front of him.

'I see. Just one moment . . .'

He began tapping at his keyboard, and she noticed a little screen set discreetly into the counter.

When the man turned slightly to one side she noticed another detail. On one of his shoulders there was a slight but very familiar bulge, a thicker garment under his shirt and well-tailored suit. She'd seen it a thousand times in her work, on herself and other people. The man was wearing a bulletproof vest. She wondered if he was armed as well.

She took a cautious step closer and leaned carefully over the counter. Her eyes slid down the line of the jacket towards the man's hips.

'That particular deposit box has two key-holders.' His voice made her jump and she straightened up unconsciously.

'Sorry?'

'You and a Henrik Pettersson. Do you know him?'

She nodded. 'He's my brother.'

'Maybe he's the one who's got the key and passcard?'

The idea of Henke having a deposit box seemed very odd. He didn't exactly own anything that was valuable enough to need this sort of protection. But, on the other hand, the bill for the box hadn't been paid, and that sounded just like him. And given the way he'd been behaving over the past few months, maybe it wasn't impossible that he had secrets he needed to keep hidden.

She shrugged her shoulders.

'Maybe . . .'

'Well, the card's no problem,' he went on. 'Because you're one of the account holders, I can order you a new one. That would cost two hundred kronor. And you'll also have to pay the overdue fee if you don't want us to drill the box open?'

'Of course, no problem, just send me the bill.'

He nodded and typed something into the computer. She guessed it was a request for a new card.

'There, the card will be sent to you within the next few days. But I'm afraid I can't help you with the key.'

'How do you mean?'

'The person who set up the contract receives all the keys. Then it's up to him or her to distribute them. The keys are copy protected, so we can't actually have new ones made, even if we wanted to. That's why we have to drill boxes open if people don't contact us.'

'B-but . . . If I'm listed as a key-holder . . .?'

'It's not unusual for the person who sets up the agreement to list several other people under the same account, as a form of insurance. In case anything should happen to them . . .'

PayTag – they were the ones behind it all. Even if he was having trouble getting the pieces of the puzzle to fit together, that fact was still bombproof. PayTag had owned ACME Telecom Services, who in turn had hosted the server farm out in Kista that he had blown sky high two years before.

The same PayTag that had wanted to buy up ArgosEye and make multi-millionaires of all its conspiring directors up in their Hötorget skyscraper office, until he had pulled the plug and sent that particular ship to the bottom with all hands.

But PayTag seemed to have just moved on, still swallowing up smaller companies at a feverish pace as its empire grew ever larger.

He had scraped together all manner of facts about PayTag that were sloshing around the deeper recesses of cyberspace. He had saved most of it on the USB stick that the cops had failed to find.

But losing it wouldn't have been a total disaster, he had memorized most of it.

He lit a fag, took a deep drag and then sent an almost perfect smoke-ring up towards the nicotine-yellow ceiling.

1992 – PayTag is founded by four dudes at an American university. The basic idea is to facilitate smooth transfers of money over the internet. There's nothing wrong with the idea, but in purely technical terms they're ten years too early and the software causes problems. In spite of this, venture capitalists pour money in and they are able to build a number of large server farms to handle the transactions they expect to have to deal with.

1997 – After five years of figures in the red the coffers start to run dry. Following a disagreement two of the founders leave. The other two decide to change direction and in a desperate attempt to exploit their unused server farms they start hiring out space to other companies that need external backup in case their own servers go down. The lads have struck gold and clients start pouring in almost immediately.

1999 – For the first time the company's accounts show a profit, and a fairly healthy one at that, making PayTag practically unique in the IT world.

2001 – BANG! All the air goes out of the global IT bubble, but seeing as the need for backup is bigger than ever PayTag still manages to make a small profit. And oddly enough in light of the stock market collapse, new capital is available. PayTag goes on a serious shopping spree among its bankruptcy-threatened competitors, and soon manages to weave itself into every aspect of the IT sector: installations, service contracts, consultancy – you name it!

2005 – The company is listed on the NASDAQ index. The largest single holding belongs to a foundation which is probably linked to the two remaining founders, but various financial machinations, along the lines of those employed by Ikea, make it pretty much impossible to work out if this is actually the case.

2009 – Another landmark! IT guru and media darling Mark Black is installed as new MD. He immediately sets to work realizing his vision – the Cloud. Clients would no longer merely use PayTag to host their critical backup, but ALL their data. Server spaces are expunged from offices around the world and instead established on the internet – or rather, in one of PayTag's heavily guarded gigantic server halls which are now popping up like toadstools in sparsely populated areas all over the planet.

But HP was almost certain that the Game began way before '92, and PayTag actually seemed to have been legitimate for a good few years. Which meant that their paths must have crossed somewhere.

The Game could have been a secret source of finance that stepped in during the collapse of the IT bubble, for instance.

Or else the mysterious foundation that owned the majority of the shares could conceal something considerably more unpleasant than just a couple of greedy little Ingvar Kamprads who didn't want to pay tax.

But the safest way to take the company over probably wasn't through holding shares, or at least not that alone.

They would need some kind of presence on the ground, someone who would make sure that things were run the way they should be, which led him to his latest theory.

The Game had probably planted a trojan inside PayTag. He knew something about trojans having been one himself inside ArgosEye. Something or someone who looked on the surface to be an asset, but who had actually brought something lethal inside the walls. For that tactic to work, the trojan would have to be implanted at the very top of the pyramid. Which meant that there was really only one candidate . . .

Mark Black.

It was under his leadership that the company had grown to span the entire world. The Cloud and the server farms were all part of Black's vision, and PayTag's owners appeared to have given him a completely free hand. Celebrities and politicians alike seemed to love the smooth bastard, and the media drooled over everything he did. No-one seemed to have worked out who Black really was. No-one except Henrik HP Pettersson.

Imagine having a little chat with Mr Black.

Eye to eye.

Player to Player . . .

He took a last drag, then stubbed the cigarette out in an overflowing ashtray on the bedside table.

A meeting with Mark Black. That wasn't actually such a bad idea.

'Mark Black, managing director of PayTag and thus indirectly our ultimate boss, will be paying us a visit in a fortnight, as you all know . . .'

Rebecca clicked to bring up the first picture of her Powerpoint presentation. It showed about thirty people dressed in white, all wearing Guy Fawkes masks and holding banners.

'The threat level is currently deemed to be high, largely as a result of the various protests seen at previous inaugurations.'

She switched to an image of demonstrators being led away by the police.

'Black's private plane, registration number November Six Bravo, will be landing at Bromma on 25 June at 19.55. Kjellgren and I will pick him up in the Audi, Mrsic and Pellebergs will be waiting outside gate number one with the support vehicle. We'll be driving straight to the Grand Hotel, where I and potentially Mrsic will accompany him to his suite. We'll decide that once we know how things look. Black evidently isn't too keen on having much visible security around him . . . We will be based in room 623, in the same corridor as Black's suite, and I'll be staying there.'

Her mouth felt suddenly dry, and she paused to take a sip of water from the glass on the table in front of her.

'Departure to the Fortress at 06.15 on the twenty-sixth. Same cars and pairings as before. The site manager and Anthea Ravel from management will be joining us . . .'

She saw a couple of the bodyguards exchange glances and went on quickly before any of them had a chance to open their mouths.

'The inauguration ceremony will begin at 09.30, followed directly by the press conference. Any questions so far . . .?'

None of the other six people in the little meeting room moved.

'Good,' she continued. 'Lindh, you and Gudmundson will meet us on site. Have you spoken to the manager there?'

Lindh, a sinewy, suntanned man in his forties, cleared his throat and glanced down at the little black notebook on the desk in front of him.

'Yes, it's all sorted. Thirty journalists have replied to say they'll be there, along with a group of local politicians, the Minister for Business and his entourage, and representatives from a couple of clients. Possibly a few more. No names that have set off any alarm bells so far, I should probably add. Obviously we've checked everyone . . .'

When the run-through was finished she took the stairs down to the floor below, said hello to a couple of faces she recognized, then slipped into Micke's cramped little office. He was crouched over his computer and hardly looked up.

'Hi!' She leaned over and gave him a quick peck on the cheek.

'Hi Becca, did it all go okay?' He spun his chair round.

'Yep, we've got Black's visit under control.'

'Good, the whole company seems a bit nervous. It's a big thing, him choosing to come here so soon after the acquisition. Will you be going up to the Fortress with him?'

She nodded just as his mobile started to ring.

He picked it up from the desk and looked at the screen. Then he stood up quickly.

'Sorry, I have to take this. We've got a crazy amount of work right now, we're completely swamped . . .'

'No problem, I was on my way out anyway. Just thought I'd ask about the pictures . . .'

'Pictures?' He had already taken a step towards the door and put his phone to his ear.

'The ones I took on Friday, in the van. You were going to try to improve the pixilation, or whatever you call it?'

40

The phone went on ringing and she could feel him getting rattled by the situation.

'Oh, no, it didn't work. Listen, I've really got to get this . . .'

She gave him a little wave and left the room.

'Hello . . .? Yes, everything's going according to plan . . .' she heard him say before the door closed behind her.

He didn't dare have a computer of his own. In his two months as an employee of ArgosEye he had realized how much of a trail you left, both on the internet and your own hard-disk. No way was he going to offer them a smorgasbord like that.

Instead he had developed a strategy where he switched between various borrowed computers at random. Short bursts where his minimal internet footprint would be hidden by thousands of other people's. Really, though, he ought to steer well clear of the internet altogether. Follow the example of Erman the hermit, cut all ties to civilization, go into hiding in a cabin in the woods and live a low-tech life way below the Game's radar.

But he had dropped that idea pretty quickly. He was born to live on tarmac, and life in the forest would undoubtedly have finished him off. Just as it had finished off poor Erman . . .

No, far better to play it cool, go along with it and make the most of the calm by gathering together as many pieces of the puzzle as possible. Preparing as best he could so he was ready when they wanted an answer.

At least that was what he had thought last winter, after his meeting with the Game Master.

Fuck it. Obviously, he should have cut back on his use of the Xbox and concentrated on reality far more than he had actually done. But up to the moment when the cops had kicked his door in, the complete absence of communication had almost managed to persuade him that the meeting out in the forest had been just a bad dream. A mad fantasy conjured up by his fucked up brain, desperate for a bit of acclaim.

Too many hours sitting with the hand controller – or his own joystick, for that matter – made it easy to lose focus.

Six months had passed since he had been given the task out at that creepy pet cemetery. Six months of decent peace and quiet, and halfway through the period of thinking time he had been promised.

Today it was the turn of the library at Medborgarplatsen. Tucked away in a corner where he could see everyone coming and going without them seeing him.

He plugged the little USB stick into one of the computer's card slots and waited for the files to load. Then he started the security program at the top of the list.

Scanning – please wait, a little dialogue box said, as a timer began to rotate. It usually took about a minute to check for spyware or any signs of surveillance. He never stayed for longer than fifteen minutes, but after the developments of recent days it was probably time to cut that down even more.

He bounced one foot impatiently as he bit on a ragged fingernail. He still had six months, one hundred and eighty days to chisel out a plan, a way out, an exit strategy that could get him out of the infernal trap he had got caught up in.

Wrong – which *they* had got caught up in . . . Because no matter how he looked at it, he couldn't get away from the conclusion that Becca was getting more and more drawn in by an old but very familiar need of her own. A distinctly uncomfortable feeling had crept up on him at the meeting in the forest when she had brought him together with the Game Master.

Uncle Tage, she had called him. Saying he was one of Dad's old comrades from the Reserve Unit. She told him that they had all – her, him and Dad – visited the old man in his summer cottage when they were little.

Obviously he had tried to explain the truth to her, but without any success.

She had never really bought the whole story about the Game, despite his several attempts to explain. But she seemed to accept whatever this Uncle Tage character told her without the slightest reservation.

Hell, her voice sounded almost tender when she talked about him, pretty much like when she talked about Dad. Time really had faded her memories as far as the old man was concerned. In a few more years she probably wouldn't even remember all the times the old sod had beaten him.

All the times the old bastard had lied to doctors and social workers, and persuaded her and Mum to back up his fabricated stories.

No, no matter how he tried, he couldn't keep a lid on the hatred that welled up inside him whenever Dad's name was mentioned. And the same applied to 'Uncle Tage'.

Hatred and – let's face it – jealousy . . .

Only a year or so before he would never have admitted that was what he felt, and had always felt, towards both Dad and Dag. As if they were stealing his Becca from him, and turning her into someone else entirely.

Someone he hardly recognized. A stranger.

Jealousy and hatred, then – a fine old combo, and only exacerbated by his already low credibility level, which effectively crushed any chance he had of convincing her of Tage Sammer's true identity.

But he could hardly blame her. The fact was his whole

43

story sounded so fucking unbelievable he occasionally had trouble believing it himself. Fortunately he had clung on to a few bits of memorabilia that he kept hidden in a safe place.

First and foremost there was the phone he had taken two years before from Kent 'Number 58' Hasselqvist, out on the E4 motorway. With the exception of the numbers on the back, it was exactly the same as the phone he had found on the commuter train, the one which had dragged him into this whole crazy business.

Then there was the passcard, the little white rabbit that had fallen out of a book in the NK department store, which had helped him to stop the clock on his normal life and granted him access to his very own Wonderland.

The third object in his collection was the hard-drive containing all the files from ArgosEye, the company that made sure the Game could stay buried in the deepest depths of the internet.

The trojan that Manga had put together, and which he had gone to great lengths to introduce into the company's computer network, had done its work. A wealth of information had been dragged out into the light: the fake trolls, the blogs that delivered pre-packaged opinions on demand, the Stasi database of people who held opposing views, and a load of other dodgy stuff that Philip Argos and his gang had going on for their wealthy clients.

But even though he suspected – correction: *knew* – that ArgosEye was protecting the Game, helping it to stay hidden whilst simultaneously keeping a record of anyone who tried to find out about it or broke Rule Number One, the leaked files still hadn't provided a single piece of firm evidence that his theory was actually correct. Maybe they had secured any information of that sort behind a second firewall, unless Manga's spyware had simply been looking in the wrong places?

The Game hadn't floated up to the surface the way he had hoped. It was still lurking down in the depths: the things he had kept proved nothing to anyone who couldn't see the whole picture. Not even the latest addition to his collection had any real value as evidence: an ordinary printed sheet of A4 that anyone could have put together. *Your final task, HP*, Tage Sammer, a.k.a. the Game Master, had said out there among the pet gravestones where they had drunk coffee together from a flask.

After all HP had done to cause trouble for the Game, the plans he had ruined and the money he had stolen, the old bastard had still seemed perfectly calm. No hard feelings, more or less . . .

But on the other hand, the task they had presented to him was no ordinary one.

Christ, what a fucking choice . . .

If he carried out the task, he was basically finished. Fucked for life, in every sense of the phrase. If he didn't do it, then his life wasn't the only one at stake . . .

FUCK!

46 of 78 files checked, no unauthorized objects found, the program informed him.

He looked at the time. More than a minute had passed, only nine left until he had to get out.

Come on, come on, come on . . . Bastard slow library computer!

Scanning . . .

70 of 78 files checked, no unauthorized objects found

He leaned forward over the keyboard, moved the mouse to the internet icon and got ready to spring into action. No search engines, oh no, just straight to the right addresses, then erase all bookmarks and cookies from the

45

computer before he logged out. Leaving as few footprints as possible . . .

An unexpected noise over by the door made him start. He raised his head and glanced cautiously over the top of the screen.

A short man in a leather jacket, dark glasses and a baseball cap pulled down over his forehead had come into the computer room.

The man stopped in the doorway as he gazed slowly around the terminals, and something about the way he looked immediately made all of HP's alarm bells start to ring like mad.

Shit!

She tapped in the number and pressed the green icon.

Connecting . . . the screen declared, but after staring at it for at least thirty seconds she realized that it clearly wasn't connecting. Annoyed, she clicked to end the call and repeated the procedure. The very latest smartphone and it was hardly capable of making a call . . .

'Police Headquarters, reception,' a voice suddenly said over the phone, without any ringing tone first.

She hesitated for a second or two, then said:

'Permit section, please.'

'One moment.'

You have reached the permit section, current waiting time is estimated to be . . . six . . . minutes . . .

She sighed and looked at her watch. For a moment she considered abandoning the call and phoning Runeberg instead to see if he could get any information about what was happening . . .

Stigsson had forbidden her to contact Henke. Not that that was actually much of a problem. Now that she came to think about it, she had been chasing Henke for weeks

46

now, months, in fact. But even though she knew he was home, he had never opened the door when she visited, or picked up her calls when she phoned.

A couple of dutiful text messages, that was pretty much it, and she was under no illusions that it would be any easier to get hold of him now.

The safe deposit box had unsettled her.

Evidently Henke had secrets that were so valuable he had felt obliged to hide them away in a high-security vault. Stigsson's crew had already emptied his flat, and all it would take was for someone going through everything they had confiscated to find a copy of the safe deposit agreement with the bank, or a letter like the one she had received. A request for a search warrant, then the drill would come out and all Henke's secrets would be dragged into the open.

Whatever was inside that deposit box, it was hardly likely to make things any better for him.

'Permit section, Persson . . .' The voice made Rebecca start.

'Yes, hello, er, my name is Rebecca Normén . . .' She glanced at the papers in front of her and tried to gather her thoughts.

'I'm phoning about an application for a weapons licence for a security company. I was just wondering how far you'd got . . .'

Cop!

HP ducked down behind the screen instinctively. The bloke reeked of plod so badly it almost made his nostrils sting.

He bent down to pull the USB stick from the computer. Like fuck was he going to let them have all the info he'd gathered over the past few months. The Security Police were bound to come up with some way of turning it all against him, locking him away on an indeterminate sentence . . .

His fingers closed around the little plastic stick, but at that moment the man in the cap burst out into a long, noisy harangue in a strange language. Another lighter voice replied almost at once, and when HP carefully peered out he saw the man in the cap leaving the room in the company of a middle-aged woman who had been using a computer a short distance from his.

He waited a few more seconds, then straightened up and breathed out.

False alarm.

God, he was twitchy!

His heart was still pounding in his chest, his hands were trembling and he had to take several deep breaths to slow his pulse down. High time to ditch the paranoia and get on with business.

The scanning program must have finished by now, and he was eager to see what the media reaction to his arrest had been.

Most of the papers were still running diet tips on their fly-sheets, but the online edition of *Expressen* ought to feature him somewhere.

> *Last night the Security Police arrested a 32-year-old man on suspicion of planning terrorist attacks.*
>
> *A source in the Security Police says the arrest has almost certainly prevented acts of terrorism on Swedish soil.*

Yep, that was how you sold more papers. The fact that they let him go after a few hours probably wouldn't be published until next week, by which time no-one would care.

The media's memory has always been short, Henrik. People can only deal with one story at a time . . .

48

Shit, sometimes he actually missed Philip and the ArgosEye life. Even though they had Anna Argos killed and almost managed to pin the murder on him, not to mention everything they did to him once his cover was blown, sometimes he couldn't help imagining what might have happened if he hadn't been found out.

Who would he have been by now?

Rilke's boyfriend?

Philip's right-hand man?

Or, even better: his successor . . . The Game Master's faithful partner, maybe even a future Mark Black. None of that sounded bad at all . . .

On the screen in front of him a little green window had appeared. The scan program must have got stuck when he nudged the USB stick. Damn, two more minutes wasted!

Annoyed, he moved the cursor to close the window and restart the scan. But just as the little arrow reached the cross in the top right corner of the window, letters began to appear. One by one, until they formed a sentence that made the hairs on his arms stand on end.

**W
a
n
t**

**t
o**

**p
l
a
y**

a Game Henrik Pettersson?

He yanked the USB stick from the computer and threw himself under the desk. On the way he hit his head, got caught in the chair and almost fell flat on the floor. At the last moment he caught hold of the desk, pulled himself to his knees and tried to turn his head away. Too late. His gaze was drawn inexorably to the screen, like an insect with a death wish drawn to a UV light.

Run! a terrified little voice was screaming in his ear.

Get the fuck out of here, moron!

But his body wouldn't obey.

Instead he remained on his knees in front of the computer, with his mouth half open and eyes big as ping pong balls, while his brain absorbed everything that was happening on the screen.

A new window opened and a series of images began to roll over it. Cut-and-paste headlines from various news sites:

The Palace reports a record level of interest from foreign media ahead of the royal wedding . . .

Huge server hall installed in old military base north of Uppsala. Rigorous security . . .

Another serious incident of hacking has been reported, this time by various companies in the defence industry. As on previous occasions, the police say that no information appears to have been stolen . . .

The Southern Link Road was closed for the second time in a week because of a computer failure which caused the failure of barriers and ventilation systems . . .

Several leading news websites are once again closing their comment sections . . .

He recognized the lot, he had looked them all up himself, cutting and pasting them onto the USB stick.

They were followed by more cuttings, things he didn't recognize:

For a third week in a row there have been reports of disruption to computer and mobile networks. The operators affected worst are 3 and Telia, but other networks have also suffered . . .

Three kilos of plutonium from Cold War projects in Sweden were recently handed over to the USA. The Foreign Minister has given assurances that it 'would not be used for military purposes'.

The EU is forcing Sweden to implement the Data Retention Directive!

The headlines vanished and were replaced by a series of short text messages:

Message received 03/04 09.55:
New job, here's my new number. Call me! /Becca

Message received 12/04 14.55:
Why don't you ever answer your phone? /Becca

Message received 02/05 16.39:
Tried to visit you again. The TV was on. Why didn't you open the door? /Becca

Message sent 06/05 22.02:
Hi Mangalito, are you back? /HP

Message received 14/05 21.13:
Where are you, Henke? Are you okay?
Please, call me! /Becca

Message sent 15/05 03.11:
Manga, call me need to talk pronto! /HP

Message received 23/05 18.36:
Henke, please get in touch!!! /Becca

Just as he realized he was reading his own text traffic, the messages disappeared from the screen and were replaced by moving images.

A familiar figure snatching an umbrella from a bag.
CUT
A cortege of horses and carriages riding through Stockholm.
CUT
A dark-clad figure on a moped.
CUT
An unmarked police car rolling over in slow motion.
CUT
An isolated cottage in flames.
CUT
Desert ravens circling above sand dunes.

Then, finally:

The silhouette of an elderly man against a snowy forest glade full of flickering lanterns.

The screen suddenly went dark. But still HP couldn't tear his eyes away. He was still kneeling motionless in front of the computer, holding his breath and waiting. When the message finally appeared he almost pissed himself:

Time to decide, Henrik!
This is your final task.
Do you want to play a Game?

Yes
or
No?

5

Ghosts from the past

Obviously she ought to try to get hold of him. He was her brother, after all. Tell Stigsson where he could stick his damn rulebook . . .

But she'd actually already tried. It felt like she'd been chasing him all spring, calling, texting, even going round to the flat and knocking on the door a few times. He was still there, she was sure of that. The flat had smelled lived in, not musty the way it had during the months he'd been away.

A couple of times she had seen the flickering light of the television from out in the street, but he still hadn't opened the door.

And at some point last winter he must have changed the locks, because her spare keys no longer worked. He was angry with her. And she knew why . . .

He didn't like the fact that she was in touch with Tage Sammer. He knew perfectly well why she liked the old man, and for exactly the same reason Henke was obliged to hate him, without even giving him a chance.

Uncle Tage reminded them both of Dad . . .

But even if Henke was an obstinate fool, she still had to try to help him.

55

Do her best to save him from himself.

She looked up the number in her contacts, hesitated a couple of seconds, then pressed call.

It was a stupid idea. But she had no choice . . .

He answered after the first ring:

'Personal protection unit, Runeberg!'

'Hi Ludvig, it's Rebecca. Sorry to call so early but I took a chance that you might be at work . . .'

'Normén, hi! Quite right, there's no time to rest up here at the moment. As you know, we've got our hands full. Are you calling to say you've changed your mind? Keen to get back to the mother ship?'

Runeberg's voice sounded the same as usual, which made what she wanted to say somewhat easier.

'Not quite. I'm still thinking about it,' she lied. 'I wanted to ask you for a favour, Ludvig . . . It's a rather sensitive matter.'

'Mmm.'

She thought she could hear his office chair creak as he rearranged his great bulk.

'It's about my brother . . .'

'Call my mobile in ten minutes.' The tone of his voice suddenly sounded very different.

'W-what . . .?'

But he had already hung up.

For the third time in five minutes he nudged the blinds apart and peered down at the dimly lit street. Everything looked okay, but he was still *certain* he was being watched. One hundred percent utterly and absolutely certain . . .

Every movement, every website he'd visited, all his text messages. They had been watching everything, in spite of all his precautions. They were playing with him, trying to fuck with his head.

And doing a pretty good job of it . . .

He let go of the blinds, walked round the sofa, once, then again. Then he sat down, drumming his fingers on one knee before noticing a fingernail he hadn't yet managed to ruin completely. The plan, in so far as he had actually had one, hadn't envisaged this scenario.

Not by a long shot!

And he'd been trying to convince himself that they had forgotten about him . . .

Epic fucking fail!

He had to get out of the flat, at once, before he started climbing the walls. It was just past seven in the morning, and ordinarily it would be several hours before he tumbled out of bed. But his experience in the library seemed to have opened all the floodgates in his head. His mind was still full of fragmentary images. As if he had dreamed an entire film with a beginning, a middle and an ending, but could now only remember a few scenes. *Memento* sequences that he couldn't piece together no matter how hard his aching brain tried.

The overflowing ashtray on the coffee table had just swallowed up his last fag, which gave him a legitimate reason to head down to the 7-Eleven at Mariatorget and get a bit of fresh air.

As soon as he opened the front door and stepped out into the street he could feel their eyes on him. He twisted his head round, checking every possible angle, but obviously they were far too professional to give themselves away so easily.

Even though it was still early, there were already four or five people squeezed into the shop. A gym-pumped guy with tattoos over by one of the shelves gave him a quick glance and HP froze mid-stride. He was almost certain he'd seen the man before. And his pretence of innocently browsing the pick'n'mix sweets convinced him: raspberry jellies didn't exactly fit into a low carb, high fat diet. HP had no choice but to turn on his heel and get out of the shop at once. Really he ought to have gone straight back to the flat, but without cigs he was finished.

Instead he carried on down Hornsgatan towards the Slussen junction, trying hard to resist the temptation to drift through the morning traffic just to give his pursuers a challenge. The walk took less than five minutes, but in spite of the fact that it wasn't even particularly warm, his t-shirt was sticking to his back and he had to sit down on one of the benches outside the underground station to catch his breath.

He was worn out, not only physically, and it wasn't until he was fishing through his pockets for a cigarette that he remembered a lack of fags was the reason for this little outing in the first place. There was a newsagent's just inside the doors to the station, and he glanced round a couple of times before getting to his feet and heading in that direction.

A train must have just arrived, because in the middle of the doors he was suddenly confronted with a great tide of people on their way out.

Office workers in suits and ties, early bird tourists and perfectly average Swedes on their way to work. He put his chin to his chest and elbowed his way through the crowd, ignoring the disgruntled complaints as he did so.

Out of nowhere he was shoved in the side and almost lost his balance. He looked up angrily, but faces were streaming past on all sides and it was impossible to tell who had pushed him.

Then the rush was suddenly over and he was left standing in the ticket hall. Instead of making his way to the little kiosk, he stood there while his brain tried to find the right synapse. One of the faces that had gone past had seemed familiar as well. The bodybuilder in the 7-Eleven might just have been a phantom, but this was something else. The eyes, forehead, the set of the face, it was all horribly familiar. But there was something that wasn't right, something missing that was stopping him putting the pieces together.

It took him another few seconds before his brain finally made the right connection.

The beard!

He took a couple of hesitant steps back towards the doors, then a few more, faster now. He rushed out into the square and even leapt onto one of the benches to get a better view, his head spinning like some fucking Linda Blair.

'Erman!' he yelled. 'Ermaaaaaan!'

But all he could see were people's backs as they hurried away from him, none of them any more familiar than all the others.

He opened his mouth to shout again, but then he noticed the looks he was getting from people around him. In spite of the bustle of the square, a small crowd of onlookers was gathering around the bench he was standing on, as if they all wanted to see what was happening but didn't dare get too close.

A couple of teenagers were pointing at him and giggling, a dad was dragging a small child closer, and some German Stieg Larsson tourists already had their cameras out.

He caught sight of his reflection in one of the station's glass doors. Bright red face, hair all over the place, eyes bulging like ping pong balls. Add a week or so's stubble and his shabby clothes, and it was hardly surprising that people were staring. He looked totally fucking mad!

Schwedisch Dummkopf, ja, ja – sehr gut!

Embarrassed, he got down quickly from the bench, fixed his gaze on the cobbles and did his best to blend into the crowd as he headed off towards Guldgränd.

He had been mistaken.

He *must* have been mistaken.

For the umpteenth time, his raging imagination had broken its reins and galloped off.

That had to be it.

'There's no such thing as ghosts,' he muttered.

No
Such
Thing
As
Ghosts

'You understand that this contravenes any number of regulations, Normén?'

She nodded.

'Absolutely. Like I said, Ludvig, I really appreciate . . .'

'Well, enough of that. You've got half an hour or so, then I want everything back by the time I've finished eating. Sunesson's in charge of stores today, I'm sure you remember him?'

'Transferred from Norrmalm? Sure. He worked as a duty officer for a while.'

'Good, there won't be any problems there, then. Just smile and wave . . . The corridors will be full of the lunch-time crowd, so there'll be plenty of people about. But Sunesson's mean, he always brings a packed lunch. Probably doesn't want to miss the lunchtime horse-race . . .'

Runeberg leaned forward and carefully pushed a folded copy of *Metro* towards her.

'This is all you need . . .'

'And you're quite sure it's there?'

'Yes, I checked the register of confiscated property after you called.'

'Good!'

For a moment she wasn't sure what to say. Even though it hadn't been mentioned explicitly, she was pretty sure she knew why Runeberg was helping her. He was best mates with Tobbe Lundh, and godfather to his son, Jonathan. The same Jonathan who, together with his friend Marcus, had created the internet phantom MayBey whom they then used to torment her for months, spreading rumours and gossip about her online, and even making her think Henke was in serious danger, until she eventually worked it all out and put a stop to the whole charade.

She really only had herself to blame: she was the one who had embarked on an affair with Tobbe Lundh, even though she knew he was a married man with a family.

Either way, Runeberg seemed to feel partly responsible for what had happened.

She suddenly found herself regretting that she was exploiting his guilty conscience like this. The entire plan was actually pretty idiotic from the start . . . Stigsson's instructions had been unambiguous:

For the duration of this investigation into terrorism, obviously you can have no contact whatsoever with your brother. I repeat: no contact whatsoever. Is that clear, Normén?

But she had no choice. She had to get into that safe deposit box before Stigsson's team got there. She only needed a quick look, then, once she had assured herself that there was nothing in there that could make things even worse for Henke, she could theoretically even tip them off about the box's existence. Give them a bit of help with the investigation. At least that was what she was trying to tell herself . . .

Runeberg seemed to notice her hesitation.

'Off you go, Normén, the clock's ticking and my food's about to arrive . . .'

A waitress was approaching with a heavy tray, and Rebecca stood up before the young woman reached their table; she picked up the newspaper and put it in her shoulderbag.

'Thanks again, Ludvig, I'm really . . .'

He smiled and shrugged.

'No problem, Normén. Now, off you go.'

'By the way,' he added when she had started to walk off towards the door, 'if this all goes to hell I'll probably be looking for a new job, so you can expect to hear from me . . .'

A brisk three-minute walk took her to the staff entrance.

She held the card against the reader beside the turnstile, holding it upside down on purpose so no-one would see Ludvig's photograph on the front.

The guard gave her a quick glance, then nodded in recognition.

First obstacle cleared.

She followed the glass walkway between the buildings, holding her head up and trying to look like she was having a perfectly ordinary day at work. That shouldn't be too difficult, seeing as she had actually worked there until last winter. In theory she was still employed at the Security Police, so there wasn't that much difference.

Yet she still felt like a stranger, someone who didn't belong. She couldn't help glancing at the little spherical cameras on the ceiling, and did her best to stay as far away from them as possible.

She turned off right into a yellow-painted corridor. At the far end she stopped at a broad metal door with a small white sign.

CONFISCATED GOODS DIVISION.

She held Ludvig's card up against the reader.

A bleep, but nothing happened. Shit!

She tried again, slower this time.

Another bleep, and this time the lock began to whirr.

Calm now, Normén!

She stepped inside a small reception area. A short distance behind the counter sat an older, slightly fat man with a pudding bowl haircut. A television screen fixed to the wall was showing a horse-race, and the man pulled an irritated face when he was obliged to look away from it.

'Hi, Sune,' she said, with exaggerated bonhomie.

'No, no, you stay where you are, I'll be okay on my own,' she went on when the man made a half-hearted attempt to stand up.

'Just need to double-check some stuff we seized last week.'

'Good,' the overweight man muttered, letting his heavy frame sink back in his chair. 'Don't forget to sign yourself in . . .'

He waved his hand towards the counter as he turned his attention back to the television screen.

Rebecca pulled the register over and scrawled something illegible in place of her name.

'Done!'

Without looking away from the screen, Sunesson raised one hand and pressed a button on top of his desk. The door to Rebecca's right buzzed and few moments later she found herself in a large storeroom filled with racks of metal shelving.

It was several years since she had last been there, and she took a few tentative steps forward as she tried to get her bearings. The smell was exactly the same as she remembered, cool air mixed with cardboard and whitewashed concrete. A few metres away against one wall was a standard issue computer and she hurried over to it.

She took out Runeberg's passcard and inserted it into the little box beside the keyboard. Then she quickly typed in Runeberg's user ID and password.

The hourglass on the screen rotated and then the database opened up.

Henrik Pettersson, she typed into the search box for names, then added his date of birth in the next box.

She pressed search and the hourglass rotated once, then twice.

Rebecca looked round, but she was alone in the large room.

She could hear the sound of Sunesson's television in the distance. The hourglass vanished and was replaced by a line of text.

Case number K3429302-12, Section 5,
Row 47, shelf 23-25.

The store was actually larger than she remembered, and it took her a couple of minutes to work out where to go.

The main aisle ran along one of the outer walls, with various smaller passageways leading off into the different sections.

Section 5 was at the far end of the store, where the light was much dimmer than near the entrance.

Only every other fluorescent lamp was lit, and she guessed there would be a switch somewhere to correct that, but she didn't have time to look for it.

The racks of shelving all round her stretched up to the ceiling, and they were almost all loaded with brown cardboard boxes that seemed to soak up the already dim light.

On the floor were pallets laden with things that were too big to fit on the shelves, and she walked past items of furniture, rolls of cable and part of what looked like a bronze sculpture.

Four of the boxes on shelf 23 were marked with the right case number. She pulled down the one closest to her and opened the lid.

The box was full of books and films, which explained why it was so heavy. She closed it and put it back on the shelf.

The next box turned out to contain exactly the same sort of thing, but the third looked more promising. A few files, random documents and, at the bottom – bingo!

A large bunch of keys, fifty or so, just as the case register had said.

They had got rid of almost all Dad's belongings after his death, but Mum had been adamant about keeping the keys.

You never know when you might need a key, so we'll keep those . . .

Presumably Henke had kept them for the same reason.

Half of the keys were so old the metal had started to decay, others were bent and worn with use, but when she looked more closely she saw that there were at least five or six keys for bicycle locks, and a couple that looked like they belonged to mopeds or motorbikes, so – just as she had hoped – it looked like Henke had gone on adding to the collection . . .

So what did the key to a safe deposit box look like?

A sudden noise interrupted her thoughts. Someone had opened the door to the storeroom.

Problems?
Don't give up, we can help you!
070-931151

The note was stuck right over the keyhole. The wording was the same as before. Probably the same note, which suggested his neighbour had worked out where it came from. But right now he really didn't care.

His brain was working in top gear. He had wandered round half of Södermalm trying to digest what he had seen.

If what he had seen at Slussen wasn't just his imagination, if Erman *had* been real, then wasn't everything he had experienced over the past two years . . . well, what?

Fucking hell!

His headache from earlier that morning kicked into overdrive and made him pinch the bridge of his nose in reflex. He tore down the note and pulled the keys to the flat from his pocket.

A noise off to his left made him jump and he stood there with the key in the lock. His heart was practically beating a hole in his chest, forcing him to take a few deep breaths to lower his pulse-rate. Fuck, he was twitchy!

Nice and easy now . . .

He glanced cautiously at his neighbour's door. The sound had come from there, he was sure of that, in fact he even recognized it from the previous day. A security chain rattling against the inside of a door. A chain didn't start to swing of its own accord, so someone must have managed to nudge it. His new neighbour was heading out.

For reasons he couldn't explain, his need to know the identity of his new neighbour was much stronger today, so he waited a few more seconds, all the while staring at his neighbour's door. But nothing happened. The door remained closed.

He was just about to turn away when he thought he saw movement through the spyhole. A vague shift from light to dark, as if someone had put their eye to the hole. And suddenly he was sure someone was standing on the other side of the door.

Watching him . . .

He quickly turned the key in the lock, forced open his crooked front door and slammed it quickly behind him.

She held her breath as she listened in the direction of the door. She thought she could hear footsteps in the distance. Even if it was just lard-arse Sunesson shuffling along in his Birkenstocks, she didn't feel like letting him know what case she was poking about in. She quickly dropped the bunch of keys in her bag and closed the box again. The steps were approaching along the main passageway.

She recognized hard heels on the concrete floor. A pair of proper shoes, unlike Sunesson's sandals or a beat officer's boots. Not many people in Police Headquarters wore shoes like that, and whoever this was, she felt no great desire to bump into him. But the only way out was along that main passageway . . .

She gently lifted the box back into place on the shelf.

The steps were slowly getting closer, steady, almost military.

She looked round and took a few quick steps further down the aisle. One of the bottom shelves on the same side was empty and, mostly on the spur of the moment, she crouched down and crept into it.

The footsteps were close now, but a large box on a pallet blocked the line of sight to the corridor. All she had to do was wait until the person had gone past and then creep out as quietly as possible.

Suddenly the footsteps stopped. Rebecca huddled up even more and held her breath.

Then the person carried on walking, but much slower

now. It took her a couple of seconds to realize where they were going. Down the passageway she was in!

She pressed against the side of the large box on the pallet. There were still several shelves between her and the far end of the passageway. If the person was heading towards one of them, she was bound to be seen.

Shit, it had been a really stupid idea to try to hide. She should have brazened it out, saying hello and pretending everything was fine.

What the hell was she supposed to say now?

Hello, yes, I just crawled in to see what things look like from down here.

The steps were getting closer, just a few metres left now.

She would have to climb out, that would be slightly more normal than being found crouching at the back of one of the shelves. Her heart was pounding in her chest.

She took a deep breath and shifted her bodyweight forward. She had to play this calm, as natural as possible.

The steps suddenly stopped. She heard boxes moving, then someone clearing their throat.

A man, no doubt about that, and just a metre or so away.

Rebecca tilted her head, leaned forward and cautiously peeped round the edge of the box.

Shit!

She pulled her head back quick as a flash. A pair of dark trousers belonging to a suit, matching black shoes, that was pretty much all she had seen. Yet she was still quite sure. The man standing in the passageway was Stigsson. He was standing in front of the boxes she had just been looking at.

She heard him lift one of them down, then the thud as he put it on the floor.

The lid came off with a dry rustle, then muffled noises, as if he were rooting around in the box.

A sudden pain in her left calf made her flinch involuntarily. Damn, the uncomfortable position had made her leg start to cramp. The pain was getting worse and spreading upwards. When it reached her thigh she had to bite her lip to stop herself groaning. Stigsson was still rummaging about in the box.

She tried to shift her weight to let some blood through to her tormented muscles, but lost her balance instead and fell against the side of the box.

The noises from the passageway stopped.

The pain in her leg was getting worse and she bit her lip so hard that she could taste blood.

Stigsson cleared his throat again.

Her back was slowly slipping down the cardboard box and she pressed her working leg against the floor to stay upright. But it was impossible to keep her balance. Her body was slowly sliding towards the edge of the box, closer and closer to the passageway.

In just a few seconds she would tumble out and land at his feet.

Suddenly she heard the sound of a box being shoved back onto the shelf. Footsteps snapped on the concrete floor like cracks of a whip, and for a moment she thought her heart had stopped.

Then she realized that the noise was getting quieter, and spent the last of her strength trying to stay upright. Just as the storeroom door slammed shut she fell flat onto the hard floor.

6

Head games

He had spent three mornings in a row with his arse parked on that fucking bench. Starting half an hour before the time of the first sighting, and staying for an hour afterwards. He had his hood up, his cap pulled down over his face and, just to be on the safe side, a cheap pair of sunglasses perched on his nose. All to make sure he couldn't be seen.

But, just like the previous two days, he'd failed to see anything, and now the whole project was starting to feel more stupid than was strictly reasonable. As his arse slowly went numb, he realized how ridiculously he was behaving. He had considerably more important problems than a possible doppelganger wandering about Södermalmstorg, and – just like his Playstation, or having a wank – this whole project was yet another way of avoiding getting to grips with the real issue.

Erman was dead, he had died by fire when the Game finally caught up with him almost two years ago. They had incinerated his cottage, his remains were found in the embers. The poor sod had tried to live outside the connected world like a hermit but by the time HP went to see him out in the sticks he had definitely wandered the wrong side of the fine line between clear-sighted genius and total wacko madness. In spite of that he had certainly been very useful. Opening HP's eyes and getting him to see what the Game was really about. And not just its most superficial and singularly unappealing levels: the Ants keeping watch, digging out information and recruiting suitable players to carry out the various tasks. Then the betting, while the tasks were filmed and broadcast live and exclusive online for internet gamblers.

No, what Erman had told him, combined with his own experiences, had also made him understand the considerably darker aspects of the Game, and what it was really capable of. No matter what the bloke's mental state might have been, HP still owed the lunatic backwoodsman quite a bit, and even if he had tried to convince himself that Erman's death wasn't really his fault, his excuses all rang pretty hollow. It was more than likely his own guilty conscience and lack of sleep, edged about with a bit of general-purpose paranoia, that had got him seeing ghosts in broad daylight.

There was no other explanation.

Or rather, *there simply couldn't be any other explanation*, he corrected himself as he kicked off his trainers and lay down on the sofa.

He landed on something hard and, after a few acrobatic manoeuvres interspersed with a lot of swearing, managed to dig out the remote control from behind his back, and zapped through a range of dreary daytime television programmes.

On the coffee table he found a half-empty box of Marlboros. He lit one and tried to direct the column of smoke towards the lamp-hook in the ceiling.

That was when he noticed it. High up, on top of his

Billy bookcase, it was lying there like a little black box. A solitary, abandoned book.

From where he was lying, all he could see was a bit of the spine, so presumably you couldn't see any of it if you were standing in front of the bookcase, which would explain why the cops had missed it.

He twisted his head and squinted as he tried to work out what book it was, but the writing was too small. It was definitely a library book, though, he could see the white classification letters at the bottom of the spine. Three letters, probably Hce – *Foreign Fiction* . . .

So the plods had missed an item of stolen property right in front of their noses, and instead filled their boxes with perfectly legitimate porn and dog-eared paperbacks.

He tried to mimic Hellström's slightly nasal voice: *Henrik Pettersson, you are being held on suspicion of crimes against the state for not returning your library books on time. How do you plead?*

Guilty as charged, fuckface!!!

He grinned and blew another column of smoke, this time aimed towards the top of the bookcase.

Suddenly he realized he was hungry. How long was it since he last ate? Properly, rather than just stuffing his face over the sink with a micro-bombed Gorby pie?

He couldn't actually remember . . .

But the rumbling from his stomach was a good sign, as if the old library book had made his brain jump track and return to more solid ground. A shower and a bit of decent food would probably do wonders for his mood. Chinese, or why not a serious kebab down at the Jerusalem? Mmm!

He glanced at the clock on the television: 10.25.

A bit early for lunch, he'd have to hold out at least

another half hour. Shower first, then. He stood up, but instead of going straight to the bathroom, he went over to the bookcase, stretched up on tiptoe and reached for the book.

His fingertips just managed to catch the edge and he shuffled the book a few centimetres closer.

The Catcher in the Rye by J. D. Salinger. A definite favourite, he must have read it at least ten times. In all likelihood the book was from the library down in Bagarmossen, which meant that the theft had passed the statute of limitation some ten years ago, if not more.

On the basis of this new information, my client wishes to change his plea to – not guiltyyy!

He reached up a bit further, got a better grip with his fingertips and tried to grab hold of the book. But instead he lost his balance and the book slipped over the edge of the bookcase. The object on top of it fell with it, hitting him hard on the head before tumbling to the floor.

A phone.

A shiny, silvery phone, with a glass touch-screen.

The passcard was white and, unlike the one she had borrowed from Runeberg a couple of days before, it didn't contain any visible information at all. No name, no logo, and certainly no photograph of its owner. Just a small, plain white card that had appeared in a padded envelope with no sender's name given.

Presumably the anonymity was another security measure. A bulky window-envelope with a bank logo on it reeked of credit card, and thus must increase the risk of it being stolen by several hundred percent.

They clearly took security very seriously.

She handed her driving licence to the man on the other

side of the counter, and he inspected it carefully before typing her ID number into the computer.

It was the same man as before but, even though only a few days had passed since her last visit, he showed no sign of recognizing her. If anything, he actually seemed even more formal that before.

'Thank you.'

He handed her licence back to her.

'Are you familiar with the procedure?'

'No.'

He moved to the corner of the counter and pointed at the door behind him.

'I'll open the door for you, and when you're inside the airlock you run your card through the reader. Then the far door opens and you can get into the vault . . .'

She nodded to show that she understood.

'Inside there are a number of rooms containing safe deposit boxes. The doors are kept locked, but the one containing your box will be unlocked. Then you will have to use your key to open the right compartment.

'You do have your key with you?'

'Absolutely,' she replied, patting the bag hanging from her shoulder while she did her best to suppress a smile.

Judging by the look on his face, she didn't quite succeed.

'Inside the compartment is a metal box. Usually clients take the box into one of the private booths at the end of the vault. There's less risk of being disturbed there than out in the vault itself . . .'

He paused for a moment, but something in her expression seemed to prompt him to go on.

'The booths aren't covered by surveillance cameras . . .' he added.

'I understand,' she replied curtly.

He pressed a button and the dark steel door behind him swung open.

Rebecca stepped inside the little airlock. In front of her, only a metre or so away, was another metal door, even sturdier than the one she had just passed through.

She turned her head slightly and glanced at the security camera in the ceiling, and tried to look as calm as possible. She actually had a perfectly legitimate reason for being there, so why was she so nervous?

The door behind her closed and the sound made her jump.

Calm, now, Normén!

She took a deep breath, held it for several seconds, then slowly breathed out.

Then she ran the passcard through the little reader. For a couple of seconds there was total silence. Then the steel door in front of her swung open.

The vault was considerably more exclusive than she had been expecting. Discreet uplights around the concrete walls and a faint smell of lemon, both presumably intended to alleviate any hint of nuclear bunker and being shut in. It worked fairly well.

A curved path of fluorescent paint on the shiny marble floor led her between a row of barred gates. In the rooms beyond she could see a great number of brass-coloured lockers. At the far end of the vault were what looked like changing-room doors. Presumably the booths mentioned by the guard.

A green lamp was shining above the fourth gate on the left-hand side. She took hold of the handle and the gate swung open without a sound. The room within was small, probably no more than a couple of metres square. Another of the spherical cameras stared down from the ceiling but she did her best to ignore it. So, which of the two hundred or so compartments in the room was hers?

She ran her fingers over the doors: 115, 120, 125 . . .
There it was, almost at the bottom of the row.

She knelt down, pulled the large bunch of keys from her bag, then inspected the brass door carefully. One of the medium-sized doors, about thirty centimetres square?

The keyhole was fairly wide, which meant she could dispense with a good number of the keys, but there were still about a dozen that might fit.

She glanced up at the camera, and imagined she could see the lens moving to zoom in on her. As if they already suspected that she shouldn't be there, that the box and its contents weren't actually hers and belonged to someone else.

No, she really did have to try to calm down. The bank had contacted *her*, and had sent *her* a passcard. And as for Henke, he clearly wasn't bothered enough about his possessions not to leave her to pay the bill for their safekeeping.

In other words, she had every right in the world to open the box.

She gave the camera another quick glance, then leaned forward and selected the first key of the ones she thought most likely.

Too big, much too big. Which meant she could dispense with that one, and another which was even bigger.

She tried a slightly smaller key. It went into the hole, but once it was in it just spun round without getting any purchase. So she discarded that one and another that was even smaller.

Four possible keys left. She inspected them carefully.

One of them was slightly crooked and looked too old, so she decided not to try it. But a couple of the others looked much more promising.

Neither of them worked, however, nor did her third choice.

She was just about to try the slightly crooked key when there was a faint noise from out in the vault. She started, and flew up to her feet, turned round and peered cautiously out into the corridor.

Empty, of course.

The door to the vault was motorised, and if it had opened there was no doubt at all that she would have heard it.

She went back to the locker and put the crooked key in the lock. It fitted, but she couldn't manage to turn it. After a couple of attempts she took it out.

Bloody hell!

Her guess about the bunch of keys looked like it had been wrong. Henke had probably hidden the key somewhere else entirely, so her best hope of opening the box was gone.

She could probably persuade the bank to drill it open eventually but, given the number of security procedures they had in place, that would be bound to take several months.

Which of course would give Stigsson and his team plenty of time to find out about the box.

So what was she going to do now?

The crooked key had at least fitted, so maybe it could be straightened?

She removed the key from the bunch, put it on the floor and put her heel on the bent part a couple of times. Then she picked it up again and looked at it carefully.

It was worth a last attempt, at least.

She put the key in the lock and carefully turned it.

The lock clicked and the little brass door opened.

The metal box inside surprised her. Not only because

it was locked, with a combination dial on the front, but also because its colour and shape really didn't seem to belong in this exclusive, almost sterile bank vault. The box had probably been green once upon a time, but the paint had peeled badly. In a couple of places she could make out the remnants of yellow letters and numbers. And the thick tin was badly buckled in places, almost as if someone had tried to open it with force. Slowly she pulled the box from the compartment. It was seventy to eighty centimetres long, and much heavier than she had been expecting, but fortunately there was a handle at the back, enabling her to pick it up and carry it over towards one of the small cubicles without difficulty.

She closed the door carefully behind her, turned the little lock and then put the box in the middle of the desk.

The combination lock looked vaguely familiar. She had an idea she had actually seen something similar in a small police station that had a safe instead of a weapons room.

You started from zero, picked a number between one and a hundred, then back to zero, followed by the next number, until you had entered the right combination.

Three numbers apart from the zeros, that was usually the case. So what should she try?

Suddenly she heard the noise from out in the vault again and stiffened. This time it was clearer. A quick little squeak, like someone treading too quickly on a marble floor with a rubber-soled shoe.

She hadn't heard the vault door open, so someone must have been inside when she arrived.

Unless there was another entrance that she hadn't noticed . . .?

She turned the lock, cautiously opened the door a crack and peered out into the corridor.

'Is anyone there?' she said quietly. No answer.

She waited a few seconds before carefully closing and locking the door.

If she was going to open the box, she had to focus on working out the combination.

She tried Henke's date of birth, but without success.

Then she tried Mum's. No good.

If Henke had picked numbers out of thin air, she would have to find another way of opening the box.

It was far too large to go in her bag, and she wondered if she could just carry it out. Was that allowed?

She stood motionless for a few moments, and realized that she was listening out for sounds from the vault. But apart from the faint rumble of the air-conditioning, everything was quiet.

Suddenly she had an idea and tried a new combination of numbers. Zero, then nineteen, back to zero, then six, back to zero, seventy-five.

Slowly she moved the dial back towards zero. The lock made an audible click.

Henke had used her date of birth as the combination!

The box had a false bottom that divided it into two sections. In the top part she found a bundle of dollar-bills. Beside the money was a little pile of small booklets, held together by a thick brown rubber band. As she picked them up the dry rubber snapped and they spilled out across the table. It took her just a fraction of a second to realize what the variously coloured booklets were.

Foreign passports, most of them a few years old seeing as she didn't recognize them immediately.

She opened one of them and found herself staring at a grainy photograph of a fair-haired man with a moustache and dark-framed glasses. He reminded her of Henke. The hairline, the set of his eyes, and his prominent cheekbones.

John Earnest, born 1938 in Bloemfontein, South Africa, according to the details in the passport.

But that was impossible. In spite of the colour of his hair, the glasses and the moustache, she was quite certain. The man in the picture was her dad.

It took him almost a whole minute before he even dare touch the phone. His hands were shaking so much he could hardly get a grip on the metal.

He could feel the numbers with his fingertips, and didn't even need to turn the thing over to check.

1

2

8

Of course. Anything else would have been out of the question.

He put the phone down gently on the coffee table, then walked around the sofa. Then walked round it again . . .

The book was still on the floor. It had brought down a couple of serious dustballs with it from the top of the bookcase, but, just like the phone, the front cover was completely clean, which could mean only one thing. Both objects must have been left up there very recently.

He got the list of confiscated property from the kitchen. Five crumpled pages of A4, where each item seized from his flat by the cops was listed in pedantic detail. Halfway down the third page he found what he was looking for.

103. One book, 'The Catcher in the Rye' J. D. Salinger.

The message was perfectly clear. Someone had retrieved the book from wherever the cops had been storing it, and put it back in his flat together with the phone. Just as Erman had said, the Game was everywhere, and the book on his living-room floor proved that not even the Security Police were immune.

Fucking hell!

He slumped down on the sofa, staring at the phone on the coffee table as he ran his fingers through his hair.

Once, then several more times, harder. Strands of hair came loose and wound round his fingers, but he hardly noticed.

The phone could be a copy.

He had given his own to Manga, two years ago, and then Becca had picked it up and buried it away in the lost property office. Then he had found out that the phone was owned by ACME Telecom Services, so presumably it had found its way back to them.

ACME Telecom Services – a proud member of the PayTag Group . . .

He stopped tearing his hair, absentmindedly pulled the loose strands from his fingers, then reached for the phone.

Its surface felt cool as he held it up to the light and tilted it until he found what he was looking for. A couple of centimetre-long scratches in one corner of the glass screen, from the time he had been dangling off a brick wall in Birkastan, with a tattooed gorilla whose door he had just defaced with a little warning message doing his best to pull him down.

Like fuck was this a copy!

He'd known it the moment he caught sight of the phone on the floor. This really was his phone.

Even before she lifted the lid of the lower section, she had a good idea of what it contained.

It was the smell that alerted her. A bitter, oily smell that she recognized all too well.

She slowly lifted the lid. A black revolver with a narrow

81

brown handle lay concealed in the lower compartment, and her heart instantly began to beat harder.

She resisted an immediate urge to pick the gun up. Instead she leaned forward and inspected the revolver as closely as she could. Unlike a lot of her colleagues, she wasn't particularly interested in guns. The police force's Sig Sauers and the compact assault rifles that were the Personal Protection Unit's backup weapon of choice were pretty much the only things she had ever fired. But compared to a pistol or an assault rifle, a revolver was a fairly simple weapon. A rotating cylinder in the middle that usually contained six bullets.

Handle, barrel, trigger and a large, visible hammer that could be drawn back with your thumb – that was basically it.

The stubby barrel made the gun look cruel, a bit like a bulldog's nose.

She carefully measured the diameter of the barrel with the end of her little finger. It was roughly the same as her own service pistol. Nine millimetres or thereabouts, but she had a feeling that the calibre of revolvers was usually measured in thousandths of an inch. She tried to work it out in her head, but didn't get very far.

There was a small reading lamp on the little table, and she switched it on and angled it so it shone down into the metal box.

Immediately above the cylinder she found some engraved lettering.

Cal .38, then a longer number, presumably the gun's serial number. Obviously she ought to write it down. She dug out a pen and notepad from her bag. She double-checked carefully as she wrote the number twice, going back over the numbers and making them thicker merely to draw out the process. To have something to occupy her mind with.

But the respite was only temporary.

What the hell had she actually found here?

She spread the passports out on the desk in front of her and looked through them.

All five had been issued in the late seventies and contained photographs of her dad.

In some of them he was wearing glasses, a moustache or beard, in one his hair colour was different. The only thing they all had in common was that none of them was issued in his real name. She glanced at the metal box, still fighting the urge to pick up the revolver.

But her police training won out once again.

The weapon was perfectly harmless where it was, and touching it without gloves would mean contaminating it with her fingerprints. But it wouldn't do any harm to have a closer look.

She stuck her pen into the barrel, lifted it up and tried to turn it around. The cylinder slipped out slightly, and when she tried to turn the gun it fell out altogether. Six chambers, just as she'd suspected, and each one held a flat brass-coloured disc. The weapon was loaded, in other words.

Two of the bullets had obvious indentations from the hammer, meaning that they must have been fired, but the other four were completely intact.

Suddenly she had an idea. She really should have thought of it at once instead of bothering with her notepad.

She put the revolver down on the desk and took out her mobile phone.

Obviously there was no coverage down there, but that didn't matter. She opened up the camera app and took several pictures of the revolver from different angles. Then she carefully returned it to the bottom of the box.

She glanced at the time: she ought to be getting off to work now. Time to make a decision.

She quickly gathered together the passports, opened her bag, and tucked them away in the inside pocket. After a few moments' reflection she put the money in as well, but she hesitated over the revolver – it was making her feel distinctly uneasy. She couldn't leave it for Stigsson's team to find, that was out of the question. But on the other hand she definitely didn't feel like taking it to work, and then home to Micke. But perhaps there was another option?

She hesitated a bit more, then closed the heavy lid and turned the combination dial a few times. Then she picked up the box with one hand, hung her bag on her shoulder and turned towards the door.

For a few moments she stood there with her hand on the handle as she listened for any sounds from out in the vault. Then she opened the little cubicle door, glanced up at the nearest camera, and headed back towards the compartment in the vault, trying to act casual. She put the box back in place, turned the crooked key with some difficulty to lock the door, then left the vault.

'I was wondering if I could have a copy of the original contract covering the lease of the box?' she asked the man behind the counter. 'I'd also like to register for another box, in my name alone. Preferably right away . . .'

He put the phone down, picked the book up from the floor, and leafed through the pages with trembling fingers.

Stockholm City Library – Bagarmossen, the stamp inside the front cover said. After a bit of searching he found the year it was printed – 1986.

But it was the message on the first page that made the

shaking of his hands shift into overdrive. Ornate, old-fashioned handwriting that looked very much like his dad's:

It's time to decide,
Henrik!
Do you want to play a Game?
Yes
or
No?

7

Just because you're paranoid . . .

He moved the glass to a different part of the wall, then pressed his ear to the bottom of it. But there was only a slight improvement. The same steady stream of vague, mumbling voices, several at once, but it still wasn't possible to make out what was being said.

Bollocks!

He had loitered about on the landing for several days, waiting for someone to go in or out, and had rung the doorbell a couple of times. Fuck, he'd even bought a box of chocolates as a polite little welcome gift.

But even though he was certain there were people inside the flat, his new neighbour hadn't opened the door. Whoever it was in there, they clearly had no desire to meet, which basically only confirmed his suspicions.

The Game was keeping a close eye on him, and knew all about his comings and goings. That meant they had to have an observation post, and a fucking good one at that. Once he realized that, the rest had been easy to work out. He could imagine them there inside the flat, a whole gang of faceless, suited Stasi agents with massive head-phones over their ears, moving microphones over the walls or drilling tiny holes so they could stick miniature cameras through the walls next to the plug sockets.

All the while muttering amongst themselves as they planned the next stage of the operation . . .

He put the glass down and took a quick walk through the flat.

Obviously he ought to take off. Get the hell out of there and hide away in some hole in the ground. But that wouldn't help, the Game was bound to find him sooner or later. As long as he was inside the flat he knew where they were. The Game Master couldn't possibly know yet that he had worked out where their secret surveillance centre was located.

Advantage HP, in other words . . .

A small advantage, maybe, but still!

And if he was going to keep hold of it, he would have to implement a few security measures . . .

Duct tape. He needed more duct tape. All the plugs and sockets in the wall may have been covered, as well as the biggest cracks and blemishes, but he still couldn't be sure. The walls were old and very uneven, and could easily conceal a microscopic little camera lens.

But in order to get more tape he would have to go out and leave the flat unguarded while he made his way to the ironmongers on Hornsgatan.

He hadn't been out for almost a week, living off tinned sardines, cigarettes and tap-water until he felt he was belching aluminium. But he didn't have any choice.

First stop, the Co-op: crispbread, fish roe, tinned food, some assorted Findus ready meals and so many packets of fags that the girl at the till was clearly bemused by the size of his request.

Then, with the whole lot hurriedly stuffed into plastic bags, back out onto the street.

He fixed his gaze on the pavement, tensing the muscles in his neck as hard as he could to stifle the urge to look round. But no matter how hard he tried, he couldn't help looking back.

He caught sight of them almost immediately. Two of them, in their thirties, standing in front of a shop window a short distance away. Chinos, sensible black shoes, staring hard at what was going on around them rather than at each other. Cops, he was pretty certain.

But they could just as easily be working for the Game. Or both . . .

He turned sharply to the right, and could feel their eyes burning into the back of his neck.

A couple of hundred metres to the ironmongers, a few rolls of duct tape, then straight back home.

Once the flat had been properly secured, he might finally get a chance to do some thinking.

The newspaper fly-sheets along the way were trumpeting the latest royal wedding news. The clothes, menu, guest list . . .

Just as he had expected, his own arrest was already forgotten. Now it was evidently all about the fact that the new prince had a 'difficult choice' ahead of him. At a guess, which charity he would pretend to work for now that the taxpayers were going to guarantee his future income . . .

He spat a gobbet of saliva into the gutter and glanced back quickly over his shoulder. His pursuers were suddenly nowhere to be seen, which probably only meant that he had more than two people following him.

Sweat was sticking his t-shirt to his skin, and he stopped outside the ironmongers to pull it away from his chest. A sour whiff of BO wafted up and made him screw up his nose. God, he stank!

He took a quick look at himself in the shop window.

His damp t-shirt was now more yellow than white, and his torn jeans were so stained they were starting to go stiff. Throw in his beard, greasy hair, the dark rings under his eyes and his crazy boggle-eyed stare, and the diagnosis was crystal clear. It was hardly surprising that people made way for him on the pavement. He looked like a raving nutter.

A sudden noise broke through the sound of the traffic, making him jump, and sending his pulse up by another twenty BPM. But it was only the air-brakes of the number 43 bus pulling up on the other side of the street, and he had already looked away when his brain caught up. Third seat from the back, the bloke sitting next to the window . . .

Fucking hell!

He ran straight out into the traffic. There was a cacophony of blaring horns, squealing brakes and skidding tyres. But none of that made him take his eyes off the bus.

He only just escaped being run over by a Saab, but the Volvo in the next lane braked a bit too late and struck him at knee-height.

He fell to the tarmac and the contents of his plastic bag spilled out across the road, but he made no attempt at all to gather them up again. Instead he used the Volvo's bumper to get quickly back on his feet.

Status check: aching pain, but – as luck would have it – no sign of any blood or jagged bones . . .

He took a couple of stumbling steps. The pain was bearable.

The driver got out of the car, his face swollen like a tomato.

'What the fuck are you playing at, you fucking mor . . .!'

HP didn't hang around for a debate.

The bus had already pulled away from the stop and was building up speed as it headed along Hornsgatan.

He got his legs going, left, right, left again. Faster and faster. He swerved to get round a car and found himself behind the bus.

He had built up speed now, almost running in top gear – but the bus was still pulling away from him. A red light at the next junction would put a stop to that.

But the bus driver showed no sign of braking, and actually seemed to be accelerating instead.

HP could see the traffic-lights now – green.

Fuck!

He must be seventy-five metres behind the bus, and cars were rushing past him on all sides with their horns blaring.

His legs ached from being hit, his lungs were burning with the sudden exertion, but he had no intention of giving up, at least not while he still had the bus in sight.

He veered across the road and carried on along the pavement. Far ahead the bus finally seemed to have stopped at Mariatorget. Yes!

He ran even faster, crossing Torkel Knutssonsgatan as he approached the back of the bus.

Fifty metres.

Forty.

Thirty.

'Hi, Nina Brandt here!'

'Hi Nina, can you hang on . . .'

She put the phone down, stood up from her desk and closed the door to her office.

'There, now I can talk.'

'Is everything okay, Becca?'

'Absolutely fine,' she lied. 'A few too many balls in the air, maybe . . .'

'So you're keen to get back to the Firm . . .?'

She forced out a laugh.

'Well, not just yet, at any rate . . . Have you managed to find out anything?' she added quickly before Nina had time to go on.

'Not really . . .'

Rebecca breathed out silently.

'There's no record of the revolver in the system. It's never been reported stolen, nor registered in connection with any crime.'

'Okay, good.'

'But my contact up in Forensics would still like to take it in for some test shots.'

'Okay, what for?'

'Because it's a .38 calibre manufactured before 1986 . . .'

'What . . .?'

'Come on, Rebecca, the revolver is at least in theory a potential OPW . . .'

'I'm not with you, Nina . . .'

'An Olof Palme Weapon.'

A short silence followed as Rebecca tried to take in this information.

'But the killer used a 357 Magnum? Holmér went on television and said . . .'

She must have seen the image at least a hundred times over the years. The press conference, with the county police commissioner confidently waving two powerful revolvers.

'Well, Holmér managed to get most things wrong, including the gun. Look, Rebecca, the .38 and the 357 have the same sized bullets, only their length is different. Some makes of .38 can be used to fire 357 ammunition, which is why Forensics are so keen to test-fire all old guns that match the OPW profile. My friend in Forensics could deal with it next week . . .'

'Okay, sure . . . Listen, I'm going to have to call you

back, Nina, I've got a call waiting . . . Thanks a million for your help,' she added. 'I'll be in touch next week and we can have lunch together . . .'

She clicked to end the call, put her mobile down on the desk and leaned back slowly. Then she opened the desk drawer and took out some sheets of paper. Since her visit to the bank vault she'd found it impossible to fit together any of the pieces of the puzzle she'd found in the box.

Not until the copy of the contract for the safe deposit box arrived.

She had been certain it was Henke's box. And she had been wrong. The agreement had been set up in 1986, and her and Henke's names had been listed in the section for *other individuals with access to the deposit box.*

In other words, Henke probably knew as little about the box as she did.

The reminders about the overdue payments must have been sent to both of them, the only difference being that his stack of unopened post had probably been seized before he had time to open it. So, the box's secrets weren't Henke's after all, but belonged to the person who was listed as the principle name on the contract. The person who had owned the bunch of keys before Henke inherited it.

Erland Wilhelm Pettersson.

Their father.

When he was twenty metres away the bus's indicator lights began to flash.

He put all he had into it.

The bus pulled away from the stop.

Ten metres left.

Eight.

Five.

The distance stopped shrinking.

Then it began to grow again as the bus picked up speed on the long slope down towards Slussen.

Fuck!

His stomach clenched and he felt the first convulsion and tried to swallow it. Forcing his legs to carry him forward . . .

The square outline of the back of the bus was getting smaller and smaller.

The second retch almost reached his mouth.

The bus disappeared out of sight.

But he couldn't give up now.

He didn't manage to catch the third convulsion, and had to take a few stumbling steps to avoid throwing up on his trainers.

The bus must have pulled up outside the underground station at Slussen at least a minute ago, which meant that he was going to get there too late. The bus would already have set off for Skeppsbron and on into the city centre.

But he'd just have to take a chance.

He'd seen the Erman lookalike at Slussen station last time, so maybe that's where he was going this time as well?

With a bit of luck he'd manage to catch up with him before he got inside the ticket hall.

All he needed were a few seconds at close range . . .

He veered off right, up into Götgatsbacken, then forced his aching legs round the corner of the City Museum.

His stomach was letting him know it was ready for a new salvo, but at that moment Ryssgården opened up in front of him and he stopped abruptly. He coughed up a mouthful of bitter vomit from his throat and spat it out from the side of his mouth. His lungs were burning and his heart was thumping so hard that he couldn't help squinting with pain, but he didn't take his eyes off the square. He was out there somewhere, among the crowd.

Well, he ought to be.

Unless . . .

He wasn't . . .

Fuck!

His pulse gradually slowed down, which helped the cramps in his stomach subside.

He took a few steps out into the square. Still no sign. Either Erman was already inside the station, or else he had carried on towards the city centre on the bus.

Just his sodding luck!

The adrenalin kick was starting to fade and all of a sudden he felt almost faint. He leaned his hands on his knees, gathered another gob of saliva and spat it out on the cobbles.

'Disgusting!' someone hissed off to his right, but he ignored them.

The cobbles beneath his feet seemed to be slowly turning clockwise, as sweat poured down his back, soaking the waist of his trousers and removing the last pale patches on his t-shirt.

He lowered his head a bit closer to his knees to improve the blood flow. He stood like that for a couple of minutes, trying to recover.

When the ground had stopped spinning he straightened up, took a deep breath and turned round.

And that was when he caught sight of him. Inside the glass box of the lift, just nine, ten metres away. White shirt, smart trousers and a pale jacket slung casually over one shoulder.

In spite of the unfamiliar clothing, in spite of the fact that the man was clean-shaven, considerably thinner and seemed perfectly normal, he looked a fuck of a lot like Erman.

Disconcertingly similar, in fact . . .

He needed to get a bit closer, to make absolutely sure.

HP took a few unsteady steps forward, then a few more, but at that moment the lift began to move downwards. He speeded up, forcing his legs to obey him.

The man's feet disappeared into the ground, then his legs, torso, and, just before his head vanished below street-level, HP looked into the man's eyes.

Fucking hell . . .

Why on earth did Dad have a secret safe deposit box with false passports, thousands of dollars in cash and a large-bore revolver?

If they'd been in a spy novel the answer would have been obvious, but this was her dad, for God's sake. A perfectly ordinary Swede with an ordinary job, a flat in Bagarmossen, and a wife and two children.

There were five passports in total spread out on the desk in front of her.

There was the South African one, then one each from Switzerland, Canada, Belgium and Yugoslavia. They all had various foreign entry stamps in them, mostly from the USA, but there were also some from other countries. On the last but one page of the Canadian passport she also found an old black and white photograph that was almost stuck between the pages. It showed some sixty or so young men in uniform, posing around a tank. The letters *UN* were painted on the turret in large white capitals.

Blue berets, Cyprus 1964, someone had written on the back in old-fashioned handwriting that looked so much like her dad's that her heart skipped a beat.

The focus of the photograph wasn't great and a lot of the faces were blurred. But one of the men, squatting in the front row, had a very familiar look to his nose and eyes. Had her dad served with the United Nations? And if he had, why hadn't he ever mentioned it?

She knew he'd been in the reserves when he was younger, that was how he and Uncle Tage had got to know each other, and the meetings of the veterans' association were one of the few things that used to put him in a good mood. But the fact that he might have served abroad and never mentioned it seemed very odd. Okay, so he hadn't been the talkative type, but at the very least he ought to have had one of those pennants, certificates or some other souvenir, like the things all her colleagues who had served with the UN usually adorned their offices with.

She had been through her childhood home in her head several times now, but couldn't recall ever seeing anything like that. Mum's collection of Spanish bullfighter dolls and jubilee plates were pretty much the only ornaments they'd had in the house, and there had been nothing among Dad's possessions after his death that gave any clue. Apart from his shirts and suits, a few bits of heavy furniture and his worn out typewriter, his remaining possessions had fitted into a plastic bag.

She had pretty much given up any idea that the revolver could have been Dad's old service weapon. Officers in the reserves in the fifties and sixties had been allocated pistols rather than revolvers, as far as she had been able to find out. Besides, the Army would have been in touch if his gun had gone missing. Nothing she had found in the safe deposit box made any sense, and there was really only one person who could help her get to grips with it.

She pulled the keyboard towards her, logged into her hotmail account and opened a new email.

To: tage.sammer@hotmail.com
From: rebecca.normen@hotmail.com
Subject: UN service

Dear Uncle Tage,
    I hope you are well.
    I have recently come across some things
of Dad's that were stored in a safe deposit
box. Among them is a photograph from a UN
mission in Cyprus in 1964.
    I didn't actually know that Dad had served
with the UN, and I was hoping you might be
able to tell me a bit more?
    Feel free to call me!

    Best wishes,
    Rebecca

He raced towards the lift, then realized it was on its way
down to the City Museum and changed direction towards
the large stone staircase a few metres away instead.

He took the steps two at a time, pushing some parents
with small children out of the way as he rushed for the
main entrance. He had lost a bit of time, but there was a
long, glassed-in corridor leading from the lift to the
entrance to the museum. There was no way the bloke
would get to the end of the corridor before he did.

The sliding doors had barely opened before he was
through them.

Just as he had expected, he got there first.

He took a couple of deep breaths, then began to walk
slowly down the long corridor leading toward the shiny
lift doors.

He jaw was clenched, and he could feel the blood surging

behind his eyelids. Any moment now the lift doors would open and he would be standing face to face with Erman.

Because that must have been Erman he saw?

Clean-shaven, nice and clean, and several kilos lighter. But it was still him, for fuck's sake.

So he clearly hadn't been burned alive out there in the bush at Fjärdhundra, it didn't look as if the allergy to electricity that had forced him to lead a low-tech life was bothering him any more.

Which meant what . . .?

Well, that was what he was planning to find out the moment the lift doors opened. Possibly rather more violently than the situation demanded . . .

He was clenching and unclenching his fists, and could almost taste the adrenalin on his tongue.

Ten seconds passed.

Twenty.

Thirty.

Okay, so the lift was the slow sort meant for the disabled, but still – it ought to have been there by now.

He hit the lift button, then looked round, wondering for a moment if he should dash back up to the square again.

But suddenly the lift made a pinging sound that almost made him jump out of his shoes.

His heart was turning somersaults in his chest as he raised his fists and got ready.

The doors slowly opened.

. . . it doesn't mean they aren't after you

'Yes, hello?'

'Good afternoon, my dear friend, or perhaps it's morning?'

'Yes, it's actually morning here. It's good that you've called. Is everything okay?'

'More or less . . .'

'What do you mean? Shouldn't . . .?'

'Don't worry, my dear friend, the pieces are about to fall into place.'

'I hope so. Failure is not an option.'

'So I've understood . . .'

'My dear Rebecca, how lovely to see you!'

'Hello, Uncle Tage, good to see you too . . .'

She was ten minutes early for their meeting, but of course he was already there.

'I thought you were abroad, when did you get home?' She leaned over the café table and kissed the old man on the cheek.

He still smelled the same. Shaving foam, aftershave, cigars and something else very familiar. Something she liked . . .

'Oh, a few weeks ago. Would you like something? Coffee, tea? No, how silly of me . . . Excuse me!'

He waved the waitress over.

'A cappuccino please, with lactose-free milk, if that's possible?'

He smiled at Rebecca, but it took her a few seconds to return his smile.

He didn't seem to have noticed her reaction.

'I'm sorry I haven't been in touch before, Rebecca, dear, but since I got home my diary has been completely full . . . These are hectic times, but of course you know that as well as I do.'

He smiled again, then sipped his coffee.

'Of course,' she mumbled. 'Absolutely,' she added in a clearer voice.

The waitress returned with her cappuccino, and she took a quick sip.

'So, how's your new job, Rebecca? I can imagine it's rather different from working for the Security Police?'

'It's good, thanks. We've had a bit of trouble getting everything set up – equipment, staff, licences and a whole load of other things. The paperwork has taken much longer than I expected.'

'The wheels of Swedish bureaucracy turn very slowly . . .'

'You can say that again!' This time his smile was easier to return.

'In which case I would guess that you've applied to be allowed to bear weapons in the course of your work. It's not usually particularly straightforward for private companies to get approval for that. The state is very precious about its monopoly on violence . . .'

She opened her mouth to say something but closed it again at once. Instead she merely nodded. She shouldn't really be surprised. Uncle Tage had always seemed to know almost exactly what she was doing, even when she worked for the Security Police, and nothing seemed to have changed just because she had a new job. The idea that he was somehow watching over her made her earlier disappointment disappear completely.

'Perhaps I might be able to help? As you know, I still have a number of contacts . . .'

'That would be great!'

She remembered very well how his contacts had helped her the previous winter. He had managed to get her cleared of suspicions of misuse of office, and saved her from getting fired. She really shouldn't be exploiting his willingness to help in such a paltry matter, but he had volunteered, and she had already had two applications for a weapons licence rejected.

The members of her team were complaining more loudly now, and it was only a matter of time before their grumbling reached the bosses. And that was something she could do without . . .

'If it isn't too much trouble, I mean . . .?' she added.

'Not at all, I'll make a couple of calls on Monday. No guarantees, of course, but I shall do what I can. What else are friends for, if not to help one another . . .?'

'Thanks very much, I really appreciate it, Uncle Tage.'

He put his cup down and gently pushed it aside.

'Now, to the matter you were asking about. As I said, I didn't really want to discuss it by email. Some things are better dealt with face to face . . .'

She nodded.

'I'm very happy to tell you about my and your father's shared past, but first it's my turn to ask you for a small favour, Rebecca . . .'

'Anything, Uncle Tage, you know that . . .'

'Good.'

He lowered his voice and leaned across the table.

'You mentioned a safe deposit box that had belonged to your father, and an old photograph?'

'Yes, that's right . . .'

He leaned forward even further.

'I want you to tell me exactly what you found, Rebecca. It's very important that you don't leave anything out!'

She was taken aback by the sudden sharpness in his voice, and leaned back slightly.

'Some documents,' she replied, fingering her coffee cup.

'What sort of documents, Rebecca?' His stare seemed to go right through her and she took an exaggeratedly slow sip of coffee to have a reason to look away. Tage Sammer was one of her dad's oldest friends, someone she trusted. Yet she still felt suddenly hesitant.

'I understand that this is rather sensitive. We are talking about your father, after all.'

His tone was softer now, more personal.

'Let me see if I can't help you a little, Rebecca, my dear . . .'

He glanced quickly at the next table, then lowered his voice a bit more.

'Might the documents possibly have been passports – foreign passports containing your father's photograph?'

She hesitated for a few more seconds, then nodded slowly.

'I understand . . .' he repeated, and this time his voice sounded almost sad.

They sat there in silence while he seemed to ponder the matter.

'A safe deposit box is actually a sort of bubble, has that occurred to you, Rebecca? Life outside goes on, things change, but in there time stands still. Much like life itself. We create our own reality, small spheres where we imagine we control what happens. In actual fact the feeling of control is just an illusion, and those spheres are nothing more than bubbles. But all bubbles are doomed to burst sooner or later, aren't they?'

He shook his head.

'You must promise to keep what I'm about to tell you to yourself, Rebecca,' he went on.

She nodded.

'You mustn't share it with anyone, not even your brother. As you know, Henrik isn't capable of keeping a secret in the same way as you or I, and if what I'm about to say were to get out, there would be consequences, serious consequences. Do you understand?'

'Of course, Uncle Tage. You can trust me.'

'Yes, I know I can, Rebecca. You're more like your father than you realize . . .'

He gave her a wry smile that made her heart skip a beat.

'It all started in 1964, in a small village in northern Cyprus. I was the company commander, and your father was one my four platoon leaders. We already knew each other from Officer Training College, and got on well. Erland might not have been the most natural leader, but he made up for it by being extremely well prepared for any possible scenario. And he was reliable and loyal, qualities which are becoming harder and harder to find these days . . .'

He turned his coffee cup gently.

'On one occasion we were despatched to protect a Turkish Cypriot village which was coming under constant fire from superior and considerably better armed Greek Cypriot forces.

'Unfortunately our presence didn't put a stop to

hostilities and we were forced to watch as the Turkish Cypriot village was blown to pieces. Erland was a man of firm principles He along with a couple of his colleagues had great difficulty accepting that we had no mandate to intervene in order to protect the weaker party.'

She nodded.

'Well, unfortunately their frustration led to them loading up two of our UN-marked vehicles with a couple of heavy machine-guns and several boxes of ammunition, with the intention of driving them over to the Turkish Cypriots. The idea was presumably to even out the fight, if only slightly. It wasn't a declaration of political intent, and even if they had succeeded in delivering the arms, I doubt they would have made much difference . . .'

He shook his head slowly.

'But they were stopped at a Greek Cypriot roadblock, and all hell broke loose . . . There was a thorough investigation, your father and his colleagues were relieved of duty immediately and the whole Swedish contingent of UN forces was reallocated at once to the southern part of the island. Erland took the whole thing very hard. He believed that he had merely been acting to protect the weaker party, according to orders. I can't pretend that I didn't sympathize with him, but the regulations were crystal-clear and not only had he broken them, but he had also damaged confidence in the whole UN mission.'

'So what happened?'

He shrugged his shoulders.

'Instant dismissal from both the UN and the Swedish Army. As his immediate superior I was forced to sign the papers. A sad day. A very sad day . . .'

He paused for a few seconds as he went on toying with his empty coffee cup.

'You see, Rebecca, your father liked being an officer,

104

part of a larger context, surrounded by peers. He had been looking forward to a long and successful career in the military. And when this was suddenly taken away from him, he became . . .'

'Bitter . . .'

He looked up.

'I was thinking of saying *a different man,* but of course you're right. Erland was never quite himself again . . .'

Empty!

The bastard lift had been fucking empty! He still couldn't work out how it had happened.

Not in the lift, not in the corridor, not in the entrance to the museum. So where the hell had the bloke gone? After all, he couldn't have pulled some magic trick and disappeared in a puff of bloody smoke, could he?

But he knew what was going on. The bastards were fucking with his head! Not content with keeping track of his every move and listening through the walls, now they were playing mind games on him. Getting him to chase a ghost halfway across Södermalm. Sneaking into the flat when he was out, planting the phone and with it the clear message that whoever put it there had police connections; most likely the Player *was* a cop.

Well, they weren't going to break him that easily! He'd started piling furniture against the door at night, and on the few occasions he went out, he stuck strands of hair across the crack of the door so he could see if they'd been in. But he'd much rather just not go out.

The whole of his living-room floor was covered with pizza boxes and newspapers and magazines. He'd pretty much stripped the newsagent's shelves, and the signs were unmistakable. Weird shit was going on all over the place: people going out to buy cigarettes but never coming home;

105

computer systems shutting down for no reason, closing the barriers in the tunnel network of the Southern Link Road, switching off the landing lights at Arlanda Airport, preventing chemists from issuing prescriptions; things simply vanishing – like that flag out at Kastellholmen that's always supposed to fly in peacetime. The newspapers seemed to think it was great fun. An innocent prank ahead of the royal wedding ... but yesterday Stockholm's pensioners blocked the Army's telephone exchange with worried calls.

As usual, the world full of average Swedes had no idea.

No flag – no peace.

In other words, war!

Well, if it was war they wanted, they could have it!

BIG TIME!!

He got up from the floor and scratched his beard as he marched over to the fridge. Time to check his supplies: four low-strength lagers, six Gorby pies, half a tube of fish roe.

The top shelf of the larder increased his assets by three slices of crispbread and a tin of frankfurters. The second shelf was full of silver duct tape. Sixteen rolls, to be precise. He did a quick calculation on his fingers. Another three days, possibly four, before he needed to go out again.

Good!

He had a lot to sort out, things to do . . .

'So where do the passports come in?'

He took a deep breath, then slowly let the air out again.

'What I've told you so far isn't particularly sensitive. You can find it all on the internet or in various books about the history of the UN. But what I'm about to say is strictly confidential. I hope you understand that?'

She nodded.

'After the Cyprus mission I continued my career in the military. We were in the middle of the Cold War and the army was larger and far more influential than it is today. Erland and I kept in touch, mostly at my initiative because I felt a certain degree of guilt about what had happened. I had been both his friend and his commanding officer, yet I still hadn't been able to help him. But as my career in the military developed, I realized that there was always a need for loyal, decisive men like Erland. I began to use him for a number of . . . small consultancy tasks, I suppose you could call them. Would you like anything else to drink, by the way? Some mineral water, perhaps?'

He waved the waitress over and ordered two bottles of Ramlösa, which she brought over at once.

'These consultancy jobs, what did they involve?' Rebecca asked after taking a drink.

'I'm afraid I can't go into the details . . .'

'You mean he was some sort of spy?'

'No, no, absolutely not.'

He held his hands up in front of him.

'Nothing of that sort, it was mostly courier work. The exchange of services and information. I really can't say any more than that . . . It's still covered by the Official Secrets Act . . .'

'But if he needed fake passports . . .?'

'I know it must sound strange, but you have to understand that times were very different. The Cold War was raging and Sweden was caught between the two superpowers. I'm sure you remember the Swedish DC-3 that was shot down over the Baltic by the Soviet Union, followed by one of the Catalina planes that was sent to search for survivors. Even the most innocent activities were liable to be misinterpreted by the enemy, so it was important to take whatever precautions were available, especially once Erland had a family . . .'

'B-but Dad had a job, he worked as a salesman, for . . . for . . .'

She tried in vain to remember the name of the company – something beginning with T, she was pretty sure of that. He let her think.

'I'd be surprised if any of you knew very much about Erland's work . . . If he ever told you anything, it was probably only in very general terms, no specifics. Something to explain his absences and long trips abroad, perhaps . . .?'

She picked up her bottle to refill her glass, but her right hand suddenly twitched a couple of times, making her spill water on the table. She used some napkins to wipe it up as discreetly as she could.

If anyone had suggested that her dad had been anything but a perfectly ordinary citizen only a few days before, she would probably just have laughed. But that was before she opened his safe deposit box . . .

'I realize that this must all feel a little . . . unreal, Rebecca.'

He leaned forward and put his hand on hers.

'Believe me, I would rather not have had to tell you any of this . . .'

She looked at him carefully, trying to find any indication that he didn't mean it. But he seemed to be completely genuine.

'S-so, what do we do now . . .?' she managed to ask. 'With the things in the box?' she clarified, dropping her right hand to her lap in an attempt to stop it shaking.

'Leave that to me. I'll make sure that everything disappears. The passports, the safe deposit box, any documentation that could connect them to your father. Just give me all the keys, codes and anything else necessary, and all your worries will be over.'

She tensed up involuntarily.

'Naturally, I shall make sure that no shadows fall across your father's memory . . .' He smiled warmly and she paused for a few moments while she considered.

'I'm not sure that's what I want, Uncle Tage,' she said eventually. 'Handing over everything, I mean . . .'

He frowned and gave her a long look.

Then he slowly pulled his hand back and straightened up in his chair.

'In which case I can't help wondering why not, Rebecca?'

The expression on his face had suddenly changed, becoming harder.

He went on looking at her for a few seconds, as his eyes slowly narrowed and his mouth grew thinner.

'There was something else in the box, wasn't there? Apart from the passports and that photograph . . .'

She didn't move a muscle, but he slowly nodded as if she had nonetheless somehow confirmed his suspicion.

'You found something else, something much more troubling . . .'

Her hand was still trembling in her lap, and she could feel her heart beating faster. She made a determined effort not to show the slightest sign that might give her away.

Uncle Tage went on staring at her, but this time she didn't look away. Instead she lowered her chin slightly and maintained eye-contact.

Five seconds.

Ten . . .

'Okay,' he eventually sighed, holding up his hands. 'There's another part of the story. Something I was hoping I wouldn't have to tell you . . . We worked together on a special . . . project, I suppose you would call it,' he went on. 'Something rather controversial, which meant that we had to be extremely careful. That's why we didn't use our own staff, but brought in freelancers like your father. People without any official connection to the project, but who were still unwaveringly loyal . . .'

'And who you could afford to lose if anything went wrong . . .?'

'That sounds rather cynical . . .'

'But it's true, isn't it?'

He shrugged.

'Your father was well aware of the rules of the game. He knew how it worked. Anyway, this project was given high priority for a number of years, and we had access to almost unlimited resources. Then suddenly everything changed, political support was withdrawn and the budget was cut drastically. But we carried on with our work nonetheless, just more discreetly. Everyone involved in the project was convinced of its importance for national security. And we also had a degree of support from some of our former sponsors, which enabled us to carry on well into the 1980s. But eventually one of our most faithful friends abandoned us, someone who had previously been our biggest supporter. Our little unit was shut down for good, the offices closed and the remaining staff reallocated elsewhere. In conjunction with this I left the service altogether. Since then I have worked for the private sector . . .'

'And Dad, what happened to him?'

'Your father was never formally employed, there was no contract, and thus no obligations . . .'

He shook his head.

'It wasn't right, considering how faithfully he had served our cause . . . Of course there were others like him, people who also ended up out in the cold without so much as a word of thanks. But I'm afraid Erland was the one who took it hardest. That was the second time he had been expelled, cast out of somewhere he felt he belonged . . .'

He paused to drink the rest of his mineral water.

'When was this? What year?'

'The late 1980s, you'd have been, what, eleven or twelve years old then . . .?'

She took a deep breath and then slowly let it out. Her right hand had finally calmed down enough for her to dare to put it back on the table.

'Do you remember much from that time, Rebecca?'

'Well, er . . .' she said, her voice catching, and she cleared her throat. 'Not much, really.'

But that wasn't entirely true. She remembered some things well. Far too well.

He didn't wake up until it was almost evening, which wasn't actually that odd. It had been four o'clock by the time he went to bed.

He had been sitting against that fucking wall listening, trying to pick up the slightest detail of the conversations that seemed to be going on in there. Hour after hour of indistinct muttering, with only random words audible.

By now his notepad was full of things he thought he had heard, but they left him none the wiser.

The words *gluten*, *labyrinth* and *carer* had recurred several times but, just like all the other words, it was impossible to piece them together into anything resembling a coherent context.

He dragged himself up into a sitting position, scratched his beard, then under his arms and his balls. Then he pulled one of the longer butts out of the ashtray on the bedside table and fumbled for his lighter. This whole situation was on the verge of slipping out of his hands. He had no plan, no defence at all, the cops were breathing down his neck and, to cap it all, he was under constant surveillance.

He hadn't spoken to Becca for several weeks, months even, which was actually no bad thing. If he stayed away from her, then she ought to be safe. The only problem was that he felt so fucking lonely!

He'd tried to get hold of Manga, but the sodding little rug-hugger wasn't answering his phone and the computer shop had been boarded up since winter when his little work experience lads got locked up. Okay, so he could have gone out to Farsta and knocked on the door of Manga's flat, but that felt like far too ambitious a project. Anyway, besides the fact that he really didn't feel like leaving the flat, he had no desire at all to bump into Manga's lawfully wretched other half, Betul the Bitch . . .

He found an old box of matches in one of the kitchen drawers and, with some difficulty, managed to light the cigarette butt.

But even the fag wasn't enough to improve his mood.

He ought to be starving, it had been hours since his last micro-bombed gourmet feast. But he had no appetite at all.

Just as he slumped onto the sofa his phone began to ring in the bedroom. He briefly considered not bothering to answer it.

But whoever was calling seemed keen to get hold of him, because it went on ringing.

He guessed it was Becca, and suddenly felt his mood brighten. He thought he might abandon his principles and answer this time, just a short conversation so he could hear her voice. That would hardly do too much damage.

He struggled laboriously up from the sofa and stumbled back into the bedroom. He'd got about halfway when he realized what was wrong. The ringtone was right, but the problem was that he'd switched his Nokia off once the cops had let go of him. He'd taken the battery out and put the phone in one of the kitchen drawers.

So it wasn't *that* phone that was ringing.

He speeded up and lurched round the doorframe into the bedroom.

The phone was still ringing, but the tone seemed to change, and suddenly sounded louder, sharper. Like a razor-blade against his eardrums. It took him a couple of seconds to identify where the sound was coming from. The pile of newspapers on the bedside table, beside the ashtray he'd just searched for butts. He tipped the whole lot onto the bedroom floor. He saw the silvery phone slide across the parquet floor, halfway under the bed. For a moment his heart seemed to have stopped.

The phone had been dead, switched off – he was absolutely certain of that!

He had even tried to bring it back to life the other night, just to make sure. Why the hell hadn't he simply destroyed it, smashed it with a hammer and thrown the pieces in the bin?

The screen was flashing and the vibrations were making the phone move, almost as if it were a living creature hiding under his bed.

HP felt the hair on the back of his neck stand up. The phone had almost spun round one hundred and eighty degrees, and he couldn't take his eyes off it.

Obviously he shouldn't answer, there were at least a thousand logical reasons why not.

WRONG! Ten thousand!

But, even so, he still sank to his knees and reached slowly under the bed. He was trying in vain to stop his hand trembling. His fingers brushed against it, slowly closing around the rectangular metal object . . .

'Hello?' he croaked.

There was silence on the line, and for a few moments he thought the person at the other end had hung up.

Then he heard music. In the distance, and he pressed the phone hard against his ear to try to work out what it was. Organ music, like a church.

It took him a few more seconds to work out what he was listening to.

The wedding march.

9

Guns, guards and gates . . .

She still didn't know what to think. The whole of Uncle Tage's story obviously sounded completely unbelievable, and if it had come from anyone else she would immediately have dismissed it as utter rubbish.

But right now his story was the only explanation she had. And in a lot of ways it fitted very well. It explained both the photograph and the fake passports, and also cast a certain light over other things, not least the bitterness that seemed to have consumed her dad from within, turning him into a different person, a person it was increasingly difficult to like. And she really had tried. Doing all she could to please him, longing for the smallest sign of approval . . .

But there were still far too many gaps in the story. According to Uncle Tage, Dad had been dismissed sometime in the mid-eighties. But as far as she knew he had gone on working, still going off on his business trips for almost another ten years before he finally came home from Spain in a coffin.

She hadn't asked Uncle Tage about that, hadn't raised any of the details surrounding Dad's death. Nor, in spite of his prompting, had she said anything about the revolver in the safe deposit box.

But the more she thought about it, the more convinced she was that he already knew about it. And that it was actually the gun he was most anxious to get hold of.

That was also why she wanted to wait before asking any more questions, at least until she'd had time to check out his story. Put a bit more meat on the bones.

But, if she was honest, her reluctance was probably just as much to do with the fact that she was worried about the answers.

Or that her brain was already full of other, considerably more pressing matters. Like the weird circumstances of Henke's arrest and Mark Black's impending visit, now only four days away.

And she hadn't been able to stop thinking about that van that had been following them. She had just found the response from the Highways Agency in her pigeon-hole. The van was a rental vehicle registered to a new company set up out in the western suburbs. Groundstone Ltd, a standard name allocated whenever the person registering a new business hadn't supplied a company name. The address was a post office box, just like thousands of other businesses. Altogether, the information in the letter didn't really help either to dismiss or reinforce her suspicions.

But at least the van hadn't shown up again, which was obviously something of a relief.

There was something else which was starting to worry her more and more though: the way her hands kept shaking, particularly the right one. Since she had almost lost hold of the bottle of water in the café, the shakes had returned a couple more times. It was probably due to lack of sleep, as her doctor had suggested. Or it could be a temporary side-effect of her new pills.

It'll take a few weeks for your body to get used to them, Rebecca, you'll just have to be patient . . .

She hadn't said anything to Micke, or anyone else for that matter. The dose she had been given was mild, but antidepressants were hardly something she wanted to boast about.

She walked along the corridor towards her office, passing Micke's door on the way.

It was closed, but she could see his back through the small glass window.

Like most mornings, he had got up early and had got to work while she was still in bed.

They spent far too little time together, she was all too aware of that, but this time it wasn't her fault alone. She'd taken the job at Sentry partly in an attempt to make things up with him after her affair with Tobbe Lundh. So that they would share more, see more of each other.

That had been the theory . . .

But for herself, she would probably rather they had had a fight about it, with him calling her terrible things, all of which she would have deserved. Slamming doors and not speaking to her for weeks, until she begged and pleaded for forgiveness.

And maybe not even then . . .

But obviously his behaviour had been far more mature. She had made a mistake, and he had forgiven her. End of story.

Much more sensible than throwing a load of accusations at her and slamming doors. But also kind of unnatural . . .

She shut the door of her office behind her and started up her computer.

While it was booting up she found herself glancing at the desk drawer.

A couple of minutes could hardly hurt. Besides, it looked like her computer was updating . . .

She opened the drawer and carefully took out the photograph. Then she switched on the desk-lamp, adjusted the beam and took the magnifying glass she had just bought out of her handbag.

The resolution of the picture wasn't great, and the almost fifty years that had passed since it was taken hadn't done anything to improve things.

But the man in the middle of the front row, who, unlike the others, was only smiling slightly, not showing his teeth, certainly looked very much like her dad.

She examined him carefully through the magnifying glass. The same pointed nose as her, the same prominent cheekbones and dark eyes. But it was impossible to be absolutely certain. The beret the man was wearing was pulled down low over his forehead, making the proportions of his face look rather squashed. And it also hid his hair, making him even harder to identify.

She moved on to the other men grouped around the armoured car.

Sixty-nine of them in total, all somewhere in their twenties, dressed in light khaki uniforms and berets. One of the men in the back row also looked rather familiar.

His face was shadowed by the men in front of him, which made it even harder to make out any details. But it could very well be Uncle Tage . . .

Her computer bleeped and she put the magnifying glass down and typed in her username and password.

Then she opened the search engine and typed in a few search terms.

Weapon smuggling, UN, Cyprus.

More than 50,000 hits.

The first took her to a Swedish military history

archive, and after a bit of searching she found what she was after:

In December 1963 fighting broke out between Greek and Turkish Cypriots, which led to the UN sending peace-keeping troops to the island. Under pressure from the UN, Sweden recruited a battalion of 955 men which was deployed to difficult terrain in the west of Cyprus. The battalion was allocated a large area with 35 observation posts, and equipped with armoured personnel vehicles to patrol the area. Late in the summer of that year the situation deteriorated and the Swedish troops found themselves caught between the warring parties and were forced to evacuate the Turkish civilian population. It was at this point that Greek Cypriot soldiers discovered that a small number of Swedish soldiers were smuggling arms to the Turkish Cypriots. The guilty men were punished and some officers replaced, stricter discipline was imposed and the Swedish battalion moved to the Famagusta region.

She leaned back in her chair, took a deep breath and laced her fingers together behind her neck. So far Uncle Tage's story seemed to fit. But how could she find more details?

She tried some of the other search results, but none of the sites was any great help.

She changed the search terms, but to no avail. But she did find a number of books about Swedish UN missions, and decided to order a couple of them. Just as she was finished there was a knock at her door.

119

'Come in!'

Kjellgren looked in.

'Morning, boss, everything okay?'

'Hmm, did you want anything particular?'

'Sanna said you wanted to talk to me about next week's rota . . .?'

'Of course, yes, take a seat . . .'

She gestured to a chair as she swept the photograph and magnifying glass into the top drawer of her desk.

Time to rearrange her list of priorities.

He was holding the phone in his hand. He could feel its cool surface against his palm as he gauged how heavy it was. He ran his fingers over the embossed numbers on the back for the umpteenth time.

1 – 2 – 8

He had been the first runner-up, the Ayatollah of Fuck'n'Rolla, the coolest dude in the Game. Just thinking about it still gave him a bit of a hard-on. Fuck, he really did have a seriously selective memory!

All the rest of it – the way they'd deceived him, making him think that he was a winner, daring him to do whatever they wanted, getting him to cross all his boundaries and then dumping him – was almost forgotten. Maybe even forgiven . . . A bit like when old blokes bang on about what a great time they had doing military service and how the bastard sergeant was actually quite a decent bloke really . . .

But the Game wasn't just a training exercise, it wasn't playing at war, firing blanks and planning everything around a lunch of pea soup and pork chops. It was totally real, one hundred percent!

120

He couldn't deny that holding the phone certainly felt good. Just for a few seconds feeling part of something bigger, something the average Swede would never get anywhere close to.

But in spite of all that, he couldn't go through with the task, he wasn't that sort of person.

Everything that had happened down in Bagarmossen was something else entirely. Self-defence, you could almost say.

Dag or Becca. Not exactly a difficult choice . . .

What the Game Master was asking him to do now was an entirely different matter. Crystal clear and straight to the point. But he couldn't do it.

He wasn't a murderer.

Not like that . . .

They were trying to manipulate him, he could see that. The cops, the message on the computer, the surveillance, the articles in the papers. The phone call, the wedding music.

It was all part of one big mind-fuck, intended to brainwash him. Make him malleable. Make him do what the Game Master wanted.

He had to regain the initiative, get the upper hand . . . Slowly he put the phone down and covered it up with some newspapers. Then he went and got his crowbar.

'Okay, if no-one has any more questions, we'll stop there. We'll meet up at 06.00 on Monday for a final run-through before we set off. As you all know, plenty of people will be watching us, which makes this an excellent opportunity to show what we can bring to the organization as a whole.'

The rest of the team nodded in agreement. No-one seemed to have anything to add.

'Good.' She stood up and gathered her papers, the signal

to the others that they could leave the table. Her hands were behaving perfectly, no trace of any trembling.

It must have been something temporary, like her doctor had said.

She took out her mobile and switched it from *silent* to *normal*. The screen flashed a couple of times, then turned blue. She muttered to herself, then pressed to switch it off. The third time this week, she really should have got it fixed before Black's visit, but if she left it on and didn't mess about with the settings it ought to work okay. Besides, they did most of their internal communication by radio.

When she got back to her office the letter was on her desk. She realized what it was at once and eagerly tore the envelope open.

Application for weapons licence: Sentry Security.

Then a load of officialese and a large stamp in the bottom right corner.

Approved.

Yes!

That meant they were now authorized to carry guns on duty, just as she had in the Security Police, and that they could now take the pistols they had used down in the firing range with them when they went out.

One worry sorted, and a big one at that. The pressure in her chest eased slightly.

Being armed was important – without weapons they could only ever be lightweight bodyguards, little better than the gym-pumped gorillas trying to keep the fans away from celebrities and pop stars. With weapons they were professionals, specialists who could defend themselves and their charges as far as was physically possible.

The letter of approval gave no indication why the issuing body had changed its decision, but that didn't really matter. She already knew.

Her phone seemed to have woken up and she scrolled through her contacts until she found the right name.

Thanks for your help! she wrote, then pressed send. Just a few minutes later the answer appeared.

Don't mention it, glad I was able to help! Have you had time to think over my proposal regarding your find? Best wishes, Uncle T.

She started a reply but stopped herself halfway through. Obviously it would be best to hand everything over to Uncle Tage. He seemed capable of dealing with most things, and the revolver was worrying her more than she cared to admit. Yet it didn't feel right to let it all go until she knew more about her dad's past.

She erased her reply and wrote a new one instead.

Need more time to think!

Then she went over to the computer to spread the good news.

He peered cautiously behind the roller-blind. Obviously he ought to wait until it got dark, but the semi-darkness of the Swedish summer wouldn't descend until eleven at night, and there was no way he could wait that long!

He carefully opened his creaking front door and listened for noises in the gloom of the stairwell. Somewhere below him he could hear the faint sound of a television, but that was all.

He took a couple of paces in his stockinged feet and put his ear to his neighbour's door. Silent as the grave.

For the first time in several days, which might reasonably suggest that the flat was empty.

Even Stasi spies probably had families waiting for them at home.

He crouched down and cautiously opened the letterbox. Dark, much darker than the stairwell, which meant that the windows were covered. The smell hadn't changed from the previous times he had checked. Sawdust. They must have done some serious work in there . . .

He straightened up, then took a couple of paces and checked down the stairs one more time, just to be sure.

Then he felt inside the sleeve of his jumper and pulled out the little crowbar.

It was surprisingly straightforward. The pointed end into the crack, just above the lock, a bang with his palm to wedge it in place, then a sharp jerk and *pop goes the weasel!*

It wasn't so strange, really. Unlike his own door, this one was wood, old wood. Fifty or sixty years' drying out had shrunk the wood badly, giving plenty of room to play with between it and the frame.

One muffled noise when the crowbar went in, then a louder one as the bolt of the lock popped out.

Open Sesame!

There was hardly a mark on the door.

HP stood still for a moment and listened. Apart from the television downstairs, there still wasn't any noise, neither from the stairwell nor the flat. He scuffed a few little splinters of wood away with one sock, nudging them up against the wall so they wouldn't stand out against the stone floor. Then he pulled a small torch out of one of his pockets, stepped inside the flat and carefully shut the door behind him as best he could.

The smell of sawdust was stronger in the flat, as he stood there for a moment fiddling with the torch.

An image suddenly popped into his head. He and Becca in front of a fire. No, a fireplace.

Sparks crackling, shooting out onto a tiled floor . . . Him chasing them, trying to catch them before they went out. Her laughter . . .

The sudden light from the torch made him jump. *Pull yourself together, for fuck's sake! Memory lane can wait.*

He swept the beam of the torch around the dark little hall. The flat looked like his, the layout was pretty much the same. He must have seen it at least a hundred times when the Goat was living there. But now it felt weirdly unfamiliar, and he padded about carefully as he let the torch light up the empty floor.

No furniture at all, not a single chair or cardboard box. The whole flat felt oddly abandoned, but he could still feel his heart beating faster. He squatted down and shone the torch over the floor, just like they did in *CSI*.

There were clear footprints in the dust. An obvious highway through the middle of the room, with hardly any deviation. He turned round and shone the torch in all directions. The footsteps led from the front door, through the hall and on towards the bedroom door, through the living room. He could make out at least three different types of shoe, two that looked like different types of trainer, and a third that seemed smoother, like a smarter sort of shoe.

All the visitors appeared to have been heading for the bedroom, which was rather odd seeing as that was the room furthest from his own flat. That must be where they had been doing most of the work, because in spite of the smell he hadn't seen a single trace of sawdust.

As he got closer he suddenly noticed a faint glow beneath the door. He froze and got ready for a rapid retreat. Then he realized that the light was far too faint to come from any ordinary lamp. Besides, it was red, so he guessed it probably came from a digital display on some electronic gadget.

He took a few cautious steps and put his ear to the bedroom door.

Silence.

The smell of sawdust was so strong that it almost stung his nostrils. Somewhere under the sweet, woody smell was something more acrid that he didn't recognize.

He paused for a few moments.

Five.

Ten.

Then he put his hand on the handle, took a deep breath, and carefully opened the door.

Snake eyes

The six guns went off so close together that the blasts almost merged into one. Double shots with just a few milliseconds between them. The targets turned away with a short hydraulic hiss.

The sound of empty magazines hitting the floor, followed by a short metallic rattle as the gunmen quickly replaced them with new ones.

The targets turned forward again.

Single shots this time, then all the weapons clicked more or less simultaneously. But none of the six bodyguards seemed at all surprised. Rapid bolt actions slid the green blanks that Rebecca had slipped into their magazines onto the ground.

Then more shots, until the clock ticked and turned the targets away again.

'Cease fire and unload!' Rebecca ordered as she removed her ear defenders.

The expensive ventilation system was doing its job, she noted. Even though sixty shots had been fired in the past minute down in the firing range, the smell of gunpowder was scarcely noticeable.

She pressed a button on the remote and the targets turned forward. Six figures made of brown card, the size and shape of real people.

But instead of a drawing of a threatening gunman, these targets merely had a round circle the size of a saucer drawn on the front. In the middle of the chest – heart, lungs, spine.

One shot in that circle on an unprotected body would in all likelihood be fatal. Two would guarantee it.

She didn't need to go up to the targets to check the results.

None of her team needed to retake the test.

All ten shots were within the circles, direct hits in the death zone, and not even the interruption to their firing towards the end had made them lose their focus.

'Nice shooting, all of you!' she said curtly as she noted the results in her file.

'Practice makes perfect, boss,' Mrsic grinned at her. 'Nice to know it wasn't wasted . . .'

She let the comment pass. She really ought to be pleased. She had designed everything down here herself, everything from the layout of the range to the demands made of each marksman.

The whole thing had cost upwards of two million kronor, and if she hadn't managed to secure the licence, that money would basically have been wasted. But Uncle Tage had come to her rescue again.

'Do you want to get your own test done, Rebecca? I can look after the targets.' Kjellgren held out his hand for the remote.

'No thanks,' she said, slightly too quickly. 'It's getting late, I'll do it early tomorrow morning,' she added, pretending to look at her watch.

'But thanks anyway, Kjellgren.' She forced herself to smile.

'Right, then,' she said, turning quickly towards the other

five bodyguards. 'You've all passed, well done!' She ticked the file demonstratively, making sure it was angled in such a way that no-one could see her right hand shaking.

It took him a few seconds to realize where the smell was coming from.

Terrariums.

Large terrariums lined up on wooden frames along the walls, with heat lamps above them. Five lamps in total, one above each tank. Only one of them was lit, but he could feel the heat from several metres away.

In the middle of the room stood a large work-table piled high with clutter.

He aimed the torch around the room, then took a couple of tentative steps forward. The door closed silently behind him, but he hardly noticed.

He was wondering what sort of creatures were lurking behind the panes of glass . . .

He directed the beam of light towards the terrariums, but they all seemed to be empty.

Good!

A sudden rattling sound from off to the right made him jump and drop the torch on the floor.

Shit!

He bent down quickly to get it, and when he straightened up again found himself looking straight into the eyes of a rat that was so fucking enormous it made the hair on his arms stand up.

It was only a metre or so away, shut inside a cramped metal cage hanging over the side of one of the terrariums, and he could see the animal's whiskers twitch as it caught his scent.

He hated rats. Vile little bacteria motels with yellow teeth and bald tails . . .

This one obviously wasn't your average disgusting sewer rat, but one of those black and white ones you could only get from the pet shop.

Bollocks!

So what the hell was the rat doing in there?

And the terrariums?

He couldn't see any sign of microphones or reel-to-reel tape-recorders. The only thing that came close to a technical gadget was something that looked like a small radio on the corner of the large work-table.

The display was on, and when curiosity got the better of him and he touched one of the buttons, he heard voices on the radio muttering to each other in a language he didn't understand. Probably just a perfectly ordinary radio tuned into some AM frequency . . . He moved the beam of the torch around the room a few more times, but couldn't see any trace of the surveillance control room he had been expecting.

Weird . . .

A loud plastic click followed by a faint whirring sound made him jump again, but this time he managed to hold onto the torch. He caught a glimpse of movement over by the rat cage and aimed the beam of light at it. One side of the cage was missing, and in its place was a sheet of wood that also formed one side of the terrarium. A small hatch between the cage and terrarium was slowly sliding up, presumably lifted by some sort of electric motor. He leaned down to look under the terrarium and saw a little dark box connected to a timer.

The hatch was almost completely open now, and the rat, which must be seriously pissed off with sitting in that cramped cage, was already exploring the opening to the spacious terrarium.

It hesitated for a moment, its whiskers twitching, but

evidently something in there smelled good seeing as it quickly scampered inside.

HP leaned forward to see better. The heat lamp may have been on, but the terrarium still seemed to be empty. All he could see was some sort of climbing frame in one corner, a bowl of water and a thick layer of sawdust. The rat took a couple of cautious steps through the sawdust, lifted its head and sniffed at its new surroundings. Behind it the motor began to whirr again and the hatch slowly closed, but neither the rat nor HP noticed it.

The animal took a step forward, then another. A sudden twitch of its whiskers and it stopped. Its little pink nose was quivering . . .

The snake appeared out of nowhere. It leaped out of the sawdust like a coiled spring and bit the rat in the middle of its back with such force that both creatures slammed into the glass right in front of HP's face.

He tumbled backwards onto the floor and the torch rolled away as his heart turned somersaults in his chest.

But instead of following his initial instinct to run away in panic, he sat there almost paralysed in front of the terrarium.

The snake was lying there quite still with its jaws clamped to the back of the struggling rat. Its dead reptilian eyes seemed to be staring right at him through the glass wall.

HP realized that he was holding his breath . . .

The rat's fight was short-lived: the wriggling stopped and was replaced by a feeble twitching that soon died away. Then a couple of jerks in its legs and bald tail. And with that it was completely still.

The snake lay there for a while before it let go. Then it twisted round, slowly put its jaws over the rat's head, and, with jerky movements, set about swallowing the rodent whole.

HP shuddered.

Seriously fucking disgusting. What kind of sick mind would come up with that business with the timer? Live food . . . What the hell was wrong with a tin of Whiskas?

He scrambled up from the floor, grabbed hold of the torch and looked round at the other glass cases. But they all seemed to be empty. No rat-cages on their sides, the lamps were all off and the hatches were all open. Presumably waiting for new tenants.

He went back to the work-table and after a bit of searching found the switch of an old angle-poise lamp that was attached to one side. There were various tools on the table: small screwdrivers, some unfamiliar-looking tongs, and several electronic gizmos and cables. For a moment he wondered if he had been right after all, that all this was something to do with the surveillance of his flat, and that all the little measuring instruments and resistors were actually microphones and cameras. But when he had checked the drawings piled up on one side of the table he realized he had been wrong.

Seriously fucking wrong . . .

What was being constructed in there was considerably more serious than that.

Hands by her sides.
Deep breaths.
In . . .
Out . . .
Focus now, Normén!
In . . .
The target spun round with a bang. Her hands moved like lightning. One hand clawed to pull back her jacket, then draw, bolt action, double shot. The target turned away. She released the trigger, lowered the gun to waist-height and took a step forward.

132

Then another.

The target spun round again. She raised the gun, fired two rapid shots. Then lowered it, released the trigger and took out the spent cartridges.

The target carried on through its pre-programmed routine, but she didn't bother completing the round. She already knew the result.

The two first shots had felt shaky, and the following two with the hammer uncocked and a harder recoil had probably not even hit the target, let alone the death zone in the middle of the chest.

Shit!

Good job she'd had the sense to send the others home.

Shooting had always been her thing, something she'd almost always been top of the class for. Ever since she got over her fear of guns at Police Academy, by practising with a replica until her fingers ached.

But now she wouldn't even get a pass. Partly it was her own fault, of course. She'd designed the test herself, making it harder than the one for the Security Police.

And now she was going to fail her own test . . .

Ironic.

She held the gun up in front of her, both hands clasped round the handle. Right arm held out straight, the left slightly bent so that it pulled the gun back towards her body. Usually the Weaver stance meant that the gun was aimed almost perfectly still at the target. But right now the barrel was bobbing all over the place and she had to fight hard to get the sights and the target to line up for more than half a second.

More practice, she tried to convince herself.

She spent too long sitting behind her desk, a few more hours on the firing range were bound to solve the problem. But she could hear how hollow the excuse sounded. Her trembling hands had nothing to do with a lack of practice.

Nothing at all.

A bomb.

He was absolutely certain of it. He was a long way from understanding all the strange drawings and symbols on the plans, but that didn't matter. Whoever owned that work-table, the tools and the snakes, was busy designing a bomb – a big one. For some reason he didn't understand it was also going to be round. A perfect circle, 1106.1 millimetres in diameter, and 224.3 millimetres thick, with a black grille on the base. Judging by all the electronic gadgetry, this wasn't going to be any ordinary bomb, if there was such a thing. No fuse or mobile phone to detonate it remotely, like the one he had set off out in Kista.

The batteries, processor and the little hard drive he thought he could see on the plans could only mean one thing. This little fucker was going to have its own AI, and would be able to make its own decisions depending on circumstances. A bomb with a brain . . .

There was a pattern in the corner of the plans. Orange-pink, 3D shapes with blue edges, linked together in a row.

Luttern labyrinth, someone had scrawled down one side.

So he'd almost heard right through the wall. *Luttern*, not *gluten*.

But what the fuck did it mean, and who the hell was the *Carer*?

Of course it could just be a codename for the bomb-maker with the snake fetish who usually hung out in there . . .

He couldn't help jumping at another noise behind him, even though by now he knew what was going on. The snake must have been starving, because the rat was more than halfway down its throat now, and it was slowly rolling back and forth in order to squeeze the rest in.

Did snakes actually have throats?

Unless that was pretty much all they had?

He couldn't help giggling out loud.

Shit, he was seriously strung out.

The snake was still staring at him with its dead eyes, and he gave it the finger before going back to the plans. The bomb fascinated him. The *Carer*, or whoever it was who was putting it together, was no idiot . . .

He leafed through the pile of papers, leaning forward to see better. His foot hit something under the table. A thick, long object, and for a moment he thought it was a large rope.

The rattling soon made him change his mind . . .

He leaned back cautiously and peered under the table.

The snake was large, its zigzag-patterned body had to be ten centimetres across at its thickest point. It was lying curled up right next to his sock-clad right foot. The arrow-shaped head was raised and the creature was flicking its tongue irritably as the sound from the rattle at the end of its tail got louder and louder.

The hair on the back of HP's neck was standing to attention, his heart pounding against his ribcage, and for a moment he thought he was going to wet himself. But at the last moment he got control of his bladder.

Run, you fool!

But the bastard snake was in the way. It was between him and the door, and he had no desire whatsoever to go any further into the room.

He had assumed that the four open and unlit glass cases were empty, but there was every chance that their occupants were somewhere in the room, hiding in the darkness under the terrariums where the light didn't reach. He began to move his right foot backwards extremely slowly. The rattling sound got even louder.

Fuck!

How poisonous was a rattlesnake, on a scale of one to ten?

Presumably poisonous enough to have had to develop its own audible fucking warning system . . .

Don'tcomenearmebecauseifyoudoyou'refuckingdead-ssss!!!

He needed a weapon of some sort, something to hit it with. But the work-table didn't have much to offer. Not one of the tools on there was any bigger than his own pathetic little torch. He needed something serious, like a hammer, or the crowbar he'd left next to the front door . . .

Oh . . . Fucking great!

But there was a drawer just under the tabletop.

He gently moved one hand towards it, a centimetre at a time. The rattling continued unabated as the snake stared at his filthy sock.

Good snake.

Nice and eeeasy . . .

His fingers reached the drawer and closed around the handle. The snake still seemed to be concentrating on his foot.

Carefully he pulled the drawer out a few centimetres.

Then a few more . . .

It took him several seconds before he realized what he was staring at. He'd been hoping for some sort of tool.

But this was better.

MUCH better!

He put his hand inside the drawer, closed his fingers slowly around the handle and felt the mesh pattern against his palm. He had to make a serious effort not to snatch his hand back.

Nice and eeeasy . . .

The snake was still rattling, but didn't seem to have made up its mind yet. He glanced at it from the corner of his eye, and saw it move its head a bit closer. His right foot was only fifteen, twenty centimetres away from its mouth. Its tongue was flicking in and out, faster now.

HP twisted his hand carefully and then pulled it back towards him. The rattling was getting louder, and the snake had drawn its head back. Getting ready . . .

He shifted his weight to his left leg, and turned his body slightly. Five more seconds, just five fucking seconds, that was all he needed . . .

Suddenly the snake's head shot forward.

HP yanked his foot back, yanked his hand out of the drawer and squeezed. The bang was so loud it jarred his ears and he shut his eyes instinctively, turned his head away and screamed out loud in terror. But in spite of all that he carried on pulling the trigger of the revolver.

Once.

Twice.

Splinters and dust flew up from the floor, and an angry ricochet buzzed off somewhere to his right. Then a dry, dull sound of wood breaking, and suddenly the whole work-table collapsed. A cloud of dust and gunpowder smoke hit him in the face and he took a couple of steps back as he tried to swallow to clear the whistling sound from his ears.

His heart was speeding on adrenalin, his diaphragm pumping his lungs so hard that his ribs creaked.

Fucking hell . . .

Warily he peered at where the snake had been. The collapsed table was covering most of the floor, but there were signs of blood and sticky black snake entrails among the wreckage. Part of the tail had broken off and lay on its own in the middle of the floor. It was still twitching spasmodically, but the sound was no longer threatening. It sounded more like broken maracas.

YES!

Eat shit and die, snake bastard!!

EAT SHIT AND FUCKING DIE!!!

It looked like he'd scored a direct hit with the revolver, and then the collapsing table had taken care of the rest. But had Sir Hiss managed to bite him?

The next moment the pain broke through the adrenalin rush in his brain and he looked down in horror.

Two tiny red marks were clearly visible on his right sock, right in the hollow between his foot and shinbone.

The Cyprus book had been waiting in an anonymous parcel on the doormat when she got home. She had already glanced through it, but wasn't really much the wiser. The arms smuggling story was dealt with summarily, as a minor and regrettable incident in an otherwise successful mission. The details were relatively thin. Just as Uncle Tage had said, it looked like a couple of Swedish officers hadn't been prepared to sit by and passively watch while superior forces from one side crushed the surrounded and badly equipped group on the other.

The whole thing looked like an impulsive act rather that a political statement, and in all likelihood the few weapons they tried to smuggle wouldn't actually have made any difference at all, apart from salving the Swedes' consciences. But the consequences of the impulsive act had been dramatic. The two officers were both dismissed immediately, and were sent home on the first plane while the rest of the battalion was hastily redeployed to southern Cyprus, away from the danger zone. She couldn't find any information about the names of the officers, but then she hadn't really expected to.

But she had found out one thing, something rather worrying.

A small photograph of a young officer with a rather hawkish appearance and a jacket decorated with little square badges of honour. *Lieutenant Colonel André Pellas*, according to the caption. But she was certain the picture was of Uncle Tage.

He'd never make it to hospital in time.

Södermalm Hospital wasn't far away, but the distance wasn't his biggest problem. He had no phone, no way of sounding the alarm.

The bangs had been loud, but the door to the snake room was thick, and he himself was the closest neighbour . . . it was quite possible that no-one had heard him.

All his instincts were screaming at him to go home. Run back to his flat and shut the door behind him. But if he did that, he'd never come out alive again.

He was already feeling seriously unwell, his foot had started to ache and he'd found it difficult to make his way out into the living room.

He had to think of something, right away. Even if he staggered out into the stairwell and screamed for help, banging on doors like a maniac, he doubted whether any of his constipated little neighbours would have the nerve to open their doors.

At best they'd call the cops, but by the time the boys in blue finally deigned to appear he'd be having a hot date with Rigor Mortis . . .

And even if, against all expectation, he managed to get to the hospital alive, it was far from certain that they'd have the right serum there. Poisonous Swedish snakes were one thing, but rattlesnake bites probably weren't the sort of thing that cropped up particularly often in the Stockholm area.

Basically, whatever he did he was fucked.

He could feel himself on the verge of tears.

Fuck, fuck, fuckety fuck!

He had to slow his pulse down – right now his heart was nothing but a pump spreading poison round his body. If he couldn't find a way to stop panicking, he'd soon be lying like some dribbling vegetable on this shitty floor.

He crouched down, checked over his shoulder to make sure that the door to the snake room was closed, and then took a couple of deep breaths.

His foot was shooting with pain, and the feeling of nausea was getting worse, but at least his heart seemed to be calming down. How much time did he have before he lost consciousness? Five minutes, seven maybe, but hardly much more than that . . .

He raised his head and looked across the dusty floor.

As he'd noticed earlier, the footsteps from the front door led straight across the floor to the snake room, with pretty much just two exceptions. The toilet and the fridge. If the Carer had snakes on the loose in his workroom, but was still the sort of person who made advanced bombs demanding total concentration, wasn't it likely that he had some sort of contingency plan?

A few syringes of serum, just in case . . . And where would you keep serum, Einstein?

He got up and swayed for a moment. His right leg was definitely stiffer now. At least the fridge was switched on, he could hear it as he got closer.

It wasn't until he put his hand on the handle that he noticed the latch and padlock.

Fucking bollocks!

He didn't even try to pull the door open. Instead he staggered back to get the crowbar he had left against the hall wall.

The poison must already be affecting his muscles, because the crowbar felt unexpectedly heavy and he had to make a serious effort to pick it up from the floor.

His right leg was hardly obeying his orders any more, and he was also finding it difficult to breathe.

He paused for a few seconds, gathering his strength. Then he tried to insert the crowbar between the latch and the fridge door. He failed and almost dropped it. His throat was now starting to feel swollen, his eyelids were burning and it was getting harder and harder to focus.

One deep, rasping breath.

Then another . . .

This time the crowbar went in, the lock flew off, but the effort still made him lose his balance and collapse on the floor. For a brief moment he contemplated staying there and having a rest – just a little rest.

But then the fridge door slowly swung open and the bright light from the internal lamp snapped him out of his trance. He struggled to his knees, leaning against the door as he tried to get up.

The fridge was empty.

Almost, anyway. In the middle of the top shelf was a neat container holding five pre-prepared syringes.

He struggled to his feet, pulled down one of the glass shelves, then another. He reached for the box of syringes, closing his fingers around its cool surface.

Then everything went dark . . .

Electric sheep

The black plane landed two minutes before it was due, but Rebecca was so immersed in her thoughts that she hardly noticed it.

'A Global Express, not bad!'

'W-what?'

'Black's plane, November Six Bravo.'

Kjellgren pointed at the runway.

'Can fly nonstop from New York to Tokyo. Someone at work said the plane's his own, not the company's. A Global Express can carry twenty passengers, but apparently Black prefers to travel alone . . .'

'Mmm,' she murmured, squinting to see better.

Kjellgren carried on about various types of plane, but she was only half listening. It was odd to see a plane that was painted completely black. Most planes were white or grey, so she guessed the colour was a statement in itself. The plane turned off onto one of the taxiways and slowly approached its gate.

She opened the car door and got out. For some reason she was feeling slightly nervous.

She liked Black right from the start.

142

It was impossible not to. Unlike pretty much every other VIP she had worked with, he came straight over to shake her hand and introduce himself – as if that were necessary . . .

He also asked her to outline the security arrangements, and even asked her what *he* could do to make things easier for her and the other bodyguards . . .

She noted that he looked taller in real life than on CNN. Younger, too, come to that.

Maybe it was because he smiled more that he did on television, flashing his brilliant white teeth in a way that was immediately infectious.

Black couldn't be much more than forty. He was at least one metre ninety tall, but in spite of his lanky body his double-breasted suit fitted him like a glove. His hair was cut short at the back, but his fringe, tinged with grey, hung down rather disobediently, so he occasionally had to run his fingers through it to push it back into place. For some reason, this repeated gesture gave his eyes more presence and intensity.

For someone who had been flying for ten hours, Black seemed almost indecently smart. Neither his shirt nor jacket showed the slightest crease, so he must have changed, maybe even had a shower?

According to her colleague's outline, Black's private plane wasn't exactly lacking in comforts. But both Kjellgren and the folder of advance information she had received were wrong on one point. Black hadn't travelled alone. A thickset man with cropped hair, a bull neck, loafers and a poorly fitting, flimsy-looking suit had also been on the plane.

For a few moments she thought he was a steward. But then their eyes met and she changed her mind at once. Bullneck was obviously in the same branch as her.

The man stayed in the background, but she could see he was listening intently to their conversation.

Once she had installed Black in the back seat of the car,

and double-checked that all the luggage was in place, Bullneck took her discreetly aside.

'Thomas,' he said without further pleasantries, and she wasn't sure if it was his first or last name. 'Chief Security Officer at PayTag,' he went on. 'Pleased to meet you, Rebecca. I've heard a lot about you . . .'

She gave a brief nod as they shook hands.

Sadly I can't say the same, she thought.

No-one's mentioned you at all.

He was running.

As fast as he could, straight ahead towards an exit at the far end of the corridor.

But even though he was trying as hard as he could, even though the office doors on either side of him were rushing past so quickly that he could hardly see them, he didn't seem to be getting any closer to his goal. He could feel his pursuers gaining on him . . .

The grey linoleum floor beneath his feet was spongy, getting softer with every step he took.

Almost like . . .

Sand.

He carried on running.

Knew they were still after him. Could hear their breathing cut through the desert night.

The snakes came out of nowhere. Leaping up from their lairs with their jaws open and teeth glinting. Dozens of them, maybe even hundreds. He did his best to avoid them, zigzagging over the sand dunes to make himself a more difficult target.

But it was impossible.

He felt teeth bite into his thigh.

Once, twice, three times . . .

More . . .

Then all of a sudden the snakes were gone.

144

He glanced back quickly over his shoulder and saw them getting closer. Hundreds of men in suits, racing over the sand. The bowler hats on their heads were pulled down low, almost to their eyebrows, but where their nose and mouth should be they had nothing but a large green apple.

The men were gaining on him, the sand was flying up around their well-polished shoes. His chest felt like it was about to burst and his legs suddenly felt heavy as lead, but he forced them to do as he commanded.

Onward!

Upward.

Towards the top.

He could see the drop opening out ahead of him and tried to change direction. But his legs were no longer obeying him. Instead they carried on straight ahead, forcing him closer to the steep edge of something that was no longer a sand dune but the roof of a building.

He could see birds waiting far below. Thousands of black desert ravens with glossy feathers and beaks the shape of scimitars.

Unless his eyes were deceiving him?

Were they actually sharp, oily rocks?

He fell.

Slowly at first.

Then faster and faster.

The ground was getting closer.

He knew it was going to hurt. More than anything he had ever experienced before. And at the precise moment that the pain shot through his body, making his limbs contract in a violent spasm, he heard their voices.

'Do you want to play a game, Henrik Pettersson?!'

Wanna play a . . .

GAME?

* * *

145

The word was still echoing through his head when he woke up.

It took him a few moments to remember where he was, then a few more to remember what had happened. Then came the panic. He opened his eyes and tried to sit up but his body wouldn't do as he wanted.

And it was dark.

Pitch black.

Paralysed, then.

Blind.

Soon to be dead . . .

So this was how it was going to end, on a filthy kitchen floor in an abandoned flat. Tears began to stream from his eyes, and he tried to blink them away as best he could.

But suddenly he noticed a subtle change on the pitch black darkness. A pale grey streak that got stronger and stronger until he was able to make out certain details. A ceiling, a lamp. Then a window covered by a roller-blind, and a crooked pine dresser in one corner. The feeling was gradually returning to his limbs and he suddenly realized he wasn't lying on a hard kitchen floor. Instead he seemed to be at home, in his own bedroom.

Howthefuck . . .?

He made a fresh attempt to sit up, and this time it went rather better.

Yep, his suspicions were confirmed. He was in his own fucking bed, with something that felt like the mother of all hangovers. His body ached absolutely everywhere, from the tips of his toes to the top of his scalp. His headache was so bad it was throbbing against his eyeballs, almost making him blink in time with it. He could feel the pressure building, so got to his feet and stumbled towards the toilet.

Unfortunately he didn't quite make it, but at least he

managed to catch most of the vomit in his hands. With a great deal of effort he clambered into the bathtub, turned on the taps and lifted his head towards the wonderful, liberating torrent of water.

He sat in the bath for more than an hour, just letting the water wash over his body. He only moved to throw up a couple more times into the drain in the floor beside the bath, and his skin had started to wrinkle by the time he had come round enough to pull his clothes off and do an inventory of the damage.

His body was shaking like mad, switching between shivering and hot flushes, but at least he was still alive, in spite of everything . . .

His ankle looked like an American football, and the two small holes made by the snake's fangs were clearly visible. So why wasn't he dead?

He found the answer higher up on the side of his thigh.

A couple of bruises the size of large coins, and a few drops of congealed blood. He must have managed to inject himself with the syringes containing the antidote after all. It looked like he'd rammed in all five of them, then crawled back to his own flat. Saving himself at the last fucking second! *Nice work, HP!!*

Another attack of the shakes made his teeth chatter, and he turned the temperature dial further to the red. The hot water stung his skin, but he was still finding it hard not to shiver.

He turned off the taps, wrapped himself up in a couple of towels, then staggered stiff-legged out into the hall, almost tripping over the crowbar on the floor. Over by the doormat he could see the torch. So he'd evidently managed to drag everything back with him from the snake flat and not leave any evidence behind.

Job well done!

Then he caught sight of the revolver lying right beside the door.

He picked it up carefully. It felt much heavier than he remembered. The acrid smell of powder was still obvious.

He peered out at the landing through the spyhole, but everything seemed quiet.

And the door to the neighbouring flat was closed as well – good!

Even in his moment of direst need, he had had the sense to shut the bastard snakes in . . .

So basically he had saved the lives of his stuck-up neighbours.

Housing Association block number 6 would like to inform all residents about the presence of one or more snakes apparently at large on the premises . . .

He tried to laugh, but all that came out of his mouth was a sad croak that made his brain slosh against his skull, so he stopped abruptly. Instead he shuffled back into the kitchen and drank four glasses of tepid tap-water.

He left the revolver in the drainer section of the sink.

Black carried on chatting to her almost the whole way into the city. Asking questions about Sweden and Swedish culture, and she found herself telling him about paid parental leave and strange midsummer rituals before they reached the Grand Hotel.

Thomas didn't say a word. He sat there in the back next to Black, and spent most of the journey fiddling with his Blackberry. But she noticed that he was carefully following all that was going on inside the car.

About a dozen reporters were loitering outside the hotel, and she spotted them from a distance.

'The press are here,' she said. 'We can use the rear entrance if you'd rather avoid them . . .'

Thomas looked like he was about to say something, but Black got there first.

'No, no, we'll take the main entrance. I presume we're in safe hands, Miss Normén . . .'

'Main entrance,' she said into her wrist microphone, and got a clipped 'Copy that' from the car behind.

They stopped at the edge of the pavement and she allowed a few seconds for the two men in the following car to stop and get out before she opened her own door.

There were something like ten, twelve people there. None of them seemed particularly enthusiastic or aggressive. They kept at a respectful distance as they waited.

Mrsic from the other car had already taken up position on the steps. He looked round and then gave her a short nod. She opened Black's door and the flashes of the cameras started to go off. But there was no great wave of them, just a few dutiful clicks, and she guessed that most of the photographers were there to take pictures of wedding guests rather than her VIP.

She walked in front, with the two men a metre or so behind her.

They could have been inside within ten seconds, but Black caught sight of the television camera.

'Miss Johansson,' he said a little too loud, shaking the female reporter's hand.

'Of course I've got a moment,' she heard him say. Rebecca regrouped immediately and positioned herself to one side just behind Black. Thomas carried on into the hotel, however, and she watched as Mrsic held the door open for him.

Two people in what looked like white overalls suddenly appeared on the edge of the crowd right next to the side of the building, and she saw them doing something with a bag they had brought with them.

Probably workmen, but for some reason their presence felt slightly unsettling.

She raised the wrist with the microphone to her mouth, ready to speak into it. She vaguely recognized the blonde television reporter as an economics specialist for one of the channels, and the woman must have said something funny because Black laughed out loud. The couple in overalls, a man and a woman in their twenties, were still occupied with their bag. Rebecca turned her head to call Mrsic over to her, but the door was unguarded. He must have gone inside with Thomas and not noticed that they had stopped . . .

'Well, Miss Johansson, PayTag exists for one single, very simple reason,' she heard Black say. 'We want to make a difference. We want to help our clients here in Sweden and around the world to store sensitive material in a way that is one hundred percent secure. Dealing very firmly with the risks inherent in the management of information. Obviously we ourselves have no interest in our clients' data . . .'

The movements of the pair in overalls seemed to be getting jerkier, more agitated. There was still no sign of Mrsic. She pressed the transmit button on her microphone. Her right hand had suddenly started to shake.

'Kjellgren, two people in white overalls over by the wall, they're doing something, can you see them?'

'I see them, on my way!'

From the corner of her eye she saw the car door open. Kjellgren was stepping onto the pavement when the pair in overalls spun round.

Obviously he ought to flee the city.

Get away, a fuck of a long way away, somewhere no bastard would ever find him.

Any time now the *Carer* or whatever his name was

would get back from his break and discover that someone had made snake stew out of one of his little darlings, nicked his revolver and used up all the serum in the fridge.

He hoped he hadn't left any fingerprints, and with a bit of luck the blood hadn't soaked through his sock, so the cops wouldn't have anything on him. Not that it mattered, seeing as he already knew the Carer would never involve the cops. No, he'd track down the closest suspect, with the emphasis on *closest* . . . and the ensuing little visit wouldn't involve asking to borrow a cup of sugar.

But there were two reasons why he couldn't just leave. To begin with, the cops had seized his passport and told him not to go anywhere. Which wasn't that much of a problem, he could always move freely among the Schengen countries. And it was always possible to conjure up a fake passport if you had the money. But the thought of ending up as an international fugitive wasn't exactly appealing . . .

Reason number two was considerably more serious. He was basically in too bad a state to travel. The snake poison combined with the serum cocktail he had injected himself with seemed to have aged him about sixty years, and even the short walk from the bed to the sofa left him utterly exhausted.

So he had no choice but to carry on hiding in his flat like some freaky Anne Frank.

A sudden rattle from the door made him start. A metallic scraping sound, as if someone was trying to open the letterbox.

He struggled up from the sofa and stumbled out into the hall.

There was no immediate danger. He'd fixed the letterbox just after the cops had smashed the door in.

He'd screwed it down so it couldn't be opened more than a couple of millimetres.

Too little for anyone to be able to push anything flammable through. That was the idea, anyway.

And it was also snakeproof.

Well, he thought it probably was.

All he could see was the corner of a letter, and after hesitating a few seconds he carefully pulled at it. A window envelope with some sort of official logo.

He opened it with one finger as he laboriously returned to the sofa.

Interview Summons

Henrik Pettersson is summoned to an interview in the matter of case number K-345456-12 . . .

He screwed the letter up and sent it flying at the wall. If the cops wanted to talk to him, they'd have to come and get him.

He slumped deeper into the sofa, found the remote and zapped slowly through the channels until he found a news bulletin.

'*Erik af Cederskjöld, former head of communications strategy for the Moderate Party and newly appointed press spokesman for the Palace: what's your view on the record low popularity ratings of the royal family? Don't they cast a rather negative light over preparations for the wedding . . .?*'

He changed channel before the slimy wanker on screen had time to answer.

A washing detergent advert . . .

Trust Vanish . . .

ZAPP

Emmerdale.

ZAPP

Another channel, another interview with another dull bastard, and he zapped again. But just before the picture changed he managed to read the caption.

He practically flew up from the sofa. He hammered on

152

the remote, making the plastic creak. *Mark Black, Managing Director, PayTag Group.*

He raised the volume until the red gauge on the screen was at maximum. But he still had trouble hearing what was being said. It felt like his ears were blocked and all he could hear was a vague mumble of unfamiliar voices. Fragments of sentences that didn't seem to fit together.

PayTag's only aim is to help . . .

Merely providing what the market wants . . .

A more secure world . . .

Preventing terrorism . . .

Don't understand the criticism . . .

High time that Sweden got modern legislation properly adapted to reality . . .

He crept closer to the television, close enough to touch the screen. He stared at it with the same horrified fascination as he had studied the snake's consumption of the rat. And suddenly he realized that the snake and Black were actually the same sort of creature.

Monsters with ice-cold, unmoving eyes, in the process of gulping down an unsuspecting prey.

He stared at Black, at the perfect suit, neatly ironed shirt and the unpleasantly reassuring reptilian smile on the man's lips. But most of all he was staring at the woman holding onto his arm.

PayTag kills internet freedom, it said on the banner that the couple in overalls unfurled between them. Neither of them said anything, they just stood there in complete silence behind the creepy white Guy Fawkes masks they had pulled on. Kjellgren had almost reached them, but she could see him hesitating. Neither of the demonstrators made any attempt to move.

Black half turned towards her and gave her a look that

immediately made her drop the hold she had just taken of his upper arm.

'Perhaps it's time to go in now?' she murmured, but he ignored her.

'Sorry, Miss Johansson.' He turned back towards the television reporter. 'Would you mind repeating that last question?'

'Never do that again, Miss Normén,' he said calmly as they were walking into the hotel lobby a few minutes later.

Four paracetamols.

Three glasses of water.

Two cigarettes.

One revolver.

He was ready. This task would be his last, he already knew that. But he had no choice.

Black was a poisonous snake, a monster created by the Game Master. Sent out to consume the whole world.

And he was going to start with Becca . . .

The scene was so familiar. Her hand on his upper arm, her steady gaze.

Becca and Dad.

Becca and Dag.

Becca and Black.

Obviously the Game Master was behind the whole thing. He had made sure Black got his claws into Becca. And, just as with that wife-beating bastard Dag, there was only one way to save her. The difference was that this time he had a proper weapon and didn't have to rely on a sabotaged balcony railing.

He pulled his jacket on, the same old army surplus coat he had used for his second task. That felt like a hundred years ago.

As for himself, he felt more than a hundred years old. More suited to a nursing home than a man on a mission.

The revolver fitted snugly into one of the deep side pockets.

He tried drawing it a few times in front of the mirror. But he couldn't quite conjure up the whole Taxi Driver vibe.

Maybe that wasn't so strange. He didn't really have the energy. And as for the way he looked . . .! His beard was sticking in different directions, his eyes were sunken and his cheeks looked like two deep pits. And his lower teeth were weirdly visible, as if his bottom lip had lost its grip of his gums.

He pulled his cap down over his forehead and covered the rest of his face with a pair of outsized mirror sunglasses. No-one would recognize him, not even Becca. He almost didn't recognize himself . . .

The revolver felt heavy, difficult to hold straight. He tested the hammer, and had to hold it tight to move it. All it would take now was a bit of pressure, a gentle squeeze of the trigger. And it would all be over . . .

Both for Black and for him.

There was no way the Game Master would let him live after something like this.

But he had no choice.

He had to decapitate the snake.

12

Deathmatch

The knock woke her up and it took her a few moments to realize where she was.

In a hotel room in the Grand, four doors away from Black's suite. She sat up and looked at the time on the clock-radio: 02.12.

Her head felt sluggish, as if it were full of some sort of goo, and she rubbed the palms of her hands over her eyes in an effort to get her brain into gear.

The knock was repeated. She got out of bed and quickly pulled on her trousers and blouse before opening the door slightly.

It was Thomas.

'Sorry for waking you, Rebecca,' he muttered, taking a step forward so that she had no choice but to let him in.

He waved the Blackberry he was holding in one hand.

'We've received a threat against Mr Black, a particularly credible one . . .'

'Oh . . .?'

She wasn't really sure what she was expected to say.

'An old friend in the Secret Service just called. They've had information suggesting that a terrorist organization is planning an attack against us during our visit to Stockholm.'

'Okay . . .' She fiddled with the bottom buttons of her blouse while she tried to get her still groggy thoughts in order.

'What organization?'

'They don't actually have a name, which probably sounds a bit odd. Terrorists usually like boasting, after all. But we've been keeping an eye on them for long enough to realize that they shouldn't be underestimated, in spite of their low profile.'

'So what's the reason for their interest?'

He shrugged.

'Terrorists don't always need a reason, Miss Normén. Fanatics have their own logic, but it's probably something to do with the recent protests. That banner yesterday evening . . .'

She nodded and turned away to open her trousers and tuck in the bottom of her blouse. At the same time she took the chance to sweep the pots of pills off the bedside table and into her trouser pocket.

She turned back and gave Thomas an apologetic smile. But the look on his face didn't let on if he had seen the pills.

'Okay, so what do we know, exactly?' she went on.

'Not much, but my friend was concerned enough to call me in the middle of the night. He couldn't say much, which probably means the information comes from a confidential source.'

'Someone on the inside?'

He nodded, as his free hand fiddled with the rather too long sleeve of his jacket.

'But in spite of that, you don't actually know what the organization is called?'

'They have slightly different names depending on who you ask. The Circus, the Event, the Performance . . .'

She shook her head.

'Never heard of them . . .'

'No, I didn't think you would have. They're pretty anonymous. Using a lot of different names is a good way to stay under the radar. But we know from past experience that they're capable of almost anything . . .' He was still tugging his sleeve, as if he were trying to make it even longer.

'Okay, well, I'll put a twenty-four-hour guard on Mr Black's door to start with . . .'

She thought for a few moments.

'And I suggest that we take a helicopter tomorrow instead of driving up by car.'

'Excellent, but can you arrange that at such short notice?'

She nodded.

'No problem.'

She grabbed her holster from the bedside table, fixed it to her belt and pulled her jacket on.

'Is there anything else I need to know, Mr Thomas?'

'Not right now. I've been promised more information early tomorrow morning, so we can go through what we know then.'

'Okay.'

She followed him out into the corridor and stopped outside Mr Black's door.

'Is he . . .?'

'He's okay, I spoke to him a little while ago.'

'Good.'

'Well, goodnight, then, Rebecca. You'll email me as soon as you've arranged transport . . .?'

'Of course.'

She hesitated for a moment. The thought had come out of nowhere, but she felt she had to say it, to get it out of the way.

'Just one last question. This organization . . .'

'Yes?'

'I don't suppose it's even been known as . . .'

The Game!

It was all he could think about.

In spite of the paracetamols, his head was throbbing so much he thought his eyes would pop out.

'You're not looking too hot, mate . . .' the taxi driver said.

No shit, Sherlock . . .

'Flu,' he said abruptly, chewing on his unlit cigarette. 'A right bastard, in the middle of the summer and everything . . .'

The taxi driver grinned.

'I bet! I get vaccinated in the autumn each year. You know, with all the people you meet in this line of work, bugs and viruses and shit floating around inside the car . . .'

He stopped the car, looked round, then did a sharp u-turn across the solid line down the middle of the road.

'Mind you, after swine flu and everyone getting sick from the vaccine, it does make you think . . .'

'Hmm,' HP agreed. The driver reminded him of someone, but he couldn't put his finger on who.

'Sometimes you can't help wondering if there ever was any swine flu, or if it was just a way of flogging a load of untested vaccine . . .' the driver went on.

If only you knew, mate!

Under any other circumstances he'd have thrown himself into the discussion, but he now hardly dared open his mouth in case he threw up a fountain of vomit.

They had reached Skeppsbron. Only another three or four minutes, with nothing to do but stick it out.

He pressed the button to open the window and get a bit of early morning air.

'. . . loads of other shit the authorities dump on us. Like this business of them keeping records of all internet and mobile traffic, have you heard about that one? Like the Post Office opening all our letters and parcels before delivering them. Another crazy EU idea that the general population only swallow because we're too busy gawping at all the inbred royals turning up here . . . It's just like East Germany, if you ask me . . .'

HP nodded distractedly.

Suddenly he realized who the taxi driver reminded him of. Manga . . .

Fuck, he missed Manga. Not a squeak since last winter. He didn't answer his phone, neither his mobile nor his landline. Almost as if he was keeping out of the way on purpose . . .

'Well, here we are, Kungsträdgården. Card or cash?'

HP mumbled something inaudible and pulled a crumpled 100-kronor note from his trouser pocket.

'What time is it, anyway?'

'Quarter to six in the morning, mate, a hell of a time to be up and about . . .'

HP opened the car door and stepped out onto the pavement, trying to get his lighter to work.

His hands were shaking so much that he almost burned the end of his nose before he got the fag lit.

The morning chill made him shiver and he took a few deep drags to warm himself up a bit. The illuminated façade of the Grand was a hundred metres in front of him. He thrust his hand into his pocket and closed his fingers around the handle of the revolver.

160

Almost there.

Almost home . . .

She stood up and stretched, then went for a short walk along the corridor. Almost four hours on that chair had made her limbs go stiff.

She stifled a brief yawn and looked at the time. It would be time to set off in a few minutes.

Room service had arrived half an hour ago, meaning that Black was now rested, showered and fed.

Unlike her . . .

She stifled another yawn and held her right hand up in front of her. Only a faint, almost imperceptible tremble.

The effects of the sleeping pill hadn't had time to wear off properly yet. The pills didn't really seem to help her insomnia, and even if the doctor had told her to increase the dose, she usually just ended up in a drowsy doze rather than the deep sleep she needed. The little pots were straining the fabric of her trousers.

One sort of pill to get through the night, another to get through the day . . .

Her thoughts were still churning. The safe deposit box, the passports, the revolver, Tage Sammer – unless his name was really André Pellas, and Henke, of course.

She had called him four times during the night, and sent him a text. A flagrant breach of Stigsson's orders. But as usual she had only ended up with the automated voice-mail service.

Obviously it could all have been coincidence, that was probably the most likely explanation. A loosely configured terrorist group occasionally known as the Game didn't necessarily have to have anything to do with the game Henke had got caught up in.

She was used to indistinct threats, that was pretty much

part of the daily diet at the Security Police. But she couldn't be certain, not until she'd spoken to Henke, heard his voice, checked he was okay. And that nothing of what was going on around PayTag had anything to do with him.

Her earpiece crackled into life.

'We're in position outside the main entrance, boss,' Kjellgren said. 'There's about a dozen people out here, reporters and a few early birds on the lookout for royalty and celebrities. No sign of any demonstrators, over.'

'Good, I want two men out on the pavement. We'll probably be on our way in a few minutes, over.'

'Copy that!'

A door further along the corridor opened and Thomas came out.

He was wearing the same suit, and the same loafers, but the shirt was new. Just like the last one, its collar was waging an uneven battle against Thomas's thick neck, and the knot of his tie was already noticeably loose.

'Good morning, Rebecca. Are we ready?'

'All ready, we'll be heading back to Bromma Airport and flying up. The helicopter can carry four passengers, so there'll be plenty of room.'

'And everything's prepared up there?'

'Two cars will be waiting for us, I sent them up right after our conversation last night.'

'Excellent, Rebecca, impressively efficient, I must say.'

She nodded and looked away.

'I've just had a message from Mr Black,' Thomas went on. 'He'll be ready in five minutes.'

'Thanks, I'll alert the others.'

Just as she pressed the transmit button she caught sight of the slight, scarcely perceptible bulge in Thomas's jacket on his right hip. It could have been his Blackberry, seeing as most Americans seemed to be unusually keen to keep them in holsters on their belts. *Agent 007, licenced to email . . .*

But she felt suddenly convinced that this bulge was something else.

Something considerably more dangerous . . .

She opened her mouth to say something, but Kjellgren's voice in her earpiece stopped her.

'Boss, I think we've got a slight problem . . .'

He was keeping his distance, watching the crowd behind the red velvet rope. To start with everything had been calm. A cluster of old ladies, a couple of tired-looking photographers.

Two black cars were parked right outside the main entrance, with two men in suits stationed on the pavement next to them. They reeked of cop even from a distance, which was why he was holding back. But a few minutes ago things started to get crazy. A number of minibuses had pulled up further along the quayside and a whole crowd of people had tumbled out of them. Twenty or thirty, maybe more, all dressed in pale overalls and white plastic masks that made them look pretty much identical. In just a few short seconds they had taken over the pavement and, as he slowly got closer, they started to unfurl banners.

PAYTAG = STASI
STOP THE DATA RETENTION DIRECTIVE!!!
BEWARE THE CORPORATE INVASION
OF PRIVATE MEMORY!
2006/24 = 1984

The cops in suits were clearly twitchy, and he could see one of them talking into a wrist microphone.

He speeded up to get closer, but was forced to slow down almost at once. What if Black regrouped and took another exit at the last minute? There was a way out on the other side of the building, wasn't there?

He'd never get there in time . . .

Shit!

He loitered by the edge of the quay as he kept a close watch on what was happening on the other side of the street. A television crew had turned up, which seemed to wake the other photographers up and set them jostling against each other. The commotion was getting more and more attention, several curious onlookers were heading over to watch.

A white van with tinted windows suddenly rolled up, blocking his view for a few seconds before stopping a short distance away.

The demonstrators appeared to have taken up positions next to the rope. They looked pretty creepy in their white overalls and masks. None of them said a word, the only noise was coming from the photographers and television crew, who now seemed to be fighting for space.

One of the suits was still talking into his wrist microphone. He didn't look very happy with the situation.

Suddenly a solitary police car came driving up from Skeppsholmen, and the other suit stepped into the street and waved it down.

HP crept in between the parked minibuses. The short walk from Kungsträdgården had left him utterly exhausted, and he had to lean against one of the buses to catch his breath.

The white van was just a few metres away, its engine running. He was hit by a stale smell of warm tarmac and diesel fumes, but was too tired to care. More spectators

164

had arrived, and now fifty to sixty people were gathered in front of the entrance to the hotel.

The patrol car had pulled over and the two police officers were now standing on the pavement.

They were standing and talking to the men in suits, and HP took the chance to cross the street.

His Nokia mobile was in his breast pocket and it took a him a minute to get it working.

His heart was beating hard in his chest, his nausea only just under control.

'Good morning, Miss Normén.'

'Good morning, Mr Black,' she replied, meeting his gaze.

No trace of the previous day's awkwardness. What a relief!

'There's a larger demonstration outside today,' she said. 'Forty to fifty people at the moment, and the number seems to be growing. My suggestion is that we take an alternative evacuation route . . .'

She glanced at Thomas.

'What's the situation right now?' he asked quickly.

'Calm, but tense. We've got two men on the pavement and there are also two uniformed police officers on the scene.'

'Media?' This from Black.

'The same as yesterday, possibly slightly more. A few photographers and a television crew.'

Black and Thomas exchanged a look.

A faint tremble ran through her lower right arm, making her fingers twitch.

Shit, not now!

'We don't want to look like the sort of people who sneak out the back way, Rebecca,' Thomas said. 'Especially not if there are media present. It could be interpreted as an admission that we have something to hide. Openness is an integral part of the PayTag brand . . .'

She nodded, as she carefully clasped her right hand behind her back in an attempt to stop it shaking.

'I understand . . .'

Her mobile began to vibrate in her inside pocket but she ignored it.

'Kjellgren, we're on our way down,' she said into the microphone on her wrist.

'It's me,' he said when her voicemail kicked in. He wasn't sure what to say next.

'I . . . er . . .'

The cops in suits suddenly leaped into action. One of them opened the door of the first car, and the other took a few steps towards the rope and the crowd.

The two uniformed officers were fiddling with their belts and didn't seem altogether sure what to do. As if on command, the demonstrators suddenly began to chant:

Don't be evil!

Don't be evil!

He ended the call and put his free hand in his jacket pocket. His fingers grazed the handle of the revolver. Somewhere behind him a heavy car door closed. The sound made him jump.

Quiet music was playing in the lift, a pan-pipes version of *The Winner Takes it All*. Clearly there was some unspoken rule that all Swedish hotels had to play Abba muzak in lifts . . .

She carefully unbuttoned her jacket and pressed her right arm to her side to check that her pistol and telescopic baton were in place. She should really have been wearing a bulletproof vest. But, against all her usual principles, she had decided against it, mainly because she didn't want to look hot and sweaty in front of Black.

A mistake, a big one, she now realized.

Bloody hell, she really did have to pull herself together, get a grip on her thoughts . . .

Her mouth felt dry, and her heart was beating faster than she had expected. Her right hand was shaking so much that she had to stuff it into her trouser pocket.

She had been involved in considerably more risky jobs than this, so she really shouldn't be nervous.

Her mobile vibrated in her inside pocket again. This was the third time, so whoever it was seemed keen to get hold of her. But they'd just have to wait. Work came first.

The lift stopped at the ground floor and the door slowly slid open. She took a deep breath.

The chanting of the crowd was getting louder.

Someone bumped into one of the brass posts, making the rope swing.

The suited man beside the rope suddenly began to shout.

'Back, get back!'

The two uniformed police officers took a few hesitant steps closer.

HP closed his fingers around the handle of the revolver.

There was no going back now.

The main doors opened and the chanting rose to a roar. But it suddenly felt like his ears were blocked.

The carpet of sound around him turned into a faint murmur, and all he could hear was his own heavy breathing.

In . . .

Out . . .

His field of vision shrank, turning into a grainy tunnel,

and for a moment he thought he was about to pass out. He squeezed the handle of the revolver even tighter, digging the mesh pattern into his palm. Hundreds of tiny, stinging needle pricks that woke him up and reminded him what he was doing there.

He had a task to carry out.

His last one . . .

And suddenly he saw him.

The snake himself.

Mark Black . . .

The roaring started the moment they opened the doors. The crowd pushed forward, she had time to notice the masks, the white overalls, the worried look on Kjellgren's face. Then the quick movements of the uniformed police officers as they extended their telescopic batons.

Leaving through this exit had been a big mistake.

'Back, we're going back,' she shouted at Thomas's thick neck.

But he didn't seem to hear her and carried on towards the car, closely followed by Black.

One of the posts holding the rope toppled over, dragging the others down with it.

And a moment later the demonstrators had broken through.

Thomas immediately floored the first person with an elbow in the face. It sounded like a whip cracking as the mask broke, sending a shower of blood and saliva over the white overalls of the nearest protestors. Thomas didn't seem remotely concerned, and merely shoved the limp body backwards to clear some space. He dealt another blow, then another.

Then she saw him bring his hand back and reach under his jacket in a way that she recognized all too well.

She grabbed the top of Black's arm with her left hand and pulled him towards her. She felt on her belt for her baton . . . Her hand was shaking so much she had trouble finding it. And then she heard Thomas yell.

He recognized him from the television.

High forehead, pointed nose and backswept, greying hair. At close quarters the reptilian feeling was even more obvious. He imagined he could see a little forked tongue dart out between the narrow lips. Getting the scent of his surroundings, preparing to attack.

The crowd was roaring now, forcing its way through the cordon. HP went with the flow. Sweat was pouring down his back.

There was a crash, and one of the white-clad figures in front of him fell backwards, leaving a gap.

Its mask fell off, revealing a shocked and very pale woman's face. Blood was streaming from her nose, soaking the front of her white overalls.

A moment later he caught sight of Becca. Right behind Black with her hand on his arm.

Far too close . . .

Slowly he began to pull his hand out of his pocket . . .

'GUUUUN!!' Thomas roared, and she saw him draw his own weapon. In amongst the white-overalled figures she caught sight of a dark figure. Baseball cap, sunglasses, a scruffy beard . . .

Hands were tugging at her clothes, trying to grab hold of Black . . .

The shout came from his left.

A guttural roar that he hardly heard. He didn't turn his

head. Instead he went on raising his hand, his eyes fixed on Black.

All of a sudden everything seemed to be happening in slow motion. She could make out every little detail in the scene playing out around her. The white-clad demonstrators that Thomas had just pushed over, the blood on their overalls.

Then Thomas's silver revolver slowly emerging from its holster.

The demonstrators in front of him raised their hands, trying to defend themselves.

She could see the suspect clearly in the crowd. The cap, the mirrored glasses, the dark camouflage jacket. The hand that was halfway out of his pocket . . .

Then her view of him was blocked briefly. Her hand reached for her own pistol and closed around the handle.

The shaking hadn't stopped. Alarm bells were going off in her head, drowning out her thoughts. Something about this whole situation felt wrong . . . The hands were still grabbing at her, trying to pull Black from her grasp.

Thomas's gun was out now, the barrel aimed directly at the man in the camouflage jacket. But the demonstrators seemed to be blocking his line of fire. He moved sideways, trying to find a gap.

The alarm bells went on ringing like mad.

WRONGWRONGWRONG!

Suddenly a gap opened up through the protestors. The man in the military jacket was standing motionless just five metres away. He was staring straight at Black, straight at her. His hand emerged from his pocket. She caught a glimpse of a dark object.

Instinct took over. Quick, practised movements.
Draw,
bolt action,
fire!

The sound came from in front of him.

Close enough for him to feel the pressure wave on his face.

A hard blow to the stomach. The next moment his knees gave way. Screaming, falsetto voices on all sides.

Someone grabbed him round the neck, dragging him backwards. Everything went black.

People were screaming in panic, throwing themselves to the ground.

She saw Thomas's head turn, and he stared at her as the figures in white scattered all around him.

In a flash she holstered her gun, grabbed Black's arm and shoved him as fast as she could ahead of her towards the edge of the pavement and the waiting cars.

Kjellgren caught up with her and helped get Black in place. Then quickly into the car.

'Drive,' she snapped at Kjellgren.

'What about him?'

Thomas was still standing on the pavement with his revolver in his hands, sweeping the barrel over the crowd as if he were looking for someone.

One of the uniformed police officers shouted something that she couldn't quite hear, then aimed his own weapon at Thomas.

'He'll have to look after himself, drive, drive!'

Kjellgren put his foot down and they shot away from the pavement with a screech of tyres.

'What the fuck was that all about?' he snarled when they reached Strömbron.

Swaying, lurching movement, so familiar.

He was lying in the back of a vehicle, a van of some sort, driving fast. Very fast.

A sharp corner pushed him up against one side, making him whimper in pain.

'He's awake,' he heard a female voice say somewhere behind his head.

He tried to turn his head, but the effort made everything go black once more.

'No, he's gone again . . .' was the last thing he heard.

13

Team Fortress

She didn't like travelling by helicopter. The jerky movement of the machine felt unnatural. Nothing like an aeroplane gently riding the currents. If the engines of a plane suddenly stopped, nothing much would happen. The pilot would lower the nose and glide for a while as they tried to deal with the problem.

But if a helicopter's engine stopped, you wouldn't be able to defy gravity for too many seconds.

She shook off her discomfort and looked at her watch.

'Ten minutes to go . . .'

Black looked up from his Blackberry.

'Okay, thanks . . .'

'Have you heard anything from Thomas?'

'Yes, he says everything's been sorted out with the police and that he'll be joining us by car later in the day.'

'Good . . .'

She took a deep breath.

'So how are you feeling,' she asked.

'Fine,' he said, a little too quickly. 'Absolutely fine,' he added. 'I'm sorry, Rebecca, I should have thanked you for what you did back there. What exactly was going on?'

He was trying to sound calm, but she had no trouble at all discerning the faint tremble in his voice. And he also seemed to have switched to calling her Rebecca instead of Miss Normén.

'I'm not entirely sure. The demonstration obviously got out of hand, but after that everything's rather unclear. I had hoped that Thomas might call me to clarify . . .'

'He's been busy with the police . . .'

'Yes, I can appreciate that. Gun laws in Sweden are very strict, I'd have been happy to explain them to him if he'd asked. But he never told me he was actually armed . . .'

'No, that probably wasn't a wise move. Thomas is very loyal. He only wants what's best for me and the company.'

She merely nodded in response.

Black straightened up and crossed his legs.

'But he didn't shoot, did he, which must count in his favour, mustn't it?'

'That's right,' she said. 'I was the one who opened fire.'

'Is that going to cause trouble for you? For us?'

'I don't know yet. We're licenced to bear arms, and I called the duty superintendent in Stockholm to explain what happened and how the police can contact me. We'll just have to see . . .'

That last bit was a lie.

She'd have a hell of a job explaining what she had done, she knew that already. Whether or not you had a licence, you couldn't just go round firing a gun, and certainly not in the middle of the city. The regulations governing warning shots were the same as firing at a target: there had to be an immediate and serious threat to life and limb.

But obviously there had been.

The man in the jacket had a gun, just as Thomas had

174

shouted, and it was quite clear that he was focused on Black.

Yet she had still only fired a warning shot . . .

She had been acting entirely on instinct, and in hindsight she couldn't really explain why she had done what she had.

In order to make the best of a potentially disastrous situation, she tried to convince herself.

It had all felt so wrong. Thomas's view had been blocked, with no opportunity to act. The gun, the attacker, the whole thing was almost a textbook example of an extreme emergency.

All the criteria were in place for firing directly at the target. But in the crowd it was impossible to shoot at the attacker without risking hitting innocent bystanders as well.

That was it, obviously.

She looked down at her hands, grabbing her knees in an attempt to keep them still.

Suddenly she realized that Black was still looking at her. Studying her face intently in a way she didn't like, and then dropped his eyes to look at her trembling hands.

'Adrenalin,' she said. 'It'll soon pass . . .'

For a moment she felt he could see straight through her.

'Two minutes to landing,' a voice said over the speakers.

'Right . . .' she said, giving Black a quick smile.

But he didn't smile back.

He was slipping in and out of consciousness.

He heard voices several times, conversations going on above him.

'He's in very bad shape . . .'

'How much has he had?'

'A triple dose. I daren't give him any more . . .'

'Have you spoken to the Source?'

'Mmm . . .'

'And?'

'He says we have to bring him back to life. That there are no other alternatives . . .'

'Okay . . . So what do we do now?'

'We wait . . .'

'Do we know anything else about the place?'

The sound of paper rustling somewhere to his left.

He must have been awake for five minutes now, but he was keeping his eyes closed. There was a rhythmic bleeping close to his left ear, which he guessed was a machine keeping a check on his pulse. Best to lie low and take slow, deep breaths.

There were two other people in the room, a man and a woman. He seemed to be lying on some sort of bunk or table a few metres away from them.

He felt a vague pressure in the crook of his right arm, which he guessed was from the needle of a drip, but other than that his body felt surprisingly okay.

There was an odd smell, ether and something musky that he couldn't identify.

'To start with, it's much, much bigger that we thought. Take a look at this!'

The woman's voice again, then more rustling which HP guessed must have been from some sort of plan.

'Right, so these red marks, are they . . .?' The man's voice sounded familiar, but he couldn't quite place it.

'Red is for guards, blue for security cameras, and yellow is different types of alarm . . .'

'Okay . . . And all this comes from the Source?'

'Yes.'

'And you trust him?'

'He's never given me any reason to doubt him. Everything he's given us so far has been one hundred percent accurate, just look at that poor sod . . .'

It took HP a few seconds to realize that the woman meant him.

'I'm still not sure. About him, or the whole thing.'

The male voice again, a bit whiny, in a way that still sounded extremely familiar. He fought the urge to open his eyes and turn his head.

Suddenly he noticed the bleeps speeding up.

Shit, he had to relax.

Deep breaths, nice and easy.

He wanted to hear more, try to work out what the fuck was going on.

'Six floors, then,' the woman went on.

'Thirty metres into the rock, each floor consisting of a hub with five tunnels leading off it like spokes, each of them fifty metres long. Five times fifty is two hundred and fifty, multiplied by six floors . . .'

'One and a half kilometres. That's a hell of a lot of space . . .'

'And each one of the spokes is ten metres wide, which means they might have several rows of server racks in them. Say, two passageways for maintenance in each tunnel. Each rack is, what, one metre deep? That makes . . .'

'Five kilometres, maybe more. Five kilometres of servers . . . That's a fuck of a lot of capacity!'

The man's voice sounded agitated.

'That's enough to supply . . .'

'. . . pretty much the whole of Europe's requirements for secure data storage.'

The site manager paused long enough for the statement

to sink in. The hundred or so visitors seemed impressed. As for her, she was only really half-listening to the press conference.

Details of the site's capacity flickered past on the large screen, interspersed occasionally with pictures of its construction. She stretched discreetly and took the chance to check her phone for messages. But the inbox was empty and the calls she had missed in the lift at the Grand didn't seem to have been registered by the phone. Weird.

In contrast to the summer heat outside, the air in there was cool, and even though they were above ground, she thought she could detect a faint smell of the rock, a bit like in the underground in Stockholm. Which wasn't really that strange . . .

During the Cold War this had been the site of an underground command base – she'd read that in the papers. And just as Kjellgren had said, there was a long tunnel which acted as both an emergency exit and a conduit for all the communication cables to the artillery bunkers on the coast a couple of kilometres away.

Now that same tunnel brought cool water from the Baltic to service the air-conditioning down in the underground chambers. That and the cool Swedish climate, the unlimited and secure supply of electricity and the extensive broadband network were evidently the main reasons why the whole installation had been located in Sweden, blah, blah, blah . . .

Obviously she ought to have been more interested, because this was her employer they were talking about here, after all. But she was having trouble concentrating on the details of the presentation. She couldn't shake the gnawing feeling that something was seriously wrong. Really she ought to be trying to call Thomas again.

Black was bound to be safe in there. All the visitors had

been registered and checked out in advance, and had been made to undergo a security check more rigorous than at any airport. All electronic gadgets except the photographers' cameras had been locked away out in the security lodge. Naturally she had been spared these security procedures, and still had both her radio and mobile on her.

But she already suspected there was no point to the call she was thinking of making. Just as before, Thomas wouldn't answer. Besides, he would be there in an hour or so.

Kjellgren was driving, and according to the text she had received a few minutes ago, they had already passed Uppsala. She wasn't looking forward to the meeting.

But she wasn't the one who had made a fool of herself, she wasn't the one who had drawn an illegal handgun . . .

'Our site basically works the same way as an old-fashioned bank vault . . .' the site manager went on as the video projector faded neatly into an image she recognized.

The bank vault on the screen was practically identical to the one she had been in a few days before. Thick concrete walls, polished marble floor and long rows of little brass doors . . . Could it be the same vault?

Rebecca straightened up in her chair instinctively. She had been trying not to think about the safe deposit box and Tage Sammer's story, hoping to set the whole thing to one side for a few days until Black's visit was over.

'A thick shell to protect against attack from outside,' the site manager went on. 'Then separate compartments inside, each one isolated from the others to allow entry only to those authorized to access the contents. But here the size of each compartment can be varied with a few simple commands from the control room. In other words we can adapt to our clients' requirements instantaneously.

The compartments become bubbles whose size can be constantly adjusted.

'Any demand to store ten, one hundred, or even a thousand times more information would be no problem at all, the changes can be made instantly. What server room can compete with that level of capacity?'

He left another deliberate pause for the rhetorical question to hang in the air for a few seconds. The projector replaced the bank vault with an image of a spacious underground chamber containing row upon row of identical server cabinets.

'Everything gathered in one location. Simple, cost effective, and – above all – secure,' the site manager went on.

The projector laid a new picture at an angle on top of the current one. An almost identical underground room, then another, and another . . . Rows of shiny server cabinets, so many that she had already lost count. Thousands, millions of secrets, all stored in the same place.

All of a sudden she felt rather unwell. It must have been the after-effects of the adrenalin rush. But at least her hands had stopped shaking.

The site manager resumed his speech as the vaults went on multiplying on the screen, but she was no longer listening.

Like shiny little bubbles, all of them doomed to burst sooner or later . . .

'Are you awake, HP?'

For a moment he wondered about carrying on pretending to be unconscious, in the hope of finding out more about what was going on.

But something in her voice made him open his eyes before he had actually made up his mind.

It took just a matter of seconds for him to recognize

her. Her platinum blonde hair was now dark, but the nose piercing and overblown eye-shadow were the same.

The emo girl with the headphones he had seen in the underground.

'Good,' she nodded to him. 'How are you feeling?'

He tried to say something, but all that emerged from his lips was a sort of dry croak.

'Here.' She handed him a bottle of water and he raised himself up on one elbow. Deep, wonderful mouthfuls . . .

'Your fever's gone down,' she said, looking at a screen beside him. 'But it'll be a few days before the infection's disappeared completely. You've been dosed up with enough penicillin to treat a horse. Quite literally.'

He didn't try to answer, and just nodded as he looked round slowly. It looked like a hospital, with the only difference that everything in there was bigger. The bunk he was lying on, the lamps and straps hanging from the ceiling.

It took him a while to work it out.

'A vet's?' he croaked.

'Yep,' she replied. 'Well, at least you're not totally out of it. My name's Nora. And you already know Kent over there . . .'

HP sat up with an effort and glanced over towards the corner where the man was supposed to be sitting.

And there he was.

'Hi, HP,' the man said. 'Or should I call you 128?'

The words echoed for few seconds in his brain.

'Hasselqvist with a Q and a V . . .' he muttered, without really being able to take it in.

'A.k.a. Player 58,' the man spat. 'Remember? You sprayed teargas in my face out on the Kymlinge Link Road.'

He flew up from his chair and sprang at HP.

'Easy now, Kent . . .' the emo girl said, stepping between them.

181

She was almost ten centimetres taller than Hasselqvist, and, judging by her posture, considerably more muscular.

'We haven't got time for wounded egos . . .'

Hasselqvist with a Q and a V glowered at her for a few seconds, then threw out his arms in surrender.

Stepping back, he muttered, 'In case you're interested, I suffered an allergic reaction and had to spend three days in intensive care . . .

'Actually, I should probably thank you.' Now he grinned at HP. 'If you hadn't got in the way, it might have been me sitting there.'

He nodded at the oversized bunk HP was sitting on.

HP ignored him.

'Where are we?' he mumbled at the emo, whose name was evidently Nora.

'The Life Guards' veterinary clinic.'

'What?'

'Lidingövägen, opposite the Östermalm sports centre. The guards' stables . . . I've got a key to the gate so we got in the back way.'

'Okay . . .'

He drained the bottle of water and tried to make sense of his thoughts. But it was impossible.

His head ached and even if he felt a bit brighter than he had over the past few days, his body still felt like it had been put through a mangle.

'So which one of you is going to tell me what the fuck I'm doing here?'

'Look, HP,' Nora said as she got him a cup of coffee from the large thermos flask on the camping table. 'We've been trying to get hold of you for a while, but you've been playing hard to get . . . Those notes on your door?' she added when he didn't seem to get it.

'Kent and I, and Jeff – you'll meet him soon – have all

been caught up in the Game. Just like you, we all did things we never would have dreamed of doing when we started . . .'

'But then we got kicked out,' Hasselqvist added. 'Or replaced by someone else, someone more suitable. A new favourite . . .' He glared sullenly at HP.

'Something like that,' Nora nodded. 'Either way, once we sobered up and got over the worst of the withdrawal symptoms from the Game, we all started to figure out that what we'd been involved in wasn't just wrong, but that we'd also been manipulated. That we'd been nothing but puppets . . .'

HP drank a quick gulp. The coffee was unexpectedly hot and burned his tongue, but he forced himself to swallow it.

'We each started trying to find out more about the Game and the Game Master, but as you know it can be dangerous to break . . .'

'. . . rule number one,' HP muttered.

'Exactly . . . We were all warned off, some more than others. But a few months ago we were all brought together by someone else . . .'

She exchanged glances with Hasselqvist.

'He used to work for the Game,' Hasselqvist said. 'We're not sure, but we think he . . .'

'No matter what we think . . .' Nora interrupted, glaring at Hasselqvist, 'this person did bring us all together.'

'And now you want revenge,' HP said. 'Give the Game Master a bit of payback for the shit he fed you? Stick a spanner in the works so you can all sleep a bit easier . . .?'

HP shook his head and emptied the cup down his throat.

'Been there, done that . . . Thanks for the coffee, but I've got much bigger problems . . .'

'Sit down, HP!' Nora said before he'd even got to his feet. To his own surprise he obeyed her at once.

'We're not just some bunch of losers wandering around without a plan. We've got a source, an insider. Someone who knows how it all fits together, and maybe even knows what's going to happen next. And, not least, why!'

She looked at him, waiting for the words to sink in.

'With the Source's help we can put a stop to the whole thing. Not just individual tasks, but the whole of their fucking Game plan. You get it?'

Before he could answer there was a knock at the door.

'That'll be Jeff, I'll get it.'

Hasselqvist walked over to the door.

'Who is it?'

He opened the door a crack to look out, but the person on the other side yanked the handle so hard that Hasselqvist almost fell over.

'Leave it out, Kent, this isn't some fucking spy story . . .' the man chuckled as he came into the room.

He was wearing jeans and a tight t-shirt that bulged impressively over his swollen muscles.

'Oh, so sleeping beauty's woken up.' He nodded quickly at HP as he took off his sunglasses. 'You managed to mend him then, good work, Doctor!'

The man – Jeff, evidently – smiled a shiny white smile and winked at Nora, but to HP's satisfaction she ignored him completely. Not that this seemed to upset Muscleman in the slightest. He pulled a chair over towards HP and sat astride it as he scratched the back of his cropped head a couple of times, revealing a serious tribal tattoo on his lower arm.

'Is there any coffee?'

'I'll get it, Jeff!'

Hasselqvist got busy with the thermos.

184

'So what do we know?' Nora asked.

Jeff shrugged.

'I got rid of the revolver and his phone.' He nodded towards HP. 'Black's in position up at the Fortress. They're busy cutting the inauguration ribbon right now, at a guess. The city's still crawling with police cars, even if they don't seem to have a clue what they're looking for . . .'

He turned on HP.

'You should be fucking grateful I got hold of you, mate,' he said, pointing a thick index finger at HP. 'If it wasn't for us you'd be dead now. That big bodyguard had you in his sights, another two seconds and BANG!'

He added a cocked thumb to the index finger and demonstrated what he meant.

Hasselqvist handed him a cup of coffee.

'Anyway, how the fuck did you come up with the idea of shooting Black? That wouldn't have solved a bloody thing . . .'

HP muttered something inaudible into his coffee cup. He had to admit that the mountain of muscle in front of him had a point. As the horse medicine did its thing, he was starting to regain control of his brain. But even though he kept rewinding and playing the tape in his head, he still couldn't really explain what had happened. It all felt very distant.

As if nothing he had experienced over the past twenty-four hours had actually happened, and had just been a dream. Correction – a nightmare . . .

'Have we heard any more from the Source?' Jeff grunted.

'He sent all the plans . . .' Hasselqvist began, but Nora cut him off.

'Not yet. First we have to find out if he wants to work with us.'

She nodded to HP.

'Okay, I am actually here, you know,' he said. 'Look . . . I'm grateful to you for helping me, but I've actually got a shit-load of my own prob . . .'

'Is one of them your sister, by any chance?' Nora interrupted. 'The one who works for Sentry?'

'What? Her job's with the Secur . . . What did you say?'

He saw them exchange a glance, and didn't like that.

'Your sister heads up a bodyguard unit for Sentry Security, to look after business bigwigs. Sentry was bought up last year by a company called PayTag. And presumably you already know a bit about them, seeing as you just tried to shoot their managing director . . .'

HP opened his mouth to reply, but Nora didn't give him the chance.

'Good, then maybe you also know that PayTag is constructing a number of huge server farms around the world? Well, perhaps server hotels would be a better description. Here in Sweden they've built a massive installation in one of the military's old underground bunkers just outside Uppsala. The place is called the Fortress, and it'll soon be storing data for pretty much every company and government body across the whole of northern Europe . . .'

HP nodded again, more forcefully this time, and suddenly he couldn't help smiling.

Becca was Black's *bodyguard*.

Of course!

She was indirectly working for the Game, which was obviously still bad news. But in his fucked-up state he had misunderstood the whole thing. He'd thought Becca was in a relationship with Black.

Epic fail!

Christ, he could be really thick at times . . .

The others were staring at him.

186

'Well, what do you say?'

'Er, what?'

Jeff leaned forward on the chair, making its plastic back creak. Suddenly HP realized that there was something familiar about the angular face. They too had met before somewhere . . .

'Are you going to help us?'

'To do what?'

More glances, dubious this time.

Eventually Nora broke the silence.

'Shut down the Fortress!'

14

Abandonware

'Hello?'

'Good evening, dear friend.'

'Ah, it's you, splendid. Is this line secure?'

'Absolutely.'

'In that case I would be grateful for an explanation of what happened.'

'I can understand that . . .'

'I don't appreciate it when binding agreements are broken. Recent events . . .'

'Aid our cause in the long run, believe me!'

'In what way?'

'In every way . . .'

'Now listen, I don't appreciate this sort of prank. You can call yourself the Game Master all you like, but don't forget who's paying for your activities.'

'Naturally, my clients' interests are always at the top of my priority list, my dear friend.'

'I should hope so! If we could try for a moment to look beyond this . . . incident. How is everything going with the rest of the plan?'

'Splendidly. We're just about to begin. You won't be disappointed, Mr Black.'

The lift had taken them down to the viewing level. A glassed-in hub with five spokes extending fifty metres straight into the rock on all sides around them. And, if she'd understood correctly, there were a number of similar levels below them.

The control room that they were looking down on, through the large glass window opposite the lifts, was undeniably impressive.

She'd been inside a couple of underground bases before, when she was working for the Security Police. The one occupied by the emergency services call centre beneath the Johannes Church in Stockholm was probably the most impressive. But that was nothing compared to this.

Thirty or so workstations were grouped in three semicircular rows above one another, so that everyone had a clear view of the gigantic screens down in the centre.

Every workplace had three connected screens, along with a mouse, keyboard and a headset neatly hung up alongside. The whole thing looked rather like the Regional Communication Centre in Police Headquarters in Stockholm, but was obviously much more up-to-date and vastly more expensive.

The control room was empty and all the screens were switched off.

'At full capacity we'll have thirty operators working in three shifts. They'll all be experts in IT security. If necessary we can reinforce them with a further ten . . .' the site manager bubbled, looking as if he might burst with pride at any moment.

Maybe that wasn't so strange . . .

The invited reporters, local politicians and members of parliament seemed just as impressed with the setup as Rebecca was. One of them asked something that she didn't hear, but it must have been funny seeing as they all burst out laughing.

Black was standing slightly off to one side, flanked by two people from the local management team and a dark-haired woman in her forties whom Rebecca had met in the office a couple of times, one of their new foreign bosses, Anthea Ravel. She didn't seem particularly pleasant, and spoke that sort of dry, patronizing English that made you feel like a lowly servant. She'd also had such a tight facelift that almost all of her facial expressions were the same.

Some people in the office had taken to calling her the Ice Queen, which was a fairly appropriate nickname.

'Good question. Naturally, we take the security of the installation very seriously indeed,' the site manager said.

'Amongst other things we've applied to be classified as a high security area, which would give our security personnel additional powers. And we're also planning a big exercise together with the National Rapid-Response Unit. Security is our main priority . . .'

Black suddenly turned his head and met Rebecca's gaze. Then he leaned to the side and whispered something to the Ice Queen, which made her look in Rebecca's direction as well.

The woman put her hand on Black's upper arm and leaned forward. She whispered something, so close that her lips were almost touching Black's ear. She went on whispering for a few seconds, before slowly pulling back. Whatever it was the Ice Queen had said, it seemed to amuse both of them, and Rebecca couldn't shake the feeling that they were obviously talking about her.

190

She forced herself to ignore them and shifted her focus back to the site manager.

'Well, the big moment has arrived,' he suddenly announced in English. 'I'd like to invite our Managing Director, Mark Black, to step forward and press the button.'

The crowd of spectators parted to let Black through to the observation window.

One employee handed Black a small box with a large red button, and Black spent a minute or so posing with this over-emphatic symbol as the cameras flashed.

'I hereby declare this installation open,' he then said.

He pressed the button and down in the control room all the screens suddenly came to life.

He should have left at once, thanked them for their help and just toddled off home. Instead he had let them show him the plans. They told him about the electrified fence, the cameras, the guards patrolling the area. He had listened with half an ear. But he noticed one thing very clearly. None of them had said a word about how they were going to get past it all, which could have had two obvious explanations:

Either they didn't quite trust him and wanted to know if he was onboard before sharing their ingenious plan with him.

Or, much more likely: these amateurs didn't actually have a plan . . .

Two years ago he had broken into a similar establishment, but that one had been considerably smaller, much less protected, and he'd also had the help of Rehyman the genius to get past all the obstacles.

'Well, what do you think?'

He saw the expectant looks on their faces and for a moment he wondered if he should hold back slightly to soften the blow. But there was no point. These muppets needed to hear the truth, the whole truth, and nothing but the truth.

'Seriously? You're all fucking mad!' He shrugged. 'Do you really think you're going to be able to get in there?' He put his finger in the middle of the control room. 'And even if by some miracle you do manage to get through, what are you going to do there, and – maybe even more importantly – how are you planning to get out again?'

'Never mind about that,' Muscleman Jeff said in a way that made HP's alarm bells ring even louder. He'd definitely seen the bloke before, but where?

'If you help us get inside, we'll take care of the rest,' Nora said.

'The Source said you'd be able to do that, he said you've done stuff like this before,' Hasselqvist added. 'That you're some sort of expert in this area . . .'

HP nodded.

'Maybe . . .' He turned it all over in his head for a few moments. Sure, it was tempting, and certainly felt very familiar. But, to start with, he already had a shit load of his own problems to deal with, and, what's more, he trusted this little trio about as much as they trusted him.

The horse doctor seemed more or less okay, but Hasselqvist was a slippery fucker, and the gorilla made him feel uneasy in more ways than one.

But at the same time they had something he might be able to make use of, something that might actually help him understand his own situation.

He took a deep breath.

'Okay, *if* I'm even going to consider helping you, I want something in return first . . .'

'You mean apart from us saving your life . . .?' Nora said before either of the others had even opened their mouths.

HP shrugged his shoulders. A vein was starting to throb in the mountain of muscle's forehead. They glared at each other for a few seconds.

'This *Source* of yours . . .' HP drew a pair of weary quotation marks in the air. 'I want to talk to him directly . . .'

'No-one talks directly to the Source,' Hasselqvist interrupted. 'We've only met him once, all communication is done . . .'

Nora raised her hand and he fell silent at once.

'So what does he look like?' HP did his best not to sound too curious.

There was a brief silence, then Nora shrugged.

'Ordinary . . .' she said, and held up her hand again, this time to stop the other two from protesting. 'Short hair, average height, not quite forty. A typical suit, I'd say . . .'

HP nodded.

'Do you know what his role is in the Game?'

'Not exactly, but Kent and Jeff have a theory . . .'

She turned to Hasselqvist.

'Well . . . it's just a feeling. Some of the phrases he uses. I think he's involved in the technical side of it. Communication, servers, something like that. The plans contain a whole load of technical details. Don't they, Jeff?'

The mountain of muscle hesitated for a moment, then nodded slowly.

'These plans are like the ones we use at work for IT projects. If he was involved in construction, there'd be ventilation ducts, plumbing, stuff like that, but there's nothing of that sort on these plans. Only details of the IT infrastructure . . .'

'So you think the Source is some sort of IT guru? Someone who was involved in setting the whole thing up?' A tingling sensation was slowly spreading from HP's stomach.

193

The two men nodded.

'And how do you know you can really trust him?'

'We're not stupid, HP . . .' Nora replied. 'Obviously we were suspicious as well to start with, but the Source has delivered on everything. He brought us together, he's supplied plans, information about Sentry and PayTag, and – not least – he helped us locate and get hold of you before you were killed or arrested. He's taken big risks for our sake, and it doesn't feel like he's lying. All of that put together means that we've decided to trust him, even if we're still wary. But, like Kent said, we only met the Source once, right at the start. So we couldn't take you to him even if we wanted to . . .'

'I see . . .' HP looked down at his lap for a few seconds while he tried to sort out his poker face.

He needed to look a bit disappointed, make it seem like he was backing down.

'I need to think about it,' he said. 'Just for a couple of days. How can I contact you?'

'Here!'

Jeff took out a mobile phone and put it on the table.

'Pay as you go, can't be traced. Call the number for *dry cleaning* in the contacts and leave a message.'

'Okay.'

HP picked up the phone, then stood up and headed towards the door.

'Hang on,' Hasselqvist shouted, and he stopped. 'Don't forget your medicine.'

Hasselqvist tossed a white plastic container to HP.

'Well done, Kent,' Nora said. 'I'd forgotten that. Take two a day for five days, HP.'

'Okay, thanks.' He waved the pills in farewell and tried to keep a straight face. 'I'll be in touch!'

* * *

She was sitting outside one of the meeting rooms in the main building, slowly turning a bottle of water in her hands.

The press had left, leaving just a few of the politicians and various managers from both the Fortress and Sentry.

Right now they were having lunch further along the corridor, and a short while ago Black and the Ice Queen had both left the gathering to hold a conference call in the small room behind her.

She glanced at the time. Kjellgren and Thomas ought to be there any minute now.

For the third time in the past five minutes she took out her mobile.

No new messages, from either Kjellgren or Micke.

She pressed the call button again, but just like last time was put straight through to Micke's voicemail. Not that that was particularly unusual . . .

For the last week or so she'd hardly had time to talk to him at all, maybe even longer than that.

Often neither of them got home till late, and then they just crashed out on the sofa.

She hadn't told him about her meeting with Uncle Tage, and only selected details about the safe deposit box. She'd said it contained a few old papers: marriage and birth certificates, a few worthless shares. He hardly ever asked her about what she got up to these days. He was probably trying to prove that he trusted her. And she was repaying the confidence by lying to him again . . .

She looked at the time, then took a little tub of pills from her bag, checked they were the right ones and fished out one tablet. She glanced around quickly before swallowing it down with a swig from the bottle.

Using antidepressant medication is nothing to be ashamed of, Rebecca . . .

Yeah, right!

That statement might make sense in the reality her doctor lived in. But in her world you couldn't show the slightest sign of weakness.

But in her private life, she at least she knew it wasn't her fault alone that her relationship with Micke wasn't working.

She had actually taken on her job at Sentry for Micke's sake, to be in the same world as he was, and she had done her best to understand what he was involved in. But it wasn't entirely straightforward trying to follow all the technical ins and outs. A whole load of different companies and official bodies were having problems with various targeted hacker attacks, she had understood that much.

DDoS – Distributed Denial of Service – was something she knew about from the time the police website had been attacked. Someone, or several people, had managed to get hundreds, and possibly thousands, of different computers to fire a mass of requests at the same server at exactly the same time, so many that it eventually stopped working.

And she understood viruses as well.

But there were loads of other security threats.

DoS attacks were related to DDoS, and then there were trojans, worms, spyware and a whole load more whose names and functions she had already forgotten.

Hacker attacks had been going on for years, but according to Micke they had become much more intensified. Most companies were worried about viruses and other hostile attacks that could affect their day to day activities. But what really scared them, and what made them turn to Sentry for help, was the risk that outsiders might gain access to their customer details: dates of birth, credit and debit card numbers, medical records, insurance history, purchasing patterns, criminal records, bank account information. The list of information hidden away in supposedly secure databases was practically infinite. And if any outsider got hold of that information, the company or official body in question would suffer a massive loss of public confidence.

One large bank had already lost several hundred thousand credit and debit card numbers, and a gambling site had thrown in plenty of other details, including email addresses and IMS IDs.

Installations like the Fortress were supposed to be the solution to problems like that. All information stored in one place, protected by the very latest technology and guarded round the clock by thirty experts in IT security. What company or official body could offer anything like that?

She heard a door close further along the corridor and shortly afterwards she saw Thomas marching along the corridor with Kjellgren at his heels.

Thomas didn't look happy.

I'll be in touch! – Not fucking even!

He already knew who the Source was, and even where he was hiding.

And there he was, thinking he'd seen a ghost and was going mad. But the pieces of the puzzle were starting to fall into place.

There was only one person who fitted that description, both physically and in terms of what he knew. The server king, the computer genius, the crazy backwoodsman, the outcast – the man, the myth, the legend:

Fucking Erman himself!

So he had survived the blaze in the outback. Managed to get himself a new identity, and then gradually returned to civilization while he finessed his plan. First finding a new hiding place, and then setting about gathering information.

Two years was a long time. Erman may have been pretty soft-boiled when they met, but there was no doubt that the guy was smart. Something of an IT genius, at least according to his own testimony. And once Erman had got himself and his head sorted, and got back in front of a keyboard, there was probably no end to the stuff he could dig out. Tasks that had been carried out, players who had failed . . .

Shit, HP had actually given the bloke the idea of wiping out the server farm because of what he'd managed to do out in Kista.

And PayTag's Fortress was obviously a hundred times bigger. The new, improved Death Star . . .

The Source said you'd done stuff like this before. That you're some sort of expert . . .

Ha!

The evidence was watertight.

Erman was the Source!

Or rather, the new, improved version of Erman was.

Slimmer, clean-shaven, short-haired, and with less of an allergy to electricity than the last version. Those idiots at the vet's seemed to think he was still working for the Game. Maybe that was part of his plan to seem credible. The truth about his real background, the nervous breakdown and the time he had spent holed up in the woods were hardly likely to inspire confidence. Better to pretend he was still part of the Game.

Now it was just a matter of finding the bastard's hiding place, and he had a feeling he'd already solved that one. It was actually ridiculously simple. After all, the bloke had said it himself out there in his cottage when he was banging on about the Game. The best hiding place was where no-one would ever think of looking.

What was the most visible place in Stockholm, the most talked about, the most over-populated?

Slussen, of course. And what was right in the middle of Slussen, surrounded by glass and granite walls in an effort to make it fit in with its surroundings?

A lift.

An innocent fucking lift for taking wheelchairs, prams and walking frames half a floor down to the City Museum.

He couldn't understand why he hadn't noticed it the first time he checked inside the lift, but now in hindsight it was crystal clear.

He'd probably been too tired, and his brain too screwed up to take in all the details.

There were four buttons on the panel inside the lift, but only two of them had floors marked next to them.

Södermalmstorg for street level, and the entrance to the City Museum one floor below.

The other two buttons didn't light up when you pressed them, which had made him think they were disconnected. Stupid, but on the other hand he hadn't been firing on all cylinders at the time.

But now that he was able to inspect the lift calmly, he noticed something else. Beside the panel of buttons there was a little card-reader. And you used card-readers to limit access – access to door, gates, entrances, and what else, if there was a card-reader in the lift, Einstein?

Other floors, obviously!

So Erman 2.0 hadn't just vanished, he'd simply used his card, woken up the dead buttons and carried on down into the ground to a floor that wasn't signposted in the lift. A secret level, to which a technical genius could surely gain access pretty easily. A dead man hiding in a place that didn't exist . . .

You had to take your hat off to him . . .

All he had to do now was wait for Erman 2.0 to show up at Slussen again, and arrange to have a little chat with him. Pump the bastard for everything he knew about the Game and Sammer, how far they'd managed to drag Becca into it, and then think of a way to get her out.

Get them both out.

Once and for all.

But first he had to make a few preparations . . .

He saw the cop car the moment he turned the corner into his street.

An ordinary Volkswagen minibus with a ladder on the roof, nothing remarkable at all. If it hadn't been for the stubby little aerial . . .

A bloke in a fleece, cargo pants, boots and a tiny, scarcely visible earpiece was standing there talking to the driver through the window.

HP turned on his heel and went back the way he had come. He had to fight hard not to break into a run.

'Hi,' she said, standing up.

Thomas didn't return the greeting.

'Is Mr Black in there?' He pointed to the door.

'Yes, but . . .'

He pushed past her and knocked. Without waiting for an answer he strode into the room and shut the door behind him.

'What the hell was that about?' she asked Kjellgren.

'He's really pissed off. The police gave him a serious going over . . .'

'Hardly surprising, is it . . .?'

She smiled but Kjellgren seemed to be avoiding her gaze.

Then the door opened again.

'Can you come in?' Thomas said to her abruptly.

'Sure . . .'

Black and Ice Queen were sitting on the same side of the conference table. She nodded to them but neither acknowledged the greeting. Nor did they ask her to sit down.

'Miss Normén, we won't be needing your services any more,' Black said bluntly.

'Sorry?'

'You're fired,' the Ice Queen added. 'Kjellgren will be taking over your job from now on. You're to take his car back to Stockholm and empty your office. At 17.00 hours today your passcard will stop working, so I suggest you set off at once.'

'B-but, I don't understand? Is this because of the Grand Hotel?'

Rebecca glanced quickly at Thomas, then back at Black. His face was impassive.

'You fired into the air,' Thomas growled. 'Instead of taking action against the attacker, you intentionally caused confusion to stop me neutralizing him. At first we couldn't understand your actions, but recent information has made the whole thing abundantly clear.'

Rebecca was having trouble understanding what she was hearing. Were they seriously trying to suggest that she had done something wrong? That she was trying to protect . . .

'Henrik Pettersson,' Thomas said. 'That's the attacker's name. And apart from being a suspected terrorist, he also happens to be your younger brother, doesn't he?'

Double play

The needle of the speedometer had hardly slipped below a hundred for the past hour.

We won't be needing your services any more . . .

The bastards had fired her!

After all she had done, all the hundreds of hours she had devoted to getting the business set up. Putting together strategies, writing manuals, recruiting the right staff – not to mention all the sleepless nights.

None of that seemed to count for anything.

Had it been any other employer she would already have called the union. Fighting fire with fire.

But who was she supposed to call now?

She was on leave of absence, after all, and hadn't bothered switching union. The police union would hardly help someone employed by a private company. Which left getting hold of a good lawyer.

But what good would that do? She could hardly force them to give her the job back, and even if that succeeded, she had no desire to stay there and work for someone like Thomas.

He'd sold her down the river, that was obvious. Let her take the hit for his own stupid behaviour.

The idea that the man in the camouflage jacket could have been Henke was clearly utterly ridiculous.

Someone must have told Thomas about Henke, before or after he was interviewed by the police.

Maybe they'd even shown him a photograph? All Thomas had to say was 'yes, that was him,' and it was all sorted.

Henke was already under investigation for terrorist activities, and if Thomas identified him as the attacker, his own actions outside the Grand would look almost praiseworthy.

Okay, so he may have committed a weapons offence, but at least he had been trying to combat terrorism.

And he would probably have succeeded, if only the terrorist's sister hadn't got involved . . .

And, hey presto, she was suddenly the scapegoat . . .!

So who had Thomas talked to up in the custody unit?

If it had all happened the way she imagined, there was really only one suspect.

She put her hands-free earpiece in, pressed one of the speed-dial buttons and waited a few moments.

'Norrmalm custody unit, Myhrén.'

'Hi, Myhrén, this is Rebecca Normén,' she said in an exaggeratedly cheery voice.

'Hi, Normén, it's been a while. What can a simple uniform do to help the Security Police?' the man at the other end chuckled. He evidently hadn't heard that she'd left, which suited her fine.

'Just a quick question, Myhrén . . .' she began.

'Shoot!'

'You brought in a bloke from the Grand Hotel this morning. A foreigner suspected of weapons offences . . .?'

'Hmm.'

She heard him rustling some papers in the background.

'Who was it who interviewed him, do you know?'

'Hold on!'

More rustling. Then he came back.

'Right, Normén. He was brought in by one of our patrols and was going to be interviewed by Bengtsson, who was on call this morning. But he insisted on talking to a different colleague. One of yours, to be more precise . . .'

'Do you know who?'

She was unconsciously holding her breath.

'Er, yes, I've got his name here. He signed in on the register . . . Superintendent Eskil Stigsson.'

It hadn't been easy getting up there.

First he'd had to circle round a load of little streets. Then clamber over a few fences and walls until he was in the right courtyard.

And now he was paying the price for his exertions. His body ached, his t-shirt was wet with sweat, and even though he'd been sitting in the alcove by the window for a fair while, his pulse didn't seem to want to return to normal.

He wondered if it was time to take one of the horse tablets that Doctor Nora had given him. But stupidly he hadn't brought anything to drink, and there was no way he was going to swallow one of those depth-charges dry. It would have to wait . . .

At least his lookout post was perfect. He was in the building diagonally opposite his own, at the very top of the stairwell, with a full view of everything going on down in the street.

The cop van was still there, but both the driver and the plain-clothes cop were gone. Probably hiding in the back.

They were no ordinary surveillance team, he'd already worked that much out. The guy with the earpiece reeked of cop too much, as did the black minibus. They were more like uniformed gorillas who'd got dressed up in civvies.

Which could really only mean one thing.

At that moment another similar minibus slowly rolled up from Hornsgatan. It stopped outside his door. The man in the passenger seat raised a microphone to his mouth. The next moment the street was crawling with cops.

The door to his building was thrown open and a gang of the heaviest orcs stormed inside. A couple of them were carrying something that looked like a battering ram.

It wouldn't take them long to smash down his already badly damaged front door.

Besides, they'd already practised once.

Yet another weird *déjà vu* to add to the collection . . .

His bladder was so full he could hardly sit still, but he couldn't take his eyes off the scene below. This time they hadn't been so ambitious with their roadblocks, and weren't shutting down the whole district.

A patrol car with flashing blue lights was blocking the street further down, and he could see people already starting to gather behind the cordon. Then he saw the roller-blind in one of his windows sway.

Fucking good job he hadn't bothered to do any cleaning . . .

So what the hell did the cops think they were going to find this time? It didn't take him long to realize . . .

Him, of course!

Stigsson could go to hell.

She was going to get hold of Henke even if it meant she had to kick his door in. She had to make sure he was okay, that Thomas's story was all rubbish. And that he was keeping well away from the Game, the Event, the Circus or whatever else it was called . . .

205

She changed lane, put her foot down and overtook three cars, only to pull back quickly into the right-hand lane and take the next exit.

The car behind her flashed its headlights at her and she responded by sticking her middle finger up over her right shoulder.

She turned into Hornsgatan, and accelerated to get over the hill.

Then she saw the flashing blue lights ahead and slowed down.

A patrol car was parked at the junction, and two uniformed colleagues were busy setting up a cordon across the entrance to Maria Trappgränd.

She crawled past, trying to see what had happened. But all she managed to see was that the door to Henke's building was open. The nausea she had felt earlier that day suddenly flared up again, and she hurriedly found a free parking space a bit further down the road.

As luck would have it, one of the officers by the cordon recognized her and, without a single word from her, held the plastic tape up to let her through.

She found the rapid-response unit in the stairwell. Six men, all dressed in civilian clothing, but they might as well have been in uniform. The holsters and bulletproof vests they were wearing on top of their clothes didn't exactly make a discreet impression . . .

A couple of the officers nodded to her, but it wasn't until she almost reached the flat that she realized which unit they were from. He was standing in the hall with his back to the doorway, which gave her a few moments to compose herself.

'Hello, Tobbe,' she said as calmly as she could.

He jerked and spun round.

'Er, h-hi Becca . . .' he said, apparently not sure where

he should look. 'I was just wondering if I should call you . . .'

'Were you? What for?' She stepped carefully over the remains of the front door.

The hall was so cramped that he had to press back against the wall so she could squeeze past.

The proximity seemed to make him even more nervous.

'The flat. I mean, we used to . . .'

'. . . meet here,' she concluded.

She turned round and looked at him. He was still pretty good looking, and for a brief moment she could almost feel the physical attraction again. But only almost . . .

There was the sound of steps from the stairs, it sounded as though several people were on their way up.

'If I were you, Tobbe, I'd stay really fucking quiet about that,' she said in a low voice.

A pair of forensics officers in overalls, each carrying a large case of tools, appeared in the doorway.

'All clear?' one of them asked.

'Sure, go ahead.' Tobbe Lundh gestured in at the flat.

The two men squeezed past and a short while later their cameras began to whirr.

'What was the thinking behind all this?' she said, leaning forward so the forensics officers wouldn't hear her. Tobbe looked quickly over his shoulder.

'There's a warrant out for your brother, suspicion of attempted murder.'

'What?!'

He nodded and glanced over his shoulder again.

'I don't know any more than that, the Security Police are in charge of the investigation, we're just helping out. They'll be here any moment. Maybe you should go . . .?'

She shook her head.

No, she had no intention of going anywhere. She wanted

to get to the bottom of this, once and for all. Henke might be an idiot, a gullible fool with an oversized ego and zero ability to control his impulses. But he was no murderer, not even a failed murderer.

Unless . . .?

In purely theoretical terms, perhaps he was, but Dag had been a different matter.

An entirely different matter . . .

She took a couple of steps further into the flat. God, the state it was in! The flat was usually untidy, but this gave the word an entirely new dimension. There were piles of newspapers all over the place in the hall and kitchen, and the stench of cigarette smoke and rubbish was so strong it made her eyes sting.

All the roller-blinds were down, and the only light came from the bare bulb in the ceiling.

The walls looked odd, all stripy, and it took her a moment to realize what the dark patches were. Duct tape. It looked like he'd taped over all the cracks and sockets.

She carried on into the living room. Same thing there, piles of papers, overflowing improvised ashtrays, and all cracks and sockets completely covered.

'Must have used at least ten rolls,' one of the forensics officers concluded, taking a few shots with his camera.

'Poor sod was probably worried about radiation . . .'

He zoomed in on one of the covered plug sockets and took another series of pictures.

'Either that or he was being bugged by aliens,' the other one said with a grin as he picked up his box of tools.

'I'll take the bedroom,' he said to his colleague, then vanished through the door.

She heard voices in the hall, several of them familiar, and took a deep breath.

Stigsson came through the door and behind him she could make out Runeberg's great bulk.

'So you're here already . . .' Stigsson said drily. He didn't even sound surprised. 'Have you touched anything in here, Normén?'

'No, of course not . . .'

'Good. But we'll have to insist that you empty your pockets on the way out. Runeberg, can you deal with that?'

'Sure, no problem,' her former boss mumbled, taking a step forward.

'You spoke to Thomas when he was in custody,' she said, fixing Stigsson with her cop stare. He didn't even blink.

'Of course.'

'Was it you who suggested that it might possibly have been Henke down at the Grand? Supplying him with a suitable perpetrator so that you could carry on harassing my brother?'

Stigsson shook his head.

'No need. The television crew who were there were kind enough to share their recording. The perpetrator is clearly visible. There's no doubt that it was your brother. On the film he's about to pull something from his coat pocket, something that Mr Thomas is certain was a gun. He might be mistaken, but unfortunately, as you know, a certain confusion broke out after your warning shot, which makes it impossible to see what happened next. Thomas is an extremely credible witness, and, considering the previous suspicions against your brother, obviously we can't take any risks. What with the royal wedding imminent, it's probably safest for everyone if he's locked up . . .'

He waited a few seconds, as if he were expecting her to say something.

'Was there anything else you were wondering about, Normén? If not, we've got work to do here . . .'

She opened her mouth to reply, but at that moment the forensics officer came back into the room.

'You should probably take a look at this . . .' he said.

He'd gone for a piss behind a bike shed in the courtyard, then found a tap and managed to get one of the horse pills down. His stomach was grumbling and he probably ought to do something about that, give up on all this and just lie low for a few days until the whole story had leaked out into the evening tabloids and he could read up about whatever the fuck was going on. Besides, he had a plan of his own to stick to: getting hold of Erman and squeezing out everything he knew about the Game.

But he couldn't quite tear himself away, not quite yet, at least.

There was certainly a degree of satisfaction to be had from being one step ahead for a change.

Hunting the hunters.

The cops had already emptied the flat in their first raid, so obviously it was him they were looking for. Him personally. The stupid bastards must have thought he was at home.

If the cops had only been a bit less obvious, they'd have been right and he'd be back in a cell by now.

Something told him he wouldn't get out quite so easily next time . . .

Installed back at his window again, he saw the car was already parked outside his door. A big, dark, stretched Volvo with little chrome flag-holders on the side of the bonnet. Not exactly a surveillance car . . .

The driver was still in the car, but the passengers seemed to have gone inside already.

The car had black number-plates with yellow lettering,

and it took him a moment to work out what that meant. The car belonged to the military.

This was all getting curiouser and curiouser . . .

One of the walls in the bedroom was almost completely covered by newspaper cuttings that had been taped up with thick strips of duct tape. Close together, so that they overlapped and occasionally obscured each other. In the middle were photographs of Black from various magazines, all with his face circled with black marker pen in a way that reminded her of the cross hairs of a sniper's sights.

There was a freestanding headline with the words *HE IS THE ONE!* above the whole lot.

Stigsson gave her a quick sideways glance.

'Do you still think your brother's innocent?'

She didn't answer. Her mouth suddenly felt bone-dry, and her stomach had contracted. Would-be assassin or not, clearly it had been Henke down at the Grand, and she hadn't even recognized him. Or had she?

If she had hesitated a moment longer, he'd probably be dead now. Thomas would have shot him.

Or another of the bodyguards. She herself, perhaps . . .

The floor lurched and for a few seconds she considered sitting down on the bed. Apart from a cup of coffee and a dry cheese sandwich she had managed to gulp down out at the Fortress, she hadn't eaten properly for almost twenty-four hours. And as far as sleep was concerned, she was even worse off.

But now wasn't the time to fall apart. Henke wasn't in a good way, that much was obvious. He needed help, as soon as possible before he did something even more stupid.

She took a deep breath and turned towards Stigsson to say something.

211

Just then two men in suits walked into the room.

One was in his thirties, thin, with short hair and dark-framed glasses.

The other man was Tage Sammer.

'Colonel Pellas, excellent,' Stigsson said, and the two men shook hands.

'You've met my colleague, Superintendent Runeberg, before, and this is . . .'

'Rebecca Normén, the suspect's sister,' Sammer said quickly, holding out his hand. 'Good to meet you, my name is André Pellas, I'm linked to the security organization at the Palace.'

She mumbled something and shook his hand as she tried to meet his gaze, but he was deliberately looking away.

'May I introduce Edler, my adjutant.'

He gestured with his stick towards the man in glasses, who nodded briefly in greeting.

'So, what do we know, Eskil . . .?' Sammer turned towards Stigsson.

'Unfortunately the suspect wasn't here, but we have been able to confirm that he was fixated upon Black . . .' He pointed to the wall of cuttings.

Sammer gave Edler a quick nod, and the younger man went over to the wall and began looking through the cuttings.

'Have you found anything of interest to the Palace?'

'Not since the video clip . . .' Stigsson said. 'But there's been a warrant out for Pettersson since this morning, and apart from this flat he basically has nowhere to go, and Normén here has promised her full cooperation.'

He nodded towards Rebecca.

She opened her mouth, then realized that she didn't know what to say. Thoughts were churning round her head, without any real coherence.

212

The Grand Hotel, events up at the Fortress, the flat, and now Sammer popping up like a jack-in-the-box, turning out to be acquainted with both Stigsson and Runeberg . . .

'Colonel Pellas, you should probably see this.'

Edler had lifted up a few of the cuttings. Behind them were other pictures, also with people's faces circled with black marker pen. He held up some of the cuttings at random. The result was the same.

Beneath all of the cuttings were photographs of the royal family.

He saw them emerge from the front door.

First a big, stiff gorilla who could have been a poster boy for the Police Academy. Then some little grey men in suits who seemed to be deeply engaged in serious discussion. He didn't recognize the shorter one, but he identified Sammer.

His heart began to beat faster.

The Game Master and the cop – hand in hand, just as he had suspected.

When Becca came out of the door his mood sank at least two notches.

Sammer, the cop and Becca wasn't a good combo, no matter how you looked at it.

But it was the final member of the group that really shocked him.

Holy . . .

Fucking . . .

Shit . . .

16

Quit while you're ahead

Welcome to Kroken dry cleaners. Please leave a message.

He was so wound up he almost forgot to wait for the bleep.

'You're fucked!' he yelled into the receiver as he jogged in the direction of Skinnarviksparken.

'The Source, the man who recruited you . . . He works for the Game Master. I just saw them together . . .'

His throat suddenly felt thick and he coughed a few times in an attempt to clear it.

'And if he works for the Game Master, then so do you . . . You can fuck right off, never contact me again! Never, got that . . .?'

Halfway out into the street he was hit by another fit of coughing and had to bend over.

A car swept past dangerously close and the driver blew his horn. He didn't even have the energy to gesticulate back.

Erman, the little bastard, hadn't come back from the dead with a plan for revenge in his back pocket. Instead he seemed to have got absolution from the Game Master . . . which was actually completely logical. After all, Erman's only crime was that he wanted to be an active participant in everything. To carry on messing about with his beloved servers. And he was one of the best in the world at what he did, which had obviously helped his case. PayTag must have been crying out for experts in servers for their massive project.

Supply and demand, and, just like magic, Erman was suddenly forgiven and back from the cold. *Capitalism rules!*

So why the hell had he gathered together that bunch of losers? And why goad them into breaking into the jewel in the Game's crown? There was obviously some sort of plan behind it all, a plan that also included him and Becca.

But, just like everything else that had happened to him in recent days, it was no longer possible to make all the pieces of the puzzle fit together. His brain had gone into overdrive, and the jog had got his pulse racing at a dangerous level, so he aimed for the nearest park bench.

This was so totally fucked up he couldn't handle it any more. The very thought that he had once dreamed of getting back into that whole crazy circus made him feel sick. The Game was obviously out to get him, and the same went for the cops . . .

All he wanted right now was to take off, get a very long way away and crawl into a hole somewhere until it had all blown over.

But Rebecca was still stuck in the shit, literally led by the nose by the Game Master, with Erman, the treacherous bastard, scuttling along behind.

Obviously that was no coincidence, nothing the Game Master did was a coincidence.

He leaned his head in his hands and struggled with another coughing fit.

His skin felt hot, not just because of the exertion, so his fever was probably back.

That was all he needed . . .

He needed grub, then a bit of cash to fix up somewhere

quiet where he could gather his strength and try to make sense of this mess.

If that was even remotely possible . . .

'As I said, good to meet you, Rebecca,' Colonel Pellas said as he shook her hand in farewell. 'And if you do hear from your brother, or get the slightest idea of where he might be, we'd be extremely grateful if you could let us know immediately.'

He handed her a business card which she tucked away mechanically.

'We'll be in touch, Eskil,' he said to Stigsson as he got into the back seat of the large Volvo.

The door closed, the driver put the car into gear, and just as it was about to pull away he gave her a quick look through the side window. She tried a tentative smile, looking for the slightest sign of acknowledgement. His face didn't move.

The car glided round the corner and disappeared, its tyres rattling on the cobblestones of the slope.

'Oh yes, Normén . . .' Stigsson said just as she was about to walk off. 'We've found a safe deposit box belonging to your brother . . .' He left a meaningful pause, and she almost walked into the trap. But at the last moment she stopped herself.

'Do you happen to know anything about that?' he continued when she didn't respond.

She shook her head.

'Henke and I haven't had much contact recently . . .'

'No, so you said at Police Headquarters, yet here you are at his flat just as we go in to search it . . .'

Once again she refrained from answering. As long as she didn't say anything, he couldn't claim she was lying.

The tactic didn't seem to bother Stigsson in the way she had hoped.

216

'You're listed as sharing it with him, Normén, so I presume you knew what was in it?'

She shook her head.

'Nothing, Normén. The box was empty.'

'Oh . . .' She tried to look as unconcerned as possible.

'Fortunately the bank has an advanced security system . . .'

She felt her heart beat faster.

'Loads of cameras, much like over in Police Headquarters . . .'

He paused again, trying to lure her into saying something, but she just stared down at the cobbles instead. What date had she visited the vault? She thought about the cameras, counting them in her head. Seven, eight, nine . . .

'Is there anything you want to tell me, Normén?' His voice suddenly sounded rather more friendly. 'According to Runeberg, you're a very good bodyguard, an asset to the department, I'm sure those were his words . . .'

She looked up and met his gaze. Stigsson had tilted his head.

'Obviously we stick up for our own. Help colleagues who find themselves in tricky situations . . .'

Another pause.

She opened her mouth to say something, then hesitated for a few seconds.

'Yes . . .?' he said, to prompt her.

'Seven,' she said.

'W-what?' At last his composed expression seemed slightly shaken.

'Seven days, that's how long the banks usually store recorded material, isn't it? At least that was the case when I worked in crime . . .'

His mouth closed like a trap. His almost paternal expression from a minute ago had vanished completely. Not that that mattered. His bluff had failed, and they both knew it. There were no pictures, nothing that could tie her to the vault. It had all been erased several days ago.

'Did you want anything else?'

Stigsson didn't answer, so she waved at Runeberg who was standing a short distance away, then turned to go.

'We've requested the list of passcards from the bank . . .' Stigsson said when she'd taken a few steps. 'It will be a couple of days before we get it, but I'm guessing we'll soon be speaking again, Normén.'

HP woke up with his whole body shaking like a pneumatic drill.

It may have been the middle of the summer, but taking an evening nap outdoors on a boat under a fucking tarpaulin hadn't exactly been his smartest move, in hindsight.

He needed to get warm, right away. But his body didn't seem to want to obey him. His head ached, his mouth was dry, his arms and legs felt like overcooked spaghetti. When he tried to roll onto his stomach he suddenly noticed the wet lump in his underwear.

At first he thought it was the bundle of notes he had dug out of the glass jar buried a few hundred metres up in the woods. But then he remembered that he'd stuffed it into one of the front pockets of his jeans.

It took another few seconds before he realized.

Fucking hell!

He reached for the railing and tried to get to his feet. The stench from his trousers caught in his nose, and his stomach cramped. It took a huge effort just to stand up.

The deck swayed beneath him, making his knees buckle.

He fell forward, hit his chin on one of the benches and ended up lying there on the deck.

Food poisoning, how fucking ironic. He hadn't eaten

218

properly for weeks, and had basically lived off tinned sardines and baked beans. But now he'd finally managed to get hold of a kebab, it turned out to be a staphylococcus bomb with extra garlic sauce . . .

His stomach cramped again, making him curl up into a ball.

Fuckingbloodyhell!

He tried to crawl to his feet but it was hopeless. All the energy had drained out of him and he couldn't stop shivering. But he had to get away from there at once, otherwise it would be autumn before Nisse or whoever owned this bastard boat found his freeze-dried corpse.

It was late in the evening, and the stretch of Pålsundet where the old boat lay was hardly a busy place even during the day.

The fall had knocked most of the strength out of him, but if he didn't want to end up like Ötzi the Iceman, he had to get away from there.

His stomach cramped again, making him pull his knees up around his ears. The cold lump of clay in his underwear moved slightly up the base of his spine.

Fuckingbastardbollocks . . .

He waited for the attack to pass, then gathered what little strength he had left and forced himself up onto his knees. The jetty was no more than half a metre away.

He planted one foot in the bottom of the boat, tensed the muscles in his thigh and got up onto his feet. His legs swayed but he stayed upright. One step forward, then another. He lifted one foot, and took aim at the jetty.

But the leg he had all his weight on suddenly collapsed and he fell backwards into the dark water.

He churned his arms like mad and swallowed several litres of water as he tried to turn the right way up. For a brief moment he was back on the prison bunk in Dubai where the cops had tried to drown a confession out of him. But then the tips of his toes touched the bottom and his panic subsided somewhat.

He dragged himself laboriously up onto the shore, crawled up into a sitting position and leaned his back against a tree. He gasped for breath a few times, then let loose a fountain of green water from Lake Mälaren. Over and over again, through both his mouth and nose, until his stomach was exhausted. Him too, come to that . . .

Forfuckssake . . .!

But, oddly enough, after a while he started to feel a bit better. As if the little swim and involuntary stomach pump had rebooted his body.

Besides, he'd had an idea. The youth hostel on Långholmen, in the converted prison. Why hadn't he thought of that before . . .?

Using the tree trunk as a support he got to his feet, and felt automatically in his pockets for his fags. He found a soaking wet stub that he tried in vain to light.

Then, with the unlit cigarette between his lips, he staggered carefully up towards the path that led to the old prison.

His office door was closed, but she didn't even bother to knock.

'I've been fired,' she said before he even had time to turn round.

'Er, yes . . . So I heard.'

He stood up, but made no attempt to move closer to her.

'Oh, so the rumour's already out. How much do you know?'

'Not much, we had a conference call with Anthea a little while ago . . .'

'And?'

He shrugged his shoulders and seemed to be studying a mark on the wall behind her.

'She just said that you'd been dismissed with immediate effect.'

He met her gaze for a moment, then looked away again.

'Something about ill-considered behaviour that had put the company at risk. That you had therefore lost the confidence of those in charge . . .'

'You don't buy that, do you?' She fixed her eyes on him.

'No, of course not . . .'

'You don't sound very convincing . . .'

'Stop it, Becca, I actually tried to defend you. I said what a hard time you'd been having lately, with the sleeping pills and all that . . .'

'You said WHAT?!'

He held his hands up in front of him.

'Nothing, just that you'd been having trouble sleeping. That's true, isn't it. Lack of sleep can have a serious effect on people's judgement . . .'

'I can't believe I'm hearing this . . .' She covered her face with her hands for a moment.

'Well, I was only trying to help . . .' he muttered.

She took a couple of deep breaths, and resisted saying the first thing that popped into her head, then the second as well.

'I have to empty my desk straight away,' she said, as calmly as she could. 'Then I'm going to contact a lawyer. They're not going to get away with this.' She glanced at her watch.

'We can talk more at home.'

'Erm.'

He seemed to be plucking up courage all of a sudden. 'I mean, Becca, I like the company. A lot, actually. I've been here pretty much from the start, and now that PayTag has pumped money in . . .'

He looked her in the eye. For a few moments neither of them said anything.

'To be honest, Becca, you and me, it hasn't been working for a long while. Not since . . .'

She opened her mouth to say something, to cut him off with some biting remark.

But instead she stood there in silence.

'Now or in two months' time, the result will still be the same, so why drag it out . . .?'

He shrugged.

The lump of ice she had had in her chest all morning suddenly felt twice the size. She wanted to protest, scream at him that he was wrong, that he was an idiot. That all this could be fixed . . .

But instead she slowly turned round. Then gave him a weary look over one shoulder.

She left the room, closing the door carefully behind her.

Her things fitted in a plastic bag.

A couple of files with her payslips, employment contract and various other formal papers. The old police cap that she'd kept hanging on the wall, along with a couple of framed photographs from the time she was training to become a bodyguard. She put the pot-plant Micke had given her when she started in the bin, then changed her mind and put it back on the windowsill.

All of her guards were out on jobs, and the office staff had long since gone home. She picked up the bag and headed downstairs.

First to the vault, where she locked her gun away, then she emptied her locker. All that remained was leaving her keys and passcard in the personnel department's pigeon-hole. But instead of going back upstairs she went onto the street through the basement door and started to walk towards the underground station.

She felt in her pockets for her travel card and found it in her inside pocket. But when she pulled it out the business card that Uncle Tage had given her outside the flat came with it. A rectangle of thick white card with a large royal coat of arms in gold, red and blue to one side of it.

COLONEL ANDRÉ PELLAS

Office of the Marshal of the Realm
Royal Household

Followed by a telephone number and an email address, but, oddly enough, no mobile number.

Then, on the back, written in blue biro:

070 – 43 05 06
/ Uncle T.

For some reason the short message put her in a slightly better mood.

He followed the brick wall for a while until he came to an opening.

Even though the place hadn't been a prison for more than thirty years, the old institutional buildings still looked really creepy, especially now, in the middle of the night. There was an Arkham Asylum vibe that was hard to shake off. The large, walled gravel yard he was standing in had once been the prison courtyard. Somewhere way ahead he could hear music mixed with the sound of traffic on the Western Bridge high above.

A few weary streetlamps in the carpark over in one

corner had company from a couple of lights in the windows of the low buildings straight ahead, which was where the music seemed to be coming from.

But all the windows of the huge building to his right were dark, and when he walked up to the door he discovered why.

The Youth Hostel is closed for refurbishment.
See you again in the autumn!

Shit! He'd been looking forward to a shower and a night in a proper bed.

But he wasn't entirely out of luck. He'd spotted a porta-cabin and a couple of toolsheds at one end of the building, and when he went round the building he found a temporary plywood door.

Two metal catches and a simple padlock were all there was to keep trespassers out, and he forced them open easily with the help of a brick.

Inside the door was a pitch-black corridor that smelled of brick dust, but at least his trusty lighter gave him a bit of light.

A few metres in he reached the large cell block. It looked almost exactly the way he had imagined.

The faint light of the summer night was falling through the skylights high up in the roof. It had to be twenty metres high. In between were several open landings lined with cell doors.

To the right was a metal staircase, and he briefly considered climbing up to look for a bed straight away. Then he realized that he really did have to clean himself up first.

His stomach was still cramping, and in spite of the involuntary bath he could still smell the shit in his trousers. In other words, a shower was priority number one.

He carried on through the ground floor, holding the lighter high enough to get a better idea of where he was.

Obviously the building was now a youth hostel. But they had retained the prison atmosphere, and in the darkness that feeling was intensified many times over. Hundreds, presumably thousands of poor bastards must have done time here over the years.

Cramped cells, thick stone walls, heavy bars over the windows. Hard labour six days a week on a meagre diet of bread and water.

Fuck, this was a long way from his own experience of prison, and that had been bad enough . . .

A sudden sound made him jump. A metallic clang from somewhere in the darkness off to his right.

He stopped for a moment, trying to move the lighter so he could see better. But the room was far too large and the flickering patch of light was quickly swallowed up by the thick darkness.

He gulped and couldn't help shuddering. Hardly surprising, really, seeing as the place really was fucking creepy, and given that he was soaked through and had shat himself.

The sound must have come from a fuse-box, or something like that.

Just to be on the safe side he waited another minute, but everything was quiet.

Time to find that shower . . .

A couple of metres away he could just make out the shape of a metal sign sticking out from one of the thick walls. He raised the light to read what it said:

Washroom

Yes!

She put her bags down inside the door and went into the living room without switching the light on.

It smelled dank.

Last winter they had talked about whether she should get rid of her flat. Micke's two-room flat was both bigger and closer to the city centre, and with the money they made from the sale they'd be able to buy the one-room flat next door and knock through.

But she had procrastinated and avoided the subject long enough for the neighbouring flat to be sold. Maybe she'd already had a suspicion that it wasn't going to work out, and that she was going to need a backup plan.

She opened the window and let in some cool night air. Then she tipped out all the belongings she had picked up from his flat onto the bed.

A failed relationship, boiled down to a toothbrush, a few crumpled clothes, a couple of dog-eared books and a few other random possessions.

Fired and dumped on the same day. Nice work, Normén...

Weirdly, losing her job hurt more. Getting fired was somehow the ultimate failure. She and Micke had been on the slide for a very long time, he had actually been right about that. There were reasons why she had preferred the time when they dating without any fuss, then later when she was going behind his back and seeing Tobbe Lundh. All the security and predictability that most other people seemed to crave made her skin crawl. Kept her awake at night.

And the happy pills hadn't been much help.

Over the past few months she had tried to find new ways of handling her restlessness. More time in the gym and the firing range, and, most of all, more work. Loads of work.

But that had all just been a way of postponing the inevitable. She simply wasn't in love with Micke any more, and maybe she never had been.

Not properly...

226

A shame, because he was a nice bloke, really nice.

But if she looked in the rear-view mirror, nice blokes didn't really seem to be her thing. According to convention, she was now supposed to shut herself away in her flat, put on her dressing-gown, eat Rocky Road straight from the tub and fast-forward through ten seasons of some American sitcom.

But what she felt was mostly just weary disappointment mixed with a few spoonfuls of relief. Besides, she didn't have time to feel sorry for herself.

The safe deposit box, Uncle Tage / André Pellas, and everything she had seen up in Henke's flat – the whole lot was probably connected somehow, and she needed to work out how.

She opened the bathroom cabinet, found the right box and took her evening medication.

Then she got the business card out of her pocket and fetched her phone.

The pills, the wet packet of cigarettes, lighter, the key to his flat and a roll of soaking wet notes from his secret stash . . .

He lined the objects up on the windowsill in the spacious shower room. The tiles on the walls reflected some of the light from outside, enough for him to get his bearings without the lighter. In one jacket pocket he found the pay-as-you-go mobile he had been given by the gang in the vet's clinic.

Shit, he thought he'd ditched it in the park.

But so what, the cheap plastic gadget was full of water now and bound to be stone-dead.

He turned on the shower, and to his surprise discovered that there was hot water. After rinsing off the worst of the dirt and mess, he moved on to cleaning his clothes.

His underpants were ruined, there was no point even trying to rescue them. But he scrubbed his jeans hard on the rough floor until most of the shit was gone.

The jacket and t-shirt were easier, and he draped everything across some hooks in the corner of the room to dry. When he was finished he sat on the floor as the water continued to rain down on him.

He leaned back against the wall and closed his eyes. The spiral of thoughts in his head slowly began to slow down.

Spinning sloooower

and

sloooooooweeer . . .

'You were very easy to find . . .'

The voice came out of nowhere.

He flinched, hitting his head on the tiles and making himself dizzy.

Then he tried to stagger to his feet as his heart raced and his brain tried to work out where he was and who the hell had crept up on him while he was asleep.

'Not very impressive, is he?'

The man's voice again, evidently addressing someone else. HP squinted at the door where the voices seemed to be coming from.

Instinctively he moved his hands to cover his crotch. The gruff voice sounded familiar.

Two dark figures emerged from the darkness and he took a step back.

'Here, we brought some new clothes . . .'

He definitely recognized that voice.

It was Nora, the vet. She dropped a gym bag on the floor beside him.

For one terrible moment he thought it was stripy, made in needlework class when he was at school, and had his

228

phone number on it. But when he touched it he found to his relief that this bag was made of nylon.

'Th-thanks,' he managed to stammer.

'Get dressed quickly, we have to go!'

Biffalo Bull from the vet's, Jeff or whatever his name was.

'What the fuck are you doing here . . .?' HP spluttered, but neither of them answered. 'How did you find . . .?'

He broke off.

'It was the phone, wasn't it?'

'Good guess, Einstein!' Jeff grinned.

'We have to get out of here, HP, right now,' Nora said. 'Every cop in the country is looking for you. If anyone in the main building works out there are people in here . . .'

'Okay, okay.' He quickly pulled on the pants, tracksuit bottoms, t-shirt and hooded jacket.

Everything fitted perfectly, even the trainers.

As if they knew exactly what size he was.

'You still look pretty rough, are you taking the pills?' Nora asked.

'Mmm,' he murmured. 'But I must have eaten something dodgy. I've had the shits really fucking badly.'

She went past him to the windowsill and picked up the pills.

'Okay, I'll give you a few more in case you threw up the last lot . . .'

He put the rest of his things in his pockets and gave his damp clothes one last look.

'Okay, I'm done. Thanks for your help!'

'Right, let's get going.' Jeff pointed at the door.

'Sorry, don't know if you'd listened to your messages, but I'm not interested in getting involved. Not my cup of tea . . .'

Neither of them moved.

229

'Listen, mate,' Jeff said in a tone of voice that was anything but friendly. 'That wasn't a request . . .'

He took a firm grasp of HP's right bicep and gestured to Nora to lead the way.

He waited a moment until she was a few metres away.

'Do me a favour,' he hissed at HP as he squeezed his arm tighter. 'You and I have a bit of unfinished business, so how about putting up a bit of resistance? Just a bit?'

'What the fuck are you talking about?'

'Number 32 Birkagatan, does that ring any bells? I had to go to A&E to get that red spray-paint out of my eyes. I was off sick for a week, and my girlfriend didn't dare to stay after you'd left your little message on our door . . .'

So that was where he knew the musclebound moron from!

Well, two years had passed, and he'd only caught glimpses of a bright red face and a tattooed arm, but now, in hindsight, it was obvious.

Remember rule number one.

The fans liked it when you fried a . . .

'Rat . . .' He blurted it out in a fit of Tourette's, and he felt Jeff twitch. The grip around his arm got even tighter, and for a moment he thought Jeff was going to hit him.

'Are you coming, or what?' Nora said.

A short silence.

'Sure, we're coming,' Jeff muttered, and shoved HP ahead of him.

Their car was parked on the other side of the wall.

'Get in!' Jeff held one of the back doors open.

'Not until you tell me where we're going!'

'Get in, I said.' Jeff took a step closer and clenched his fists.

'Like fuck will I.' He looked over his shoulder, trying to find an escape route. But unfortunately he was on an island, and he had serious doubts about his ability to cope with a long run.

'Okay, calm down, both of you.'

Nora again. She put her hand on Jeff's shoulder and the intimacy of the gesture made HP dislike the body-builder even more.

But it seemed to work, because Jeff lowered his hands.

'We're going to a meeting,' she said curtly. 'It's not far, then afterwards we'll drop you wherever you want to go.'

He didn't move.

'Come on, HP, you can hardly be scared of a meeting . . .'

She winked at him, and suddenly he found himself trying not to smile. He stood there for a few more seconds, pretending to think about it. But really he was far too tired to think about anything.

'Okay,' he sighed with a shrug. 'Let's do it . . .'

The dark Volvo pulled up outside her door.

The driver hardly had time to put the handbrake on before she was out on the pavement.

She had already been waiting fifteen minutes in the dark stairwell, and having to wait had done nothing to improve her mood.

She jumped into the back seat and slammed the door hard behind her.

'What the hell is going on?' she snarled.

'Calm down, I'll explain everything. Just give me a chance, please.'

Tage Sammer held his hands up in such an exaggerated way that she had trouble staying angry.

'Okay,' she said, then took a deep breath. 'I'm listening . . .'

'As you already know, I work with security issues. I have done ever since I left the military. The Palace, or rather the office of the Marshal of the Realm, is one of my clients.'

'Yes, I worked that out,' she snapped. 'So why didn't you say so when we last met, and why are you called André Pellas instead of Tage Sammer? And how does my brother fit into the picture . . .?'

He put one hand on her arm to get her to stop.

'We can set off now, Jonsson,' he said unnecessarily loudly to the chauffeur.

'Of course, Colonel.' The chauffeur put the car into gear and pulled away from the kerb.

Tage Sammer leaned closer to her.

'You have to understand, Rebecca,' he said, 'just like your father, sometimes I have to use different names. André Pellas is the name I went by earlier in my career.'

'Military Intelligence, yes?'

It was dark in the back seat, but she thought she could see his face twitch slightly.

'I found an old picture of you in a book about Cyprus,' she added.

'I see . . .'

A brief silence followed.

'Well, I should have known better than to underestimate you, Rebecca,' he said with a wry smile.

'Your father was also very diligent in his work, preparing everything very thoroughly, never leaving anything to chance . . .'

He took a deep breath.

'After the attack in Kungsträdgården two years ago, the Palace realized that they needed to improve their handling of security and intelligence. The Marshal of the Realm and I are old acquaintances, which is why he contacted me. As you know, His Majesty has had a number of . . .'

He paused and seemed to be searching for the right words.

'. . . PR-related difficulties, one might say.'

'You mean that muckraking book, and the friends who employed gangsters, and the rumours about . . .'

'Perhaps we needn't go into detail . . .' he interrupted. 'But any decrease in public support goes hand in hand with an increased level of risk, and with an event like the princess's wedding just around the corner, everyone is rather more nervous than usual.'

'I can understand that, but the Security Police are already on top of all that . . .'

'Naturally, of course they are. But the incident in Kungsträdgården a couple of years ago showed that there were clear deficiencies both in the evaluation of the threat level, and in communication between the Palace and the Security Police. My role is to act as a link. To bridge potential differences of opinion, if you understand what I mean?'

He brought his fingertips together to illustrate his point, and suddenly she couldn't help smiling. The gesture was so obvious, and so familiar.

'I am also able to contribute the experience and network of contacts I have built up during my thirty years or so in the world of international security,' he went on. 'Offering a second opinion, so to speak . . .'

The car climbed to the crown of the Western Bridge, then continued down towards Hornstull.

Down to their right they could make out the dark edifice of the old prison on Långholmen.

'We believe that the attack in Kungsträdgården was carried out by a particular network. A group calling itself the Circus, the Event, and occasionally . . .'

'The Game,' she interjected.

'Exactly! I presume you heard about it from Henrik?'

She nodded.

'To begin with I thought it was just talk. Another one of his stories . . .'

'But as time went by you became more convinced?'

'Yes, especially after I'd talked to . . .'

She bit her lip.

'. . . Magnus Sandström?' Sammer concluded. 'Or Farook Al-Hassan, as he calls himself these days.'

She didn't answer.

'Don't worry, Rebecca, we know all about Sandström. We've had our eyes on him for quite a while. We know that one of his tasks was to recruit people whom the Game might find useful.'

'People like Henke, you mean?'

'Precisely. Your brother is an excellent example of an active participant. But Sandström and his like also recruit other more . . . passive resources.'

'Such as?'

He leaned even closer and lowered his voice almost to a whisper.

'Such as you, for instance . . .'

17

Game change

They parked in a garage near Södra station.

'Here.'

Nora handed him a pair of cheap sunglasses.

'And pull your hood up as well.'

He didn't really understand why until they passed a tobacconist's and he saw his own glazed expression from his passport photograph staring out at him from the wall.

SWEDEN'S MOST WANTED MAN! the flysheet screamed, so loudly that he felt like covering his ears.

'Okay?' Nora said quietly.

'Sure . . .' he mumbled, without sounding at all convincing. 'Is it much further?'

She shook her head.

'We're heading to Fatbursparken first, then we're almost there.'

They walked round some portacabins and made their way along a fence surrounding a building site.

The music and noise from the pavement cafés up in Medborgarplatsen were clearly audible.

Jeff stopped for a moment and looked around.

'Through there,' he said, pointing to an opening in the fence.

They went down a rough tarmac path, looping downwards in a semicircle. Just as they disappeared below ground level the path turned to gravel and they found themselves in a narrow gulley with rock walls on either side. Weird . . . he thought he knew Södermalm like the back of his hand, but he'd never given any thought to this particular corner.

He must have crossed the footbridge he could see seven or eight metres above them hundreds of times without ever thinking about what was underneath. Probably because the vegetation growing from the sides of the gulley formed a canopy that blocked the view.

The gulley stopped abruptly at a rock wall. In the middle was a large metal gate, and cool, damp, cave air hit them as they got closer.

Jeff looked over his shoulder again, then glanced up at the buildings just visible above ground level.

'Okay?' Nora said.

Jeff nodded.

She took a large key out of one of her jacket pockets and unlocked the gate.

Once they were inside she locked it again.

Jeff pulled out a torch and shone it into the cave.

Ten metres in, there was a folding door.

Nora marched quickly over to it and began fiddling with the lock, but HP didn't move.

He was tired, exhausted, unable to walk another step, at least not until someone told him where the hell they were going.

'Come on.' Jeff tugged at his arm.

He opened his mouth to tell the king of the bodybuilders to go fuck himself, but at that moment a row of lamps lit up on the other side of the door, revealing a long tunnel that led into the rock.

He hesitated a few more seconds, then curiosity got the better of him.

The tunnel was big, judging from its height and width it looked like it had probably once been used for trains. The roof was bricked over, and every fifteen metres there was an old fluorescent light-fitting, giving off just enough light to see by. The sides of the tunnel were mostly bare rock, but here and there water had trickled through, polishing the surface.

The tunnel curved to the left, and the ground sloped gently down. HP's tired legs were grateful for any help they could get. Their steps echoed off the walls, and once they'd walked about fifty metres the folding door behind them vanished from view.

'So where are we going?' he asked Nora. Jeff answered.

'We told you back on Långholmen. A meeting . . .'

'Yes, but I thought . . .' He didn't finish the sentence.

What had he actually thought?

He scarcely knew. His whole system had rebooted, and only now did his head seem to have started working normally.

They had entered the tunnel up by Fatbursparken, and it curved down and to the left. They must have walked about two hundred metres now, which meant they should be somewhere under . . .

Sankt Paulsgatan.

The chauffeur pulled up in a free parking space. Then, without a word from Sammer, he got out onto the pavement and closed the car door behind him.

'You must have an awful lot of questions, Rebecca, and believe me, nothing would please me more than to be able to answer them all. But, as I'm sure you can appreciate, that is sadly not possible . . .'

He looked at her in a way that made her nod unconsciously in agreement.

237

'But, because I trust you, I will do my best to satisfy your curiosity. Tell me what you know, and I shall try to fill in the gaps . . .'

She opened her mouth to speak, then closed it again.

The fact that Sammer was working for both the Palace and Security Police explained a fair amount. But she had plenty more questions, a great deal more, and now she had to try to reformulate them.

'The safe deposit box . . .' she began. 'You knew there was a gun in it, didn't you?'

He hesitated for a moment, then nodded slowly.

'I certainly suspected as much. As I said, your father had begun to act on his own, and made a number of ill-considered decisions. It would be extremely unfortunate if the weapon were to be traced back to . . .'

He gestured towards the window.

'. . . events in the past.'

He fell silent and looked at her.

'A safe deposit box is in many ways a sort of bubble, Rebecca. A place where time has stopped and all the normal rules have ceased to apply. But as you already know, bubbles have one thing in common . . .'

'Sooner or later they're bound to burst,' she said.

He nodded.

'And the passports?'

'There's less risk attached to them, but I'd still be grateful if you could let me have them, along with the gun. Not least to protect your father's memory . . .'

She didn't answer, and tried instead to put her questions together into something resembling a narrative.

'That piece of paper you gave Henke, out in the cemetery. You said you wanted to give him a message, that that was why you needed to get in touch with him . . .'

Sammer didn't respond immediately, and seemed to be

waiting for her to say more. She waited silently for an answer to her question.

Finally, he let out a sigh.

'I promised your father that I'd look after you. Both you and Henrik. When we started to receive information which suggested that Henke was seriously involved in the Game, I decided to break the rules . . .'

'Something happened out there by the Kaknäs Tower, didn't it . . .?' she persisted.

He glanced briefly out of the window.

'I suppose you could say that I decided to use rather unorthodox methods . . .'

'Come on, this is my little brother we're talking about! You have to tell me, Uncle Tage!'

He lowered his voice and leaned forward.

'Henrik doesn't like me, does he? He doesn't like the fact that you and I are close?'

'Er . . . what?' The question took her by surprise. 'Well, maybe not. But not because of you.'

'I'm afraid it is, Rebecca . . .'

He took a deep breath and appeared to think for a few moments.

'Let me explain. Most participants in the Game become afflicted sooner or later by severe paranoia. They have difficulty seeing the difference between fantasy and reality, and begin to see conspiracies round every corner . . .'

He paused, and she couldn't help nodding.

'Just as I feared, I'm afraid this applies to Henrik. He has long since passed the point where it was possible to appeal to his common sense . . .'

She went on nodding, more firmly now.

'Unfortunately, the only way to save him is to make use of his condition. It's not something I would do if there

239

was any other way of reaching him, Rebecca, I hope you can understand . . .'

'But what did you do?'

'I managed to persuade Henrik that I was actually the Game Master.'

'W-what . . .?!'

He held up his hand to stop her.

'Rebecca, I thought my deception was the only way to save him. It was a shock tactic. I gave him a task, one that was so unthinkable that Henrik would be unable even to consider carrying it out. He would be jolted into a return to reality, so to speak, and would feel a need to break free of the Game's grasp. Then he would once again be reachable, possibly even . . .'

'Willing to cooperate!' she interrupted. 'You wanted to get him to spill the beans about the Game, to become an informer. Was that why he was pulled in by the Security Police?'

Sammer nodded slowly.

'But Eskil acted a little prematurely. Henrik wasn't ready, and once that lawyer showed up . . .'

'. . . Stigsson got cold feet and let Henrik go.'

She took a deep breath.

'So the plan was to put Henrik under so much pressure that he'd jump ship. But instead you pushed him over the edge, and for some reason he ended up trying to attack Black. And now you're worried it's all going to get out. That's why you wanted to get to Henrik first, to make sure he didn't give you away . . .'

He held up both hands as if to prevent her finishing the sentence.

'No, no, absolutely not, you misunderstand, my dear Rebecca, you really must believe me when I say that I only want the best for you both. You and Henrik. Erland was

240

a friend, a trusted comrade who was always loyal to me and our cause. The fact that I wasn't in a position to save him from himself is one of my greatest regrets in life. The forces that have got their claws into Henrik are closely related to Erland's fate, and that is why I chose to take such drastic measures . . .'

Her heart suddenly began to beat faster.

'You mean that Dad was also being used by the Game?'

Sammer grimaced.

'You can't answer that, can you?' she said.

He glanced out of the window again.

The chauffeur was still standing a short distance away on the pavement, and to judge by his body-language the night air was pretty cold.

'We don't have much time left, Rebecca,' Sammer went on.

'What was the task?'

'I'm sorry?'

'The task you gave Henrik out at the pet cemetery, the "unthinkable task." What exactly was it?'

He was looking out of the window. The chauffeur had turned round and was on his way back to the car. Just as he was about to open the door, Sammer leaned closer to her, so close she could smell his aftershave.

'He was supposed to carry out an attack on the royal wedding.'

They had gone another two hundred metres or so, and the tunnel was sloping downwards more steeply.

There were noises now, a vague rumble from a ventilation system. A large grille in the right wall of the tunnel suddenly blew out a gust of air, and a few seconds later an underground train rattled past on the other side.

In the distance he could hear the announcement from the platform.

Far ahead in the tunnel he could make out what looked like builders' huts. One on each side of the tunnel.

And suddenly he realized where they were going.

Bloody hell!

He stopped dead and looked back quickly over his shoulder. Nora had locked the gate up there, and the key was in her jacket pocket. And he'd never be able to run all the way back.

'Are you coming, or what?' Jeff took a step closer.

HP leaned forward and put his hands on his knees.

'Wait a moment,' he muttered, trying to sound exhausted, which wasn't exactly difficult. His pulse had been racing for a while and it felt like the air was getting harder to breathe.

He needed to buy himself some time, get a few moments to think.

They had been veering left the whole way, and had been going down, which meant that the underground station he could hear had to be Slussen.

So those huts up ahead had to be right underneath . . .

'We're going to meet the Source, aren't we?' he said, looking up.

Neither of the others had much of a poker face.

'Come on,' Jeff said, taking another step closer.

HP didn't move.

'Your source is called Erman. I met him a long time ago. Back then he was hiding out in the bush and claiming to have been thrown out of the Game.'

He spat a gob of saliva onto the floor of the tunnel.

'Erman's working for the Game Master. I saw them together just a few hours ago with the cops. And before that I saw him go down in the lift that comes out over there.'

He gestured towards the huts.

242

Jeff tried to say something but HP ignored him. Instead he stared straight at Nora, trying to catch her eye.

'This whole thing is a trap, Nora . . .' he said as calmly as he could. 'At best the Source has sold you out, getting you to run errands for the Game . . .'

She didn't respond, but a little frown had appeared above her nose.

'. . . or else you've been working for the Game Master all along.'

He couldn't quite make out the expression on Nora's face, but he was still pretty convinced that she was just as disconcerted as he was. But right now that really didn't matter.

'Either way, the Game's been trying to find me. They're desperate to get hold of me at any cost. And you're about to deliver me to them, exactly as they want. Don't you get it?'

He paused for breath.

'Bollocks,' Jeff growled. 'So you expect us to believe that you've met the Source *and* the Game Master?'

He grinned and tilted his head towards Nora.

'We've got a real heavyweight here, eh . . .?'

'What does he look like?'

It took HP a moment to realize that Nora was talking to him.

'W-what? Who?'

'The Game Master, of course, who do you think?'

'Er, well . . . he's around seventy, well dressed, walks with a stick . . . A typical grey old man . . .'

He slowly straightened up.

'He calls himself Tage Sammer.'

'And you've met?'

HP nodded. Her tone of voice and the expression on her face reinforced his theory. There was no way she was consciously working for the Game.

'I even had coffee with him out at the pet cemetery just

243

beyond the Kaknäs Tower. He had a check-patterned flask in a little camping box, typical old man stuff . . .'

'And you seriously expect us to believe that?'

Jeff again, but HP ignored him.

It was Nora he had to convince, and not just for the simple reason that he didn't want to be handed over to Erman and the Game Master. He actually wanted her to believe him. Properly.

'Well, what do you say?'

He held his arms up towards Nora and fired off his most charming smile.

'You're right,' she said, and he noticed Jeff twitch. 'The Source wants to meet you. He's waiting down there . . .'

She gestured over her shoulder, towards the huts.

'He's usually incredibly cautious, but as soon as we told him you were backing out, he wanted to set up a meeting. That has to mean something . . .'

'It just means he wants to get hold of me . . .!'

Without warning Jeff suddenly grabbed HP by the arm and tried to get him in some sort of police hold.

But HP was ready. He resisted for a fraction of a second, then took aim and spun round to the right.

Just before they collided he raised his left leg and planted his knee hard into Jeff's crown jewels.

The man collapsed like a house of cards, almost taking HP down with him as he fell. But at the last moment HP managed to pull free.

He took a couple of stumbling steps, then regained his balance and started running towards the huts.

Nora stuck out her arms in an attempt to stop him, but the tunnel was wide enough for him to dart past without any problem.

Fifty metres to the huts and lift.

His heart was already pounding in his chest.

244

Running straight towards danger wasn't exactly the best idea, but he didn't have any other options.

With a bit of luck Erman was hiding in one of the huts not daring to look out.

Thirty metres, and suddenly he could hear steps behind him.

It had to be Nora, Jeff would hardly be in a fit state to run.

'HP, stop!' she yelled, and he fought the urge to look back.

Twenty metres now.

Fifteen.

His throat was burning, shrinking to the size of a drinking straw.

The footsteps were getting closer.

Ten metres left.

The tunnel narrowed to a path between the huts, and beyond that there was a pale rectangle in the rock-face that had to be the door of the lift.

It was open!

'HP, stop!'

Her voice was sharper now, and this time he couldn't resist the urge to turn his head.

She was six or seven metres behind him, close, but still further away than he had imagined.

It might just work . . .

It was going to work!

The next moment he saw movement from the corner of his eye.

He started turning his head to the front again, and just had time to see the door opening right in front of him.

Then everything went dark.

'Is he okay?'

'Yes, he's coming round . . .'

He felt something cool and wet over his eyes and forehead.

His head ached, his nose was blocked and he was having to breathe through his mouth.

Long, rattling breaths.

'Can you hear me, Henke?'

The object over his eyes vanished and he blinked up at the light.

Nora's face was floating above him, and for a few moments he felt full of a sense of wellbeing. She was calling him Henke, just like his sister . . .

Then suddenly he remembered where he was.

And why!

They must have dragged him inside one of the huts . . .

He tried to sit up, pulling his legs towards him to get to his feet.

'Easy . . .'

She was holding onto him, trying to stop him, but without putting much force into it.

'The Source . . .' he panted. 'Erman, I've got to . . .'

Then he caught sight of him.

He was sitting on a chair a few metres away, leaning forward. Thin, receding hair, with dark-framed glasses, just like the description. Their eyes met and for a few moments HP's brain tried to take in what he was seeing. What it meant.

But it was impossible.

Completely.

Fucking.

Impossible.

'Hi, HP. Good of you to drop by . . .' Manga grinned.

18

Impossible things before breakfast

'HOW . . .
    THE . . .
    FUCK . . .
    CAN . . .
    YOU . . .
    BE . . .
    HERE . . .?!!!'
He was sitting astride Manga's chest, his fingers clasped tightly round his throat and neck as his beat the balding head against the floor.

'Steuurrp . . . H . . . P . . . Furrrfurck . . .!!' Manga gurgled, his arms flailing.

HP didn't care.

Someone was pulling at his shoulders, grabbing his arms. Nora was screaming in one ear, but he wasn't listening. He was going to kill the lying little fucker . . .

A powerful arm suddenly wrapped around his neck and got him in a grip that instantly shut off the blood-supply to his brain.

His vision started to turn black, his fingers began to twitch spasmodically and he lost his grip round Manga's throat. The next moment he was dragged onto his feet. The stranglehold round his neck eased slightly, just enough for his eyesight to return.

He could see Nora leaning over Manga.

'Okay, mate, are you going to calm down, or what?' Jeff snarled in his ear. 'If not, I'll be only too happy to break your neck . . .'

HP tried to resist, feeling behind him with his hands in an attempt to grab whatever part of Jeff he might be able to damage. But it was hopeless. Jeff's grip was rock-solid and his pathetic attempts at resistance just led to Jeff lifting him up so his toes were only just touching the ground.

All his energy drained away. His arms and legs felt heavy as lead and he could no longer hold them up, could hardly hold himself up.

Jeff dragged him a couple of metres and then dropped him down on a small sofa.

It took him a few seconds to gather the strength to sit up.

Manga had got to his feet, and was feeling his neck as he drank a glass of water that Nora seemed to have conjured up out of nowhere.

HP could have done with something to drink, his throat felt parched and right now thirst was the only sensible feeling he had to cling onto.

Manga was the Source.

Manga
Was
The
Source.

Which meant . . .

WHICH MEANT???

He closed his eyes and put his hand over his forehead.

Tears were pricking his eyes, and he screwed them tight shut to stop anything leaking out.

Fuck.

Fuck!

FUCK!!

Manga picked up the chair he had been sitting on and put it in front of HP.

'Here!'

He held out the glass of water, still half full.

HP just stared at him.

'Come on, HP! No need to be scared, you're among friends . . .'

HP grabbed the glass and gulped down the contents. The water was ice-cold and made his throat sting.

'How long?'

'What?'

'How long have you been involved in the Game, Manga, or Farook, or whatever the hell you're calling yourself this week . . .?'

Manga shrugged.

'Quite a while, actually . . .'

HP put the glass down, leaned forward and rubbed his temples. He was still trying in vain to get his brain to make the right connections. But it was totally fucking impossible.

'W-what, why . . . well . . . er.'

He carried on rubbing his face, harder and harder. Digging his fingers in until his skin stung.

'From the start?' he finally managed to say towards the floor. 'Were you involved right from the start?' he said in a slightly clearer voice as he straightened up.

Manga took a deep breath.

'I've been involved longer than you. Considerably longer, in fact . . .'

'So you were the one who dragged me into it . . .?'

Manga shook his head.

'No, to be honest, it wasn't me. I didn't know you were involved until you showed up in the shop that time and pulled your phone out. Not even then, in fact, because I thought you'd just found it by accident, that some other Player had lost it. Then when I did realize that you were involved . . .'

He held his hands out.

'B-but I don't under . . .' HP cleared his throat and tried again.

From the corner of his eye he could see Nora watching him.

'H-how did you get involved? What do you do? Are you a Player, or an Ant? You've got to tell . . .'

'Later, HP, right now we don't have much time. The whole city's looking for you, the cops, the Ants, everyone . . .'

Manga turned towards Jeff.

'Can you keep an eye out in the tunnel?'

'Sure.'

'All I can tell you right now is that I've tried to help you . . .' Manga went on once the door had closed behind Jeff.

'Help?!' HP could feel the blood rushing to his head. 'For fuck's sake, you could have told me you were involved, and explained how lethal it all was. Told me to stop! Shit . . . you're supposed to be my best friend!'

'Yeah, right, like that would have worked . . .'

Manga shook his head.

'Besides, you know what happens if you break rule number one . . . You weren't the only one who received a warning shot.'

Nora reappeared with more water, a glass each this time.

'The arson attack on the shop, remember?' Manga added

when HP didn't seem to get it. 'That was aimed at me, not you. A little reminder from the Game Master about what would happen if I didn't stick to the rules. It probably wasn't even meant to start a real fire. They just wanted me to realize what was at stake.'

Nora accidentally tipped one of the glasses and spilled some water on HP's trousers, but he hardly noticed.

His brain was still searching for solid ground.

'S-so . . . how much of all this has been real?' he stammered.

'How do you mean?'

'I mean . . . Well, what the hell do you think I mean?! Everything I've been through, the fire in my flat, the bomb on the E4, the server farm I blew up out in Kista, running away, all that crap in Dubai, and everything that happened with ArgosEye. How much of that was real? Properly real, I mean?'

'All of it, of course . . .'

Manga took a sip of water.

'But maybe not real in the way you thought . . .' he added, shifting slightly on his chair. 'You could say that you never really left the Game . . . That you've actually been working for them the whole time. Or, well . . . For us . . .'

HP put his glass down and covered his face with his hands.

Manga was still talking, but his voice suddenly sounded tinny and distant, as if he were in a different room.

The situation was unreal, dreamlike to the point where he ought to be pinching holes in his arms.

Working for them . . .

His brain was stuttering, trying desperately to keep to the facts: he'd blown up their server farm, escaped from their conspiracy to frame him for murder, and sunk their business partners at ArgosEye with all hands . . .

251

Unless he was wrong?

Had he actually been . . .

Working for them?

He stared at Manga. Boring, dependable, balding Mangalito. The coward. His old friend, his BFF.

The world lurched.

For a brief moment he was back in the eighties, sitting on the sofa in front of the television, with yellow cheese-puff fingers and eyes wide open. On the screen the shower door had just opened and Bobby Ewing was looking out.

Working for . . .

Us . . .

'What the fuck am I doing here, Manga?' he whispered.

'Give us a couple more minutes, please, Jonsson!'

The chauffeur got in and closed the car door without a word.

'Now do you understand why I'm so keen to get hold of that gun?' Tage Sammer said in a low voice.

She nodded.

'I think I do, anyway.'

'Good. I'd appreciate it if you could empty your father's safe deposit box as soon as possible and hand the entire contents over to me. Can I ask that of you, Rebecca? You have my word that the gun will disappear, that neither it nor the passports will ever crop up anywhere that they could be misused.'

She thought for a few seconds.

'The gun isn't in the safe deposit box any more . . .'

'What?'

'I moved it to another one the day I found it, I opened a box in my own name.'

'Ah, I see. Good thinking, Rebecca!'

'I have the passports at home. I'll go to the bank first thing tomorrow morning. I'll call you as soon as I'm done.'

'Excellent, Rebecca, you never let me down! If only more of my colleagues were like you!'

He patted her knee and she found she was grateful for the slightest touch.

'No problem, Uncle Tage,' she mumbled.

'Back to Fredhäll, please, Jonsson,' he said, tapping on the chauffeur's shoulder. 'Miss Normén needs to get to bed, she's had a rather trying day . . .'

'Okay, HP, let me explain,' Manga began. 'You're here for the reasons Nora has already given you. We're going to close down the Fortress, and stop PayTag and the Game Master from gaining an unlimited monopoly on people's pasts.'

'Er, hang on a minute . . .'

Manga held up his hand and stopped him.

'I know you've got loads of questions, HP . . .' He looked at his watch. 'But time's marching on. I had to come up with somewhere to meet at short notice, a place they wouldn't think of.'

He gestured towards the roof with his hand.

'This is one of the Game's own meeting points, which is why it's free from prying eyes and ears. But we can't stay here long. We hadn't exactly counted on you passing out . . .'

He glanced at his watch again.

'I signed up a long time ago. I had friends who were already involved in the Game, and I pretty much got an invitation to help out. Just like with you, it started off small, a cool thing to do. As time passed I got more involved, and I liked the feeling of being part of something bigger, something that most people knew nothing about.'

HP nodded reluctantly.

'I'm listening.'

'The big thing we found out early on was that through the Game it was actually possible to influence events, make a difference. Shine a light on things other people would rather conceal. Secrets that those in power want to hide. Investigations that have been buried, reports that have been swept under the carpet or silenced. Lots of little tasks all slotted together, then we could tip off the media or post what we'd found out on various whistleblower websites. We did a lot of that at the start . . .'

'But?'

Manga glanced at Nora.

'My friends and I only saw a fraction of what was going on. That's always been the case.

'The whole Game is divided into small cells, so that the Game Master is basically the only person who can see the whole picture. As time went on, it became clearer that he was changing direction. The Game was getting more and more closely managed, as the Players' choices became fewer and the tasks increasingly murky. Gradually the rest of us lost whatever influence we had, and everything started to pass through the Game Master. It was becoming more and more obvious that he was exploiting the Game to gain power for himself. Then when PayTag . . .'

'Where do I fit into the picture?!' HP interrupted.

Manga looked clearly disconcerted by the unexpected question, and it took him a moment to collect his thoughts.

'Well, to get straight to the point, you could probably say that most of what you've accomplished has been within the boundaries of the Game. Serving the Game Master's purposes, so to speak . . .'

Manga smiled uncertainly at HP as if he were waiting for a reaction.

254

'B-but I blew up the server farm. I gave them one fuck of a serious kick in the balls, shut them down for months, emptied their bank account, sank ArgosEye . . . Didn't I?' he added when Manga didn't reply.

He could hear how hollow his voice sounded.

'Like I said, I've been trying to help you, I was actually trying to get you out,' Manga mumbled.

'But after the fires . . .' He exchanged a quick look with Nora. 'After the fires I agreed to help. The Game Master promised to let you go when it was all finished.'

He looked down at the floor.

'They emptied the building in Kista the day after you and Rehyman were there. Moved to another, more secure site. You blew up an empty building, that's all. I wanted to explain everything to you a thousand times, but as long as they were watching you it was impossible . . .'

HP took another deep, stuttering breath.

'So the whole thing was planned, they just let me get away with the money? But why?'

'The Game needed an attack, something that could never be traced, to tie in with the EU summit. The money was your reward for surviving your own End Game and, just as they expected, you took the money and fled the field. No witnesses, no trail . . .'

He shook his head slowly.

'So far everything had gone exactly as the Game Master had promised. Both you and Becca were out.'

'What about later – Dubai, ArgosEye?'

Manga grimaced.

'Obviously I should have realized that the Game Master is the one who sets the rules. That he's the one who decides when the Game begins and ends. Evidently you were too valuable an asset for them to just let you go. I was away and heard by chance that you were involved again, but by then there wasn't much I could do. I asked a friend to keep an eye on you and send me reports about what was happening . . .'

'Who?'

Manga shrugged.

'Does it matter? Anyway, you soon got in touch yourself, when you wanted the trojan. You told me about ArgosEye. That put me in one hell of a difficult position. Should I help you directly, or check with the Game Master first?'

Manga twisted his hands in his lap.

'You called the Game Master . . .'

HP thought for a moment:

'So that was why I couldn't find any information about the Game. You designed the spy program so that it only leaked information that wasn't about them.'

Manga shook his head.

'I did actually suggest that to the Game Master, but he said it wasn't necessary. I was instructed to help you as much as I could. It took a while for me to realize . . .'

HP opened his mouth to speak, but it took a while for him find the right words.

'Okay, hang on . . . S-so, you mean ArgosEye . . .'

'. . . was never actually hiding any of the Game's secrets . . .' Manga concluded.

'B-but . . . they were the Game's partners? PayTag was going to buy them out, and . . .'

Manga shook his head.

'Think about it, HP. Who told you about the PayTag buyout? I bet it wasn't Philip Argos or anyone else working there, was it?'

HP's mind drifted aimlessly and it took him a while to find the right thread.

'Er, no. It was Monika, Anna Argos's sister, she told me

256

out on Lidingö. She said Anna had opposed the sale and that was why they had her killed . . .'

'Okay,' Manga nodded, 'let me explain . . .'

He exchanged another glance with Nora, looked at his watch, then leaned closer to HP.

'PayTag was never interested in ArgosEye. They'd already bought another company in roughly the same line of business for peanuts, and they were in the process of putting together a decent management team. What Philip Argos was planning was a perfectly ordinary stock-market flotation. If it had been a success, then PayTag would have had unwelcome competition . . .'

HP flinched.

'What, you mean Monika Argos lied to me? Pretending that the flotation was actually a buyout? Why the hell would she have done that?'

'Two fairly simple reasons, in fact . . . First and foremost, because you were in position and leapt at the chance to help her sabotage Philip Argos's plans . . .'

HP nodded wearily.

'And the other reason . . .?'

'Well, ask yourself, whose idea was it? Who was likely to get a kick out of the idea that Philip Argos was paying you way over the odds for the shares? It was a real bonus when the trojan actually sank Philip's ship and he ended up with a ruined reputation and no financial backing . . .'

Manga looked at HP as if he were expecting an instant answer. But HP's brain was way, way behind.

'Think, HP . . .' Manga said, more slowly. 'Who hated Philip Argos enough to cook up one hell of an advanced way to get revenge?'

He pulled out a shiny metal phone with a glass screen and HP flinched involuntarily.

On the screen was a picture of a woman with dark hair

cut in a bob, sitting at a restaurant table. She was holding a glass of wine in her hand and seemed to be drinking a toast with a man who had his back to the camera.

The woman looked vaguely familiar, but he couldn't quite place her.

'Take a closer look, and ignore the colour of her hair,' Manga said.

HP did as he was asked. And suddenly he saw something. Her posture, the way she was looking at the man. But it was unthinkable. Impossible!

'Forget Monika,' Manga went on. 'We're talking about a seriously cold person. Someone who would literally step over dead bodies to get what she wanted. Even her own . . .?'

He brought up a fresh picture on the phone and this time the man was more visible. It was Mark Black. But HP could not immediately take this in.

'She calls herself Anthea Ravel these days,' Manga continued patiently. 'She's working for PayTag, in fact she's here, getting their new business up and running. Ravel. A fitting surname in a lot of respects, actually. A Janus word . . .'

'What the fuck are you talking about,' HP grunted distractedly as he sat there with his eyes glued to the screen.

'A Janus word can mean its own opposite. Like *screen*, which can mean both to conceal and to show. Janus, after the Roman god with two faces . . .'

Manga held the phone even closer to the end of HP's nose.

'Two faces, get it?'

'Anna Argos,' HP muttered, unable to quite believe what he was saying.

'You must be careful, Rebecca, promise me that,' Tage Sammer said as the car pulled up beside the pavement and the chauffeur got out to open the door for her.

'Not just when you go to the bank. The Game has eyes and ears everywhere, and Magnus Sandström is an extremely dangerous person. You can't trust anything he's told you. In all likelihood he's been cultivating the pair of you. Planting stories, arranging meetings . . .'

She shook her head.

'I just can't believe it. We've known each other since we were kids. Manga was nice, a good lad.'

'Of course, I appreciate that it's hard to take in. But Sandström has been working for the Game for a long time, a very long time. These days he has a senior position, possibly even the most senior. Henrik has already slipped out of our hands, and now I'm afraid that Sandström is using him and is well on his way to turning our own weapons against us. We would dearly love to get hold of them both before the wedding, before history repeats itself . . .'

The car door opened and he stopped abruptly.

'Promise you'll take care of yourself, my dear Rebecca. If you hear from your brother you must call me at once. I'll try to help you both as best I can, but until Henrik is in safe custody I'm afraid we can't have any further direct contact.'

She nodded.

'I understand.'

'Good. I really am sorry that it's come to this, Rebecca, from the bottom of my heart. Some of the responsibility for this falls on me, I know. If I was going to use unorthodox tactics I should have made sure Stigsson left HP alone, but I had hoped to make him see sense. Now you have to deal with all this. I wouldn't have wished this sort of trial on anyone, least of all you. Truly, I hope that you can forgive me.'

She didn't answer, but leaned over instead and gave him a peck on the cheek.

The car door closed behind her and a few moments later she was standing alone on her street.

'Bingo!' Manga smiled. 'Not a bad package deal, is it? Anna Argos gets revenge, PayTag gets rid of a competitor and the Game Master gets paid. All that was needed to seal the deal was a suitable Player and a way of motivating him into going back into the hornets' nest. And suddenly your early retirement was over . . .'

HP was shaking his head in disbelief. What Manga was saying obviously sounded completely mad. A conspiracy theory of the first order . . .

But, on the other hand, the boundaries of logic were so far behind him now that there was no point even trying to work out where they were.

Anna Argos, still alive . . .

In which case the fucking bitch had got him locked up and tortured on suspicion of murdering her, then deported, and all to wind him up to the point where he'd want to get his own revenge. And the whole time she was living a life of luxury on a beach somewhere with a new name while she waited for the plastic surgery scars on her face to heal.

'So the whole business of bringing down ArgosEye was pointless . . .?' he mumbled.

'No, no, absolutely not!'

Manga shook his head with exaggerated vigour.

'Philip Argos may not have been a killer, but he was still a fully paid-up bad guy. Just think about what they did to you. And what they were doing with the business really did stink . . .'

'But now PayTag and Anna Argos are doing the same thing, just under a different name . . .'

'Unfortunately it looks that way, which takes us back

to what I was saying about the Game Master's wobbly moral compass . . .' Manga pulled a face.

'What's PayTag's new company called?'

'Sentry Security . . .'

His brain made the connection between the right synapses almost immediately this time.

'Sentry? Shit, that's where . . .'

'. . . Rebecca works. Exactly. Are you starting to see how it all fits together?'

Manga checked the time for what must be the tenth time.

'Sorry, but we have to leave soon. Kent's fixed a place where you can lie low until we're ready to get going. You'll have to . . .'

'Listen, right now I'm about a millimetre away from having a massive stroke, so don't tell me what I have to do! As you probably realize, your credibility really isn't that fucking high right now. Give me one reason why I shouldn't just go and crawl into a hole until this has all blown over.'

'Because we need you, HP!'

Manga held out his hands.

'I get it, I can see why you're sceptical. I can't deny that I've deceived you really badly. No question! But everything I've done has been to help you and Becca, I swear!'

The door opened and Jeff looked in.

'Someone just used their passcard upstairs,' he hissed. 'The lift's on its way down, so we have to go, now!'

Manga and Nora stood up at once.

But HP didn't move.

'Come on, HP, we have to leave! I'll explain more on the way. If they find us down here we're finished . . .'

'Not until you tell me who *they* are . . .'

'Local transport staff, the cops – who cares?' Jeff snapped. 'Get a fucking move on or I'll carry . . .'

Manga raised his hand and Jeff stopped instantly.

'I'll tell you more later, HP, I promise. But right now we have to go. I know it's a lot to ask, but you have to trust me. If the cops get hold of you, we're fucked . . .'

HP looked hard into Manga's face for a few seconds before reluctantly getting up.

They jogged through the tunnel. Nora first, then him and Manga, with Jeff bringing up the rear. HP couldn't help looking back over his shoulder.

He tried to say something to Manga, ask more questions, but their speed and the uphill slope were keeping his exhausted lungs fully occupied.

The huts disappeared beyond the curve of the tunnel and after a few more metres Nora slowed down.

'I can't make sense of it,' HP panted to Manga. 'The Game owns PayTag. Black works for the Game Master . . .'

He was gasping for air.

'No, no, absolutely not,' Manga replied. 'PayTag is owned by a secretive foundation. We have our theories about who's behind it, but that's a different story. To start with PayTag was just one of many companies that employed the Game. But for the past year or so they've been pretty much the Game's only client . . .'

Nora stopped short and the others were forced to do the same.

She held one hand up. For a few moments the distant noise of the air vents and HP's laboured breathing were the only sounds.

Then there was a faint, rhythmic scraping sound somewhere ahead of them.

It was easy to recognize. Footsteps, probably from more than one person.

A shrill, three-note signal echoed off the rough walls and made them all jump.

'A radio, must be Underground staff!' Jeff growled.

'Back,' Nora said quickly, and started to jog back the way they had come.

'But then we'll run straight into the arms of whoever . . .' Jeff protested.

'Quiet!' she snapped. 'Just keep up . . .'

They set off at a run.

'So you and your friends are planning a rebellion. A little Palace coup . . .' HP hissed.

'Something like that,' Manga replied. 'The Game could still be used in a good way. But we have to cut ties with PayTag and get rid of the current Game Master.'

'Old Sammer?'

Manga flinched and almost stopped.

'You've met him?'

'Last winter, out in the pet cemetery beyond the Kaknäs Tower . . . Becca thinks he's one of Dad's old colleagues. Is he?'

'Here!' Nora suddenly stopped and pointed at the tunnel wall. There was rusty metal hatch hidden between two thick pipes.

Jeff pushed in front of them. From a small holster on his belt he pulled out a multipurpose tool. A few moments later he had the hatch open, revealing a dark hole.

They were hit by a warm gust of fetid underground air.

Nora didn't hesitate, just snaked past the pipes and through the opening.

'Go with her,' Manga said, pointing at the hole. 'Nora will look after you. Jeff and I will stay behind to close the hatch after you. There's another way out through the station at Slussen, with a bit of luck we'll make it in time . . .'

'B-but . . . er, hold on,' HP protested.

'Get moving,' Jeff snarled. 'They'll be here any minute.'

HP gave Manga an angry look.

'You and I have more talking to do . . .'

'Absolutely, I promise, HP. We'll sort everything out, but until then you have to trust me. Now go, for fuck's sake!'

HP hesitated a couple more seconds. The noises from further up the tunnel were clearer now. Heavy steps, probably boots. Voices drifting through the darkness, followed by the unmistakable crackle of a radio. HP took a deep breath, then dived into the darkness.

19

Being Earnest

She should really be asleep.

It was middle of the night, her day had been eventful, to put it mildly, and it was more than an hour since she had taken her sleeping pills.

But in spite of that, she was wide awake.

Her laptop was sitting on the little kitchen table beside a plate holding the remains of the microwaved Gorby pie she had forced herself to have as an evening meal. Thoughts were flying around inside her head.

She no longer knew what to believe.

Uncle Tage's story was pretty astonishing, but at the same time far from impossible. When you looked at all the evidence and threw in a number of other events and indications, it actually held up.

Claim number one: *Dad and André Pellas / Tage Sammer served together in Cyprus.*

The photograph from the safe deposit box and the other one she had found in the book both seemed to support that theory.

Claim number two: *Dad and some colleagues tried to*

smuggle arms in an attempt to stop the losing side from being massacred.

The event itself certainly happened, and if you accepted the fact that Dad served in Cyprus, then the claim could very well be accurate.

Then what?

Dad was supposed to have carried on working for the military in some capacity . . . as a courier who needed fake passports because of the sensitive nature of his work?

That wasn't actually quite as unlikely as she had initially thought. Until very recently, the Cold War had felt very distant to her, the sort of thing you only saw in films and television documentaries.

But back then, in the sixties and seventies, it had been very real indeed.

The post-war period had started to fascinate her more than she liked to admit. A few hours on Wikipedia was all it had taken to get a better idea of what things had been like. Sweden had had one of the largest air forces in the world, with vast underground hangars, like the one out in Tullinge.

There weren't many people, now or then, who doubted the fact that the enemy was off to the east, and Sweden's friends to the west. Sweden had feigned neutrality, but at the same time the National Defence Radio Institute was monitoring the Soviet Union and, in all likelihood, passing the information to NATO. None of this was exactly news, but it wasn't the sort of thing you normally chatted about over coffee, except perhaps the other year when divers found the wreckage of one of the surveillance planes shot down by the Russians over the Baltic Sea.

But the part that fascinated her most was something else entirely, something she'd had no idea about until just a few weeks ago. If it hadn't been for the newspaper cuttings on Henke's bedroom wall she would probably never have made the connection.

Sweden had recently handed over three kilos of plutonium to the USA. According to the official statement, the plutonium had been used in research projects during the sixties and seventies, and since then had been lying hidden in an underground military base, probably somewhere much like the Fortress.

A Swedish project conducting research into nuclear weapons, and then sitting on several kilos of potentially lethal plutonium for something like forty years, sounded utterly incredible. The whole thing must have been top secret!

Apart from recent newspaper articles about the handover, to her surprise she found that Wikipedia had a great deal to say on the matter:

There had been two different threads to the research.

The S-programme was supposed to develop ways of counteracting a nuclear attack. Which seemed entirely logical, given the spirit of the times. She had seen black and white public information films on the Discovery Channel dating from the time of the Cuban Missile Crisis, American schoolchildren diving under their desks.

Duck and cover!

As if that would help . . .

But the considerably more confidential L-programme was a different matter entirely: research into the development of Swedish nuclear weapons. If there hadn't been so much documentary evidence she would have dismissed the whole idea as fantasy. Like that television mockumentary claiming that the 1958 World Cup didn't actually take place in Sweden, or the theory that Neil Armstrong was really bouncing around in a sandpit in a Hollywood studio rather than on the surface of the moon.

267

But the remains of the first test reactor were preserved in the rock beneath the Royal Institute of Technology, pretty much slap bang in the middle of the city. That much was confirmed by the Institute's own website.

A second reactor out at Älta, just outside the city, was intended to develop high-grade plutonium. Just like the Iranians were attempting to do, fifty years on.

But it had turned out to be more difficult than anticipated. So the military had begun to procure plutonium from other sources. And this was where Wikipedia started to get really interesting.

> On 6 April 1960 the US National Security Council decided that American policy would not support Swedish nuclear armament, nor any Swedish programme to develop nuclear weapons, because it was thought more beneficial to the defence of the West against the Soviet Union if Sweden were to devote its limited resources to conventional weapons rather than a very costly nuclear weapons programme.

In other words, the Americans had formally rejected the L-programme. So, no help from them with nuclear weapons. But the following paragraphs made the hair on her arms stand up.

> In spite of the policies outlined in 1960, Swedish representatives in contact with the US military were granted access to confidential information during the 1960s, partly regarding nuclear weapon tactics and the demands these made on surveillance resources and

rapid decision-taking, and partly other data about nuclear physics.

Among other things, Swedish representatives were able to inspect the MGR-1 Honest John missile system, which could be armed with the W7 and W31 nuclear warheads. The USA had also developed the W48 shell to be fired from 155 mm howitzers, with an explosive effect of 0.072 kilotons. No plans for such small-scale Swedish nuclear weapons have ever been found, however.

Honest John.
Earnest John.
John Earnest . . .
John Earnest from Bloemfontein, South Africa, with loads of entry stamps from the US in his passport. And whose photograph was a picture of her dad . . .
That could hardly be a coincidence.

They must have been crawling through the pitch blackness for at least three quarters of an hour.

The floor of the tunnel beneath him was rough, and his hands and knees were protesting increasingly loudly. To the left of him ran a number of thick pipes, and one of them was seriously bloody hot.

He'd already burned his left arm a dozen times, and sweat was starting to drip down his back and face. He could have done with a break several minutes ago, but he had no great inclination to appear pathetic to Nora. If she could do it, then so could he!

He was keeping as close to her as he could, listening out for her movements and breathing in the tunnel ahead of him.

He felt movement over the back of one hand and for a moment he thought he'd got too close to her. Then he realized that it didn't feel like a leather boot, but something damp and furry.

A tickling motion against the inside of his calf make him jerk and bang his arm against the hot pipe again.

'Bollocks!' he yelled.

'Are you okay?'

A faint bluish light appeared ahead of him, then swung round towards him. She was using her mobile phone as a torch.

'A fucking rat,' he muttered. 'I hate rats . . .'

'We can stop for a bit if you like?'

'No, no, it's fine. Let's carry on.'

But Nora seemed to have realized how tired he was. She turned round and sat across the passageway, pulling her legs up and pressing her boots against the hot pipe. Out of her trouser pocket she pulled a tub of chewing tobacco and, without showing the slightest sign of offering any to him, tucked one of the tiny pouches under her lip.

'We probably haven't got far left . . .' She put the tub back in her pocket.

'Where to? The station at Slussen, or what?'

He stretched his stiff limbs and tried to sit in the same position as her.

'I thought that to start with, but the tunnel's curving in the wrong direction. We're heading south. I think we must be getting close to Medborgarplatsen . . .'

'Okay . . . And when we get there, where do we go after that? Where's this flat Manga mentioned?'

'You'll see . . .'

He tried to look hard at her, but the mobile was facing towards him and her face was in shadow. She was actually pretty cool. Clearly the smart one of the group.

Kent Hasselqvist was a pathetic little approval-junkie, and Muscleman Jeff lived up to all his prejudices about tattooed gym-freaks with cropped hair. But Nora was different.

'So, what was your role in the Game?' he said in a tone of voice that was supposed to sound relaxed and not uncomfortably interested.

'I mean, were you a Player or an Ant?' he added rather less confidently when she didn't answer. 'Or some sort of Functionary like Mangelito?'

Still no answer.

'Okay, Greta Garbo. Sorry I asked . . .' he muttered and resumed the crawling position.

'Shall we?' He nodded at the tunnel ahead of them.

She sat still for a moment longer.

Then she shifted round and switched off her mobile.

'A Player, just like you,' she said, and began to crawl away.

Rebecca carried on scrolling down the page. Most of the information seemed to come from the Royal Library, so a visit there felt like a natural next step.

In 1968, four years after her dad was fired from the military and, according to Sammer / Pellas, started work as a consultant, Sweden signed the non-proliferation treaty and gradually began to dismantle its nuclear weapons programme, which officially ended in 1972. But the following section on Wikipedia appeared to contradict that:

However, activities related to nuclear
weapons continued at the National Defence
Research Establishment even after the
dismantling work had been concluded in
1972, albeit on a considerably smaller scale.
(Resources in 1972 were approximately one

third of the 1964-65 level.) Research into
ways of protecting against the effects of
nuclear weapons, unconnected of any
research into active construction or an
independent capability, continued.

All of this fitted perfectly with what Uncle Tage had said. A large, top-secret research project requiring clandestine contact with other countries. A project which was later closed down but continued on a smaller scale, even more secretly than before. Rumbling on below the surface with the tacit approval of those in power.

In 1985, however, a newspaper article attracted a lot of attention and the Palme government suddenly got cold feet. An official investigation was set up, and took two years to conclude that there were no conclusions to conclude seeing as all research into nuclear weapons really had stopped in 1972, just as the government had been claiming all along.

Two years allowed plenty of time to shut things down, cut off all contacts and erase all traces for good. A solution that suited all parties. Or at least *almost* all . . .

If she was right, if the L-programme and its even more secret successor had been Sammer's and, by extension, her dad's project, then this would mean that they were both conclusively removed from it in 1985 or 86.

The safe deposit box contract had been signed in 1986, and that was also the period when Dad began to change. He became bitter, angry – and considerably more violent. Was that when he got hold of the revolver, or had he had it much longer, possibly from Uncle Tage as a form of security?

The nuclear weapons programme was originally under the auspices of the air force, and, in contrast with the army, their personnel were issued with this sort of revolver, .38 calibre.

That would explain why Uncle Tage was so keen to get hold of the gun, apart from wanting to keep it away from Henke.

He wanted to get shot of the revolver for good.

Before it could be traced back to events in the past . . .

Now what had he meant by that?

Then there were his cryptic words towards the end of the conversation that she hadn't really taken in before she was out of the car. Something about *not letting history repeat itself.*

She closed her eyes, rested her head in her hands and massaged her temples.

God, what a story!

'Did you get far up the rankings?' he gasped towards her legs. 'I was first runner up, Player number 128. I was actually in the lead for a while, but I suppose you know all that . . .'

No answer.

She really was playing hard to get . . .

Without any warning Nora suddenly stopped and he almost hit his head on her backside. Not that that would have been a wholly unpleasant experience.

He was about to open his mouth to say something clever when she cut him off.

'Shhhh!'

Now he suddenly noticed the faint light ahead of them.

It was coming through the roof of the tunnel, through some sort of grille or something. There was a vague sound of voices in the distance.

'What time is it?' he hissed.

'Half past five.'

For a moment he thought she meant in the evening. That they had spent a whole day crawling through the darkness. But that obviously wasn't the case. They'd picked him up from Långholmen in the middle of the night, then they'd walked through the tunnel just in time to see the last trains rumble home before the system shut down.

Add a few hours for talking and crawling, and it would soon be time for breakfast.

Nora carried on moving forward carefully, stopping just below the grating. She got up into a crouch and carefully stretched out, reaching towards the light. Her head disappeared from view and for a moment, even though he could see the rest of her body, he felt strangely abandoned.

Then she was back.

'Come on!'

She waved him forward.

'Quick!' she added when he failed to move fast enough.

He crept forward and got up beside her, so close he could feel her breath on his cheek.

'Medborgarplatsen underground station.' She pointed upwards. 'The platform's empty, but the station must be opening any time now because I can hear voices. We have to get up before they let in the morning rush . . .

'Otherwise it would look a bit odd, wouldn't it?' she added, when he didn't seem to get what she meant. 'Two shabby-looking people crawling out of a hole in the ground . . .?'

'Sure, of course,' he mumbled.

God, he was being slow!

She stood up, flicked some sort of catch, and then raised the grating.

She did a little jump and climbed out.

'Here!'

She reached one hand down towards him.

For a moment he considered ignoring it, because

274

obviously he could get himself out of a fucking hole without any help. But his body was completely knackered and he had no desire to get stuck halfway up, like some geek doing circuit training. So he took her hand, pushed off from the floor and jumped towards the hole. She pretty much pulled him out onto the platform.

'Come on, they've started letting people in, I heard someone rattling keys . . .'

She hadn't let go of his hand, and pulled him up on his feet, then dragged him after her towards the middle of the platform.

From the staircase leading down from the entrance at the far end they could hear a metallic sound that seemed to be getting closer. But there was still no sign of any early morning passengers.

Two pairs of legs in blue trousers appeared in their field of vision.

Then weapons belts with jangling handcuffs, followed by blue uniform jackets and two capped heads.

Cops – one male, one female.

Heading straight for them!

Shit!

For a moment he was seized by an instinct to run. But Nora was still holding his hand, forcing him to calm down.

'Pull your hood up,' she whispered, then slowly began to slip towards the nearest flight of steps up from the platform. There seemed to be voices coming from up there.

He did as she said and slowly pulled his hood over his head.

'We'll already be late, get a move on!' someone above them growled.

Presumably the station staff, about to open up.

HP glanced cautiously over his shoulder. The cops were getting closer, gaining on them with every step.

They seemed to be aiming straight for them.

Suddenly he realized how filthy his hooded top was. Dirty stains all over it and brown scorch marks along one sleeve. Nora was in a similar state. It was hardly surprising that the cops seemed interested, they looked like a couple of down-and-outs.

Nora squeezed his hand and he found himself squeezing back. The stairs were still ten metres away, and the cops were much closer than that.

They weren't going to make it. Unless they ran for it . . .

He tensed his body, tried to free his hand and get ready to sprint.

But she wouldn't let go.

Just as the cops caught up with them she pulled him to her, pressed her lips to his and started kissing him hard.

The kiss took him completely by surprise, but after a couple of seconds he got used to the idea and started kissing her back. Her lips and tongue were just as soft as he had imagined, even if the faint but not unpleasant taste of tobacco surprised him.

He put one arm round her lower back and pulled her towards him.

A gust of wind from the tunnel caught her hair, and it tickled him on the cheek.

But he hardly noticed.

'Get a room . . .' the female cop smirked as they walked past.

A few seconds later a train thundered into the station.

People came running down the stairs, forcing their way past them even though the carriage doors hadn't opened yet.

Nora pulled back and let go of his neck and hand.

276

'Here,' she said, fishing a crumpled envelope out of her trouser pocket.

'Take the train out to the Woodland Cemetery, Kent's sorted out a flat there. The key and address are in the envelope. We'll be in touch in a couple of days.'

'Er, okay,' he mumbled, not sure what he was expected to say, or do, for that matter.

'This is your train,' she said with a smile, pointing towards the carriage a metre or so away.

'Er, okay.'

Same words again. He really did have the gift of the gab today. A real ladies' man.

The Woodland Cemetery, of all places. Almost back on home territory. The little basement where the Fenster ran his stolen goods racket, where HP had financed pretty much the whole of his adult life.

He stepped into the carriage and turned round.

For a few moments they stood there looking at each other.

'Fires,' she said just as the doors began to bleep.

'What?'

'You asked what I did for the Game.'

'Right . . .'

The doors slowly started to close.

'I started fires . . .'

20

A Friend

A scarf round her head, big black sunglasses, gloves, and a blue raincoat. Like something out of a fifties magazine, and definitely not her. But, on the other hand, that was the whole point of this little masquerade.

She said hello to the guard in reception and held out her passcard. It was a different man to last time, or at least she thought it was.

'You can go through,' he said once he'd drawn her card through the reader.

'Thanks.'

She carried on to the airlock. The large beach-bag she was carrying over her shoulder was chafing slightly, but she gritted her teeth. She used her card again and tried to stop herself from glancing up at the little round camera in the ceiling.

The plan was simple: open the new locker, put the green metal box in the bag and disappear out of the door, never to return.

There was no time to lose. Sooner or later Stigsson and his henchmen would get hold of the passcard register and join the dots. She couldn't let them find the revolver, because they'd link it to events at the Grand and use it as incontrovertible evidence that Henke really had meant to kill Black. The simplest solution would be to hand the gun over to Uncle Tage, just as she had more or less promised. But right now that thought didn't feel quite so appealing as it had during their conversation in the car. Oh well, she could decide later, once she'd managed to get the revolver out of the bank.

The door at the other end of the airlock opened and she stepped inside the vault.

It looked exactly the same as last time, but just to be sure she stood still beside the door, listening for any sound of other visitors.

Everything was silent, and after a few seconds she headed off down the central passageway.

She walked slowly at first, then speeded up, as if she was afraid she wasn't going to make it in time. The sound of her heels bounced off the walls and created odd echoes in the rooms off to each side of the main path.

As she passed the gate leading to the room containing the old box she couldn't help looking over at it. The hole in the brass door where the lock had once been was clearly visible.

She fought a sudden urge to stop and take a closer look. Instead she carried on, past two more gates until she reached the one with its green lamp illuminated. Her heart started to beat faster and she paused for a couple of seconds to look round. One of the dark, spherical cameras was almost immediately above her head, and she had to make a real effort not to look up.

As soon as she got inside the little room and found the door to her own safe deposit box, she felt much calmer. Everything was okay, the lock was intact and there was no sign that anyone had tried to force it open.

She put the key in the lock, then looked over her shoulder one last time just to be sure. Then she turned the key.

It took several seconds for her to register what she found.

The tin box was gone, and the locker was all but empty. Empty except for the little round object in the middle of it. A small glass sphere, maybe five centimetres in diameter.

She carefully took it out, holding it between her thumb and forefinger. Her right hand suddenly began to shake and for a moment she was worried she was going to drop it.

She quickly switched hands, then held the sphere up to the light and examined it carefully as she tried to get her head round the situation. Everything suddenly felt very unreal, almost dreamlike. She could see right through the sphere as she carefully rolled it between her thumb and forefinger.

At its centre floated a small bubble.

The flat couldn't have been more than twenty-five square metres in size.

A tiny kitchen that reeked of frying, and another room with a spongy cork-matting floor, fitted out with a folding bed from Ikea and a roll of wank paper. Not exactly the Hilton. And it was also hot as hell.

The morning sun was blazing down on the windows, and the roll-blinds seemed to be absorbing the heat rather than deflecting it.

He held up the transparent little pill bottle in front of him and shook it. Five big pills bounced around inside. For what must be the tenth time in the past five minutes, he popped the lid open and pulled one of them out.

Obviously he really ought to clamber out of bed, pour himself a glass of lukewarm water from the wonky tap in the kitchen, and swallow the bastard.

Long overdue too, for that matter, seeing as he'd spent almost twenty-four hours asleep in there, so he was behind on his medication. His head was aching in a rather disturbing way, and in spite of the heat he had found himself shivering a few times.

Yet still he hesitated.

She must have put the bottle of pills in his pocket while they were kissing. That was the only realistic explanation he could think of.

He put the pill back in the bottle, fished out the box of Marlboros he had picked up on the way from the station, and lit one.

I started fires . . .

Nice girl . . .

Really nice . . .

There were a number of fires to choose from. Erman's cottage. Manga's shop. Not to mention his own flat . . . Take your pick, basically . . .

The first time he took one of those horse pills he got ill. He'd had food-poisoning before, but this had felt different, he realized now in hindsight. And his involuntary stomach pump out in the water of Pålsundet had made him feel better almost immediately, which definitely wasn't what usually happened after an overdose of kebabylococcus.

If he hadn't suddenly fallen ill, he'd be a long way away by now. He'd have taken off to the countryside and hidden himself away in a hole deep enough to make Saddam Hussein jealous. But instead he had ended up wandering round Långholmen, feeling like shit until he came up with the bright idea of having a nap on a boat.

And then all they had to do was reel him in, basically.

And now he was here in their flat. Exactly where they wanted him.

And all thanks to Manga.

Fucking bloody Manga, who had obviously shafted him royally. No, *imperially*! But now he was expected to just forget everything that had happened, and swallow the story that he had been doing the Game's bidding the whole time.

FUCK!!

He threw the bottle of pills at the ceiling, where it made a dent in one of the plasterboard tiles before bouncing over towards the front door.

If only he had a computer, he could do a bit of googling and check out some of the details of the shit soup Manga was trying to feed him.

But no, here he was with no broadband, telephone or even a sodding television.

Like a suburban variation of Erman the Hermit.

Ah yes, Erman . . .

The Game Master's little buddy, who was clearly one of the people who used that underground office when he needed to. An outcast who had come in from the cold, and had managed to carve out a place for himself right next to the stove.

If he had ever really been frozen out, of course.

It was through Manga that he had hooked up with Erman in the first place. Manga, who he thought he knew inside out. The same Manga whose first Commodore 64 HP had procured from the Fenster in exchange for three stolen car stereos.

Manga, who always helped out no matter how much you took the piss . . .

Ohforfuckssake . . . !

He flew up from the bed, trying desperately to find something to take his frustration out on, but ended up just pacing up and down the worn floor. His headache got worse with every step.

A decision.

He basically just had to make a decision.

Swallow the pill, and with it Manga's story that he, Nora, Hasselqvist and Muscles were the good guys. That they had formed a resistance group to depose the Game Master.

Or else he didn't buy it . . .

Time to make a decision, Mr Pettersson.

Red

or

Black?

The revolver was gone. Someone had opened her safe deposit box without leaving any trace, and had removed both the gun and the tin box. Apart from her, there was only one person who had known where the gun was. So he had decided not to wait, or, even worse: he didn't trust her.

All bubbles are doomed to burst sooner or later . . .

She took her phone out of her bag, scrolled through the contacts until she found the right number.

'Hi, it's Rebecca,' she said when the voicemail kicked in. 'I know I'm only supposed to call this number in absolute emergencies.'

She paused for a moment and drew a deep breath.

'But I think Henke's in trouble. Really bad trouble, and I'll do anything I can to help him. Anything at all . . .'

The noise made him leap out of bed. At first he couldn't remember where he was, but once he'd figured it out, and what he was doing there, he tried to make sense of the noise.

It had come from the hall. The doorbell, of course.

He took a few cautious steps towards the front door, but before he got to it someone opened the letterbox. He stopped automatically, then took a couple of steps back into the living room.

The flat was on the third floor, too high to jump.

If there was a fire, he was fucked.

'It's me . . .' a voice hissed through the letterbox. 'Kent.'

HP breathed out. He went into the hall and unlocked the door.

Hasselqvist with a Q and a V slipped in and squeezed quickly past him. An acrid burst of nylon-shirt sweat hit HP's nostrils.

'Don't worry,' he said before HP had time to open his mouth. 'I wasn't followed, I pulled every trick in the book.'

He went into the kitchen, poured himself a glass of water and gulped it down.

Then another glass.

'Here,' he panted, putting a supermarket bag on the draining board. 'Thought your supplies were probably starting to run out.'

HP opened the bag.

Milk, baked beans, ready meals, some vegetables and – YES! – cigarettes! Christ, what a relief! He suppressed a sudden urge to kiss Hasselqvist, tore open a pack and pulled out a Marlboro.

'So, what's happening?' He took a couple of deep drags.

Hasselqvist didn't answer, just gave HP a disapproving look.

'If you have to smoke, stand under the extractor fan . . .'

'Sure . . .'

284

HP shrugged, but moved a bit closer to the cooker.

'The others are on their way,' Hasselqvist said. 'They'll be here in the next hour or so. You'll find out more then. Jeff's got a plan to get us into the Fortress.'

'Okay. So you haven't dropped that idea yet . . .'

'Why would we do that? If we can shut down the Fortress, it's all over . . .'

'Yeah, right . . .'

HP took another drag.

'W-what do you mean?'

'Nothing, Kent, we can talk about it later. I'm going to heat up some grub, do you want anything?'

'No thanks, had a hotdog on the way.'

'Okay, your loss . . .'

HP chucked the Findus version of a hamburger into the microwave and blasted it with full force.

'By the way, I'm not pissed off.'

'What?' HP turned round.

'About what happened out on the E4. The tear gas and all that,' Hasselqvist elaborated.

'Okay, that's good . . .'

'I mean, it wasn't really your fault . . . Just wanted you to know.'

'Okay.' HP wasn't sure what he was expected to say.

'After all, it wasn't personal, was it?'

'Nah, course not . . .' HP blew a column of smoke towards the greasy extractor fan.

A short silence ensued.

HP was squirming slightly. He had sprayed Hasselqvist full in the face with teargas, kicked him in the bollocks when he was already on the ground, and, to top it off, had threatened to smash the bloke's skull in. But back then he was Player 58, HP's strongest competition, and someone he suspected of any number of things. Now, in

285

hindsight, things looked very different. If fact he should probably . . . well . . .

'Listen, Kent . . .' he began.

But the ping of the microwave interrupted him.

The dialogue box popped up a few seconds after she switched the computer on. At first she thought it was some sort of automated program update, and clicked the button in the top right-hand corner to minimize it.

But the window stayed open.

She tried again, but when that didn't work she tried closing the programme entirely.

But the window refused to obey. A two-tone bleep rang out, and then a message appeared:

Farook says: Hi Becca, Manga here. I got your message but can't call you back. What's happened?

For a few moments she wasn't sure what to do. The dialogue box didn't belong to any of the usual chat programmes, she was sure of that, so he must have managed to install the programme on her computer remotely. But how had he managed to get hold of her IP address?

A new message appeared:

Farook says: No need to worry, this programme is encrypted and our conversation can't be bugged . . .

Farook says: Tell me, what's happened to HP?

She moved the cursor and clicked inside the little text box, which was now showing her name.

Becca says: How involved in the Game are you?

It took a minute or so for his reply to appear.

Farook says: Who have you been talking to?

Becca says: An old friend.

Farook says: I thought I was an old friend.

Becca says: So did I, Manga . . . ☺

Another pause, slightly shorter:

Farook says: Okay, I deserved that. You're right, Becca, I haven't been honest with you, or HP. I was part of the Game long before he got involved. But everything I've done has been meant to help him. Help you. You have to believe me!

Farook says: You've been talking to Sammer, haven't you?

Now it was her turn to hesitate. Manga was better informed than she had expected. She was rather taken aback. But, considering what Uncle Tage had said about him . . .

Becca says: That's right.

Farook says: Okay, now I can understand why you're worried. He must have told you a whole load of stuff. That I'm one of the people behind the Game, and that HP's in great danger?

Becca says: Is he?

Farook says: I'm not going to lie to you, Becca. HP's in trouble. But we can help him, you and me. If we work together.

Becca says: You lied to me before, pretending you didn't know anything about the Game. Why should I trust you now?

Farook says: Because the alternative is trusting Sammer.

Becca says: And that would be bad because . . .?

Farook says: Because he isn't who he says he is, Becca.

Becca says: And you are?

Another pause, two minutes this time.

Farook says: Sorry, got to go, I'll be in touch again soon. You've got to be careful, Becca. Really careful!!

They arrived just a couple of minutes apart, which made him suspect that they'd actually come together. That Nora had hung about out on the stairs so HP wouldn't work out that they were an item.

He felt like putting a stop to their little performance, and couldn't help wondering what Jeff would think about his girlfriend snogging him in Medborgarplatsen underground station.

'Okay, now we're all here we might as well get going,' Nora said as she hung up her coat. 'Let's sit in the kitchen.'

'What about Manga?' HP muttered.

'He's not coming, too dangerous,' she said, without meeting his gaze. 'But he can still join in . . .'

She pulled a black smartphone from her pocket, fiddled with it for a few seconds, then put it on the windowsill with its screen facing towards them.

'Two more minutes. Can you get the plans out in the meantime, Jeff?'

The mountain of muscle pulled out a bundle of papers from the bicycle bag he had brought in with him, and put them on the table. HP couldn't help seeing the stamp on the front.

Classified information!

'He's online now,' Hasselqvist said.

Everyone looked at the small screen of the smartphone, where Manga's face suddenly appeared.

'Okay, I'm here. I can see you all fine, can you hear me okay?' he said, almost in a whisper.

'We can hear you,' Nora said.

'Good! HP, it's a relief to see you looking a bit better.'

HP didn't answer, and he was gratified to see that this seemed to unsettle Manga.

'Well then, as we discussed before, the Fortress is our target,' Manga went on after a slight pause.

'A company like PayTag can't afford to lose the trust of its clients, and even a rumour that they've been infiltrated will be enough to pull the ground from beneath them forever.

'What we need to do is introduce the trojan I call Big Boy into their system. It's designed both to erase and mess up the information on their servers – to cause as much chaos as possible in the shortest possible time, if you follow?'

The three conspirators in the room nodded, but HP didn't move a muscle.

'It's impossible to implant Big Boy from the outside,' Manga went on. 'Which means that we need a way in. Jeff, you've been looking at the various possibilities . . .?'

Muscles straightened up.

'Yes, Kent and I have been through all the options. Every gate, door and camera, and we've come to the conclusion that the place is extremely well-guarded. . . .'

No shit, Sherlock. Evidently it took two sharply honed minds to come to that obvious conclusion . . . Or else you could just take a look at the plans. The description *High security site – application pending* in one corner ought to give a bit of a clue. These two morons were the perfect poster boys for a campaign against cousins getting married . . .

'HP, you look like you want to say something?' Manga interrupted.

'No, it's nothing,' he muttered.

Muscles gave HP an irritated glance before going on.

'We've concluded that the only way in is through the underground tunnel. It used to carry the cables linking the base to the artillery installations along the coast, but now they've extended it out into the Baltic Sea . . .'

'The Fortress uses the tunnel to bring in cold water . . .' Hasselqvist went on eagerly, digging out some documents from the bottom of the heap.

'Here are the pictures . . .'

All that could be seen were some steep black cliffs and a whole lot of churning seawater.

'The opening is under there, about five metres below the surface. It's probably covered by a grille, but Jeff can get that open . . .'

'I did my military service as a diver, ordnance clearance,' Muscles said in a self-satisfied tone of voice that lowered HP's already lousy mood to new depths.

'I can cut through the grille, then we can swim through the tunnel into a small cold-water reservoir here.'

He pointed at the map.

'From there we probably need to climb four or five metres up the side, and then we blow open a door so we can . . .'

'Hang on a minute . . .!'

He had promised himself that he was going to keep his mouth shut, but it was impossible to hold out any longer.

'I'm mean, I'm sorry to interrupt Batman and Robin here, but underwater welding, diving, a bit of climbing and then blowing a door open – seriously?'

He leaned back in his chair, folded his arms and shook his head very pointedly.

'Someone here has been watching far too many of a certain sort of film . . .'

He grinned at Jeff, and was rewarded with an angry glare.

'HP . . .' Manga began.

'No, no, hang on. I'd love to hear how Jason Bourne the Ordnance-Clearing Diver here is going to explain how we're all going to get past those cliffs and then swim how far? Two, two and a half kilometres through that fucking tunnel?'

'Two point three,' Hasselqvist sighed, earning him another glare from Jeff.

'Thanks, Kent. So, two thousand, three hundred metres of underwater swimming, in total darkness, I'm guessing.

Apart from Jason here, is there anyone else who's got so much as a Open Water certificate from a diving holiday in Thailand?'

No response.

'No? Thought as much. So, if – against all expectation – we don't end up as drowned cats inside the tunnel, we round off our little swim with a bit of free-climbing followed by blasting open a door?'

He grinned and shook his head.

'You're all fucking mad, that's insane . . .'

Jeff opened his mouth as he began to rise from his chair.

But Nora pre-empted him.

'So what would you do, then, HP? I presume you have a brilliant suggestion . . .'

'Sure, just give me a minute to think. Anything would have to be better than that.'

'Good, well you carry on thinking, HP. It wouldn't hurt to have a backup plan. And I have to say I agree with you, at least in part. Underwater swimming doesn't really make sense. Are we sure the tunnel's full of water?'

She turned to Jeff.

'Well, er, it's an underwater tunnel. It says so on the plans . . .'

'Yes, I can see that, but if you look at the elevation here . . .' she pointed at one side of the plans, '. . . then at least the roof of the tunnel is above water level the whole way. Or am I reading it wrong?'

She glanced at Hasselqvist, who leaned over the plans.

'No, you're right, Nora. The inflow is below sea level, but at least half the tunnel is above. Which ought to mean that we can swim instead of diving.'

'Inflatable dinghy,' Jeff muttered. 'We take an inflatable dinghy with us, dive in through the end of the pipe, then blow it up inside the tunnel. Then we wouldn't have to swim . . .'

'Good,' Nora said. 'That sounds much more manageable. Have you got anything to add, HP?'

HP slowly shook his head.

'Okay, let's say that, then. We'll pick you up here the day after tomorrow . . .'

'Okay, okay.'

HP practically had to shove Hasselqvist out of the flat. The other two had already left, a couple of minutes apart. Jeff had hardly said a word after HP complained about his lunatic plan. But it had actually been for everyone's benefit. Him excepted, the gang was made up of cheery little amateurs. If they were going to stand the slightest chance of success, the plan would have to be as simple as possible.

HP couldn't help admiring Nora, and not only because she'd had the good taste to agree with him. It had only taken her a quick look at the plans to discover something that the other two idiots hadn't noticed. It was a bit odd that she and Jeff hadn't discussed the matter before the meeting, but perhaps they hadn't had time.

The way she'd managed to turn his protests into a task was also bloody smart. That way she didn't trample on Jeff's toes too much, at least not right now. But things would be very different once she saw the alternative plan that he was already starting to piece together. All it would take was a couple of little excursions and a visit to the Fenster's basement. He had two days. That ought to be enough.

He locked the door carefully and put the safety chain on.

A sudden noise from inside the flat made him jump. Two little notes, like a text message arriving. He went out into the kitchen. Nora's smartphone was still sitting on

293

the windowsill. The little icon for a received message was flashing on the screen.

He picked up the phone, holding it in his hand for a few moments while he considered what to do. Nora had obviously forgotten it, which probably meant she'd be back shortly. For some reason the idea appealed to him. But on the other hand there was always the risk that she'd show up with her *boyfriend*, Jeff. If they really were an item . . .

There was one easy way to find out. He touched the screen with his finger and opened the inbox. The message was short, just four words.

You must be careful!! / A.F.

Okay, that wasn't exactly what he had been expecting.

No little *where are you?* or *see you at Medborgarplatsen*.

A.F. – who the hell was that? He didn't know Jeff's surname, but his first name didn't fit either of the initials. But maybe they used different names for lovey-dovey stuff . . .

The phone buzzed again and for a brief moment he almost dropped it.

Are you there?

He thought for a few seconds, then pressed the *reply* icon. An empty text box opened up. He paused again.

I'm here, he typed, then pressed *send*.

The reply came almost immediately.

I'm starting to think one of them is playing a double game . . .

He noticed he was holding his breath and forced himself to put the phone down. This wasn't good. Why

294

the hell had he replied . . .? But the message fascinated him.

The sender had to mean their little group, nothing else made sense. So which of them had he meant? Hasselqvist, Manga, or himself . . .?

Another message appeared in Nora's inbox.

Promise me you'll be careful. There's a lot riding on all of you, as I'm sure you appreciate!

Shit, what was he supposed to do now? If he didn't answer, A.F. – whoever that was – would get suspicious.

He hesitated a few more seconds before replying:

I promise!

The answer came by return.

Good!

He breathed out. In the distance he heard the outside door of the building slam. Probably Nora on her way back up. Menu button, *erase conversation*. Perfect!

He'd made it out into the hall when the phone buzzed again. At that moment the doorbell rang.

Best not to look, just open the door and hand the phone over to Nora as if nothing had happened.

Pretend everything's fine, play it cool.

But, on the other hand, reading the message could hardly hurt . . .

As soon as he saw the text he regretted it.

Good luck, HP!

His heart suddenly began to beat so fast he could feel it against his ribs.

Whatthefuck . . .

Who are you? he wrote, without thinking.

The doorbell rang again, followed by a careful knock.

'It's me, open up,' he heard Nora say.

Who are you!!??? he wrote again, pressing so hard that his thumb went white.

But he didn't get an answer.

21

Time bubbles

'Hello, Rebecca here . . .'

'Good morning, Rebecca, this is Uncle Tage.'

'Oh, hello . . .' She tried to hide her disappointment.

'I was expecting to hear from you yesterday, but you never got in touch. Did everything go as planned at the bank?'

'I daresay you can tell me, Uncle Tage . . .'

There was a short silence on the line.

'I don't understand, Rebecca . . .' The surprise in his voice sounded completely genuine, and suddenly she felt unsure. Anyway, hadn't he said that they should avoid direct contact? In which case, what was he doing, taking the risk of phoning her?

Unless . . .

'So you haven't got it, then . . .? The revolver, I mean?'

'I'm sorry?!' His surprise still seemed quite real.

Bloody hell!

She took a deep breath before going on.

'I went to the bank yesterday morning, just as we agreed, but someone had got there before me. The box was empty, all that was in it was a glass ball with a bubble inside it . . . I thought it might have been you . . .?'

Another short silence.

'My dear Rebecca, I think you might be overestimating my powers,' he said in a sombre tone of voice. 'Besides, I would never do anything of that sort to you.'

She shook her head.

'No, I see that now. Sorry, Uncle Tage.'

'So the gun is missing, and we have no idea who has it . . .?'

'Yes, but an idea occurred to me just after I left,' she said. 'The box could only have been emptied within the past few days. Stigsson's team were there recently and seized all the recordings from the cameras. Do you think that you might be able to . . .?'

He seemed to consider this for a moment.

'I'll see what I can do, Rebecca . . .'

His shopping list was almost complete.

Just as he had hoped, the Fenster was still running his little business, and all he'd had to do was disguise himself as best he could and walk a couple of blocks, and he was back among old friends.

He laid everything out on the floor in front of him.

White overalls – check.

Hard plastic rucksacks – check.

Protective masks – check.

Taser – oh yes!!

Sweet!

He ran his fingers over the weapon, which looked like a big remote control with two metal prongs at the end. Pressing the button gently was enough to send a little blue arc dancing between the prongs.

BZZZZT!

Fifty thousand fucking volts, right up the Moomin Valley!

And it fucking hurt, he knew that from experience from

298

the time Philip Argos's little helpers had fried him. But this time he was the one in charge . . .

BZZZT! BZZZT! BZZZT!

He couldn't help trying it out over and over again.

The smell of electricity spread through the flat.

Best plug it in to recharge . . .

He pulled out a large sports bag and carefully began to pack all his equipment away inside it.

There was only one thing missing, albeit a very important one. After that, his backup plan would be complete. All he could do was hope that the Fenster's suppliers would come up with the goods.

The security check surprised her.

No handbags or briefcases, and all your other belongings packed into a transparent plastic bag before you were let in.

As she waited in the queue she took the opportunity to look for cameras. She managed to locate three of them before it was her turn. Dark little spheres up in the ceiling or stuck to the thick stone walls. Exactly the same sort as the ones she had seen in Police Headquarters and down in the bank vault.

'ID,' the woman on the door said.

'What?'

'I need to scan your ID,' the woman said. 'It's the Royal Library's new security policy. You probably heard about the thefts . . .'

Rebecca muttered something and fished out her driving licence. The woman placed it on a flat glass screen set into the counter. There was a flash of light, then a bleep.

'There you go!'

Rebecca put the licence away.

'By the way,' she said as the woman was about to

turn to the next visitor, 'what do you do with the information?'

'Sorry?'

'The data, the information from my driving licence. What happens to it?'

'You'll find a copy of our data policy over there.'

The woman pointed to a notice board and turned away.

All data relating to visitors is stored for security purposes for thirty days before it is purged of all personal details.
The anonymized data is used to help plan our visitor strategy.
The Royal Library does not share information with any third parties.

She couldn't help glancing up at one of the little round cameras in the ceiling. For a moment she thought she could see movement behind the dark glass. She shivered.

Pull yourself together, Normén!

She shook off the sense of unease and carried on into the reading room.

It took her about ten minutes to find the books she wanted. A couple of dry as dust official parliamentary reports, and a thick history book. On her way back to her desk she stopped at the coffee machine.

'The nuclear weapons programme, there's a lot of people interested in that right now! Probably because of that business with the plutonium . . .'

The voice made her jump.

An elderly man in a white shirt, tie, and knitted tank-top was standing behind her. Evidently he had been looking at the books under her arm.

'I'm sorry, I didn't mean to startle you . . .'

'Don't worry,' she mumbled as she got herself a cup.

'Thore Sjögren,' the man said. 'But I'll refrain from shaking hands.' He held up his hands, both of them clad in white cotton gloves.

'It looks like you've already found what you were looking for, but just say if you need any help.'

The man seemed rather too old to work there, but maybe he was a regular. A lonely old bloke keen for a bit of social contact. Well, she didn't have time for that sort of distraction.

'Of course, thanks very much, Thore.' She allowed herself a polite smile, then set off towards her desk.

'It was an exciting time,' he said as he put a coin in the machine. 'Until we got shut down, I mean . . .'

She put her cup of coffee down and turned round. He took his time at the machine, tentatively adjusting his cup in an attempt to keep his white gloves clean.

'Did you work on the nuclear weapons programme?'

He nodded, then blew gently on his coffee.

'Would you mind telling me about it?'

'Of course not.' He looked round. 'I even have a few photographs, if you're interested.'

He held up his passcard to a reader, then held the door open for her. So he did work there after all.

'We want that lift over there.'

He used his passcard in the lift and pressed one of the buttons.

'We're heading for minus three,' he said. 'There are five floors in total. Five library buildings stacked on top of each other, plus the one above ground. Everything printed in Sweden since 1661 is kept here. As soon as anything comes off the printing press – newspapers, journals, books, even audiobooks these days – a copy must be sent here, according to law. It's fantastic, don't you think? Millions

301

of little time bubbles, all with their own stories from the past. But of course Swedes love their time bubbles, have you ever thought about that? In the midst of all this change, all this modern technology that we're so keen to adopt, we still want certain things to remain the way they have always been.'

Rebecca shook her head. The word *bubble* had caught her attention, but she realized that Thore Sjögren's bubbles were quite different to the ones Uncle Tage often mentioned.

'Donald Duck on Christmas Eve, national heats for the Eurovision Song Contest, communal singing at Skansen. Not to mention the royal family. Just look at the fuss everyone is making about the princess's wedding . . . Of course it all requires a huge amount of storage space, the fifth floor is all of forty metres down into the bedrock . . .' Thore Sjögren went on.

Rebecca was only half listening. All this was doubtless very interesting, but right now she had other things on her mind. Why couldn't he just get to the point?

The little man didn't seem to have noticed her lack of interest, and carried on about how much shelf space there was, how many pages. Without even pausing long enough to drink his coffee.

Finally the lift stopped and they emerged into a long, well lit corridor. The dark globe of the camera in the ceiling was unmissable . . .

'My little cubbyhole is at the far end,' Thore said, gesturing with his free hand towards the other end of the corridor.

He set off, and she followed a metre or so behind him.

A strange little character, slightly shorter than her. Thin grey hair arranged in a neat side parting. Reading glasses on a cord round his neck. Tank-top, white shirt and tie, even though it must be thirty degrees outside, and then those white cotton gloves.

His clothes accentuated the impression that he was a cosy little old uncle. But it only took her a few seconds to notice that his neatly ironed shirt collar was worn and frayed, and that his well polished shoes could have done with new heels a while back. The sense of creeping but inevitable decay suddenly made her feel rather depressed. She'd seen this before, at close quarters.

Dad. Everything seemed to begin and end with Dad.

Thore Sjögren pointed to a double door just ahead of them on the right.

'And in there is the apartment . . .' he whispered.

'What?'

He stopped and turned round.

'The apartment. Nelly Sachs's apartment, exactly as it was when she died. Down to the very last detail. The ultimate time capsule or bubble. Fascinating, don't you think?'

He pointed towards the double doors again.

'Just the way it was when she died.'

Rebecca nodded, not entirely sure what she should say. But this time he seemed to pick up on her cool response.

For a moment it looked almost as if the little man was blushing.

'But the story of Nelly Sachs actually has some connection to the subject that interests you.'

He stopped at a small door, pulled out a key and unlocked it.

'Please, do go in, Nelly . . . No, no, of course I mean Rebecca . . .' he quickly corrected himself.

She stepped inside. The room was little more than ten square metres in size, and the slightly claustrophobic atmosphere made her think almost immediately of the interview rooms in Police Headquarters. Most of the space was taken up by a desk covered with papers, some bulging bookshelves along one side, and two office chairs.

The little man closed the door behind her. The thick concrete walls seemed to absorb the sound, making it sound muffled.

'Well, as I was saying,' Thore went on. 'Nelly Sachs became a Swedish citizen in 1952, the same year that we started to build the first nuclear reactor in the bedrock below the Royal Institute of Technology. Please, sit down . . .'

He gestured to one of the chairs.

'In 1966, the year she got the Nobel Prize, Sweden signed the non-proliferation treaty where we promised to stop work on developing an atomic bomb of our own, and by the time she died in 1970, the shut down was well underway. Two years later almost everything had been dismantled and closed down . . .'

'But not quite everything . . .' Rebecca added quickly.

He gave her a long look, and took a first sip of his coffee.

'No, you're right. Part of the project continued. It was called defence research . . .'

'But it was actually something completely different?' she said.

He shook his head slowly.

'You shouldn't believe everything you read on the internet, my dear . . .'

He patted the lid of a folded laptop, a fairly old model, that was sitting in the middle of the desk.

'Their activities were severely restricted, and limited to defence research.'

'I see. So what was your role, Thore?'

'I was a research assistant in what was known as the

L-Project, trying to produce plutonium – without much success.'

She glanced at her watch.

He suddenly stood up.

'But forgive me, my dear, can I offer you something else? A little mineral water, perhaps?'

He leaned down and opened a small cupboard in one of the bookcases, from which he conjured up a bottle of Ramlösa and a glass.

She opened the bottle with the opener he gave her, poured a glass and drank it in silence. The bubbles stung her tongue and she was starting to get a very strong feeling that she was wasting valuable time.

'Now, let's see, photographs . . . most of my papers are here. Maj-Britt didn't want them at home. I was thinking of writing a book . . .'

He shuffled the piles of paper on his desk, evidently looking for something. High time to get to the point, before he started up again:

'Thore, did you ever work with anyone called Erland Pettersson?'

No reaction, he didn't even look up, which actually felt like something of a relief. But at the same time it didn't.

'Or Tage Sammer?'

Still no response.

'No, I'm afraid neither of those names sounds familiar . . .' he muttered as he stood up and went over to the files in the bookcase at the other end of the room.

She was close to swearing out loud with relief and disappointment. Then another name occurred to her.

'What about André Pellas?'

He stopped.

'You know him, don't you?' She could hear how eager she sounded.

'Well, I didn't know him, I was aware of him . . .
Lieutenant Colonel Pellas was a section head in the
programme . . .'

'Which one, which section?' She was fighting a spon-
taneous urge to leap up from her chair.

'They were called the I-Group. I think that meant
Information and Intelligence, but I'm afraid my memory
isn't quite what it used to be . . .' He shook his head.

'And what was their role in the programme?'

'I don't really know. But there was a monthly report,
where we would register problems that had arisen.
Instances where we had ground to a halt entirely used to
be marked with a large 'I'. A week or so would pass, and
then we would be given a detailed description of what to
do in order to solve the problem. The report would be in
Swedish, but every now and then you could tell that it
had been translated from English. It was mostly just a
feeling, certain words and expressions . . . of some sort.
We would get advice from the I-Group on various problems we had with the project, and it was clear the reports
were written in collaboration with non-Swedish experts.'

'The Americans?'

'That's the logical answer. Even if the politicians might
have liked to suggest the opposite, there had been strong
military ties between Sweden and the USA ever since the
war. The American OSS, the forerunners of the CIA, for
instance, financed secret military activities along the
northern part of the Norwegian border. The main purpose
wasn't to fight the Nazis, but to have troops ready once
the Germans had withdrawn. To prevent any potential
Soviet annexation of Norway,' he clarified. 'The operation
would never have been possible without the help of the
Swedish military and intelligence services . . .'

He broke off mid-sentence and smiled apologetically.

'I'm sorry, my dear, I've wandered off the point once again, but I was trying to show that Swedish and American militaries had been cooperating, albeit unofficially, long before our project began . . . and it would never have been possible in the first place without the help of the Swedish military and intelligence services . . .'

She nodded.

'Do you know what happened to the I-Group later, after 1972?'

He paused for a few seconds as he drank his coffee.

'Like I said, the project was shut down, and the military personnel were transferred to other duties. Those of us who were civilians had to try to find work elsewhere. Very sad, of course, so many dedicated colleagues, so much work just abandoned. All in vain . . .'

He sighed.

'I myself moved to Västerås and got a job at ABB as an automation engineer. I was there until I retired. They were a fantastic company to work for, so you could say that it turned out for the best in the end. You see, we developed processes that . . .'

He carried on, but she was no longer listening to what he was saying.

She had been right. Uncle Tage *had* worked on the nuclear weapons programme, handling the exchange of information with the Americans.

'Now, let's see . . .'

Thore Sjögren took out an envelope and spread its contents across the desk. Photographs, most of them black and white, but a few in colour. Judging by the clothes and hairstyles, most of them were taken in the sixties and seventies.

'My wife, Maj-Britt,' he muttered, putting down a photograph of a smiling, sun-burned woman in a sundress sitting at a table in a restaurant.

'She passed away three years ago . . .'

'I'm sorry . . .'

He went on looking through the pictures.

'Here!'

He laid out several black and white pictures. Typical group shots that could have been from any business. Lots of sombre men in suits, some in white coats. Sixty or seventy of them in total, lined up in three rows on a broad flight of steps.

'That picture was taken in 1966 or 67, I seem to recall . . . That's me.'

He pointed to a young man with a side parting in the middle row. The resemblance was striking.

'Young and fashionable,' he laughed. 'These days I've only got the *and* left . . .'

He ran his finger across the rows of faces.

'There,' he said, but she had already spotted him.

Back row, third from the left. Suddenly she felt sick.

'Colonel Pellas,' he said, pointing, but she was staring at a different face altogether.

Her father's.

22

And those we've left behind

They were standing in a clearing among the trees. Even though it was dark and he was a long way off at first, he had no trouble recognizing them. The old man with the stick, straight-backed.

Beside him Manga's slouched silhouette. Steam was rising from their coffee cups.

As he approached them through the snow he gradually noticed more people in there among the trees. Dozens, possibly even hundreds of silent silhouettes that seemed to be watching him. He could feel the snow crunch beneath his feet, but oddly enough there was hardly any sound. The two men now had company in the clearing. Four more figures, all in white Guy Fawkes masks, with painted, curling moustaches and goatee beards.

'Welcome, Henrik,' the Game Master said when he stepped into the clearing.

'Would you like some coffee?' Manga held out a plastic cup towards him, and he took it without saying a word.

'Who are they?' He nodded towards the four people in masks.

'Don't you know?' the Game Master chuckled.

'Two of them are completely uninteresting, but the other two could turn out to be vitally important.'

The first of them took a step forward and held out his hand. In spite of his bulky winter clothes, it was possible to make out the square, muscular body. They shook hands.

'Friend?' HP asked, but received no answer.

The next person stepped up.

'Enemy?' he asked.

Still no answer.

The third person was a woman, he was sure of that.

'Friend?' he asked again.

For a moment he thought she shrugged her shoulders.

He held out his hand towards the fourth figure, but the person leaned towards him instead and whispered something in his ear. The voice was so familiar, so sad, that it actually felt painful.

'The Luttern labyrinth,' she whispered. 'You have to save us. The Carer . . .'

A raven croaked in the distance. Twice, in an ominous way that sent a shiver down his spine. The shadowy figures in amongst the trees suddenly began to move. They stumbled towards the clearing like dark-clad zombies. And all of a sudden he realized who they were . . .

'More,' they hissed.

'MOOOORE!!!'

A moment later he was running. Snow was flying around his feet, his heart pounding in his chest.

The lights from the road lay far away on the horizon.

'See you in the Luttern labyrinth, number 128 . . .' the Game Master called after him. Unless it was actually Manga's voice that he had heard . . .?

Rebecca emerged onto the steps library and took a few deep breaths.

310

The fresh air made her nausea subside and after a couple of minutes she felt considerably better.

She could think. About the nuclear weapons programme; the betrayal of the Palme government. Dad's violent rages. The safe deposit box in Sveavägen, set up in 1986. The wide-bore revolver with its two fired cartridges that made Uncle Tage so uneasy. Which mustn't be traced to . . .

Events in the past . . .

1986.

Dad's rages.

The revolver is an OPW, an Olof Palme Weapon.

She took her mobile out of her bag. Her fingers didn't seem to want to do as she told them, and it took two attempts before she managed to tap in the correct pin-code.

The email from Uncle Tage arrived almost at once, but it took another minute for the attached file to download. A black and white recording from the bank vault, lasting thirty-two seconds, which must have come from one of the cameras in the corridor.

The man walking down the corridor before turning off into the room containing her box was wearing sunglasses and had a baseball cap pulled down over his face.

But she didn't have any problem recognizing him.

It was Manga.

Bloody hell, he'd been having some creepy fucking night-mares. Last time they'd been caused by the snake venom, and this time by the pills, at a guess. They were meant for horses, not people, which probably explained quite a lot.

The long wait in the flat was driving him mad. No Xbox, Playstation or any other games console to while away the time with, and all he'd managed to come up with by way of television was a huge old box with just the basic channels. He couldn't handle any more *Emmerdale* or *Days of Our Lives*, and he'd already had two anxiety-driven wanks, and a third was guaranteed to give him friction burns on his joystick. But, as luck would have it, at least he had a decent supply of cigarettes.

He lit yet another Marlboro and set off on his little stroll round the flat. Living room, kitchen, hall – then back again.

A few seconds' respite, to give him time to think.

One of the gang was supposed to be a traitor, if he was to trust the mysterious A.F. who had sent him the message – through Nora's smartphone.

A.F.

Friend?

No-one outside their little group knew that Nora's phone had been in the flat he was borrowing. So, logically, A.F. should also to be one of the group.

A friend.

An enemy.

The problem was that no-one could be ruled out.

Jeff had hated him since the incident in Birkagatan, and their relationship had hardly improved over recent days.

Hasselqvist with a Q and a V may have declared that bygones were bygones, but that could very easily be a complete lie. He had demolished the guy out on the E4. Sprayed teargas in his face, humiliated him, and snatched his End Game away from him.

You didn't forget an injustice like that, not even if you were an obsequious little Kent.

Nora was harder to make out. She had evidently been behind the fires, probably both the one that almost killed him up in his flat, and the smaller one in Manga's shop.

And he hadn't entirely dropped the idea that she might have poisoned him with those pills.

The last name on the list was his old friend, Farook Al-Hassan, a.k.a. Magnus Sandström.

Good old mythomaniac Manga who, with the blessing of the Game Master, had stuffed him so full of lies that he couldn't even begin to work out how much of everything he had experienced over the past two years was actually real.

All in all, not a bad collection of suspects – good luck with that case, Columbo!

So, why not just stay at home? Why take the risk of getting involved in this lunatic project? Yep – another two questions that he had no good answer to . . .

Peter Falk would obviously have to put in a bit of overtime.

Rebecca reached the bottom of the escalator just as the warning signal went off, and she made it inside the jam-packed underground train seconds before the doors closed.

Sweaty tourists, most of them with bum-bags, caps and bottles of water, so they were probably Americans. She found herself in the middle of a group of people, with nothing to hold onto.

Someone pushed into her from behind and she tried to move as far as she could to one side.

To judge by the noise, at least the air conditioning seemed to be switched on, but, together with the sound of the train, it made it hard to hear what anyone was saying.

The person behind her pushed again, and she was just about to turn round and explain that she couldn't move any further when she heard a familiar voice in her ear.

'Don't turn round!'

'Manga, what the f . . .?'

She glimpsed a baseball cap and pair of sunglasses from the corner of her eye.

'No, no, for fuck's sake, don't turn round . . .!' He put his hand on her back.

'Okay.' She went on staring in the opposite direction.

This was ridiculous, to put it mildly, and if he hadn't sounded so worried she would have ignored his plea.

'I've sent you something,' he whispered. 'Read it and you'll understand how everything fits together . . .'

'Really, Manga, this is completely . . .' She turned her head.

'No, no, you mustn't turn round. They're watching you, *he's* watching you!'

'Who is, Manga? Who's watching me?'

'Sammer, of course!' His voice sounded scared.

'And why would he be doing that, Manga? As far as I can work out, he's got his hands full looking for you. I daresay he'd be quite pleased if I brought you together . . .'

The carriage lurched and for moment she almost fell, but the tightly packed bodies around her helped her stay upright.

'Don't make jokes about that, Becca,' he said quietly.

'I'm not joking, Manga. Henrik's already tried to convince me that Uncle Tage is the Game Master, so now it's your turn. But, unlike the two of you, Tage Sammer has actually *helped* me, he's saved my skin a couple of times . . .'

The loudspeaker announced a station that she didn't catch the name of, and the train began to slow down.

'Besides, you've got something of mine, Manga,' she said.

'W-what?'

'Don't act all innocent. The bank vault on Sveavägen. You stole a metal box that belonged to my dad out of my safe deposit box. I saw a clip of you . . .'

'I don't know what you're talking about, Becca,' he said, a little too quickly. 'Let me explain . . .' He leaned closer to her ear. 'The Game is like a Rorschach test, those ink stains, you know? The brain comes up with its own interpretation and then fills in the gaps itself. You only see the things you want to see, Rebecca . . .'

The train pulled in at the platform, braking sharply, and once again she almost fell.

The doors opened and people pushed past her in all directions.

Once she'd regained her balance and looked round, he was gone. It was several minutes before she discovered the mobile phone he'd slipped into her pocket. A smooth, silvery thing with a glass touch screen.

23

Spheres of reality

She had most of the puzzle worked out now.

Or at least she thought she did. Her dad, André Pellas, the nuclear weapons programme, the safe deposit box, Tage Sammer . . . Everything was connected, and the chain could be made even longer if you added the unthinkable: the revolver, Sveavägen and Olof Palme . . .

For the time being she was trying to keep a grip on her galloping imagination. She went on reciting the chain that she had started putting together a few days ago:

Dad and André / Uncle Tage work for the UN together.

Dad is unfairly dismissed for an action he believes is justified.

Uncle Tage employed Dad on the secret nuclear weapons programme. Sent him on secret missions to the USA to exchange information with the Americans. This carried on for years, long after the defence project was officially shut down. Until a newspaper starts snooping about in the mid-1980s. Then everyone panics, the project is buried once and for all, and without warning Dad was shoved out into the cold again, like he'd been shoved out of the UN . . . everything he believed in ended up in the bin.

And it's all the fault of the Palme government . . .

The nausea that had been stalking her since she had seen the photograph of her dad in Thore Sjögren's claustrophobic little office wouldn't go away. She got up from the sofa and went over to open the window. The street below was dark, no movement at all. The crowns of the trees opposite made it impossible to see more than ten metres into the park. For a few moments she imagined she could see someone standing down there in the shadows, someone watching her. She knew it was just her imagination, but she still couldn't help drawing one of the curtains before she went back to the sofa and her laptop.

It only took a minute or so to dig out the description of the suspect on Wikipedia:

A man, acting alone and suffering from a personality disorder, who is driven by his hatred of Palme. He has probably had difficulty forming relationships all his life, particularly with anyone in positions of authority. He is introverted, lonely and mentally unstable, but not psychotic. His condition is closely connected to the fact that he feels he has 'failed' in life. Adversity makes him depressed, and this has developed into paranoia. When and if people of this sort begin to commit violent crimes, they are usually between 35 and 45 years old . . .

In 1986 Dad was 45 years old. Motivated, disappointed, a failure and paranoid. And the sort who never forgot an injustice, real or imagined.

Never, ever . . .

317

All that was needed was a gun, an OPW. And a bit of help . . .

Because what if he wasn't alone? What if he got a gentle shove in the right direction from someone he trusted? A phone call, information about a time and a place. Maybe that was all it would have taken? Maybe Dad thought he was being given another chance? That he was going to be part of something bigger once more, where his services were still in demand. That he was still a Player.

Back in the Game.

History repeats itself . . .

But there was something that wasn't right, a little piece of the puzzle that didn't quite fit. The only problem was that she couldn't work out which piece.

The white van climbed over the brow of a hill, then pulled up in a small paved yard surrounded on two sides by a ramshackle L-shaped farm building.

'This is it.'

Nora gently put her hand on HP's shoulder, but he'd woken up a while back, when the van turned off the tarmac and onto the narrow gravel track.

The sliding door of the barn was already open and Hasselqvist backed the van in with millimetre precision. Manga's little red Polo was already parked inside.

Jeff jumped out quickly and closed the barn door behind them. HP took his time getting out of his seat. He double-checked the lock on the sports bag he had put on the floor, then stretched and breathed in the ingrained smell of cows and old hay.

It took a while for his eyes to get used to the gloom.

In one corner of the barn he could see several large white plastic sacks, and beside them a row of pallets full of old tyres, a couple of oil-drums and random clutter. A

318

bit further away stood a bit of rusty agricultural machinery. The place looked like it hadn't been used for the past ten, fifteen years.

Maybe longer than that.

'Hello, and welcome!'

'Hi,' he muttered, without looking Manga in the eye.

'Follow me . . .'

Manga skirted round a couple of stalls to reach a door at one end of the barn. The others followed him, with HP bringing up the rear.

'Just mind your feet, the floor isn't that great.'

Manga opened the door and they headed down a short corridor to a small kitchen.

The room smelled of fresh coffee and damp.

HP had a sudden flashback to Erman's little cottage out in the bush. But that had been in a considerably better state than this place. Old wallpaper was peeling off the walls, and in a couple of places water had come through the yellowing ceiling. Here and there the floorboards had given way, revealing dark holes. A camping table with five folding chairs had been set up in the middle of the room.

'So this is where you've been hiding,' HP muttered, pointing at the camp bed and sleeping bag in one corner. 'Has Betul chucked you out then, or what?'

Manga shrugged his shoulders.

'Right now it's safest like this . . .' he said. 'There's coffee, if anyone wants any . . .'

He took a paper cup and got himself some coffee from the thermos in the middle of the little table. While the others followed his example Manga sat down. He took out a small laptop, opened it up and then turned it so that everyone could see what was on the little screen.

'Okay, everything's ready. Operation Puncture starts in exactly . . .'

He looked at his watch.

'. . . nine hours, twenty-seven minutes and eleven seconds . . .'

Everyone except HP adjusted their watches.

'We'll take the van, and leave my car here.'

'No, we'll need both . . .' Jeff interrupted him in an authoritative voice. 'I did a recce. The last bit by the cliffs is just a soft forest track, and the van will get stuck. Unless we want to carry everything the last five hundred metres, we'll have to load it all into the Polo. It's a lot lighter, and it's front-wheel drive, so there shouldn't be any problems there.'

'But, er . . .' Manga sounded like he was trying to protest, then changed his mind. 'Okay, that's what we'll do. Good thinking!'

He nodded at Jeff, who smiled with satisfaction.

'Let's go through the whole thing one more time,' Manga went on. 'Then I suggest that we get changed and make sure we're familiar with everything, say for half an hour before we set off. But we have plenty of time to kill. It's an hour and fifty-three minute drive from here, then twenty minutes to unload. If anyone wants to take a walk, there's a lake round the back. And there are sandwiches and cold drinks in the fridge over there . . .'

He pointed to one corner.

'The toilet doesn't work, but there's an old outdoor privy behind the farm.'

'Ah, old-school shithouse . . .' HP grinned, but got no response.

Humourless tossers!

But what the hell . . . He had seven hours to work out who in here was a friend and who an enemy. It would be just as well to make a start.

He had a whole load of mysteries to unravel, and not just concerning the gang he was with.

Who was the Carer? And what was the Luttern labyrinth, where it looked like the bomb was going to be placed? Who was it going to be aimed at?

And, maybe most important of all: how did Becca fit into all of this?

The letter was lying on her doormat beside the morning paper.

A window envelope with her name on, and at first she thought it was a bill. So she didn't open it until she had poured a cup of coffee and sat down on the sofa. But when she opened the envelope she found that it contained something very different. The sheet of A4 with her name at the top consisted of just two lines. The first was the address of a web page. The second contained two sad smileys.

Manga. It could hardly be anyone else.

Taking the letter with her, she went and sat in front of the computer, typed in the web address and pressed enter.

A log-in window with boxes for username and password appeared. After a bit of hesitation she typed in her full name in the top line. But she had no idea what password the page wanted. She turned the envelope inside out, but couldn't find any clues.

Manga, she finally wrote, and pressed enter.

Wrong password, the site informed her.

Shit!

She tried again, this time with *Henke* as the password.

Wrong password, one attempt left.

Only one more chance.

She went out into the hall to check that she hadn't received another letter containing the login details. But there was nothing there.

Just to make sure, she read the letter again, holding

both it and the envelope up to the light in an attempt to see if there were any hidden messages.

But the only unusual thing she found was that the sender had spelled her first name with 'ck' instead of 'cc'.

Surely Manga of all people ought to be able to spell her name?

Unless . . .

She typed *Rebecka* into the password box and pressed enter. The window changed colour and suddenly she was in.

The site looked like a Wikipedia page, in fact was so similar that it was hard to see the difference. But she was pretty sure this particular page wasn't available on the online version.

The Game
also known as the Circus, the Event or the Performance – is the name of a secret military project that was set up in the USA, probably sometime during the 1950s.

The Game was originally a subordinate part of the so-called MK-ULTRA Project which was established to conduct research into various forms of brainwashing and mind control (see also *Manchurian candidate*).

Unlike the MK-ULTRA Project, which used different types of drug and compulsion to force its subjects to act in certain ways, the researchers involved in the Game applied a diametrically opposite methodology.

By using various forms of powerful positive stimuli, including affirmation, praise and idolatry, researchers successfully encouraged many of their subjects to carry out actions which they had declared at the outset of the experiment that they would never do.

In the Game, the research subjects – who all demonstrated narcissistic personality characteristics – were placed in different types of scenario suited to their individual psyches.

Some were led to experience the feeling of taking part in a sporting occasion, others of being in a film or a significant political event. What all the subjects had in common was that they were treated like stars, and that they were manipulated into believing there was a large audience watching and admiring their actions and following every step they took.

By enhancing the test subjects' exaggerated self-image in various ways, and making them the central characters in a larger context, the researchers soon managed to persuade many of them to shift their boundaries voluntarily and carry out numerous dramatic actions.

Some members of the military personnel connected to the project even began to bet on how far each test subject would be prepared to go, hence the origins of the name the Game.

Both MK-ULTRA and its subsidiary projects were shut down in the 1970s, but there is evidence to indicate that the Game escaped and developed a life of its own.

This evidence suggests that the Game, led by an individual known as the Game Master, has used various forms of advanced psychological manipulation to persuade apparently ordinary people to carry out inexplicable and occasionally drastic tasks. The same sources indicate that the Game has recruited a cadre of assistants, so-called Ants, to provide information and carry out simpler tasks. They prepare the ground for the more active participants, who are known as Players.

There are several well-known events which are occasionally attributed to the Game, including murders, arson, sabotage or theft, but, as with most other conspiracy theories, there is a lack of conclusive evidence . . .

This absence of proof is believed to be the result of the Game devoting much of its energy to ensuring that it remains hidden. As a result, this very lack of evidence is – paradoxically – taken by some as an indication in itself of the existence of the Game.

Rebecca read the page three times, then did a screen-dump and printed out several copies.

It all fitted perfectly with Henke's fragmentary descriptions and her own observations, but also with the information that Uncle Tage had confided to her.

There really was a Game, which manipulated people into carrying out various acts. Which could incite people to do completely insane things.

Poor, self-obsessed fools who didn't think the world properly appreciated their unique talents and significance, and were prepared to do almost anything to get a bit of approval.

People just like Henke.

And her dad . . .

But whose version of the story was the right one?

Uncle Tage had helped her, in the aftermath of events in Darfur when she was under suspicion of gross misuse of office, but also with the weapons licence and, most recently, the recording from the bank vault.

He had told her about her dad's dark past, and – even though she'd had to drag it out of him – he had finally revealed more confidential information to her than he should have.

On the other hand, she had known Manga all her life, and the idea that he might be a criminal mastermind still felt unreal, to put it mildly. But Manga had demonstrably lied to her face, and had admitted as much himself. All he had given her was the information on the webpage, information which didn't actually prove anything.

So whose version was true?

Who could she trust?

Which of them could help her rescue Henke?

She leaned back in the sofa and went through everything that had happened in the last few days once more, but she still couldn't shake the feeling that she was missing something.

Even though it was the middle of summer, the wooden seat still felt ice-cold on his arse.

The planks of the toilet door had shrunk, and let in enough light for him to see the earwigs running about at the foot of the door.

Jeff and Hasselqvist had got busy with the equipment immediately after the run-through. He had hoped to get a private chat with Nora, but she seemed to prefer hanging out with Manga in the kitchen. So mother nature got his undivided attention instead.

It was actually pretty sweet, taking a dump outside, at least in the summer. Obviously there was no toilet paper, but there was a bundle of old newspapers that would probably do the job. And – handily – they also fulfilled his almost obsessive need to read something while he took a crap.

Upsala Nya Tidning. Uppsala's new newspaper . . .

Well, this one was from 1986, so it wasn't that new any more.

33-year-old released from custody
Police: no comment

The 33-year-old . . . Wasn't that the first bloke arrested for Palme's murder? Ended up getting shot in the States, if he remembered rightly . . . Speaking of the USA, PayTag were devious bastards. Together with the Game Master, they'd managed to fuck him over more than once, getting him tortured in Dubai, then using him to sink ArgosEye so that they could turn the merry widow, Anna Argos, into their new superstar . . .

And what had he got in return?

A couple of million as a sticking plaster, but that was probably loose change for a company like PayTag. A shitty little accounting error!

And now they'd spent the past few weeks trying to break him, and had come pretty fucking close to succeeding. And now every police force in Sweden was looking for him . . . So why the hell was he stupid enough to consider sticking his head into the lion's den again?

Well . . .

Revenge was obviously one motivation, and a fucking strong one at that.

Just the thought of the look on the Game Master's face

when their main sponsor suddenly discovered a spoke in their wheel was worth the risk. He, Black and Anna Argos all in the same room, shouting at each other. So fucking sweet!

But there were other factors.

The excitement.

The thrill of the chase.

Besides, he had a whole load of mysteries to unravel, and not just concerning the gang he was with.

Who was the Carer? And what was the Luttern labyrinth, where it looked like the bomb was going to be placed? Who was it going to be aimed at?

And, maybe most important of all: how did Becca fit into all of this?

She's sitting in the passenger seat.

Dad's driving, Mum and Henke are in the back.

They're weaving through a maze of narrow streets, and only when she sees the huge church on the hill to their left does she realize where they are.

Döbelnsgatan, next to Johannes Church, on their way up the Brunkeberg ridge in Stockholm.

Henke is no more than six or seven years old, and he's making a fuss in the back seat. Mum's trying to keep him quiet, telling him it's not far now. Dad says nothing, but she can see his jaw clench.

Henke whines, and she turns round to help Mum.

That's when she sees him.

He's standing completely still a short way into the darkened churchyard, and seems to be watching them as the car slowly glides past. In one hand she can make out the glow of a cigar. In the other he is holding a stick. Without really knowing why, she raises her hand to wave.

'Do you know John Earnest, Rebecca?' her Mum asks gently.

'Quiet!' Dad suddenly roars, and Henke starts crying.

'Make him shut up, for God's sake!' She sees his knuckles turning white on the steering wheel. Mum shouts back something that she doesn't hear.

She raises her hands and presses them to her ears.

But the voice goes on whispering inside her head.

Do you know John Earnest, Rebecca?

The car carries on through the slush, and suddenly she realizes where they're going.

As they reach the top of the hill and Döbelnsgatan turns into Malmskillnadsgatan, the scenario suddenly changes.

Now it's her adult self sitting behind the wheel.

The sound of Henke crying is still coming from the back seat, but when she looks in the rear-view mirror she sees Tage Sammer's face instead.

'Forward, Rebecca, not backward. You have to look forward,' he says in a tone of voice that's so sad it pains her heart.

And, just as she looks back at the road, he's suddenly there, right in front of the bonnet. A man dressed in a dark jacket with the collar turned up around his face. He must have come up the steep steps off to the right. The steps that lead down to Tunnelgatan, where a prime minister is lying, dying.

She slams on the brakes, the wheels lock and the car carries on sliding forward through the slush.

Straight towards the man.

Henke's crying is turning into a scream.

She releases the brakes, then slams them on again.

Trying to get a grip.

But it's hopeless.

The man turns his head, holds his hand towards her, as if to protect himself. Then she sees the revolver in his other hand.

328

'Daddy, noooo!!' Henke screams.
Or is she the one who says it?
Then she hears another voice, far away.
It's calling her name.
Rebecca, Rebecca.
And the very moment she wakes up, she finally realizes
what it is that's wrong.
The name.

She lay still on the sofa for a few minutes, thinking, fitting the new information into everything she had been through over the past few days.

Then she got up, fetched her mobile and scrolled through the contacts until she found the right number.

'It's me,' she said as soon as the man at the other end answered. 'I think I understand how it all fits together now. Dad, Henke, the Game – everything.

'Just tell me what you want me to do!'

24

Corporate invasion of private memory

He'd just taken the first drag of his morning cigarette, and was on his way round the corner of the barn when he heard their voices and stopped abruptly.

'He can't be trusted, don't you get that?' Jeff snarled. 'He's way too involved, he's done too much . . .'

'Like me, you mean?'

Nora's voice, just a metre or so away.

HP pressed against the wall and pricked his ears.

'That's different. This guy's got no scruples at all.'

Ah, so the loving couple didn't trust Manga either, or at least one of them didn't. Maybe he'd have to upgrade Jeff a bit, the bloke clearly wasn't as stupid as he looked.

'Everyone deserves another chance, Jeff. Besides, we need him.'

'I have no problem giving people a second chance, Nora, but they have to show some sign of regret first. Show they've changed. But he still doesn't think of anyone but himself, don't tell me you haven't noticed that?'

HP couldn't help grinning. A lovers' tiff out here in the bush . . .

'You're just annoyed because he spray-painted your door . . .'

HP's smile died instantly.

'I had to spend seven hours in A&E because of that, if you remember?'

'Yes, and I really do appreciate you doing this for me, Jeff . . .'

HP pulled a face. As if it wasn't enough that it was him they were talking about, Nora's voice also had a tender quality that he didn't like.

'I'll always be grateful to you for helping me. Without you I'd still be stuck in the Game . . .' she continued.

Then there was a short silence, and HP suddenly got the feeling they'd realized he was eavesdropping on them.

But then she went on.

'You know this is important. Not just for me, but for everyone they've exploited and are still exploiting. If we can do this, then it's all over . . .'

Jeff muttered something inaudible.

'Give him a chance, Jeff, that's all I'm asking . . .'

Fuck!

The burned-out cigarette was searing his fingers, and he was forced to drop it in the grass and stamp on it hard several times to put it out.

When he looked round the corner Jeff and Nora were gone, but at least he was a bit wiser.

Jeff obviously wasn't a fan of his, not that he had ever had any reason to believe that he was, which pretty much meant the musclebound hunk could be removed from the list of candidates for A.F. But, on the other hand, Biffalo Bull could still be a traitor, at least as long as the treachery didn't affect Nora.

He walked round the corner and slipped slowly into

the barn. Hasselqvist was busy doing something right at the back of the van.

'Hi, Kent,' HP shouted through the open side-door. Hasselqvist jumped and dropped whatever it was he was holding.

A round object, a bit like an ice-hockey puck, came rolling across the floor towards the door. Hasselqvist leaped at it but HP was quicker.

'So what have we got here, then?' he said jokily, holding the puck up.

Hasselqvist grabbed it out of his hands.

'None of your business!' he snarled, and HP took an involuntary step back.

'Sorry,' he muttered.

But Hasselqvist pulled the door shut right in his face. But no matter, he'd had time to read the inscription on the side of the little puck.

Elite GPS 512.

Interesting.

Very interesting . . .

He carried on through the barn and into the house. Manga was bent over his laptop but looked up as soon as HP came into the kitchen.

'Hi,' he said, slightly too loud.

HP merely nodded in response.

'Look, I know you're pissed off with me, HP . . .'

'No shit . . .'

'. . . and you've got every right to be. I lied to you, more than once. And I really am sorry about that . . .'

He smiled uncertainly.

'But, like I keep saying, I really was trying to help. I've been watching your back . . . Yours and Becca's . . .'

'What do you know about Becca?!'

Manga grimaced.

332

'Not as much as I'd like. I have a well-placed source close to Sammer, but all I really know is that he and Becca have met a few times. Sammer seems very interested in her, that much is pretty obvious, but I still don't know exactly how she fits into the picture. But right now she's not in any immediate danger, I know that much. Sammer seems totally fixated on you . . .'

'Okay, good . . .' HP took a deep breath. 'What's the Luttern labyrinth, and who's the Carer? How do they fit into the picture?'

'W-what?'

'Come on, Manga, don't act stupid. The flat next to mine, the workshop, the snakes . . .?'

He fixed his eyes on Manga, looking for the slightest sign of weakness. But he couldn't see any, not a flutter of the eyelids or an involuntary twitch.

'I genuinely have no idea what you're talking about, HP . . .'

'And you expect me to believe that, just like that? Your credibility isn't particularly high right now, Manga . . .'

'Come on, HP, I've said I'm sorry . . .' Even Manga's voice passed the test. Not the slightest tremor . . .

'I don't know everything that's going on – like I said, the Game Master doesn't let anyone else see the whole picture. All I've got are fragments. Please, tell me about the flat. Everything's connected, one way or another . . .'

HP glared at Manga as he considered what to do.

Okay, so Manga was a liar, but the lies had actually been meant well. And they were old friends . . . correction: best friends.

He'd always thought of Manga as a bit of a coward, a computer geek, and – more recently – a hen-pecked husband under the thumb of his dragon of a wife. But, even though it hurt to admit it, he had been wrong. Manga was no coward, and had actually shown himself to be a pretty capable guy.

Besides, now that he came to think about it, he had actually suspected Manga from day one – in fact, from the moment he found that bloody phone on the train. So, looking at it one way, he hadn't been *completely* taken in. He hadn't been totally blind.

But it still made sense to keep some things to himself. Having a slight advantage when it came to information wouldn't hurt at all.

'That can wait,' he finally said. 'So, remind me again why I should go along with this idiotic plan?'

'Sure, no problem.' The disappointment in Manga's voice was obvious. 'Take a look at this.'

Manga reached for the table and turned the laptop so HP could see the screen.

'I've made a list of clients who have already begun to store their data down in that bunker. Sit down . . .'

Manga pointed at one of the chairs. He opened an Excel file and started scrolling through the list.

'The Highways Agency, the Tax Office, the Police, Customs, three different bio databanks, one of which already has over 500,000 DNA samples in its register. Dental records, the National Population Register, the electoral roll, and a whole load of smaller official bodies. Pretty much all telecom and internet providers signed up before the EU directive was passed, which means that all telephone records, and all IP addresses and text messages are already stored in the Fortress.'

'Okay, that's more or less what I thought . . .' HP mumbled.

'What?'

'A few weeks ago they replayed all my computer records, as well as all my texts to you and Becca. A little warning, just to let me know they were keeping an eye on me. I couldn't quite work out how they got hold of everything so quickly from so many different sources. But now I get it. All they had to do was press a couple of buttons . . .'

Manga nodded.

'Go on . . .' HP waved one hand.

'Okay, so you've already worked out the basics, but before too long the big supermarkets will be joining in, followed by pretty much every other company that runs a loyalty card scheme. They're all terrified that their information is going to leak, with the ensuing loss of customer confidence. But what's most interesting is probably what's hidden right at the bottom of the bunker . . .'

'Hi Ludvig, it's Rebecca, sorry to call so early . . .'

'Er, no problem. I was awake anyway . . .'

She could tell he was lying, and gave him a few seconds to come round.

'So, what can I do for you, Normén?' he said, in a slightly less sleepy voice.

'I want to come back to work.'

'Er, okay. That shouldn't be a problem. Call the personnel department after nine o'clock and they'll help you. It'll probably take a couple of weeks to sort out . . .'

'No, no, I haven't got time for all that. I want to come back now, right away. The wedding's tomorrow, and you told me yourself that you needed every bodyguard you could get hold of.'

'Of course, yes. But surely you can see . . .'

He cleared his throat.

'Well, as long as this business with your brother is still going on, I can't take you back, no matter how much I might want to. Stigsson would go mad if I so much as suggested it . . .'

'Ask!'

'What?'

'Call and ask him!'

'I'm not quite with you, Normén . . .?'

'I'm asking you to call Stigsson and ask him if it's okay for me to return to duty. Please, will you do that, straight away?'

There were a few moments of silence.

'Sure,' he muttered eventually. 'But I already know what the answer's going to be.'

Me too, she thought.

'The lowest level of the bunker is reserved for one particular client. The whole thing's top secret . . .'

Manga looked over his shoulder, as if he were worried that someone was listening.

'To be honest, I think this particular client is more than just an ordinary customer. It could be that the secret tenant in the lowest level is actually behind the whole PayTag Group. But instead of risking their own valuable brand they're using PayTag as a front, a windscreen for the insects to smash themselves to death on, while those with the real power are sitting nice and safe in the passenger seat on the other side of the glass.'

'And who might they be?'

Manga shrugged.

'Who do you think? Which companies have the most influence within the information-gathering industry? Which ones are constantly designing new services to tempt us into saying what we're doing right now, where we are, which search terms we use most often, or even – what we're thinking?'

HP thought for a moment.

'There are plenty of candidates. Search engines, social media sites . . .'

'You're on the right track, young Padwan . . .'

Manga closed the laptop.

'Google, Facebook, Twitter and a few more have worked out what we're too stupid to realize.'

'Which is . . .?'

'That information is the new currency. If you can get hold of enough information, in the end everyone will want to do business with you. Just look at Facebook's stock-market valuation. It may be lower than they were expecting, but it's still three of four times the value of Ericsson.

'But do you know what their assets are, HP? Have a guess! What do you think? Not telecom systems, or years of research, or tens of thousands of patents. What Facebook owns, and what makes it worth all those billions, its very greatest asset, is . . .'

'Its users,' HP muttered.

'Exactly! Or, to be more precise, the *information* that its users volunteer. Everything gets stored – comments, shares, pictures, games, likes . . .'

Manga's face was starting to go red.

'How do you predict the future, HP? By looking back at the past, that's the starting point for any forecaster. The more information you have about the past, the more reliable your predictions for the future will be. Just think . . .'

Manga paused for breath for a moment.

'What if the past, *everyone's* past, was stored in one and the same place? State databases, medical records, patterns of consumption, social networking and search engine preferences. All of it in one massive database? All you'd have to do is collate the information. Then all you have to do is type in a search word, anything you like, and you'd be able to watch the trends. How many people had cancer in a particular year, how many people prefer white cars to blue ones, what age groups are most likely to commit

337

crimes, or look for particular brands, are most active on Twitter, where they live, what music they listen to, what books they read, and what they usually buy in the supermarket on the last Wednesday before payday . . .'

He paused for breath again.

'*He who controls the past controls the future*, Orwell wrote in *1984*, and he certainly had a point. Although I'd have to say that the PayTag project is even more refined that that . . .'

He paused again, and HP couldn't help leaning closer.

'He who controls the future, HP, without any shadow of a doubt . . . is actually the person who *owns* the past. And that's exactly what the whole PayTag project is about!'

HP lit a cigarette. He deliberately took his time, to give himself a chance to think.

All of this was pretty hard to digest. Besides, it was hardly the first conspiracy theory he'd ever heard. Last time it had been Erman going on about the Game, and now it was Manga and PayTag.

But if there was one thing he had learned over the past two years, it was that no theory, no matter how far-fetched it might seem, could be written off entirely. No smoke without fire, at least not where the Game was concerned.

And everything Manga had said fitted in pretty well with the little demonstration he had been given on the computer in the library. Moreover, it also fitted with the little backup plan he'd been working on. In fact it actually made it even better . . .

He took a deep drag, then slowly exhaled the smoke.

'Okay Manga, I get what you mean, but to be honest I don't give a shit what PayTag's up to. All I want is to deliver a decent kick in the bollocks to the Game Master, Anna Argos and Black. And that's where our interests seem to coincide. It looks like we've got a mutual enemy . . .'

He took another drag, then stubbed the cigarette out on a cracked old saucer on the draining board.

'It's like this, Manga: if you want my help, I need a favour in return. I need to get hold of Rehyman, preferably straight away. I need to talk to him with no-one else listening . . .'

Manga looked up from the laptop.

'W-what? Why?'

'I'd rather not say right now. You asked me to trust you, and the same applies here . . . But, for the sake of appearances, I suppose we could call it my price for taking part in all this . . .'

He gestured towards the yellow ceiling with one hand.

Manga gave him a long look as he seemed to consider the proposal.

'Okay, I suppose that's fair enough . . .' he muttered.

He tapped at the computer, then dug out a pen and paper and wrote down a number.

'Here, he's online so you can call him right away. There are some pay-as-you-go phones in that box over there. When you've finished, smash the SIM-card and scatter the pieces out in the woods, okay?'

'Sure, no problem . . .'

Manga gave him another long look.

'You do know what you're getting into, don't you, HP? This isn't a game. If it goes wrong . . .'

'Sure, don't worry, I've got everything under control. This isn't the first time I've gone up against the Game Master . . .'

'Well, I guess that's true. But it is the first time you're doing something that doesn't suit the Game's plans . . .'

'Good job I'm not on my own, then,' HP grinned. 'If it goes to hell, then we all get fucked at the same time!'

Quests

'Here.'

He handed her the key to her gun-cabinet.

'I presume you've got your ID and passcard in there as well?'

She nodded.

'Okay, get your stuff out and then head straight down to the firing range. You'll need to do the test again before we can let you out on duty. You soon lose it if you don't practise . . .'

'That won't be a problem, Ludvig.'

'Okay, good.'

'Was there anything else?'

He nodded.

'Before you go, Normén, I just have to ask. How the hell did you get Stigsson to agree to reinstate you?'

'Oh, you could say I had a bit of help from a mutual friend.'

She smiled and he gave her a long look.

'And is that something you'd like to explain to your boss?'

She took a deep breath.

'Not right now, Ludvig. But sometime . . .'

'Okay . . .'

He was still looking at her hard.

'You do know what you're doing, Becca?' he finally said in a low voice.

'Don't worry, Ludvig. You wanted me back and now I'm here. Just be happy with that for the time being,' she smiled.

The target turned when she was ten metres away, and long before the conscious part of her brain had registered the fact she had gone into action. Clawing her jacket open, both hands down to her holster.

Gun out, left hand on the bolt. Then push forward and up, feeding a bullet into position. The steadying hand coming up beneath the barrel. Then the sights, and the target.

Two rapid shots.

The target turned away.

She released the hammer with her left thumb, and continued to move forward. A new target turned, this time far off to her right. She squeezed off a shot, not even thinking about the result. Quickly released the hammer and carried on. Two targets began to turn at the same time, and she'd already shot a hole through the first before they stopped turning.

Then her gun clicked.

She hit her left hand against the base of the magazine, then performed the bolt action to release the trapped cartridge onto the floor. Three quick shots.

The targets turned away.

'Stop, cease fire, unload!' the instructor yelled.

'Unloaded!' she said.

She pulled out the magazine, flipped the bolt and caught the cartridge that was ready to fire. Then she let go of the

341

bolt, holstered the gun and took off her ear protectors. All the targets popped up with a loud hiss, but she didn't look at the results. The shooting instructor walked past her, did a quick check of the targets, then came back. She heard him whistle.

'Well, Normén, that went pretty well. What do you say?'

'Yep,' she said.

'I didn't actually time you, but I'm guessing you were somewhere close to the record for the course. I'll call Ludvig straight away and tell him your shooting is . . . approved. Can you sort them out yourself?'

He handed her a roll of little black stickers.

'Sure.'

He turned his back on her and headed towards the door.

She tore off four small stickers the size of a stamp and put the roll down.

On her way to the targets she picked up the little green blank cartridge that the instructor had sneaked into her magazine, which had caused the break in her shooting.

All the shots were in the dead zone. Three of the pairs of holes were so close together that they were touching, and the other two had just a millimetre of paper between them.

'Good, then you'll be in touch? Thanks for your help.'

He ended the call, opened the back of the phone and pulled out the SIM-card.

He had just snapped it in two when Hasselqvist came round the corner.

'Er, hi, HP. Listen, I just wanted to explain something . . .'

'Sure.'

He turned his back on Hasselqvist and sent one half of the SIM-card into the nearest clump of nettles.

'That thing in the van . . .'

'You mean the GPS?'

He tossed the other half in amongst the fir trees.

'Yep, that's right . . . You see, I'd just found it when you appeared at the door . . . it had been underneath a bag and just rolled out.'

'Okay . . .'

'Is it yours?'

'W-what?' HP turned round.

'The GPS transmitter, is it . . .?'

'Yeah, I get it, Kent. No, it isn't . . .'

'Okay, I just wanted to check. You were the one sitting right at the back, so I thought . . .'

HP shook his head.

'Nope, not mine. Maybe it belongs to the van?'

'I doubt it . . .'

'In that case I suggest that you get rid of it at once.'

'Sure, I just want to check with Jeff first, it may be his . . .'

Hasselqvist drifted away and HP waited another minute before pulling a new SIM-card from his trouser pocket. He inserted it into the phone he had got from Manga, switched it on and tapped in his pin-code.

The text arrived almost immediately.

Done!

Hidden number, but he knew who it was from.

Fuck, Rehyman was fast!

They got changed in silence. Tight black wetsuits, rubber shoes, then neoprene ski masks that made the heat intolerable, and which HP pulled off at once. Total fucking madness, on a massive scale!

'Everything's ready,' he heard Manga say from round the back of the Polo.

343

'I still want to double-check,' Jeff said.

'But it's getting . . .'

'We've got time,' Jeff interrupted. 'There's always time to check your equipment . . .'

Manga seemed to give up, because when HP walked round the car the back door was already open.

'Diving gear, inflatable dinghy, welding equipment, explosives . . .' Jeff was saying to himself as he moved his hand over the various black bags in the boot.

The word *explosives* startled HP. He had a sudden flashback to the E4 motorway two years before, when he had plugged his phone into a similar bag. A bag stuffed with so much explosive that it was enough to blow an entire building sky-high.

For almost two years he had believed that he'd blown the Game's brain to kingdom come. But, according to Manga, that had been nothing but an illusion, a very clever one that the Game Master had implanted in his head. The real Death Star wasn't located in an old office building out in Kista, but deep underground in a bunker little more than a couple of kilometres away.

But if everything he had experienced up until a few days ago was just an elaborate mind game, then what guarantees did he have that what he was experiencing now was any more real?

He had been wrestling with that particular dilemma for several days.

Even if he decided to trust Manga, there were no guarantees. Manga seemed to be telling the truth, because – as far as it was possible to tell – he genuinely appeared to believe his own story. But what if it wasn't his story?

What if someone else was playing mind games with Manga, in exactly the same way they had done with him?

That what they were heading towards now was actually nothing more than part of an even more elaborate plan?

That was the trouble with conspiracy theories. Once you started to accept their existence, it was impossible to say where they really stopped.

Just because you're paranoid, doesn't mean they aren't after you . . .

'Quiet!' Jeff suddenly said, raising his head from the boot.

'Did you hear that?'

No-one said anything.

'What is it, Jeff?' Hasselqvist quacked after a few seconds. 'There!'

A faint humming sound was approaching from the east.

HP realized what it was immediately. He took a couple of quick strides, grabbed the heavy sliding door of the barn and began to close it.

'What the hell . . .?' Jeff yelled.

HP ignored him.

The sound was getting closer very fast, throbbing like a pneumatic drill on his eardrums.

The door was almost closed, just a metre or so left, and HP was leaning his entire weight on the handle. But the door was slowing down, began to catch, and finally stopped with a loud screech.

The throbbing noise was suddenly echoing off the buildings, amplified until he could feel the vibration in his ribcage, and only now did the others seem to get it.

A helicopter, flying extremely low, was about to appear over the treetops any second now. HP made another attempt to close the door. But the wheel at the top seemed to have jumped its track and the door sat fast.

He bent his knees and pulled on the handle as hard as he could, with one leg on each side of the door. Suddenly and without warning the door jolted loose and came racing towards his chest. He threw himself to the side and only just escaped getting his head caught as it slammed shut.

'Sorry!' Jeff shouted, his hands still on the other end.

A moment later the helicopter thundered across the yard, and the pulsing rotor blades practically deafened HP.

Both he and Jeff crouched down instinctively as they tried to catch sight of the helicopter through the broken barn roof.

It seemed to be hovering a few metres above the barn.

HP glanced quickly at the others. Jeff seemed utterly focused on the helicopter, as did Nora. But Hasselqvist slipped quickly inside the van.

'We need to go, now!' he yelled as he scrambled into the driver's seat.

'B-but, we're not ready . . .' Nora cried.

The helicopter was still hovering above them, and the downdraft from the blades was making what was left of the roof begin to shake. Slowly at first, then faster and faster.

Fragments of tiles came loose and fell into the barn.

'Kent's right!' Jeff roared. 'Any minute now this roof's going to collapse on top of us . . .'

A large piece of tile hit the roof of the van with a thud.

'I'll open the door, then you lot get going . . . Just drive, don't stop and wait for me,' Jeff yelled in HP's ear.

HP nodded, and tried to run towards the van in a crouch.

A small piece of tile hit him on the head and he raised his arm instinctively to protect himself. There was a loud bang, then another. Probably one of the helicopter's runners hitting the roof.

'Come on, Nora!' he shouted when he reached the door of the van.

346

But she seemed to be hesitating.

Jeff roared something at her that HP didn't hear. He waved his hand towards the van. Another bang, more forceful this time. A large tile crashed to the floor right in front of the van, sending splinters in all directions.

Hasselqvist started the engine.

'We have to go, come on!' he yelled again.

Jeff had turned away and was bracing himself against the door. Tiles crashed down, the air was full of flying fragments. HP put his arm across his eyes as they thudded down onto the van. When he looked up Nora was lying on the floor.

Shit!

He leaped out of the van, but she was back on her feet before he could reach her.

'Into the van, HP, come on!'

She pushed him in ahead of her. More tiles rained down and seemed to pull part of the roof with them. Blood was running down Nora's face from a wet patch on top of her head. He pushed her down into one of the seats.

'Jeff!' she groaned.

'Never mind your boyfriend, we've got to go . . .' he snapped.

Through the windscreen he saw the door slowly open.

Hasselqvist revved the engine.

'Brother . . .' she groaned.

'What?'

'He's my older brother, you idiot . . .!'

Jeff had almost managed to get the heavy door open. His back and neck muscles were straining against his t-shirt, threatening to split it.

The van suddenly leaped forward.

Her brother . . .

He grabbed hold of the headrest of the nearest seat, then hung out of the door.

'JEEEFFF!' he roared.

The mountain of muscle spun round and met his gaze. The van's wheels were spinning on the dirt-covered concrete floor, trying to get a grip . . .

HP reached out as far as he could, holding out his hand. Jeff took a couple of quick strides.

The collapse was spreading across the roof, section after section of tiles was giving way and sending showers of razor-sharp fragments clattering against the body of the van. One piece, big as a hand, flew past HP's nose but he hardly noticed.

Jeff leaped forward . . .

The tyres suddenly got a grip and the van shot out of the barn like an arrow. A moment later the entire roof fell in.

The dark car was waiting outside her building when she got home. As she approached the chauffeur opened the door and got out. But it wasn't the same man as before, this one was considerably younger, and it took her a few seconds before she could place him.

'Hello Rebecca, my name's Edler, I'm Colonel Pellas's adjutant . . .'

He held out his hand.

'We met very briefly in the flat in Maria Trappgränd . . .'

'Hello,' she mumbled, shaking his hand.

He opened the door to the back seat.

'Good evening, my dear Rebecca,' Tage Sammer said. 'I'm sorry to arrive unannounced like this, but I have good news . . .'

She hesitated and glanced at Edler.

Sammer seemed to have read her thoughts.

'We can talk freely, I have no secrets from Edler . . .'

'Good . . .'

Then, after thinking for a couple of seconds, she added:

'Perhaps we should go up to the flat instead? A bit more pleasant than sitting in the car . . .'

'Thanks for the invitation,' he smiled. 'I'd like that, on another occasion, but today I would prefer the car. Inside flats one never knows who might be listening . . .'

He patted the seat beside him and Rebecca had no choice but to climb in.

Edler got in behind the wheel, started the car and pulled away slowly towards Rålambsvägen.

'Have you found Henke?' she asked before he had time to open his mouth.

'Not yet, but we think we know where both he and Sandström are. We're expecting them to be picked up shortly.'

'Okay, good. Well, good is probably the wrong word . . .'

'I know what you mean, Rebecca. All this is for Henrik's own good, and we're very grateful that you're helping us. We have to get hold of him before he does anything really silly. You see, this isn't just about the revolver . . .'

He glanced towards Edler.

'We have information about a bomb . . .'

'What? Then you have to postpone the royal wedding . . .'

'No, no, that's out of the question. The Palace is quite clear on that point.'

'But the risk?'

He took a deep breath and then shrugged his shoulders.

'The risk is considered to be acceptable under the circumstances.'

'Acceptable, seriously? A bomb . . .'

'The information is as yet unconfirmed. We have too few details to be in a position to suggest anything so drastic as postponing the wedding. Bomb threats are a regular occurrence, and my employers . . .'

349

He sighed.

'There's a lot at stake, Rebecca, much more than you can imagine. Popular support for the royal family has halved during the past fifteen years, parliament is full of republicans who are simply biding their time, and if the figures continue to decline at the same rate . . .'

He paused and shrugged once more.

'Of course, factors of that sort can't be taken into account when you're evaluating the level of threat, but you know how that works as well as I do. All large organizations are the same. Somewhere there's always someone who's worried about losing his job, and who therefore hesitates to take unpalatable but sometimes necessary decisions.'

He held his hands out.

'There's hardly anything that increases support for the royal family like a wedding, my employers taught me that a few years ago. Unfortunately all the articles in the papers, however wrong they might be, have wiped out almost all of the upturn.'

'What about the christening? That wasn't long ago.'

He shook his head.

'A christening is far too low key, it doesn't give the same warm glow. Nowadays I'm afraid there are only two things that raise support for the royal family – weddings and national crises. In other words, it would take a very great deal indeed for anyone to decide to rein in the festivities, let along postpone them. Anyway, as far as this potential bombing is concerned, we have very few details so far.'

'So what do you know, can you tell me?'

'Not really, Rebecca . . .' He paused for a few seconds, exchanged a quick glance with Edler in the rear-view mirror, before going on.

'A few hours ago we received a tipoff about a flat. We got a warrant and searched it, and found certain indications that a bomb could have been constructed there . . .'

'And how is this connected to Henke?'

Sammer took a deep breath.

'The flat was in Maria Trappgränd, right next door to Henrik's . . .'

Her heart began to beat faster, but she did her best to hide her agitation.

'Hang on, you're not suggesting that Henke . . .? Well, you can drop that idea. He can hardly put together a Billy bookcase, let alone a bomb . . .'

'I agree with you entirely, my dear Rebecca.'

He gently patted one of her knees.

'We don't believe that Henrik constructed the bomb on his own either. But, on the other hand, it can hardly be a coincidence that the workshop was located in the flat next door to his. And we've also found a couple of his finger-prints in there . . .'

Rebecca shook her head reluctantly.

'As I said before, Henrik is in dangerous company at the moment. Extremely dangerous company. The people he has surrounded himself with are experts at manipu-lating other people, they've done it many times before. And sadly Henrik is, as you know, rather . . .'

'Gullible . . .'

'Precisely.'

The car stopped at a red light on the roundabout at Lindhagensplan, and they sat in silence for a moment.

They were only a couple of hundred metres from the place where the car she and Kruse were in had crashed after Henke dropped a rock through the windscreen from the motorway bridge above. Admittedly, Henke hadn't known she was in the car, but that was fairly irrelevant. Someone had manipulated him into doing it, getting him

351

to completely ignore the inevitable conclusion that other people would be hurt as a consequence of his actions. Could that really happen again?

Under the right circumstances – absolutely.

'So what do you want me to do, Uncle Tage?' she said as the car approached the motorway bridge.

His voice sounded sad:

'A lot of people's lives are at risk, Rebecca. If we don't manage to catch Henrik tonight, then we will all have to do whatever we can to stop him. And I do mean whatever, if you understand me?'

He paused briefly.

'Obviously, you can choose not to accept the assignment. No-one would blame you. I can have a word with Eskil Stigsson . . .'

They passed under the bridge and she couldn't help glancing up at the railing above. For a few moments she imagined she could see someone up there. A dark-clad figure in a hood.

'No!' she said, a little too loudly, and saw Edler looking at her in the rear-view mirror.

'No, thanks, Uncle Tage. That won't be necessary,' she said, as calmly as she could. 'Just as you say, there's too much at stake. I'm very grateful for everything you've done already . . .'

'Don't mention it. We need the right people in the right positions. People we can rely on. We all agree on that, Stigsson, my employers and I.'

He patted her knee again.

'You're so like your father, Rebecca, have I already said that? Conscientious, loyal, reliable, no matter what the circumstances. Those qualities are getting harder and harder to find in today's egocentric society . . .'

She couldn't help blushing.

In the gloom of the back of the car, if she squinted slightly Uncle Tage looked very like Dad. His posture, his slightly archaic way of speaking, even the way he smelled was almost the same.

Cigars, aftershave, and something else.

Something that brought a rather sad lump to her throat.

He was pinned down on the floor, with Jeff lying motionless on top of him. The van was bouncing and lurching along on the gravel track, the strut holding one of the seats digging into his leg all the way. Weirdly, he couldn't hear any sounds around him above the high-pitched whistling tinnitus noise that seemed to be rebounding round his head. He pressed his hands against the floor and tried to pry himself free.

Suddenly he felt Jeff move, and a moment later the heavy body rolled off him.

At the same time his hearing returned.

'What the fuck happened?' he yelped.

'The barn!' Nora shouted.

'W-what?' He tried to get up off the floor.

'The barn exploded,' she yelled, trying to wedge herself against one of the side windows.

'The roof fell in, then there was an explosion . . . The sky was full of smoke and there was no sign of the helicopter. Don't know what happened!'

'The explosives . . .' Jeff coughed. 'The explosives and detonators were in the Polo, next to the welding tubes. The boot was open. And there was chemical fertilizer in those white sacks in the corner . . .'

HP struggled up into the seat next to Jeff. The big man's eyes were closed and HP could clearly see his muscular chest rise and fall under his soaking wet t-shirt.

The van flew over a bump and HP found himself on the floor again.

353

There was a thud, then the van veered sharply to the left, and suddenly the sound of the road changed.

'Nice driving, Kent!' Nora yelled towards the front seats, and Kent muttered something in reply.

'We're out on the main road,' she said, helping HP up.

'How's your . . .?' He nodded to her blood-streaked face.

She put her hand to her head, then stared at the blood on it.

'Shit!' she said. 'I hadn't noticed, must be the adrenalin. I've got the first-aid box in the front . . .'

She clambered past him and slipped into the front passenger seat.

He leaned forward to ask if she needed help, but a hand pulled him back.

Jeff had his eyes open.

'Thanks,' he said quietly.

'No worries,' HP mumbled.

Jeff nodded, then shut his eyes again.

'There's a petrol station up ahead, can you pull in there?' Nora said to Hasselqvist.

HP leaned over to look out of the side-window. A large plume of smoke was clearly visible above the forest, but there was no sign of the helicopter.

'There's a car-wash shed round the back, pull in there. We can lie low till it gets dark,' Nora went on.

Hasselqvist drove through the forecourt of the petrol station and around the back of the shop to the car-wash shed, a corrugated metal box with a row of vacuum cleaners and buckets along one wall. A lone pensioner was washing the windscreen of his old Saab, but otherwise it was empty. Hasselqvist stopped the van and they sat in silence for a few moments.

Nora was using the mirror behind the sun-visor to inspect the wound to her head.

'Ow, shit . . .' she muttered as she used a pair of tweezers to pull a razor-sharp splinter the size of a one-krona coin from the wound.

'Can you press here, please, HP?'

'Sure.'

He leaned over her head.

'Right, take this compress and hold it down, as hard as you can.'

He did as she said, trying to get his hands to stop shaking from the adrenalin rush.

'We're fucked,' Hasselqvist suddenly blurted out. 'They know where we are, what van we're driving. We've got no chance . . .'

No-one said anything.

'Because surely no-one thinks it was a coincidence that that fucking helicopter showed up?' Hasselqvist's voice was steadier now. 'If we set off now, we can be back in the city by midnight. We can come up with a new plan, find another way to . . .'

'There is no other way, Kent!' Nora snapped. 'And you know that perfectly bloody well! If we give up now, we might as well not bother. And that means the Game will win. Is that what you want?'

Hasselqvist didn't answer.

'We haven't got any stuff, Nora, all our equipment just went up in smoke,' Jeff muttered. 'Without it we don't stand a chance of getting into the Fortress . . .'

Total silence descended inside the van.

'Actually, we do,' HP said after a while, but they all seemed too upset to hear what he said.

'You asked me to put together a backup plan, remember?'

He looked at Nora, and finally got a reaction.

'I know how we can get in, but it means you'll have to do as I say . . .'

Far in the distance they could hear sirens getting closer. It sounded like several of them.

'We have to go,' Hasselqvist whimpered.

'Hang on,' HP said. 'The cops always switch their sirens off when they get close to their target . . .

'So they don't scare the bad guys away . . .' he added when no-one seemed to get what he meant.

'So as long as the sirens are still on, they haven't got to where they're going. Get it?'

The sirens were close now, at least three of them, maybe more.

Nora glanced at HP.

Hasselqvist moved his hand to the ignition key.

HP put his hand on his shoulder.

'Just relax, Kent. It's the fire brigade, I swear,' he said quietly.

The sirens were so close that the sound echoed round the little tin shed, making the old boy look up from his insect-smeared windscreen. Then they slowly diminished in strength. Thirty seconds later they vanished altogether.

'You can get moving now, Kent,' HP said, patting Hasselqvist on the shoulder. 'Head north . . .'

He leaned back in his seat and tried to gather his thoughts.

'By the way, there's something we've forgotten . . .' he said as they pulled out onto the main road.

'Did anyone see how Manga got out?'

26

Game change

The new van smelled of car-freshner. Jasmine. Or possibly just new car smell . . .

It had taken him ten minutes or so to steal it from a multi-storey carpark, which meant he was losing his touch. As an extra precaution he had nicked a couple of licence plates from another car, in case the van's owner was quick to report it stolen.

They had spent about an hour in a run-down industrial estate, getting changed and sorting out the new van. White overalls and full-face protective masks that he pulled out of the sports bag, along with a couple of large stickers for the van. Two identical rucksacks made of rigid plastic, fastened in four different places across the chest, making them look like something from a science fiction movie. One for him and one for Jeff. And everything courtesy of the Fenster's little emporium.

The forest track they were now parked in lay almost opposite the road leading to the Fortress. The lamps surrounding the steel gate were just visible a few hundred metres away through the dark forest.

Everything was ready.

Time to get moving . . .

'Okay, let's get going. Keep your fingers crossed that it's going to work.'

Three nods in response, two confident, from Nora and her brother, and one more hesitant from Hasselqvist.

'And you've got everything ready? Name-badges in place?'

More nods.

'How's your head, Nora?'

'Okay, the skin adhesive seems to be working.'

'Good!'

HP took a deep breath.

'Okay, off we go then . . .'

Hasselqvist seemed to hesitate for a moment, then started the engine and put the van into gear.

'Shame about Manga,' Nora said once they'd started to move.

'Yeah,' HP muttered.

'Are you sure there's no way he could have got out?' Hasselqvist said.

'No chance. When everything went up he was still shut in behind us . . .' Nora said.

HP swallowed to clear the lump in his throat.

'Besides, we must have called his mobile at least twenty times, and he hasn't answered.'

They turned onto the newly surfaced tarmac road and drove up towards the gate, a massive thing fixed to solid concrete pillars on either side. As if that wasn't enough, there was a saw-toothed metal bar set into the tarmac, stretching right across the roadway. On top of the pillars were double rows of floodlights, and, just below them, aluminium camera boxes. Trying to force the gates with anything less than a tank would be utterly futile.

There was a large yellow warning sign on the end of

the concrete bunker that was evidently the gatehouse. The sign was partially obscured by black plastic, but the wind had shredded it enough for the text to be clearly visible.

STOP
High Security Area
No admittance without permission
No photography, recording or surveillance
without permission

Hasselqvist stopped the van at the clearly marked line, just a couple of metres from the saw-toothed metal bar.

HP opened the door, jumped out and went over to the glass hatch in the gatehouse.

A sour-faced woman in uniform glared at him through what looked like a double layer of bulletproof glass. He carefully adjusted his fake glasses, then gave her his friendliest smile.

'Yes, how can I help you?'

Her voice was surprisingly melodic, almost disconcertingly so. Hell, she ought to be on the radio, not sitting out here in the middle of nowhere.

'Er . . . E-Erik, Erik Andersson . . .' he began.

Fuck, the smooth radio voice had almost made him forget his assumed name.

'From Andersson Sanitation,' he added quickly. 'Apparently you've got trouble with a couple of blocked filters. They said it was urgent . . .'

'Are they expecting you?'

'I certainly hope so . . .' he nodded, throwing in what was supposed to look like an innocent smile, and trying not to glance at the camera fixed to the window just to the left of her.

'One moment.'

359

He watched as she turned to her left and began typing on a keyboard.

'Have you got some ID, Erik?'

He nodded again, removed his fake ID from its plastic holder on the breast pocket of his overalls, and put it in the metal drawer that slid out below the window.

The drawer slid back in with a whirr.

He could hear the faint sound of typing over the speaker.

He looked back quickly over his shoulder.

The van looked fine, almost better than he'd expected it to.

The stickers with the words *Andersson Sanitation* could have been a bit straighter, but what the hell . . .

They hadn't had any time to waste on details, and besides, it was hardly noticeable when the sliding door was open.

Jeff was visible in the doorway, with Nora just behind him.

More typing.

Come on, for fuck's sake, Rainman. Show us your magic!

'Would you mind looking into the camera, Erik?'

'Of course.'

He adjusted his glasses and tried to look relaxed. To judge by the reflection in the window, he more or less succeeded . . .

What if they had one of those face-recognition programs?

Shit, he hadn't even thought of that until now!

Fake glasses might stop you looking like the guy in the newspapers, but no way would they fool a piece of software . . .

He glanced over his shoulder again, then looked into the camera. A bead of sweat broke from the back of his neck and trickled down between his shoulder blades. Then

360

another one. And in just a few moments very similar beads of sweat would begin to appear conspicuously on his forehead . . .

The guard reappeared.

'Right, Erik . . .'

He smiled again, a nervous, loose-bowelled smile. He didn't need to check his reflection to know that.

'Here are your cards. The email said five people in total. The lads in Operations will be responsible for letting you in and out, and I don't want to hear about you blocking any of the doors to keep them open, is that understood?'

'Absolutely,' he nodded.

'Good. Okay, carry on down the slope and follow the signs for the Operations Division. You'll have to turn right, but you'll see the sign. Don't forget to hand your cards back when you leave . . .'

'Okay, thanks!'

The drawer opened and he pulled out his ID and the five cards marked *Visitor* before turning and heading back towards the van.

A loud click startled him, but it was only the saw-toothed bar being lowered.

As he got into the van the gate began to swing open.

Hasselqvist put the van into gear and they rolled slowly through the gate and down the hill. The road was cut deep into the rock and soon they could no longer see the edge of the forest.

'Shit, it actually worked. . . .' Hasselqvist sounded slightly happier.

'Yep, Kent, my mate Rain . . . I mean, Rehyman, is a bastard when it comes to security. It only took him ten minutes to spot the weaknesses in their system. Ordinary, unencrypted email between the Fortress and the gatehouse. All Rehyman had to do was find out the addresses, then set up a cloned account that looked like it came from the Fortress . . .'

'Then, hey presto, it looked like we were expected, yeah, we got that bit when you told us. But we're not home and dry yet. The hardest bit's still to come . . .'

HP opened his mouth to say something cutting, but changed his mind at the last moment. He was still holding Manga's superfluous visitor's badge in his hand. He stared at it for a few seconds, then slowly slipped it into one of his breast pockets.

'There's the sign.'

Nora pointed to the right.

'Shit, what a place . . .'

They reached the end of the cutting and emerged into a large gravel yard. Right in front of them was a two-storey building and something that looked like a garage. Behind and above the buildings, the rock face rose up vertically at least thirty metres.

'There's only one way out of here . . .' Hasselqvist muttered, glancing in the rear-view mirror.

They parked to the right of the building, next to a loading bay with the correct sign.

One of the garage doors on the building opposite was open slightly, and HP thought he could see something that looked like a dark minibus inside. His heart was beating faster and faster.

Somewhere a dog was barking, and the noise echoed around the little hollow before fading away into the gloom of the summer night.

For fuck's sake, HP, calm down and stick to the plan . . .

He took a deep breath and put his hand in his pocket, fingering the handle of the taser.

'Put your breathing masks round your necks. Everything has to look genuine,' Nora said. 'Jeff, are you ready?'

'Sure, I'm ready,' her brother mumbled.

'Okay, let's get going. This time I do the talking . . .'

She gave HP a quick nod. Then she opened the door.

'Okay, as you all know, it's the big day tomorrow. The happy couple seem to have the weather gods on their side, no rain forecast, which means they'll be sticking to plan A: open carriage instead of the covered coach we recommended. The Palace PR department, however, want the young couple to be close to the public and not hidden behind glass . . .'

Runeberg shrugged.

'On the other hand, they're going to be spending the rest of their lives behind glass, so I suppose we shouldn't begrudge them this last taste of freedom . . .'

He pressed the remote and changed the picture.

'We'll be using runners, exactly like we did with the last royal wedding. Six in total, three on each side of the carriage. Two teams, running half the route each.'

He pointed at the picture showing six bodyguards in suits running on either side of the royal carriage.

'As you can see, I'm getting more and more handsome as the years go by.'

He placed the laser pointer at the easily recognizable figure at the front on the right. Quiet laughter filled the room. Runeberg must have been talking on his radio, to judge by his peculiar expression in the picture.

'We'll have three vehicles following the second troop of Horse Guards. Two as backup in case of an evacuation, and the van for the runners, just like last time. Any questions so far?'

None of the thirty bodyguards in the room said anything.

'In that case, I'll hand over to the head of security at

the Palace. I'm sure he has plenty to tell us, and I would advise everyone to listen very carefully.'

Runeberg gestured towards Tage Sammer, who was sitting a short distance away. Rebecca had noticed him when they entered the hall, but her heart still began to beat faster when he stood up and buttoned his jacket.

The man on the other side of the little counter leafed through his papers.

'Replacing filters,' he said into his radio. 'Have you heard anything about that, over?'

The radio crackled.

'No,' the voice at the other end said.

'Have you checked the daily log, over?'

'Yep, there's nothing here. No alarms in the system either, over.'

There were a few moments silence.

The man shrugged and smiled at Nora.

'Sorry, but I can't let you go down without securing authorization from the boss . . .'

'I understand,' she said. 'Obviously, we can turn round and go home, but it sounded urgent when the bloke called . . .'

She pretended to look at her watch.

'And we're already late. If the system overheats . . .'

The man grinned again.

HP had taken against him the moment they stepped inside the little office: very fit, with greasy, back-combed hair, a smarmy smile, prominent cheekbones. A bit too good-looking for a place like this . . .

He took a couple of slow steps forward so he could look at the other side of the little counter.

Dark blue ribbed sweater, matching trousers covered with pockets, polished black boots. On a table behind him there was a pile of yellow protective helmets, and an assortment of hi-visibility jackets were hanging over a rack full of radios. All the things you might expect to find in an Operations Division.

Yet there was still something not quite right . . .

The radio crackled again: 'Okay, look, I can't get hold of Jacobsson over the phone. He must be busy with all the other stuff. What we do is – you park them up there for the time being, then head down to the ventilation room and check, over.'

'Can't one of us go with you?' Nora said before the man had time to reply. 'Then at least we can say we checked the filter on site, to keep the boss off my back. You know how it is . . .' She smiled at him and tilted her head slightly. To judge by the man's inane grin, the trick seemed to work.

'Listen, they're asking if they can send someone along so they can tick some boxes. Maybe that would make sense, over?'

'Okay, that's what we'll do, over.'

'Over and out!'

The man put the radio down and winked at Nora.

'Okay, the two of us can go down . . .'

'Nice idea, but I'm afraid only Jonas here has full authorization to carry out this sort of inspection . . .' Nora put her hand on Jeff's arm.

'I see . . .' The man's disappointment was obvious, but HP hardly noticed. The nagging feeling that something wasn't right was getting stronger and stronger.

Busy with all the other stuff . . .

'Don't forget me, if it's a UV filter then it'll take two of us to check it . . .' HP said.

Nora gave him a quick look, and he held her gaze, nodding almost imperceptibly. She appeared to think for a few seconds.

365

'Of course,' she said. 'I almost forgot. It takes two to hold the frame.'

'Surely I could do that . . .?' the technician protested.

'I'm sure you could, but if it slips you could lose a couple of fingers. Remember what happened to Kalle?' She turned to the others.

'You mean Three-Fingered Kalle from ABB . . .?' Hasselqvist shot back like lightning. 'Ouch. And the insurance didn't cover it either . . .'

The technician's smile died instantly.

'Okay, you can come as well,' he said, pointing at HP. 'The rest of you wait here, there's a coffee machine over there . . .'

He got up, walked round the counter and headed over to a heavy metal door set into one wall. He pulled out a passcard that was attached by a coil to his belt, tapped it against a reader and then held the door open for them.

'This way, gentlemen . . .'

A guard with cropped hair and neat red goatee was sitting in a cubicle between the lift doors. As they approached he gave them a quick look, then went back to staring at the screen in front of him.

'I'm taking these two visitors down to the ventilator room,' the man said.

'Sure.' Without looking up from the screen, the guard pressed a button and one of the lift doors opened.

They stepped inside and the technician repeated the card procedure with another reader, then pressed one of the buttons. The door closed and the lift slowly began to move.

No-one said anything. HP looked round cautiously. There was bound to be a camera hidden behind the mirror in the ceiling, but that wasn't what interested him most.

366

The control panel showed six floors below the entrance level. The floor they were heading for was minus one, and had a small sign saying *technical services.*

Beside the button for minus two was a sign saying *control room.* The lower levels had no labels.

The lift braked so sharply that HP's stomach lurched. From the corner of his eye he saw Jeff starting to feel inside one of the pockets of his overalls . . .

'Right then . . .' their guide said.

'We're not getting out here,' Jeff said coldly.

'What?'

Jeff pulled out the revolver and aimed it at the man's head. HP recognized the gun straight away, it was the one he had taken down to the Grand. He'd had a feeling that an aggressive bloke like Jeff wouldn't get rid of a perfectly functional weapon . . .

'Control room, now,' Jeff ordered.

The technician didn't move.

Oh, for fuck's sake . . .!

HP leaned forward and slowly lowered Jeff's arm. Then he pulled the passcard from the man's belt and tapped it against the reader. Then he pressed the button for minus two.

'Just take it easy . . .' He read the name under the photograph on the technician's passcard.

'. . . *Jochen*, and everything will be fine.'

The man looked like he was about to say something, but at the last moment he seemed to change his mind and buttoned his lips.

HP glanced at the mirror in the roof of the lift.

The only question was how long it would take the guard up above to realize that something was wrong.

But, if his suspicions were correct, then all the guards' attention was focused elsewhere. He slowly took off the fake glasses and put them in his pocket. The masquerade was over, or very nearly, at least . . .

The lift stopped at minus two and the doors opened. The large lobby was empty, and through the huge windows around the sides they could make out long, illuminated tunnels containing rows of server units. But it was the windows facing the control room that interested HP most. Something like thirty workstations arranged in what looked like a semicircular amphitheatre, with large screens at the front instead of a stage. He could see the backs of at least eight people down there.

Jeff pushed Jochen the technician ahead of him.

'Door.'

This time the man didn't protest. He tapped his card to the reader beside the heavy steel door, then stepped to one side.

HP opened the door and gestured to the other two men to step in. His mouth suddenly felt bone-dry.

'Nobody move,' Jeff roared, holding the revolver in the air.

Lights, camera, action!

27

Prineville

'Good morning, everyone. My name is Colonel André Pellas, and I'm afraid I have some disturbing information to share with you. It would appear that there are advanced plans afoot to disrupt the wedding. We suspect that these individuals are involved in some way.'

He nodded to Runeberg, who changed the picture.

A photograph appeared on the projector screen, and she bit her lip unconsciously.

'Henrik Pettersson, alias HP, or Number 128. Pettersson is known to the police, not least for a conviction for manslaughter. He is suspected of being behind the attack in Kungsträdgården two years ago, and is, as you may know, wanted in connection with a failed attack at the Grand Hotel one week ago.'

She saw the officers around her nod, and did her best to look unconcerned.

'The other person is a more recent acquaintance.'

Runeberg changed the picture again.

'Magnus Sandström, also known in some circles as Farook Al-Hassan. Sandström is probably the brains behind an autonomous group known as the Game. He's highly intelligent, with a manipulative personality, and should be regarded as extremely dangerous. We are currently trying very hard to locate these two gentlemen, and we believe that we are closing in on them. So there is a good chance that we will have apprehended them before the wedding tomorrow, but if for some reason we should fail, you will all be issued with their pictures.'

He looked at Runeberg.

'Their pictures are actually in the folders in front of you, along with maps, the official schedule and various contact numbers, including Colonel Pellas's mobile number,' Runeberg said.

'Thank you, Superintendent. Well, allow me to wish you all the very best of luck for tomorrow, and to add that I personally, along with the Marshal of the Realm and His Majesty the King, are extremely grateful for your efforts. Let us hope that we have a calm and peaceful day ahead of us . . .'

Eyes like saucers, mouths wide open, pale faces.

Jeff pushed the technician aside and took several firm steps down the narrow staircase leading to the floor of the room. His revolver was still pointing at the ceiling.

'Who's in charge here?'

'I am.' A thickset man in a short-sleeved white shirt, with a pen-case in his top pocket, stood up from his chair.

'Sit down!' Jeff aimed the revolver at the man.

He hesitated for a moment, then obeyed.

Jeff carried on down the steps until he reached the man's desk. HP followed slowly, looking round the whole time. No cameras in here, just as he had suspected . . .

The unions didn't like it if you filmed people at their desks . . .

A couple of the operators exchanged glances, then nervous smiles, as if to reassure each other . . .

370

Jeff had stopped beside the manager's computer. HP hung back a bit while Jeff slowly pulled at the velcro to open one of the breast pockets of his overalls.

'Here.'

He pulled out a chunky USB memory stick and put it on the desk next to the man.

'Plug that in, then open the file entitled Bigboy.exe. Then you'll receive new instructions . . .'

'Okay . . .'

The man in charge put his hand on the USB stick and slowly pulled it towards him. HP glanced quickly over his shoulder. He caught the looks on the other operators' faces.

Fear?

Maybe, but that wasn't the dominant feeling. More like . . . Anticipation . . .!?

The manager leaned over towards the USB ports on the side of one of the screens.

Jeff's Adam's apple was performing a vigorous dance. The hand holding the revolver was shaking noticeably.

From the corner of his eye HP noticed Jochen the technician slowly moving closer. The manager turned the stick the right way up, and moved it closer to the USB port. As he leaned forward his shirt sleeve rode up, revealing the lower portion of a tattoo. A drop of sweat freed itself from one of the man's sideburns and slowly trickled down his cheek.

'STOP!' HP suddenly said.

The manager jumped and dropped the stick on the desk.

'W-what?' Jeff turned towards him.

'DON'T put that stick in! Don't you get it . . .?' HP snapped as the man picked up the USB stick from the desk.

'B-but wait. Big Boy . . .?' Jeff began.

371

'Do you seriously think it's possible to plug in a stick containing a virus, just like that?'

HP stepped forward and snatched the USB stick from the man's hand.

'Tell us what would happen . . .' he said to the man in charge.

The man stared at him dumbly.

HP pulled the taser from his pocket and pressed the trigger halfway in, making the blue lightning perform its jerky dance between the metal prongs.

'Tell us what would happen if you plugged that stick into the system, otherwise I'll send fifty thousand volts up your fat arse!'

'Er, wait, I mean . . .' the man protested.

HP jabbed the prongs at the man's chest, and he immediately began to jerk wildly.

'AAAARRGH!!'

HP pulled the taser away and let the man slip onto the floor. His body continued to convulse for a couple of seconds before lying still. A faint smell of burned hair spread through the room.

HP turned round slowly and pointed the taser at the technician, who backed away at once.

'What the fuck are you doing, HP?!' Jeff's face was ghostly pale, but HP ignored him.

The atmosphere inside the room had suddenly changed, and the fear was now tangible.

He took a few steps up towards the closest operator and raised the taser.

'What would have happened if the stick had been plugged in?'

'The system would have shut down at once . . .' the man replied instantly.

'Excellent! What else . . .?'

'Er, the lights would have gone out, the electricity would have shut off, the lifts would have stopped. The alarm would have gone off, then the guards . . .'

The man gulped a couple of times but HP waved the taser in front of him to encourage him to go on.

'Guards, cops, the military . . . the whole lot!'

HP turned his head towards Jeff. But Muscles didn't seem to be keeping up.

'This is a trap, Jeff. They knew we were coming. Didn't you?'

He moved the taser closer to the operator's face and once again made sparks crackle between the prongs.

'Not like this . . .' The man held up his hands and leaned as far back in his chair as he could. 'Th-the tunnel, you were supposed to come through the tunnel . . . It was all . . .'

'It was all what?!' Jeff seemed to have regained the power of speech.

'A t-test, some sort of exercise. That's what they said. Not . . .'

The operator glanced over the railing at his floored boss, who was now curled up and sobbing quietly.

'. . . like this.'

'FUCK! FUCK! FUCK!!'

Jeff didn't seem to know what to do with himself.

HP gave him a couple of seconds to calm down.

'It's all fucked! If we can't plug the virus in, we might as well . . .'

Jeff slowly shook his head. He lowered the arm holding the revolver towards the floor and HP noticed Jochen the technician creeping gradually closer.

'Take it easy, Jefferson,' HP muttered. 'We're not finished yet. Just keep an eye on our little hero over there.'

He put the taser in his pocket, turned away from Jeff and began to fiddle with the oversized catch of his rucksack.

Jeff looked up at Jochen, realized that he had moved, and quickly raised the revolver again.

'Get back!' he snarled.

Jochen held his hands up in front of him.

'Take it easy, mate, you've got no chance,' he said in a sterner and considerably less jocular tone of voice than before. 'You managed to get in, against all the odds – congratulations. But our response unit will be in place upstairs now. The alarm will have gone out by now . . .'

He took half a pace forward.

'Jeff, that's your name, isn't it? Listen, Jeff. You'll never manage to sabotage the system. It's idiot-proof, the slightest attempt to introduce anything into the system makes it shut down. Anyway, there's nowhere for you to go . . .'

Another half step.

'The best thing you can do now is give up!'

Jeff's arm was trembling even more than before.

'The response unit will be on their way down the stairs by now. They'll be breaking in any moment, and I'm not sure I'd want to be holding a gun when that happens, if you get what I mean . . .?'

Jochen was trying to establish eye contact with Jeff, and took another pace forward. He reached his hand towards the barrel of the revolver.

'Come on, Jeff. I promise I'll help you. Everything will be . . . GAAARGH!!!'

The electric shock made the man shake like a pneumatic drill. His mouth opened and closed, and his eyes rolled back until only the whites were visible.

HP held the taser against Jochen's arm for a good five seconds before letting go.

All of the man's muscles stopped working at once and his body collapsed to the floor where a puddle of urine quickly spread from beneath it.

'That was a really stupid thing to do,' HP said coldly to the unconscious technician as he nudged him with one shoe.

'Probably military, or used to be . . .' he said to Jeff as he put his rucksack on the desk. Jeff seemed too shocked to react at all. 'No technician has such clean hands, and he talked in a military way. Like my dad . . .'

Jeff still didn't say anything. HP shrugged and after a couple of attempts successfully undid the fiddly combination lock of the rucksack, and managed to open the stiff lid.

'Here!'

He pulled out a rubber-padded portable hard-drive from the rucksack, then a pair of handcuffs, and then a bottle of water and tossed it to Jeff, who caught it, and for a moment seemed unsure what to do with it. Then his brain finally switched track, and he opened it with his teeth and took a couple of deep gulps.

'Could I suggest that you put your musket away, Jeff,' HP said. 'These guys seem to realize we mean business – isn't that right?'

None of the operators said anything, but the terror in their eyes was answer enough.

'And our would-be hero was probably right,' HP said, looking up at the large clock on the far wall. 'The response unit is bound to be on its way . . .'

He put the hard-drive on the desk in front of the nearest operator.

'Plug this in, please.'

The operator reached for the square hard-drive. His hands were shaking so much that he had trouble getting hold of the lead sticking out from the back of it.

'W-wait!' Jeff finally spoke again . . .

Ignoring him, HP nodded to the operator, waving the taser to underline his order. The man leaned forward and plugged the lead in. The screens on the desk in front of him flickered. Everyone in the room seemed to hold their breath. The second-hand on the clock ticked forward one second.

Two.

And carried on . . .

'Good to have you back, Normén,' Runeberg grinned as they headed down the corridor. 'But I still don't quite get it. I mean, Henrik Pettersson is . . .' he paused while they walked past a couple of other bodyguards. '. . . your brother. Why do you want to . . .?'

'It's pretty straightforward, really, Ludvig. No-one knows Henke better than I do, no-one else knows how he works . . .'

'Sure, there's a certain logic to that, but what happens if . . .'

They passed an open door and she caught a glimpse of Stigsson and Sammer inside, together with a third man that she recognized vaguely from television.

'I'm prepared to do whatever it takes to stop Henke and the people behind him,' she said, rather too forcefully. 'But I'm afraid I need to ask a favour, Ludvig,' she added once they were past the door. 'A very big favour . . .'

Nothing happened.

'Open the Excel file called *R-day*. Then do a search for the ID numbers listed there,' HP said, as calmly as he could. His heart was pounding so hard he imagined he could see his overalls moving.

'Use the databases kept at the bottom of the bunker. Criminal records, search engine results, parking fines, texts, telecom records, emails, Facebook, medical records, their supermarket loyalty cards – I want the fucking lot!'

The operator opened his mouth to say something but HP interrupted him.

'If I were you, I'd protest a bit less and work a bit more . . .'

He made the taser crackle just in front of the man's face.

The operator thought for a moment, then pursed his lips and nodded. He typed in a couple of commands on the keyboard.

'You see, Jeff, we aren't going to introduce anything into the system. That's exactly what they're expecting,' HP went on, trying to sound a lot calmer than he actually was. 'So, instead of following our original plan, trying to put a stop to something that can't be stopped and then sticking our hands up, we're going to do something completely different. We're going to take something with us when we leave, something seriously fucking valuable. Something this place is crammed with. Get it?'

HP raised his eyebrows in an encouraging grimace.

'Information,' Jeff muttered. 'But how's that going to help us? How can a bit of stolen information put a stop to PayTag?'

'Look, there must be five hundred names on this list,' the operator interrupted.

'Almost right, my good man,' HP smiled.

'The first tab has a hundred names. All the leader writers for every newspaper in Sweden, as well as the heads of news for every radio and television station you can think of, and a few people whose surnames just happen to be Bonnier or Wallenberg.'

'And the others?' Jeff suddenly looked a bit brighter.

'The other list contains three hundred and forty-nine names. Exactly. Are you starting to get the idea now?'

28

Ninjas

'Ready for the final act?'

Jeff nodded.

'Okay, let's get going. Keep your fingers crossed!' He put the hard-drive in the rucksack, locked the lid and fastened it round his chest. He attached the passcard with the technician's photograph to one of the straps. The blue top was a couple of sizes too big, and the uniform trousers were soaked in piss, but they'd have to do.

'Guys, the best thing you can do now is lie still under your desks for about ten minutes and try to breathe through your noses,' he called out to the men in the room.

He pulled the protective mask over his face, took out the smoke grenade, removed the safety catch and set it off. In less than thirty seconds the room was full of thick, irritating smoke.

He opened the steel door, set off another grenade and tossed it into the lobby in front of the lifts.

They waited a few seconds. An alarm went off somewhere in the distance.

'Now!'

They went out into the smoke-filled lobby. They could

hardly see as far as their hands, and their masks weren't exactly making things any better.

Jeff reached up on tiptoe and smashed the little round camera in the ceiling with the butt of the revolver. They felt their way to one corner of the hall, sat on the floor and pressed their backs to the wall.

Right beside them was a metal door with the symbol of a staircase on it, and a green sign marked *emergency exit*.

They could hear noises on the other side of the door, boots clanging on steps, radios crackling.

'Any minute now,' HP hissed. He pulled the handcuffs from his pocket.

'Fire at will, Jeff!'

Jeff aimed the revolver at the ceiling and let off a couple of shots. The stone-clad surfaces of the room served to amplify the noise and make it even more deafening.

'Shots!' someone on the other side of the door shouted. 'Get ready to go in!'

Jeff slid the gun away across the floor and put his hands behind his back.

HP quickly slipped the handcuffs on, but left the key in the lock. A moment later the door flew open in their faces, shutting them in the corner.

Through the crack in the door HP watched as a number of armed, dark-clad men in protective masks and helmets stormed in.

He and Jeff carried on pressing themselves against the wall, trying to make themselves invisible. The men disappeared into the smoke, and they heard clipped commands over by the metal door leading to the control room.

'GO!' someone shouted. There was a crash as the door to the control room was smashed open, and at that moment HP and Jeff got to their feet, rounded the door and ran out into the stairwell.

379

They raced up the stairs, two at a time.

'We've got a couple of minutes at most before they work it out,' HP hissed through his mask.

The door to the ground floor was open and they could hear voices and radios crackling above them.

They paused to catch their breath on the last floor before the surface.

HP pulled Jeff's mask off.

'Last bit, are you ready?'

'Yep, we'd better get going before they find Jochen with no clothes on . . .'

He nodded towards HP's baggy uniform and looked as if he were about to say something, but HP had already begun to drag him up the stairs with a firm grasp on the handcuffs.

Three men dressed in black were clustered round the door. As HP and Jeff approached they raised their assault rifles.

'One captive,' HP roared as loudly as he could through the protective mask. 'The second is still at large. Keep the door covered so he doesn't sneak out!'

The men stared at HP, glancing between his clothes, the ID card on his chest and Jeff's cuffed hands.

Then they stood aside and HP was able to squeeze past.

As they passed, one of the men in black slapped HP on the back.

'Take him out through the front to the others . . .'

HP carried on through the hallway, shoving the handcuffed Jeff ahead of him like a shield.

He pushed his way past firemen, paramedics and an assortment of other people who were talking into radios or mobile phones.

He was aiming for the main entrance, where he could

already see the floodlights out in the yard shining through the glass doors.

Suddenly someone grabbed him from behind. A thickset, square bloke with cropped hair, wearing a suit and loafers.

'Is this one of them?' the man said loudly in English.

'Yes,' HP barked, and tried to move on, but the man kept hold of him.

'Good work, man. What's your name?'

'Andersson,' HP shouted through the mask, and tried again to pull free of the man's grasp.

'My name's Thomas, I'm head of security for the PayTag Group. Come and find me once you've got him locked away, I want to hear more. You're exactly the type of colleague we want in the business!'

'Yes, sir!' HP shouted.

The man let go and HP and Jeff carried on out through the main doors.

The turning circle was full of vehicles. Police cars and vans, ambulances, fire engines, and several black minibuses with tinted windows.

There were lights shining from all directions, floodlights from the buildings, car headlights. People walking round with torches, even though the summer night was hardly dark. A gang of black-clad police in full riot gear were talking together but stopped when they caught sight of HP.

'Another one caught!' he barked. 'Where are you holding the others?'

'Over in the van,' one of the police officers said, nodding towards a vehicle a short distance away. 'We'll take care of this one now. Nice work!'

Two huge policemen stepped forward and grabbed Jeff's arms.

As they did so HP turned the key and unlocked the handcuffs.

Jeff shot off like a rocket. He knocked the two officers in front of him flying, and carried on across the yard. His legs were pumping like pistons, sending the gravel flying around his feet.

'He's making a run for it!' HP roared, and, just as he had hoped, the cops all took up the chase immediately.

'Get him, for fuck's sake!'

'Stop! Stop, you bastard . . .!'

Jeff tore off along the road with what must have been at least ten police chasing him.

HP waited a couple of seconds, then ran over to the van the officer had pointed out, a big, dark thing with double doors at the back, just like the one that had been parked outside his building.

He put his hand over the back window and peered in through the mesh. Nora and Hasselqvist were sitting inside, opposite one another, both with their hands behind their backs. Fucking good job he'd kept hold of the hand-cuff key . . . He resisted the urge to tap on the glass and jogged round to the driver's side instead.

The cop in the driver's seat was halfway out of the van when HP jabbed the taser into his stomach. In contrast to the two men down in the bunker, the officer just let out a sigh of surprise before collapsing. Presumably the taser was running out of juice . . .

HP dragged the man between a couple of other vehicles, then jumped into the driver's seat.

It wasn't worth trying to take the rucksack off. Anyway, he wanted to keep it close to hand, just in case.

He put his hand to the ignition.

Shit! No keys, and nothing tucked in the sun-visor either.

The cop must have had them on him, he should have checked. But he didn't dare get out to check the man's pockets. He ducked down under the wheel and yanked the plastic moulding off. He searched out the right leads as his heartbeat thundered in his ears.

This was the second van he'd stolen that day. Practice makes perfect . . .

Somewhere far off in the darkness beyond the flood-lights he heard a roar, followed at once by several more.

The cops had probably caught up with Jeff, and were now trying to wrestle him to the ground. Good luck with that . . .

His hands were twitching from the adrenalin, but he forced them into submission. He found the right leads, wound them together, then connected them to a blue one he'd already identified. A little spark, then the starter motor began to click. He pressed the accelerator pedal, once, twice . . .

The engine spluttered into action.

When he looked up, the square security chief was running straight at the van. He was closely followed by a whole pack of black-clad cops. HP revved the engine, then looked round, trying to work out the quickest way out of there.

To his left two fire engines were blocking the way, to the right another cop van.

The only way out was forward. Straight towards the pack.

His heart felt like it was going to burst out of his chest.

Here goes!

He put the van into gear and slammed the accelerator pedal to the floor. The square man stopped abruptly and stood there quite still, right in HP's path.

The van's engine roared as the distance between them shrank rapidly.

Twenty metres.

Ten.

The man didn't move.

HP hugged the wheel, looking for another way out but failing to find one.

He moved his left foot above the brake pedal.

The square man wasn't showing the slightest sign of moving.

Fuuuuck!!

Just as HP took his foot off the accelerator, two of the cops threw themselves at the square man and dragged him out of the way. The path was suddenly clear.

'Chicken!!!' HP yelled as he floored the accelerator again.

He felt sudden exultation beginning to bubble in his chest, and the taste of adrenalin was stinging his tongue.

This might actually work!

This might actually fucking work!!

The van flew up the ramp and hurtled towards the gate.

There was a pile of black-clad cops halfway up the hill, but they seemed to be far too busy trying to wrestle Jeff to the ground to pay any attention to the van as it veered round them.

HP felt with his hand over the dashboard, and found some switches towards the top that seemed promising. He pressed as many of them as he could.

The blue lights above the windscreen began to flash, and the gas-driven siren joined in a moment later.

The gate had already begun to swing open before he actually caught sight of it.

The bubbling in his chest rose up and reached his mouth just as the van drove through the gate, and he burst into hysterical laughter that almost deafened him.

Elvis has left the fucking building!

29

Information is power

'Hello?'

'Good evening, my friend, or, to be more accurate, good morning. But I daresay that you don't think it particularly good. I can imagine that you might be a little upset . . .'

'Upset isn't the word!'

'I understand, and obviously I deeply regret that things didn't go according to plan.'

'You . . . regret?'

'Of course, I'm as mortified as you are, but at the same time I would like to assure you that we're doing our utmost to reclaim the stolen information.'

'Your assurances are worth very little right now. As soon as we get this situation under control, you'll be our top priority. If I were you, I'd shut down the entire operation and find somewhere to hide, a very long way away. Because when we're done . . .'

'Let's not be too hasty, Mr Black. You are angry at the moment, which is entirely understandable. But don't allow that to make an enemy of a friend. After all, it is impossible to know in whose hands the hard-drive will finally come to rest . . .'

'You mean if you manage to get hold of it first?'

'If that scenario were to occur, I can put your mind at rest already, Mr Black. Naturally, I would personally guarantee that the information would remain secure. And that you and PayTag would be in no danger . . .'

'Ah, now I get it . . . And your guarantees would obviously come at a price?'

'Nothing in the world is free, Mr Black, and you of all people should know how valuable information can be, don't you think?'

'I'm warning you . . .'

'Think very carefully, Mr Black. If I were you, I would be weighing my words with the utmost precision. So, what was it that you were about to say?'

'. . . Nothing.'

'Good. It would seem that we understand each other. I shall be in touch again shortly, when I hope to have rather better news for you. But, for now, goodbye.'

'How the hell could you possibly have known . . .?' Hasselqvist was rubbing his wrists. 'That they were expecting us, I mean?'

It was starting to get light, and the birds in the trees around them had already kicked off with *Now That's What I Call Pine Forest* . . .

HP shrugged, pulled on his hoodie and gobbed into the nettles.

'Just a feeling, really. There always seemed to be someone one step ahead of us. First down in the tunnel, then that helicopter. Like they always knew where we were, keeping an eye on us. Besides, I got a tipoff . . .'

'Who from?'

'Oh, let's just say from a friend . . .'

He bundled up the technician's urine-stained uniform, stuffed it under one of the seats and pulled out a cigarette. The violent adrenalin rush that had given his hands

Parkinson's for the whole of the past hour seemed to have subsided for now. Hasselqvist still didn't seem entirely satisfied.

'But where the hell did you get everything from, the taser, the hard-drive with all the ID numbers . . .? When did you find the time to sort all that out?'

'I've got an old friend who lives out near the Woodland Cemetery . . .' HP cupped his hands round the cigarette. 'He can get hold of pretty much anything if you're prepared to pay,' he muttered from the side of his mouth while he struggled to get his lighter to work. 'All I had to do was turn up, see if he was in, and ask nicely. You did ask me to come up with a backup plan . . .'

He finally got the cigarette lit, took a deep drag and then blew the smoke up towards the treetops.

Sweet!

'What about Jeff?' Nora this time.

'No need to worry, he'll be fine. Unlawful threats, trespass, a bit of resisting arrest combined with violence against a public official. If he hasn't got any previous convictions, he'll get away with a fine. Two months' prison max . . . Open prison, at that . . .' he added, when she didn't seem quite as relieved as he had hoped.

Why could he never learn just to keep his mouth shut?!

'I still don't see why . . .' Hasselqvist whined. 'Why didn't they pick us up ages ago? Why let us get anywhere near the Fortress?'

'For fuck's sake, just think about it, Kent!' Nora snapped. 'What better PR could PayTag dream of than catching a group of internet terrorists red-handed? A chance to show the world how effective their security apparatus is, and simultaneously how desperate and evil we, their opponents, are? *If you're not with us, you're with the terrorists* – that trick's worked before. Shit, how come I didn't see this coming . . .?'

387

She picked up a stick and began to draw some lines in the grit on the track.

'The EU Data Retention Directive would have swept through every parliament in Europe, just like anti-terrorism legislation did after 9/11. Then PayTag could sit back and rake in the profits. The Game Master came up with a suspected terrorist, and fixed him up with a few other suitable scapegoats. People who had already outlived their usefulness . . .'

She scratched over the lines she had drawn, turning them into crosses.

Four of them . . .

No-one spoke for a while.

Then Hasselqvist opened his mouth again, but Nora beat him to it.

'It must have been him. You get that, don't you?'

HP didn't answer.

'W-who? I don't get it!' Hasselqvist whined.

'The Source, Manga. It must have been him deceiving us.'

'We don't know that,' HP muttered.

'Of course we do . . .'

The penny finally seemed to have dropped for Hasselqvist:

'The whole thing was his idea! It was him who brought us together, me, Nora, Jeff . . .'

'And you, HP,' Nora said quietly as she went on drawing lines on the ground.

'There could be other explanations. He might have been tricked himself, the Game Master might have . . .'

'You just don't want to see it,' Nora snapped, throwing the stick into the undergrowth. 'We got fucked, properly fucked by someone who's an expert at mind games like this. For all we know, Manga could have been working directly for the Game Master. Maybe he could even . . .'

She broke off.

'What? What were you going to say, Nora?' HP snapped back. 'Let's hear your brilliant deduction . . .!'

'I know Manga is your friend, but you have to consider the fact that he could actually BE the Game Master . . .'

'Impossible!'

'Why?' Hasselqvist seemed to have taken Nora's side.

'Because I've met the Game Master, I told you. His name is Tage Sammer, and he's about seventy . . .'

'How do you know he's the Game Master? Did he say so?' Nora again. They were working as a team now.

'Yes. Well, no, not in so many words . . .'

He could hear how flaky it sounded.

'Look, it's like this: I met him out in the middle of a forest. He gave me a task, a totally mad one that I couldn't possibly carry out. He wanted me to attack the royal family, okay?'

No-one said anything, the other two seemed to be waiting for him to go on.

'They've been chasing me ever since, trying to send me mad . . .'

'Was that when you decided to shoot Black?' Nora said.

'Erm . . . yes, and no. I mean, I wasn't really myself . . .'

'But what did the Game stand to gain from you going mad? I mean, if they wanted you to carry out a task . . .?'

He had to admit that he had no answer to that.

'Manga is dead,' he said bluntly. 'That, if anything, proves . . .'

'Do we actually *know* that?' Hasselqvist was sounding very agitated now. 'Okay, so Nora saw the barn explode. But what if Manga managed to get out . . .?'

'Hmm. I'm inclined to agree with HP on that,' Nora said. 'No-one could have survived that!'

A short silence followed as Hasselqvist reflected on this.

'Okay, how about this: the helicopter was there to give

Manga a chance to escape. Create a diversion so that we'd all leave without him. But they hadn't counted on the explosives going up, because they were supposed to be in the van. Don't you remember how Manga protested when Jeff said we had to move everything into the Polo?'

Hasselqvist was sounding more and more heated.

'That must have been it. The helicopter would have given him a chance to get out, leaving the rest of us to head off to the tunnel on our own. And that fits with the GPS transmitter I found in the back of the van. They needed a way to keep track of us once we were on our own, without Manga . . .'

Nora looked like she wanted to say something, but Hasselqvist carried on.

'Then, when we switched vehicles, they lost us. So they were left staring at the tunnel while we snuck in through the main entrance. It all fits . . .'

HP didn't respond, just stood up and marched straight out into the forest.

'Where are you going?' Nora called after him.

'Need a piss,' he muttered, mostly to himself.

He had no desire at all to continue this discussion. Manga was dead, Sammer was the Game Master. If Manga *had* somehow been involved, the short-sighted little snake had in all likelihood been shafted as well, just like him and the two muppets by the van.

He stopped, whipped out his joystick and took aim at an anthill. Someone had betrayed them, that much was crystal clear. But if it wasn't Manga, then who was it . . .?

Another question he had no answer to . . .

'So what do we do now?' Nora said when he returned to the van with a fresh cig in the corner of his mouth.

'We head back to civilization, find a computer with a decent internet connection, and send the contents of that hard-drive to every newsroom we can think of. And to the email address of every MP, of course.'

He took a deep drag.

'That ought to give them something to think about before the vote on the EU directive. It's a pretty shocking experience,' he went on, 'getting all of your electronic footprints thrown back in your face like that. And the papers will have a field day. Just think of all the goodies hidden away on that hard-drive.'

He nodded towards his rucksack.

'Affairs, tax fiddles, all sorts of unsuitable connections. You name it!'

He grinned and shook his head.

'It might even lead to a new election . . . In which case . . .'

'. . . PayTag, Black and the Game are fucked!' Nora concluded.

Her voice sounded a bit brighter.

'There's no way they could recover from something like this. Not just because the most wanted man in Sweden managed to fool them and get in and out of their ultra-secure underground bunker . . .'

HP muttered something, finished his fag and ground the butt into the dirt.

'. . . but because the hard-drive proves that they really did have the tools to cream off their customers' information. Picking out anything of interest, then refining it into a saleable asset. Just as we suspected the whole fucking time!!! There's no way anyone would want to work with them after this . . .'

'So it's all over . . .' Hasselqvist sighed.

'We won, they lost. Game over!'

HP was about to say something, but stopped and held up his hand. Far in the distance there was the sound of sirens.

Then they suddenly fell silent.
'Into the van, quick!' he hissed.

Clear blue sky, hardly a cloud in sight. The kitchen window
was open, letting in a breeze of summer air. Perfect wedding
weather, the happy couple deserved congratulations for
that.

She had woken up long before the alarm clock went
off, and a song by Kent seemed to have got stuck in her
head during the night. Even though her mind had plenty
of other tracks to choose from, the lines continued to
replay in her ears. Over and over again . . .

You know nothing about me.
I know nothing about you.

She inserted a pouch of coffee into the Nespresso
machine, then waited patiently as the golden brown rat's
tail trickled into her cup before she picked it up.

The coffee went down easily enough, which was more
than could be said for the sandwich. Her nerves had
already shrunk her stomach to half its normal size, and
there wasn't a lot of room left.

She shut her eyes and took a couple of deep breaths,
put the coffee cup down, then held her hands out in front
of her. The song was still going round her head.

You know nothing about me.
I know nothing about you . . .

Only a few hours left, and she still hadn't made her
mind up.

Unless she had, a long time ago . . .

Jocke Berg was still singing inside her head:

How do you feel now?
Do you feel anything?

Good question!

A bloody good question, actually.

Surprisingly, she felt strangely calm for the first time in ages.

She went through the timetable in her head, trying to picture the route before her. Every turn, every new street. Trying to imagine the sounds, smells, impressions. The bulletproof vest against her body, the earpiece of the radio in her ear – the gun at her hip.

It helped briefly, but the song was back a minute or so later.

I know nothing about you . . .

She opened one of the kitchen cupboards and took out a small tub of pills without even thinking. She weighed it in her hand, listening to the little tablets rattling around inside.

Time to decide. What was it to be?

Red or black?

She pulled the lid off.

You know nothing about me . . .

'How the hell did they find us so quickly?'

'Don't know,' HP growled as he tried to cling onto the seat.

The heavy police van was lurching over the gravel track.

'Maybe the van can be traced, but I didn't think the cops were that advanced . . .'

They flew over a bump and for a fraction of a second the van left the ground. As it landed HP hit his head on the side window.

'Fuck!'

He tried to look through the little window of the holding cell at the back of the van, but all he could see was dust flying up behind them.

'How many?' he yelled at Hasselqvist.

'Two, at least. Must be more on the way!'

'Hang on, shit, we should have done this earlier . . .'

Nora undid her seatbelt and clambered into the passenger seat. She fiddled with the police radio and suddenly excited voices began to pour from the speakers.

9150, they're heading straight for you, over.

Copy that!

Hasselqvist slammed on the brakes, spun the wheel and slid the van into a side track. Say what you like, but the guy could drive . . .

Control, 9127, they turned left, now heading north . . .

Copy that, 9127, all cars from control, now heading north, towards Nybygget . . . The radio operator in the Regional Communication Centre sounded considerably less excited than the officers taking part in the chase.

The van's engine was roaring and the track in front of them narrowed to a thin line. But Hasselqvist didn't seem particularly concerned.

'In two hundred metres I'll be turning sharp left, so hold on . . .' he yelled.

'How the fuck do you know where . . .?' HP managed to splutter as he clung on as best he could.

'I did some rally driving up here a few years ago . . .' Hasselqvist replied.

He slammed the brakes on and did a controlled hand-brake turn.

Control, 9127, they've just turned off, we've lost . . . hang on.

HP held his breath.

No, we've got contact again, now heading west.

Copy that, 9127, the helicopter's on its way.

'If the helicopter picks us up we're finished,' Hasselqvist snarled through his teeth.

He spun the van into another side track.

'There's only one option,' he said over his shoulder. 'You'll have to jump out.'

'What?!'

'YOU'LL HAVE TO JUMP OUT!' Hasselqvist shouted, without taking his eyes off the track. 'I'll stop and let you out, then I'll carry on. There's half a tank left, and I can keep going for at least another half hour, forty minutes. If they don't figure out where you jumped, they'll never find you . . .'

'B-but, we're in the middle of the forest . . .' Nora began.

'The railway line's over there.'

Hasselqvist gestured towards the window beside her.

'Find it, then head south. It's a couple of hours' walk to the nearest station. Then you can just catch the train back into the city.'

'But we can't just leave you . . .'

'Kent's right. We don't have a choice,' HP interrupted. 'If we get caught, the hard-drive will be in the Game Master's hands in less than an hour, and then everything, all this, will have been in vain . . .'

Nora bit her lip.

'Okay,' she conceded. 'Just tell us what you want us to do, Kent.'

'We need a bit of breathing space, some sort of diversion so I can stop for a moment . . .'

Control to all cars, the helicopter will be with you in approximately five minutes.

They're currently heading west. It looks like they're listening in, so we'll switch to the backup frequency. Backup frequency from now on, over and out!

The radio bleeped and suddenly went silent.

'The fire extinguisher . . .' Nora turned to HP and nodded at the floor.

It took him a moment to catch on.

He loosened his belt, braced himself against the seat and leaned over. There was a fire extinguisher on the floor on the side of the van. He quickly untied the rubber strap and pulled it loose.

At the same time Nora scrambled back over her seat.

'Open the door!' she yelled, and he did as she said.

The heavy sliding door slipped from his grasp and flew open.

He stared through the opening at the trees flying past just a metre or so away.

'Don't worry!' she yelled. 'I'll keep hold of you!'

But he hesitated.

'The helicopter's almost here,' Hasselqvist shouted from the front of the van.

HP closed his eyes.

Now or never.

He loosened the nozzle of the extinguisher and pulled out the safety catch.

Then he stood up.

Nora grabbed hold of his belt.

'Hold on, I'll slow down and let them get closer . . .'

Hasselqvist took his foot off the gas and suddenly they could hear the sirens of the cars behind them.

'Now!' Hasselqvist shouted.

HP put one foot on the step, then leaned the top half of his body out of the van.

His belt cut into his left kidney and he felt Nora's grip tighten against his hip.

The first police car was only ten metres away.

He raised the nozzle of the extinguisher, took aim . .

Suddenly the wheels on one side of the van hit a pothole, the van lurched and his head slammed against the roof. He lost his balance and for a couple of weightless seconds was floating free.

Then Nora grabbed his arm and dragged him into the van.

Fuck, that was close!!

'Now, now, NOW!!' Hasselqvist screamed from the driver's seat.

HP stood up again, leaned his torso out through the door and braced himself against the step.

He raised the nozzle and slammed the lever down.

A shower of powder flew out of the hose, got caught in the van's slipstream and landed in the middle of the police car's windscreen like a big white blanket.

The driver put his foot on the brake but HP carried on spraying powder until the police car vanished in a cloud of smoke behind them.

Then he threw the extinguisher out and let Nora drag him back inside the van.

Hasselqvist put his foot down.

'There's another side track in a hundred metres,' he yelled. 'Jump out when I slow down to turn. Then just lie low until they've gone past . . .'

'Copy that!' HP moved closer to the door again.

'Good luck, Kent. You're hot shit when it comes to driving!' he yelled at Hasselqvist, and got a quick wave in response.

'Don't forget the rucksack,' Nora said close to his ear.

Of course . . . shit!

If he'd jumped without the hard-drive . . . Epic Fail!

He snatched the rucksack from the floor, and pulled it onto his back.

'Straps!' Nora said, pointing at his chest.

He muttered something to himself, but did as she said, fastening the clumsy metal catch between the two straps.

The van slowed down, then turned sharply to the right.

'NOOOW!' Hasselqvist yelled.

30

*Underneath the spreading
chestnut tree . . .*

She cycled slowly along Rålambsvägen, then turned off into the park, following the path across the grass.

Seagulls and crows were squabbling as usual over the previous night's rubbish and leftover food, but a team of cleaners from the council had already arrived.

The city had to put its best face on now that at least part of the world would be watching it.

Apart from them, the only people in sight were a couple of dog-walkers and an early-bird jogger.

She changed down the gears to get up the steep slope leading to the bridge over Norr Mälarstrand. An empty bus with blue and yellow flags on its roof passed below her.

She carried on up to Fridhemsplan, wove her way through the red lights and stopped next to the gatehouse. The feeling of pulling her police ID from her pocket was unexpectedly comforting.

'Good morning,' the guard said in an over-cheerful voice before waving her through.

Just as she passed the gate and was starting to roll down the tunnel leading beneath Kronoberg, her mobile buzzed.

She waited until she had parked her bike in the garage before checking the message.

> Good luck today, Rebecca.
> Your father would have been very proud of you!
> When this is over, I promise to explain all about him.
> Uncle Tage

She couldn't help smiling. Then she saw that there was another text in her inbox.

Just three words, with no sender's name or number.

> Don't trust anyone!

She deleted it at once.

Outside the changing room she bumped into Runeberg.

'Have you heard anything?' she asked, skipping the preliminaries.

'There was a car chase early this morning north of Uppsala. At least ten cars, helicopter, road blocks, the works. It took them an hour to put a stop . . .'

'And?' She held her breath.

Runeberg shook his head.

'They got away. They're probably hiding, lying low up there in . . .'

'. . . the forest,' she concluded, but he was only half listening.

They'd chatted a bit at the start, mostly about which way they should go, but for once he had been fairly taciturn and the conversation had died out.

But now she evidently wanted to make another attempt.

'What did you say?' he mumbled.

'I said we should soon be out of the forest. I thought I just heard a church bell . . .'

'Mmm.'

It had taken half an hour to find the railway line, then they'd spent more than two hours walking through the trees along the side of the track. In spite of its thick, padded straps the rucksack was digging into his neck and shoulders. His legs felt heavy and he'd already fallen flat on his face a couple of times after tripping over roots and rocks as they rushed into the trees to hide from passing trains.

He was a child of the tarmac, not some fucking tree-hugger . . .

She turned round and gave him a quick glance.

'You look knackered. When did you last get any sleep?'

He didn't answer.

Now that the adrenalin had faded things were starting to fall into place. Things he hadn't thought about before.

They walked on in silence.

'Shame about Manga,' she said eventually.

'W-what?' He looked up and stopped abruptly.

'A shame what happened . . . With the barn . . .' she added when he just stared at her like an idiot.

'Yeah, okay . . . You've said that once already.' He looked away.

'You're angry with him, aren't you?'

He didn't answer, but that didn't stop her going on.

'You do get it, don't you? That Manga shafted us somehow . . .?'

'I don't want to talk about it . . .'

'Mind you, you could be right, maybe Manga got shafted as well? If the Game Master tricked him the same way he tricked us, making him believe he was really doing something good . . .'

400

'Just a couple of hours ago you seemed pretty convinced that he *was* the Game Master . . .' HP kicked at a stone, then another one.

'I know, I'm sorry about that. Stress makes you say weird things. Manga had the wool pulled over his eyes just like you and me,' she said. 'At least that's how I'm choosing to look at it.'

He was still kicking stones from the track into the undergrowth.

'Manga isn't the sort who'd sell out a mate . . .' he muttered, but without sounding quite as convinced as he should.

Or *wasn't*, he silently corrected himself.

Shit, Manga, how did everything get so fucked up?!

With everything that had been happening, he'd hardly had a moment to think about the barn and the explosion. Instead he'd been using his tried and tested method of getting his brain to skip past anything that was too unpleasant to deal with. But right now his superpowers were waning.

High time to change the subject.

He set off again, and she quickly turned round and they ended up walking beside each other.

'One more thing . . .' he said. 'I've been wanting to ask ever since Medborgarplatsen . . .'

'You want to know if I was the one who set fire to your flat?'

He started, but before he'd worked out how to reply, she'd trotted a few steps ahead.

'Over there, can you see it? A station!'

'Okay, good people!'

The police officers gathered in the conference room fell silent at once when Runeberg entered the room.

'One last run-through before we go live. The ceremony in the cathedral ends at 13.30, and the cortege will set off shortly after that. We'll be heading down Slottsbacken, then round to Norrbro. Then right towards Kungsträdgården, and into Kungsträdgårdsgatan . . .'

He paused for a moment and several of the bodyguards exchanged glances.

'We've got extra plain-clothed officers stationed along Kungsträdgårdsgatan, in case anyone fancies trying a copycat attack . . .' Runeberg went on. 'Then left into Hamngatan, to Sergels torg, then right onto Sveavägen, as far as the Concert Hall . . . Any questions so far?'

'Any news about the suspects?' one of the bodyguards at the front asked, probably one of the new ones. 'Pettersson and Al-Hassan, I mean,' he went on in a confident tone of voice.

'I was going to take that later, but since you ask,' Runeberg muttered, clearly annoyed at having to change subject.

'A fair bit has happened since yesterday. Farook Al-Hassan, or Magnus Sandström as he's also known, is believed to be dead. His car was found at the site of an explosion in a barn north of Uppsala, along with remains that forensics are fairly sure are his. There were also traces of explosives and chemical fertilizer at the scene, so it may be that a homemade bomb accidentally detonated early. We'll be hearing more about that shortly.'

Runeberg nodded towards Tage Sammer, who was sitting on one of the chairs closest to the door. Stigsson was sitting next to him, and when Runeberg started talking again Stigsson leaned forward and whispered something in Sammer's ear. Rebecca felt a lump in her throat and swallowed hard a couple of times to get rid of it.

'As far as the others are concerned, we have recently

apprehended an individual in a stolen police van. But two of the suspects are still at large, including our other prime suspect.'

Runeberg glanced in her direction.

'By that I mean Henrik Pettersson, also known as HP.'

They were in luck. The next train to Stockholm was only ten minutes away, giving just enough time for Nora to buy tickets and get something to eat from the station's vending machine.

HP stayed hidden behind one of the pillars on the platform, keeping an eye out for pursuers.

He gulped down two Snickers bars as he stood there, and just had time to wash down these delicacies with the half-bottle of Coke that she passed him before the train pulled into the station.

Once they'd found two empty seats he was so tired that he forgot to take the rucksack off before crashing down onto the window seat. To make matters worse, the metal catch was playing up, and he swore so loudly that several of the other passengers glared angrily in their direction.

'Hang on, I'll get it.' Nora slipped into the aisle seat and leaned over to help him. 'You have to lift them up first, then twist the two flat pieces apart.'

Her head was right next to his face, he could feel her fingers against his chest, and for a few moments he thought he could smell her shampoo.

Strange how the artificial scent of flowers could make him feel a bit better . . .

'There!' Nora said as the straps slipped apart.

He pulled the rucksack off and slid it onto the floor. Just to be on the safe side he leaned it against one of his legs so he'd feel if anything happened to it. Then he leaned back, massaged his aching shoulders and resisted a sudden urge to close his eyes.

The train had built up speed and the gentle rocking motion was almost impossible to resist.

But he was going to try.

He turned towards Nora. She was just putting a little sachet of chewing tobacco in her mouth, and he waited politely for her to slot it into place under her top lip.

'We'll be back in the city in less than two hours,' he said in a low voice. 'There's an internet café with a decent connection at Hötorget, I've used it a couple of times before. I can send from there.'

She nodded as she adjusted the position of the tobacco with her tongue. The movement fascinated him, almost making him lose his thread.

'That sounds good, HP, we'll aim for that. Have you thought about what we're going to do after that?'

He shook his head.

'I don't really give a shit. Once the files are out there PayTag will sink like a stone, probably dragging the Game Master down with it, maybe even the whole Game. They're going to have their hands full trying to save their own skin . . .'

'And you think they'll just forget about us?'

'That remains to be seen . . .'

He shrugged.

'So, how about telling me how you got involved in all this?' he said a few moments later, without really knowing why.

She put the lid back on her tub of chewing tobacco and slowly put it away as she thought about her response.

'It's quite a long story . . .' she said.

'I'm not doing anything for the next hour or so,' he replied, and tried to conjure up his most charming smile.

'Okay, but it'll have to be the short version. We could both do with a bit of a rest . . . I used to play top-level handball. It was going pretty well, I even got selected for the national squad. Trained practically every day . . .'

He nodded to demonstrate his interest, which was easier than he'd expected.

'I lived for sport, for the camaraderie of the team, the competition. Then I picked up an injury.'

'Ouch.'

He could have kicked himself. Time for some serious empathy, and the best he could come up with was *ouch* . . .?

But Nora didn't seem bothered.

'The cruciate ligament in one knee became detached, and the doctor told me my body just couldn't handle that amount of training. I was determined to make a comeback, did the whole rehab thing, but it was never the same again. Once you've had problems with your ligaments you never get back to where you were. From having been one of the best, I came back as no better than average. So I trained even harder, which was obviously really stupid.'

She shook her head.

'So I kept picking up more injuries, and ended up spending more and more time on the bench. In the end I decided to quit, before I got dropped . . . I didn't want to give anyone the satisfaction, better to go before I was humiliated – at least that was my reasoning. Now in hindsight that wasn't particularly smart . . . Can you imagine the withdrawal symptoms?'

He nodded. His eyelids suddenly felt heavy, but he really did want to hear the rest. He thought he had a pretty good idea where the story was heading.

'So I ploughed my energy into my studies instead, got my degree and started work as a vet. But I missed sport so fucking much. Nothing else even came close. So when the Game Master contacted me, offering me a new sense of belonging, a new game plan . . .'

She shrugged.

'How did that come about? I mean, how did he get hold of you, the Game Master?'

'It started with a simple email, an offer . . .'

'. . . *to take part in a completely unique experience, unlike anything you've ever done before* . . .'

'Something like that, yes.' She smiled. 'It wasn't until much later that I realized they'd been checking me out. They knew all about who I was, what I'd done. How I worked, what buttons they had to press . . .'

He nodded.

'Sounds familiar . . .'

HP's head was feeling heavier and heavier, and he had to struggle just to keep his eyes open.

'Look, that business with the fire in your flat . . .' she went on.

'We don't have to talk about that now . . .' he mumbled.

'I know, but I want to. You're right, it was me. But you were never supposed to get hurt, I called the fire brigade before I even started the fire. I wanted to be sure they were on their way . . . But obviously that doesn't make it okay. My only excuse is that I wasn't thinking straight. All I wanted was to move up that list, get to the top . . .'

He waved one hand.

'You really don't have to explain . . .'

'Okay, but I feel like I should. I don't want you to think I . . .'

'I don't, it's fine. Trust me, the Game Master got me to do far worse things . . .'

The door at the end of the carriage suddenly opened and a man in a dark jacket came in.

406

He looked round the carriage in a way that made HP dodge below the back of the seat in front.

The door opened again and the man was joined by a woman.

They seemed to discuss something for a moment, then returned to the carriage they had come from.

'False alarm,' Nora said. 'They were just looking for empty seats . . . Look, what I was saying, I'm sorry about the fire,' she went on. 'You've got to believe me. I wasn't thinking straight . . .'

'Nora, it's okay.'

His head suddenly felt like it was full of porridge and he was having trouble holding it upright.

'Look, I'm wiped out, how about getting some rest?' he muttered. 'We can swap more war stories later . . .'

'Sure,' she nodded. 'No problem.'

He leaned his head back and she was quick to follow his example.

A couple of minutes later she cautiously opened her eyes. She listened to his heavy breathing, then leaned forward and gently pulled out the rucksack from where he had put it on the floor.

Then she slid silently out of her seat and left the carriage.

'I'm very pleased to have caught you, Miss Normén.'

It was Sammer, closely followed by Stigsson and the vaguely familiar man she had glimpsed in the office the previous day.

'Both I and Superintendent Stigsson are extremely grateful for your cooperation. We are both deeply impressed by the strength of character and loyalty that you've shown.'

She smiled uncertainly, partly because she was having trouble with this whole charade, and partly because she wasn't sure how she was supposed to react to the unexpected praise.

'T-thanks,' she managed to say.

The third man in the group held out his hand.

'Erik af Cederskjöld, press spokesman for the Palace. Good to meet you. Colonel Pellas speaks very highly of you,' he smiled.

His handshake felt damp, and his smile only reached halfway to his eyes. She had no difficulty seeing through his fake politeness.

'Nice to meet you,' she muttered. 'I'm afraid I have to go, we're on our way now.'

'Of course,' Sammer / Pellas said. 'I just wanted to wish you good luck, Miss Normén . . .'

She met his gaze, and, just as the other two men turned away, he gave her a quick wink.

He was in a labyrinth, he realized that pretty much straight away. The pink walls around him didn't quite reach all the way to the ceiling, and seemed to start and stop without any discernible logic.

He had no idea how he'd ended up there, nor how he was supposed to know who was chasing him. The passageway behind and in front of him was empty, and there wasn't a sound to be heard anywhere. Yet he still knew they were out there, that they were making their way towards him on all sides through the maze.

The straps of the rucksack were cutting into his shoulders and the pain was so bad it was making him screw up his eyes, but he kept going. Somewhere inside this labyrinth was the solution to everything, he was convinced of that.

If only he could get there first, everything would be all right.

When he turned a corner she was just sitting there. A little girl with a red hair-band, and he knew at once who she was. She had her hands over her face, but looked up as he came closer.

'Is this the Luttern labyrinth?' she said, and her voice was just as he remembered it.

'Of course it is,' he heard himself reply. 'You can come with me, if you like?'

He held out his hand but she didn't take it.

'I daren't,' she said. 'He says you're dangerous . . .'

'Who? The Carer?'

'No, I don't know him.'

The next moment he heard steps approaching. Sounds from all directions. Polished black shoes on tarmac. And he knew who they belonged to. The hair on the back of his neck stood up.

'Come on,' he said to the girl. 'You have to come with me . . .'

She shook her head.

'If I go with you, we'll both die.'

'But you have to. The Carer . . .' All of a sudden his voice sounded whiny, like a small child's.

She stood up, and suddenly it was as if they had both changed and swapped roles. She leaned over him, stroked his hair and kissed his cheek.

'Forget the Carer. People only come to the Luttern labyrinth for one reason, little Henke,' she whispered. 'They come here to die . . .'

He was sitting two carriages away, and as soon as he caught sight of her his face burst into a smile.

'Well done, Nora, I knew you could do it.'

'Thanks.'

She sat down in the empty seat beside him and handed over the rucksack. He put it down on the floor without showing the slightest inclination to open it.

'Are you okay?' he asked.

'Sure,' she muttered.

'What about him?'

No answer.

'We had no choice, you know that, Nora . . .'

'Yes, I know . . . How's Jeff?'

'Don't worry about him, he's perfectly safe where he is. So, how long have we got?'

'Half an hour, maybe a bit longer. I put half a Rohypnol in his Coke, and together with his lack of sleep . . .' She shrugged.

'Good, plenty of time. It's up there.'

He gestured towards the luggage rack above them.

'What about her, his sister?' Nora said.

'She's exactly where she needs to be . . .'

He looked at her for a few moments.

'You like him, don't you?' he finally said. 'HP, I mean . . .'

Nora didn't answer.

Instead she stood up, got the object down from the rack, and put it over her shoulder.

'He thinks you were manipulated,' she said curtly. 'That you meant well, but were deceived as well. He'd rather believe that than the alternative, Manga . . .'

31

Point of no return

They were in position outside the cathedral.

Six of them around the carriage. Runeberg in front on the right, with her in the same position on the left.

Two troops of Horse Guards in ceremonial uniform were grouped around the Obelisk in front of the Palace. The horses were stamping anxiously at the cobbles, the sound of their hooves echoing between the buildings.

For what must be the tenth time, she ran through her equipment. Baton, radio, pistol. All of it fastened to her belt under her jacket.

The wire from the radio ran up her back, and turned into a curly little telephone cable above her collar before reaching the earpiece in her left ear.

In the other ear she had the speaker connected to the mobile in her inside pocket.

She tried jogging a few steps down the slope in front of the Palace.

No problem, everything was where it should be.

She glanced at the time.

Forty minutes left.

* * *

'Wake up, HP!' She shook him gently on the shoulder.

He opened his eyes reluctantly, and it took him a few seconds to realize where he was.

'We're almost there,' she said.

'Okay.' He sat up, rubbed his eyes, then looked down at the floor for the rucksack.

It was gone!

Panic-stricken, he leaned down so quickly that he banged his head on the seat in front. Then he realized it had just slid under his seat slightly.

'You were talking in your sleep,' Nora said.

'Oh?' He sat up again, rubbing his head.

'The same words, over and over again.'

'What words?'

'*The Luttern labyrinth*. What does that mean?'

He shrugged his shoulders.

'You tell me. I've been trying to work it out for weeks now. Luttern is a region in northern Germany, in Westphalia, to be more precise. That's all I've managed to find out.'

'Okay, well that explains the street name . . .'

'What?'

'Westphalia was Swedish once, that's why they named a street after it.'

'Hang on, what are you talking about? There's no Lutternsgatan in Stockholm . . .'

'No, not any more, there isn't. They got rid of it when they built Kungsgatan. They did away with another road at the same time, Hötorgsgränd . . .'

She was interrupted by an announcement over the tannoy.

We will shortly be arriving at Stockholm Central Station. The platform will be on the left hand side of the train, facing the direction of travel.

412

We at Swedish Railways would like to welcome you to Stockholm, and once again, we apologize for the late arrival of this service . . .

Nora stood up from her seat.

'Time to go . . .'

He stretched, then squeezed out of the window seat.

'So where was it, then, Lutternsgatan?'

'Where Malmskillnadsgatan crosses Kungsgatan, I think.'

The train was slowing down jerkily, making the carriage sway.

'I did a unit on the architecture of Stockholm at university, in case you're wondering . . .' she added. 'The only reason I remember Lutternsgatan is that we were given half the day off to go and take pictures of the sign . . .'

'The sign?' He pulled the rucksack on.

'There's a sign under the Malmskillnad Bridge . . .' She helped him with the straps. '*To commemorate the breaching of the Brunkeberg Ridge and the successful union of separate districts of the city*, something like that. It was part of the test . . .'

She carefully did up the metal catch across his chest, and pulled up the hood of his jacket. The other people in the carriage were making their way to the exits, but Nora took HP's hand and forced her way through to one of the doors. The train pulled slowly into the platform.

They saw the men as the train moved slowly along the platform. Two standing at the end of the platform, another two in the middle, all of them in dark suits and sunglasses, their earpieces clearly visible. Nora squeezed his hand.

'Ready?'

He nodded.

She turned towards him and started fiddling with the thick flap of material above the catch of the rucksack,

413

adjusting the velcro several times before she was satisfied. It felt bulky against his chest, as if it had grown while he was asleep.

'There, now you'll be able to run without it rubbing.'

The train made a few last jolts.

'If we get separated don't wait for me,' she said. 'The mission comes first. Whatever happens you have to get to that internet café, okay?'

He nodded.

'Good.'

Just as the door began to bleep, she leaned forward, put her hand behind his back and kissed him.

'Thirty minutes to go, are you ready?'

She nodded to Runeberg as he marched towards her over the cobbles, but he didn't respond.

'Over here, everyone.'

The other four bodyguards joined them.

'We've just received new information. The two remaining suspects are not longer thought to be in the forest outside Uppsala. They may have managed to get back to Stockholm.'

'Are we cancelling the cortege?' one of the other bodyguards asked.

Runeberg shook his head. 'The threat is not judged serious enough . . .'

He gave Rebecca a quick look.

'Someone really wants this cortege to go ahead. At almost any cost, it would seem . . .'

She let a few eager passengers out first before pulling him onto the platform.

The train on the other side of the platform must have just arrived as well, because the platform was soon full of people heading in all directions.

They zigzagged their way towards the exit, trying to keep their heads down.

The exit was getting closer.

A loud cry behind them made him look back.

Two men in suits were heading straight for them.

'Come on!'

Nora dragged him after her, forging ahead faster and faster.

Off to the left in front of them two more men were trying to elbow their way through the crowd of passengers. Nora broke into a run, pushing a couple of people straight at the two men. One of the passengers fell over right in front of the suits. But Nora didn't stop. She pulled his hand harder, speeded up and found a gap along the edge of the platform.

The exit was getting nearer.

Then he caught sight of the man from the Fortress. His square frame was unmistakeable. The security chief, the man he'd almost run over . . .

The man wasn't moving, he was just standing there waiting by the exit. Staring straight at them. His knees were slightly bent and he had his hands out in front of him, like an American footballer.

HP pulled Nora's hand, then looked back over his shoulder. Their pursuers were just a few metres behind them.

No chance of turning back, that escape route was completely cut off . . .

Ten metres away from the man, and HP thought he could just make out a hint of a smile. A creepy, snakelike smile that made HP shudder.

But Nora carried on straight ahead without seeming to realize the danger.

The man steeled himself, thrusting his shoulders out . . .

At the last moment Nora let go of his hand. Her long legs pumped a few times like pistons on the platform . . .

Then she jumped.

She crashed straight into the man. Their bodies collided with a muffled thud.

He heard Nora yell something, saw her hands rise and fall as she made an all-out attack on the man, and HP was overwhelmed by an instinctive urge to help her.

Then he realized that she wasn't shouting at the man.

She was yelling at him.

'Keep going, keep going, keep . . .'

One of the man's massive hands grabbed Nora by the neck, lifted her from the ground and cut off her cry. HP looked straight ahead and aimed for the exit. But it was impossible not to look back. Nora was struggling wildly, trying to loosen the man's grasp round her neck.

HP looked forward again to avoid running into the doorpost. When he emerged into the hall he looked back one last time and just managed to see the massive man toss Nora's limp body aside as if it were a ragdoll.

The feeling took him by surprise. It came out of nowhere, and it took him just a fraction of a second to identify it. Hate.

White hot, burning hate!

His pursuers were still close behind him. HP raced through the concourse, aiming for the main exit. But just as he was about to swing left through the glass doors leading to Centralplan he caught sight of a police car outside, and carried on straight ahead instead. Someone shouted something behind him, but he ignored them.

Shit, obviously he should have run down into the underground network instead of heading straight for the nearest exit like some fucking rat . . .

The south end of the concourse was rapidly approaching

416

and all the exits were behind him. There was nothing but restaurants at this end, no decent escape route anywhere.

A quick look back.

Two muppets in suits ten metres behind him, then another group led by the square-framed man.

The door to the restaurant was getting closer but he made no effort to slow down.

Instead he stormed past the reception area and carried on towards the back of the room.

A swing door opened to his left and a waiter came out carrying two plates. HP raced past him with the narrowest of margins and shot through the swing door into the kitchen.

Two men in aprons looked up in surprise.

'Exit?' HP yelled.

One of them pointed with a spatula.

'Thanks!' he managed to splutter before rushing on.

There was a serving trolley parked by the wall and he pulled it over behind him to slow his pursuers. But he didn't waste any time looking at the result. Instead he crashed into the door with full force, hammering the handle down and lurching out into an enclosed yard. In front of him, on the other side of the fence, stood the ten-metre tall cement pillars supporting the Klarastrand flyover.

Out of reflex he ran to the right, and it took him several seconds to realize that the way out was back to the left.

Fuck!

The men chasing him crashed through the door, but he'd just spotted another way out. The end of the station building was covered in scaffolding, and there was a ladder not far ahead of him. He scampered up it to the first platform like a chimp on acid, and just as the first suit put his hand on the ladder he kicked it away as hard as he could.

417

The ladder fell to the ground and he heard swearing below him, but didn't stop to see if it had landed on anyone. He raced off along the planks until he found some more steps, and shot up them to the next level.

The railing of the flyover was clearly visible now.

Up another level, and now he could feel the scaffolding shake as his pursuers ran along the platforms below him.

Another level, and now he was the same height as the railing.

The only problem was that there were two metres of empty air between it and the scaffolding . . .

One last ladder and he was at the top of the scaffolding.

Fuck, it was high!

Someone shouted something in English. The platform was shaking badly, and he guessed that everyone chasing him was now scrambling up the scaffolding.

The flyover was about a metre below him, but at least two metres away. Difficult, but not impossible. Well, that was what he hoped, anyway . . .

But of course he did have the rucksack on his back now.

It felt heavier than before, but that could well be because he was weaker.

The scaffolding was shaking more and more.

He kicked the safety rail away, then took a step back and pressed against the wall of the building.

The next moment the first of his pursuers reached his level, and he pushed off as hard as he could, taking a single stride and then leaping out into thin air . . .

'Well, good people, that's the ceremony over,' Ludvig's voice said over the radio in her ear. 'Ten minutes for the bride to freshen up, then it'll be time. We'll be moving the carriage to the outer courtyard any minute now . . .'

He was standing ten metres away, in a cluster of uniformed colleagues with plenty of gold on their shoulders. She tried to catch his gaze, but without success. Her heart was suddenly pounding in her chest and her mouth felt dry.

A moment later her phone rang.

She pressed the button on the handsfree earpiece.

'Yes,' she said abruptly.

'I just wanted to check how you're getting on . . .'

'No problems.'

'Good . . .'

'How about you?' she said.

'Fairly well. One slight difficulty, but nothing to worry about . . .'

'What sort of difficulty?' she asked.

But he had already hung up.

He scraped over the railing by the smallest of margins and landed on the pavement.

The momentum of his landing carried him on into the road, and he only just managed to avoid being hit by a bus which missed him by a matter of centimetres, horn blaring.

He staggered back to the pavement and looked at his pursuers on the scaffolding. None of them seemed particularly eager to repeat his jump, and he couldn't help waving to them. Then he saw the square-framed man step forward.

'You there, don't fucking move!' the man roared.

HP responded by sticking his middle finger up at him.

'Shoot him!' the man ordered the closest muppet in a suit.

'No way,' the man replied. 'He's unarmed . . .'

'Which side are you on, man? He's a fucking terrorist, shoot him. That's an order!'

419

The suits seemed to flinch.

'You're not our boss . . .' one of them muttered. 'And this is Sweden . . .'

The square-framed man swore loudly, then cast a quick glance at HP, shoved the suits aside and braced himself against the wall.

Shit! The crazy bastard's really going to jump . . .

HP spun round, crossed the carriageway and began to run.

When he was halfway down the slope he realized that he really should have chosen a different route.

The slope was taking him straight down onto the Söderleden motorway, and, to make things just that little bit worse, the traffic was heading towards him.

Cars came racing at him, many of them sounding their horns madly, as he cursed his stupid decision. But it was too late to turn back. Instead he kept as close to the edge of the bridge as he could.

He peered over the railing, down at the swirling water.

There was no way he was going to jump into the Strömmen, swimming really wasn't his strong point and he'd probably end up as a swollen corpse caught in the sluice gates over by the Parliament building. Not to mention the unhappy combination of water and hard-drive . . .

Much better to keep running.

He was halfway across the motorway bridge before he dared to look back. The square-framed man was fifteen, twenty metres behind him.

His face was bright red and his short, muscular legs were pumping against the tarmac. But even though he was wearing a suit and loafers, unlike HP, who was far better dressed for running, the man still seemed to be gaining on him.

The rucksack, of course.

420

That was what was slowing him down, and if you threw in the exertions of the past few weeks, then it really wasn't all that surprising that he didn't have much strength left in his legs.

Strömsborg was his only hope.

But before he had even got close to the little island he realized it was hopeless. Even if the distance wasn't that great, the railing of the bridge made it impossible to take a run-up. And there was no way he could let the hard-drive get wet.

So he carried on running.

The square-framed man was still shrinking the distance between them.

The closest island was now Riddarholmen, but to reach it he'd have to cross both carriageways, then the railway line, and find a way of getting up a steep rock face. But he didn't have any other option. He let a couple more cars go past, then ran straight out into the roadway. A Passat almost clipped him, but at the last moment the driver swerved and swept past him with just half a metre to spare. He swung over the concrete barrier separating the carriageways and landed on the southbound side. His lungs were burning in his chest and his throat seemed to have shrunk to the size of a drinking-straw.

He carried on running along the road, this time in the same direction as the traffic.

The big brick palace on Riddarholmen was casting long shadows over the road.

'Now I've got you, you bastard!' the square-framed man roared behind him.

'Okay, let's get to work!'

Runeberg's voice over the radio again, and a few seconds later the newlyweds emerged through the western archway.

They didn't look quite as pleased to be married as she had expected. More like nervous, in fact. Maybe that wasn't so strange, given the media frenzy. Live broadcast on television, both in Sweden and a handful of other countries that were fascinated by monarchy.

And now the married couple had to get through the journey in a cortege and a drawn-out formal banquet before the day was over. It probably wouldn't be much of a wedding night . . .

A man in livery held the door of the carriage open and another helped the bride sort out her dress before she sat down.

The bridegroom was waiting outside the carriage, and gave Rebecca a quick glance, then smiled at her uncertainly. She gave him a quick nod in response.

HP ran into the shadow, and carried on a few more metres along the roadway.

The rock face was out of the question as well now, the man was too close and would be on him before he reached it. His heart was pounding fit to burst, he could taste blood, and the first vomit wasn't far off.

He stopped abruptly and turned round, bent his knees and got ready to fight.

The man slowed down and stopped a couple of metres away, then grinned at HP.

'You think you can take me, boy?!' he shouted.

HP didn't answer, and was just staring at the traffic rushing towards them behind the man's back.

Cars were streaming past on both sides of them, their drivers frantically sounding their horns, but the man didn't seem remotely bothered. HP took a couple of cautious steps back, and suddenly the sun shone on his neck, only to vanish again after a couple more steps.

A big lorry was approaching in the distance behind the man.

And suddenly something resembling an idea popped up . . .

'Come on, boy, let's do this the easy way . . .' the man yelled over the noise of the horns and the traffic.

HP met the man's gaze, then took a couple more steps back before stopping and holding up his middle finger.

The man crouched, getting ready to pounce. His lips drew back in a carnivorous leer.

'Any last words?' he growled.

'Yippikayee, mothafucker!' HP yelled.

Then he threw himself down on the roadway and covered his head with his hands.

The lorry hit the square-framed man from behind with full force. It looked almost like a film.

One moment he was there – the next he was gone.

The lorry carried on, its brakes shrieking, over the top of HP, and rolled another fifty metres or so before the driver finally managed to stop.

The first thing HP saw when he cautiously raised his head was a single, empty loafer.

32

Insignificant bearer

He jumped down from the roof into the underground station, hanging from one of the sturdy beams and dropping onto the platform. The landing was softer than he expected, and the platform was pretty much deserted.

He could hear sirens up on the Söderleden motorway, several of them, but they were soon drowned out by the sound of the approaching train.

He got on and collapsed into the nearest empty seat. The rucksack hit the back of the seat and he fumbled at the catch with shaking fingers for a few seconds before giving up.

The adrenalin kick was massive, his whole body was shaking like mad, and he felt like throwing up. He leaned forward and tried to hold his head as low as possible.

Fucking hell!

He'd never seen anyone die before.

Not like that, anyway.

Actually, maybe he had . . .

Just like with Dag and the balcony railing, he'd planned the whole thing. Finding a patch of light on the bend in the road where a driver would be momentarily blinded as his

424

eyes adjusted to the shadow. Then luring his pursuer into the right spot . . .

But, just like with Dag, he'd felt he hadn't had a choice. Back then it had been to save Rebecca, and this time to save himself.

Wrong . . .

To save them both.

Now all he needed to do was send the contents of the hard-drive to the papers, and the Game and PayTag would be history. Then he, Becca, Nora and the others would be free.

Nora . . .

She had sacrificed herself for him, throwing herself at the square-framed man even though she must have realized she didn't stand a chance. Taking a hit for the team. No-one had ever done anything like that for him. When this was all over, he'd find a way to thank her.

If she was still alive, of course . . .

The train thundered into T-Central and he crouched down in his seat instinctively. But just like Gamla Stan, the platform was almost empty.

Ghost town.

Weird . . .

Where the hell was everyone?

Slottsbacken was full of people, and there were even more waiting when they swung left, passing below the Palace garden. Video recorders, cameras, hundreds of phones.

By the end of the day she would be on thousands of pictures and film clips, whether she liked it or not.

Their speed down the hill had been gentle, but once the whole cortege was on flat ground the riders switched from walking pace to a trot. The horses pulling the carriage followed suit and Rebecca and the five other bodyguards around the carriage broke into a jog to keep up.

She caught sight of the first mask as they crossed Norrbro.

HP threw open the door of the internet café and walked straight up to the counter.

'I need a computer with the best connection you've got, for two hours, maybe more . . .' he said to the receptionist, but the bloke scarcely looked away from the television screen hanging above the counter.

'Sorry mate, internet's down . . .'

'What?'

'Yep.' The receptionist turned towards him. 'Broadband, ADSL, the mobile network, *tutti*. Everything's been down since sometime last night. They're saying it's a programming error somewhere, but I reckon it's got more to do with the wedding, personally . . .'

'With what?'

'The wedding, mate!' He gestured towards the television, which was showing a picture of a carriage and load of horses. 'Big brother doesn't want any protests, so they've shut down the net, just like they did in Egypt, yeah?'

'Right,' HP said distractedly.

Something on the screen had caught his attention. One of the goons in suits around the carriage looked vaguely familiar. The camera zoomed in . . .

HP felt a sudden chill.

'Where are they going?' he snapped, grabbing the man's washed-out t-shirt.

'Back to the Palace, where else? Take it easy, mate . . .'

'No, you moron, I mean what route? That looks like Kungsträdgården . . . Which way are they going after that?'

'Sergels torg, then past here up Sveavägen, then right into . . .'

Kungsgatan!!
Fucking shit!!!

The second and third masks were in Strömgatan, close to the Opera. Chalk white Guy Fawkes masks with black goatees and curled moustaches, just like the ones outside the Grand Hotel a few days before.

The white-clad figures wearing the masks didn't move, just stood completely still, which only made things even creepier.

'You've seen them, haven't you, Ludvig?' she said into the microphone on her wrist.

'Yep,' he replied curtly. 'Keep your eyes open, good people, here comes Kungsträdgårdsgatan . . .' he went on.

The cortege swung left.

HP dashed out of the café, raced round the corner and tore off towards Hötorget. In the distance he thought he could hear people cheering.

Four more masks at various points along Kungsträdgårdsgatan, five along Hamngatan, but no sign of any trouble.

Maybe that wasn't so strange. As well as all the various soldiers and volunteers lining the route, she had seen at least twenty uniformed officers, and more in plain clothes. But the masks were growing in number.

One more for each street they passed. That couldn't be coincidence. Something was clearly going on.

They turned right at Sergels torg, skirting round the glass obelisk, and the cheers were so loud she could hardly hear her radio when it crackled into life.

Hötorget was full of people, and he had to elbow his way through. The closer he got to Sveavägen, the thicker the crowd got, and he realized he needed an alternative plan. The underground, of course!

He turned round and ran back down Sergelgatan, then veered between two of the skyscrapers, trying not to look up.

He leaped over the barriers, took the steps in three strides and raced along the platform to the northern end of the station. As he ran he pulled his mobile from his jacket pocket.

'All bodyguards. A person matching the description of one of the suspects has just been seen at Hötorget.'

The voice on the radio was Stigsson's, she was almost certain of that.

Her mouth felt bone dry and she swallowed several times in an attempt to moisten it. To no avail.

'Is everything okay, Normén, over?'

'Fine, Ludvig . . .'

'Good, everyone, stay alert. These masks are worrying me . . .'

Sveavägen now, seven masks.

One more than Sergels torg. The front part of the cortege began to swing down into Kungsgatan.

Her mobile started to ring, but she ignored it.

No answer, fuck!

He emerged from the north exit of the station, pushing his way out through the crowd onto the pavement.

The street was lined with people in uniform, but they seemed largely there for decoration.

The Malmskillnad Bridge was just fifty metres away to the right.

He pulled his hood up over his head, got his sunglasses

428

out of his pocket and put them on. Then he started to force his way through towards the bridge.

In the distance he could hear the sound of horses' hooves.

She saw the biggest group of masks just as the carriage started to turn. They were standing in a row this time. She could see eight of them, then even more.

A lot more . . .

'I don't like this . . .' Runeberg muttered on the radio.

Her phone was still ringing in her right ear.

He was fifteen metres away when he saw the pattern under the arch of the bridge. Three-dimensional orange-pink geometric shapes edged with blue curled upwards in a hypnotically regular pattern. Just like on the plan, the pattern looked like a labyrinth.

The Luttern labyrinth!

He'd found it!

The sound of hooves was getting louder, echoing off the buildings and merging with the cheering of the crowds.

A moment later he caught sight of the large, black air-vents at either end of the arch. Five metres above the pavement, at a perfect angle to the roadway.

Two circular grilles, exactly matching the description on the Carer's plan, approximately one metre in diameter. Or 1016.1 millimetres, to be precise . . .

FUCKING BOLLOCKS!!!

The first horses in the escort had almost reached the bridge. He put his mobile away and pushed the people in front of him out of his path, elbowing his way out into the road, and then started running towards the cortege.

His rucksack was still bouncing up and down on his back. It felt heavier than ever . . .

She saw him from a distance.

Dark clothing, scruffy beard, sunglasses and a hood pulled over his head. The light grey straps of a rucksack were clearly visible across his chest. He was running straight towards the carriage, towards her.

Waving his arms and shouting something.

Her hands went straight to her belt. Grabbed the handle of her pistol. Draw – take aim . . .

'BOMB!' he yelled. 'THERE'S A BOMB OVER THERE!'

But she didn't seem to hear him. Instead he saw her and the other bodyguards aim their guns at him. As if he were the real threat.

A moment later he saw the masks. All around them, lining the street, a hundred, more. All still. As if they were waiting for something. And suddenly he realized . . .

The world went into slow motion as the pieces of the puzzle in his head flew into the air, breaking up the image he had so carefully put together, and forming a new one in its place.

One that was far more horrifying.

The tunnel, the bomb, the explosion in the barn. Strong arms dragging him out of the snake flat, injecting him with serum. Someone standing outside the door of the flat out by the Woodland Cemetery and sending text messages. Warning him about a traitor.

The explosion, Rehyman, running away.

Nora, fastening his rucksack so carefully. Giving him the location, the last piece of the puzzle. The fatal kiss . . .

He stopped abruptly and raised his hands. Voices were

430

echoing back and forth inside his head, drowning each other out. Some of them clear, some of them muffled.

This is your last task, Henrik!

Red or black?

You are to carry out a deadly attack against the royal wedding . . .

Wanna play a game, Henrik Pettersson?

Luttern, not Gluten.

The Carer, I don't know him . . .

Are you absolutely sure?

Not the Carer . . .

He backed away slowly, pulling at the straps to get the rucksack off. But the lock wouldn't budge.

'GET BACK!' he yelled as loudly as he could.

People come to the Luttern labyrinth to die! the voice in his head whispered.

Not.

Carer.

But . . .?

Bearer!

'THERE'S A BOMB IN THIS RUCKSACK!' he yelled.

She took aim at the centre of the death zone, right where the straps of the rucksack crossed his heart.

'BOMB!' someone yelled over the radio, and for a moment she thought it was Tage Sammer's voice she'd heard. But the warning was completely superfluous.

She squeezed the trigger.

Breathed in . . .

Like a punch in the chest – that was pretty much what it felt like. In a weird way the blow seemed to slow everything down even more. All of a sudden he could appreciate the tiniest details around him. The gun aimed at his chest, the drawn out, panic-stricken screams from the surrounding crowd. All around him, bodies crushed together in slow motion. Trying to get as far away from him as possible.

But in spite of the evidence, in spite of the gunpowder stinging his nostrils and the shot still reverberating on his eardrums, his brain refused to accept what was happening. As if it were fending off the impossible, the unthinkable, the incomprehensible . . .

This simply couldn't be happening.

Not now!

She had shot him . . .

SHE

HAD

SHOT

HIM!!!

The pistol was still pointing straight at his chest. The look on her face behind the barrel was ice-cold, completely emotionless. As if it belonged to someone else. A stranger.

He tried to raise his hand towards her, opened his mouth to say something. But the only sound that passed his lips was a sort of whimper. Suddenly and without any warning time speeded up and returned to normal. The pain spread like a wave from his ribcage, out through his body, making the tarmac beneath him lurch. His knees gave way and he took a couple of stumbling steps backwards in an attempt to keep his balance.

His heel hit the edge of the kerb.

A second of weightlessness as he fought the law of gravity.

Then a dreamlike sensation of falling freely.

And with that his part in the Game was over.

33

Mastermind

The explosion was so powerful she felt it in her chest. It echoed between the buildings before it was followed by a second, then a third.

Above her, plumes of light shot up into the night sky, white, red, blue. Other fireworks followed.

Over in the distance, near the Palace, the crowds roared.

'Spectacular, isn't it?'

'Yes.' She climbed the last few rungs to the platform and joined him at the railing high above the NK department store. A few metres above their heads the massive neon sign rotated, as the green NK logo was replaced by a red clock.

'My dear Rebecca, I'm so very sorry, from the bottom of my heart . . .' He turned to her and held out his arms. 'Obviously some of the responsibility must fall on me.'

She went over and put her arms round his neck.

'Thanks, Uncle Tage . . .' she said into his shoulder.

'Is there anything I can do, my dear?' He leaned back and gently grasped her upper arms.

'No, not at the moment, anyway.'

She looked away, towards the Palace, where more rockets were shooting up.

'Losing a brother like that. And having to do it yourself . . .' He shook his head.

She didn't reply, and tried to swallow the lump in her throat.

'My dear Rebecca, I can't begin to imagine how you must be feeling . . .'

The sadness in his voice cut through her like a knife, and for a moment her feelings threatened to overwhelm her. But she quickly pulled herself together.

'My plan went wrong, terribly wrong, and in spite of all our efforts I'm afraid Henrik couldn't be saved,' he went on. 'Henrik was carrying a bomb, and it was only thanks to your judicious intervention that he didn't have the chance to set it off. He knew about it, even shouted out that he was carrying it . . .'

Tage Sammer held his hands out and took a step back.

'Henrik had made his choice, and you were forced to make yours. You saved a lot of lives this afternoon, I hope you realize that. Sometimes the good of the many has to take priority over that of the individual . . .'

She gulped hard, then nodded slowly. Tears were pricking her eyes, but she did her utmost to restrain herself. To keep control . . .

More fireworks shot up into the night sky.

'Brave decision, to carry on with the wedding festivities,' she muttered. 'And he made a good speech . . .'

'Yes, it's easy to underestimate His Majesty. It's at times like this that people show their true mettle. His televised speech was fine proof of that.'

'Mmm,' she said.

'The nation needs a uniting force,' he went on. 'Someone

434

who can help us stand strong in the face of the trials ahead. His Majesty understands that . . .'

'Or his PR department does . . .'

'I'm sorry?'

'Nothing,' she mumbled. 'It just all felt so premeditated, as if . . .'

'As if what, Rebecca . . .?'

He tilted his head and looked at her curiously.

'Nothing . . .' she said quietly. 'Sorry, I'm not quite myself, Uncle Tage.'

'My dear Rebecca, I quite understand. You have nothing to apologize for . . .'

She turned towards the railing and they stood in silence next to each other for a while.

'S-so, what happens now? With the investigation, I mean?' she finally said.

He shrugged.

'Magnus Sandström and your brother are gone, and the other three are locked away. Even if a few details remain, the case is fundamentally solved. The Game has been crushed and the guilty will get their punishment . . .'

'It can't be quite that simple, Uncle Tage . . .'

'How do you mean?'

'There must be something more behind it, there must be more people involved. For instance, who made the bomb in Henke's rucksack, and who were all those people in masks?'

'Well, as far as we know any one of them could have been behind the bomb. Sandström is probably the likeliest candidate . . . The masked protestors along the route might well have been sheer coincidence. Sometimes conspiracy theories are just a convenient way to avoid having to deal with the difficulties of reality . . .'

'What about Dad?'

435

'How do you mean?'

'He worked for you, did everything you asked of him. Pretty much like me . . .'

Her stomach lurched and she had to break off.

'That's true, Erland was a particularly loyal colleague. There's always room for people like that in most organizations, Rebecca.'

He waited for the words to sink in.

'Are . . . are you offering me a job, Uncle Tage?'

He smiled gently.

'If I were, would you accept, Rebecca? I think we could be an excellent team. Someone with your decisiveness, your self-control. Who doesn't hesitate to do what is necessary, however unpalatable it might be. There's room for that sort of person in every organization . . .'

She took a deep breath.

'I already have a job, you know that. Once all this has died down I think I'd like to go back to it. Try to help find out exactly what happened down there . . .' She gestured towards the two towers on either side of Kungsgatan, by the Malmskillnad Bridge.

Sammer nodded slowly.

'I didn't really expect any other answer, Rebecca . . .'

He bent down and picked up a check-patterned thermos flask from beside the railing.

'Let me at least offer you a cup of coffee before we part.'

'Thanks . . .'

He conjured up two cups and filled them.

'Have I told you why I'm so fond of this spot?'

She shook her head and blew gently on the hot coffee.

'My father worked for ASEA. He helped construct the clock in 1939. But back then it was mounted on the telephone company tower in Brunkebergstorg.'

He pointed across the rooftops.

436

'My father used to take me to look at it. Telling me how they got it up there. The tower was forty-five metres high, you see, a dizzy height in those days . . .'

She nodded, and slowly raised the cup to her lips.

'I was very proud of my father, I even used to boast to friends about how he had constructed the clock all on his own . . .' he chuckled.

'Then, in 1953, the tower caught fire, and the clock was taken down and placed in storage. My father died a couple of years later . . .'

She studied his face in profile, the eagle-like hook of the nose. The taut skin over his cheeks, the dark eyes that reminded her so strongly of her father's.

'Fortunately, with the help of a few contacts, I eventually managed to get this mast constructed. And in that way my father's clock could be restored to its rightful place . . .'

Sammer turned and smiled at her.

He was still holding the cup in his hand, but didn't seem to have touched his coffee.

'Thanks for telling me the story, Uncle Tage, but I'd rather you . . .'

'Talked about *your* father, yes, of course I can understand that. That's why you're here. You're worried about what Erland might have done with that revolver. What the consequences of it might have been. So worried that you can't sleep at night, is that right?'

She nodded heavily, her head moving up and down as if it didn't really want to obey her.

'Poor Rebecca.' He smiled. 'The past few years can't have been easy for you. Everything that's happened: the crash at Lindhagensplan, the attack against the American Secretary of State. By the way, the police van containing the bomb *was* being driven by Henrik, but you'd probably already guessed that . . .'

She opened her mouth and tried to say something.

'Shh, don't worry.' He put a gloved finger to his lips. 'That can stay between us. Henrik has been involved in a number of violent actions, some of which you know about already. I'm actually going to miss him,' he chuckled. 'In fact I daresay we all will . . . But my dear Rebecca, are you all right . . .?'

The plastic cup had fallen from her hand and hit the mesh floor with a clatter.

'Perhaps you should sit down . . .'

He gestured to the steps.

She followed his advice, sank down on the top step, and leaned her head against the railing. The metal felt cool and soothing against her temple.

'Poor Rebecca,' he said, walking slowly over to her. 'Suspected of misuse of office in Darfur, fired from your job, and then your boyfriend left you. And today you were forced to shoot your own brother. So terribly tragic . . .'

He gently stroked her forehead.

The green letters on the sign above their heads turned into a clock, casting a red glow over his face. He leaned over and began to unbutton her jacket.

'Such a shame that it has to end this way, my dear, but in my branch I'm afraid one can't afford to leave any loose ends. In fact I'm almost rather surprised that your colleagues let you keep your gun, in light of what's happened.'

He felt around her belt, then pulled her service pistol from its holster.

She made no attempt to stop him.

'There's no knowing what you might do, my dear Rebecca.'

He turned the gun over, inspecting it for a few seconds.

A tear seeped out of one of her eyes, then another.

'Perhaps it would actually be a relief not to have to worry about it all any more? The poor police officer, under such stress, shooting her own brother. The media won't show any mercy. When you look at it like that, you might even say that I'm doing you a favour.'

She looked at him, tried to open her mouth.

'The . . . the coffee,' she finally said.

'Oh, don't worry. It's the same substance you're already taking. Just a little stronger. Look, it even says your name on the label . . .'

He pulled out a little tub of pills and shook it between his thumb and forefinger. Then he put it in her pocket.

'Time to say goodbye, I'm afraid . . .'

He raised the weapon and performed the bolt action. Then he put the gun to her temple and fired.

34

The Red King

The gun clicked.

He pulled it back, performed the bolt action again and fired once more.

Another click.

Sammer stared at the pistol, unable to understand what was happening.

Rebecca raised her head and met his gaze. Then she put her hand over the barrel, stood up and twisted the gun from his grasp.

He took a stumbling step backwards, then another. For the first time since she met him, his carefully controlled persona seemed to waver and for a moment he almost looked scared. It passed in a matter of seconds, then he collected himself.

She held the gun in both hands, performed the bolt action once, then a second time.

Two little green blank cartridges flew out, bouncing off the grilled floor and finding their way through the gaps to the roof twenty metres below.

She lowered the gun to waist height, but kept it pointed at him.

'Live . . .' she said bluntly, waving the gun. 'In case you were wondering. By the way, I've given up the pills, and instant coffee . . .' she added. 'Someone told me they weren't good for me . . .'

His mouth narrowed. 'I see . . .'

He looked at her for a few moments.

'What was it that . . .?'

'Oh, a tiny detail. Something so insignificant that it took me several days to put my finger on it . . .'

He didn't respond, just went on studying her.

'The safe deposit box, your story, the passports, everything fitted together perfectly. Everything fell perfectly into place, and what Thore Sjögren told me in the Royal Library tied the last loose ends together beautifully. Like I said, it was all perfect . . .'

'But?'

'Perfect, if it hadn't been for the name . . .'

'I'm not sure I quite understand . . .?' He tilted his head.

'Thore was busy with a little digression and happened to call me by the wrong name, then very quickly and politely corrected himself. A silly little mistake, that's all. There was just one problem . . . I never told Thore what my name was, so he must have known already. He must have known what I looked like, that I was going to show up at the library. The only person who knew that was you.'

'And that was enough to make you suspicious . . .?'

'That, and the fact that I was becoming more and more convinced that someone was tracking my phone. Keeping an eye on where I was and who I contacted. In the end I got some help from an old friend . . .'

'Oh . . .'

He stood there in silence for several seconds, and seemed to be thinking.

'Sandström?'

'His name is Al-Hassan these days.'

'Of course . . .'

'Aren't you going to ask if he's alive, Uncle Tage? No, of course not, the explosion in the barn was part of your plan, after all. A way of removing him from the break-in at the Fortress. Manga switched the hard-drive for the bomb, exactly as planned, but to be on the safe side he made sure that the charge in the rucksack could never be detonated.'

She glanced up at the NK clock.

'Three minutes ago he sent all the information on the hard-drive to all the news media . . .'

Sammer nodded slowly.

'In my position you must always be prepared to be betrayed. There's always someone younger, someone hungrier waiting for their chance. Up to now I have successfully managed to survive coups of that sort. But Sandström wasn't on my list. He struck me as being rather too timid for that sort of power politics. Too soft . . .'

She shrugged. 'Fear can be a powerful motivator . . .'

'Naturally, but a plan like that requires someone considerably stronger, someone who has what Sandström lacks . . .'

He gave her a long look.

'Evidently he found that person. You knew what was going on, Rebecca, yet you still played along. You let me pull the strings to get you back into the bodyguard unit. And put yourself at the front of the cortege so that . . .'

He shook his head.

'You shot your own brother in order to get at me . . .' His tone was almost admiring. 'I clearly underestimated how determined you are, Rebecca. Your father would have . . .'

'Don't talk about my father!' she snapped, raising the pistol towards his face. 'You manipulated me, using my memories of Dad to make me trust you. Like you, even . . .'

She squeezed the trigger gently.

'But there is no Uncle Tage, no André Pellas, no John Earnest or secret missions for the military . . .' Her pulse was pounding against her temples. 'No conspiracy, no Olof Palme Weapon, no fake passports in a forgotten safe deposit box. All there is, is you. An old man and a mass of lies. Uncle Tage . . . Even your name is a joke, almost as if you were laughing at me. Tage Sammer – *Game Master.*'

She spat out the last two words.

'Everything that happened was part of your plan. Henke, me, everyone else – we were just pawns. At least two different task-masters in desperate need of help. Black with the Data Retention Directive, the Palace with the popularity of the royal family. Who knows, maybe there were even more behind them, people wanting tougher legislation, more resources, more opportunities for surveillance . . .'

She slowly lowered the gun. Suddenly the sound of sirens could be heard in the distance.

'The Grand Hotel was merely a demonstration, a sales pitch, to show what you could do, how much power you had. You let Henke steal that information from the Fortress so that you could seize it yourself. Then you'd have a serious stranglehold over PayTag, Black and their secret owners, not to mention every single MP . . . *Information is the new currency.*'

She took a deep breath before she went on.

'But to soften the blow you did actually deliver what was at the top of everyone's wishlist, something that would

443

make them forgive your little transgression. A home-grown wanted terrorist prepared to launch an attack on the very symbol of Swedishness, and who, appropriately enough, gets shot and killed by his own sister before he can tell his own incredible story. After something like that, everyone will flock to the royal family, and parliament will rush through pretty much any legislation. No-one will protest, and no-one will ever doubt your power. The perfect game . . .'

She paused for breath again.

'Tell me – am I wrong?'

He stood still for a few seconds, then shrugged.

'My dear Rebecca, you disappoint me. You might very well think that, I couldn't possibly comment.'

He let out an exaggerated sigh.

'The crook is supposed to confess at the end so that the audience can have all the answers. So that the film ends happily and everyone can go home happy and satisfied. I daresay you're even wearing something so banal as a hidden tape recorder?'

He shook his head.

'My only response is that you and everyone else are free to believe whatever you choose to . . . Obviously, I couldn't possibly comment . . .'

The sirens were getting closer, at least four or five vehicles, possibly more.

'So what are you going to do now, Rebecca? Take me back to the station in handcuffs? Show the world how clever you've been?'

'Well, I've certainly got enough on the tape to arrest you for attempted murder.'

She patted her inside pocket.

'Your position at the Palace, your close collaboration with Eskil Stigsson and af Cederskjöld the spin doctor, all

444

of that will be examined in minute detail. By the end of the week at the very latest all the air will have gone out of your good friend Black and his company. I daresay the same will apply to the Data Retention Directive, if it even lasts that long . . .'

'I see . . .' His voice was dry, but the note of bitterness was still obvious.

'And if that isn't enough, there are all the witnesses. Manga, me, the three who were up at the Fortress.'

She paused for a moment.

'And then of course there's the most compelling testimony of all, from a person who can explain the details of the tasks you gave him . . .'

It took him a moment to understand what she meant. Then he slowly shook his head.

'Your brother – of course, how could I have imagined anything else,' he smiled. 'I presume you had Runeberg's help arranging that charade in Kungsgatan? The esteemed superintendent would do almost anything you ask, wouldn't he?'

He took a deep breath, then held out his hands.

'Congratulations, Rebecca, well played. I admit defeat . . .'

He turned and leaned heavily against the railing.

For a few seconds he stood quite still, then he turned to her and looked up at the rotating sign above them.

'I'm proud of my work, Rebecca. I've achieved things that other people can only dream of . . .'

The red clock turned into a sign again, casting a green light over his face.

'But I never broke the rules of the Game. Are you aware of them?'

She shook her head.

There were sirens everywhere now, echoing between the buildings and rooftops around them. Blue lights were reflecting off the windows of the buildings.

'First and foremost: never discuss the Game with anyone. The second is that the Game Master is in control he decides how and when the Game ends. That's really al you need to remember . . .'

He took a final look at the rotating sign, then placed one foot on a cross-brace and climbed up onto the railing

She made no attempt to stop him.

For a moment he stood on top of the railing, balancing there with his arms outstretched.

As the clock completed its circuit and turned the light from green to red, he fell slowly forward into the darkness.

Seconds later his body crashed through the glass roof then carried on through the atrium of the department store before landing with a thud on the marble floor some fifty metres below her.

35

Just one more thing . . .

Rebecca slowly holstered her pistol, then picked up the flask and mugs before heading off down the spiral staircase.

When she reached the roof at the foot of the mast she took out her phone. A shiny, silvery thing with a glass touch screen.

He answered on the first ring.

'Is it over?'

'Yes . . .'

'And?'

'Much as we thought.'

'Are you okay, Becca? I mean, considering . . .?'

'I'm okay, Manga. Surprisingly okay, actually . . . Better than I have been for ages.'

'Good to hear it.'

'How is he?'

'Mad as hell, and badly bruised across the chest, but he'll survive. People like HP always survive. He's with Nora. I still don't understand how you dared to shoot. I mean, the buckle and the Kevlar casing were no bigger than the palm of your hand . . .'

A short distance away she could hear voices, radios crackling, keys jangling. She jumped nimbly onto the next roof, opened a small door and disappeared into a dark stairwell.

'So what do we do now?'

'You can do what you like, Becca. Go back to your old life, meet someone new, have kids, and live to be a hundred . . .'

A moment later he added:

'Unless you'd rather do something else entirely . . . Something that would really make a difference. You decide . . . Red or black?'

'Nothing's ever going to be the same, is it?' she said.

'Is that really so wrong, Becca?'

'Maybe not . . .'

She took a deep breath.

'Look, Manga . . . I should probably call you Farook . . . What is your name these days?'

She could hear him laughing, far away.

'What do you think of . . . Game Master?'